WOMEN
ON
THE
EDGE

BOOK YOUR PLACE ON OUR WEBSITE AND MAKE THE READING CONNECTION!

We've created a customized website just for our very special readers, where you can get the inside scoop on everything that's going on with Zebra, Pinnacle and Kensington books.

When you come online, you'll have the exciting opportunity to:

- View covers of upcoming books
- Read sample chapters
- Learn about our future publishing schedule (listed by publication month *and author*)
- Find out when your favorite authors will be visiting a city near you
- Search for and order backlist books from our online catalog
- Check out author bios and background information
- Send e-mail to your favorite authors
- Meet the Kensington staff online
- Join us in weekly chats with authors, readers and other guests
- Get writing guidelines
- AND MUCH MORE!

Visit our website at
http://www.kensingtonbooks.com

WOMEN
ON
THE
EDGE

Edited by Martin H. Greenberg

KENSINGTON BOOKS
http://www.kensingtonbooks.com

Contents

Author Notes

Sara Paretsky's rise to preeminence in the mystery field has been steady and certain. Her latest novel, *Guardian Angel*, was both a national best-seller and a critical benchmark. Paretsky's work, is, in turn, influencing a whole new generation of female private-eye writers . . . and bringing thousands of new readers to the mystery field.

While **John D. MacDonald** is deservedly celebrated for his novels about Travis McGee, some feel that his best work was done as paperback originals back in the fifties and early sixties. Such novels as *The End of the Night, One Monday We Killed Them All, Soft Touch,* and *The Price of Murder* are fine, gritty crime novels that should be made more accessible to MacDonald's present-day readers.

Howard Browne has been a successful fiction editor, a fine mystery novelist and a celebrated screen and TV writer. His Paul Pine novels, particularly *The Taste of Ashes,* are among the best private detective novels written in the forties and fifties. His story here will demonstrate why his books are finding a receptive new audience in the nineties.

Barbara Michaels is one of the great unsung stylists of mystery fiction. Like Rex Stout, she rarely receives her due because her prose does not show off or promote itself . . . it simply shines through with clarity, wit and its own kind of unassuming beauty. Her story here is an example. She has written dozens of novels, the best of which is, perhaps, *Smoke and Mirrors*.

Loren D. Estleman writes the best Chandleresque private-eye novels of our time. His many fans argue over which Amos Walker is best . . . but the nice thing is, they're all good. Estleman is at least as talented with the western story, as well, his *Mr. St. John* being one of the most important western novels of this past half century.

Ed Gorman has been called "One of the world's great storytellers" *(Million)* and "The poet of dark suspense" *(Bloomsbury Review)*. His most recent crime novels include *The Night Remembers* and *A Cry of Shadows*.

Barbara Collins is a new writer who is just beginning to make her mark in mystery fiction. Most of her terse, ironic tales would have adapted well to Alfred Hitchcock's old half-hour TV show. She has a long and lucrative career ahead of her.

Bill Pronzini is the creator of the Nameless detective series of private-eye novels that *Mystery Scene* called "One of the most unique and lasting contributions to the field of crime fiction." Pronzini is equally as good with short stories, having won the Shamus and been nominated for the Edgar.

Bill Crider's *Blood Marks* was one of the best crime novels of the past season. In addition, he also found time to write both a Sheriff Dan Rhodes novel and a western novel as well. Crider's fiction is sleek, wry and quietly innovative.

Max Allan Collins has his own niche in private-eye fiction. The Nate Heller novels combine serious history with first-rate storytelling. *Stolen Away*, Collins's take on the infamous

Lindbergh kidnapping, is a feast of fact, fiction and first-rate writing. He always gives readers great pleasure.

Nancy Pickard's "Afraid All The Time" is one of the most important stories in the history of crime fiction. It demonstrated that serious social stories can be done in the genre without getting self-consciously literary. Pickard is just now starting to get her due as one of the field's most serious yet readable authors.

Wayne D. Dundee's tales of the working class are finding more and more readers. Dundee is a solid pro, imbuing his stories with color, pace and a strong sense of place and social caste. He is an important voice in the nineties.

Richard T. Chizmar is a young writer of dark suspense who is just now finding an audience for his stories. While you can spot certain influences in his work, he is already his own person so far as voice goes. He is at work on a first novel, and is publishing the fine magazine *Cemetery Dance* and selecting books for his CD Publications line.

Back when women private eyes were little more than gimmicks, **Marcia Muller** wrote a novel called *Edwin of The Iron Shoes* which not only launched her career but also would eventually change the face of mystery publishing. In a very real sense, Marcia made it all right for other women to write serious private-eye stories. Since then, she's gone on to write ever richer, more thematically complex novels. Like Sara Paretsky, Marcia has inspired a whole new generation of mystery writers.

Introduction

Nancy Pickard

Picture a solid cube.

See its six sides; roll them over in your mind like a die in your hand. Feel the eight corners as sharp as the points of eight pocket knives, sharp enough to prick your skin, to make the blood run in tiny, warm rivulets down the length of your fingers. Run your imaginary fingers along the edges of this cube, down each one of its twelve edges, and feel on the tips of your wounded fingers the terrible cutting contrast of the angles with the smooth, glacial, searingly cold expanse of the four sides, the top, and the bottom. But which is the top, the bottom, the sides? It's all of a oneness. Or maybe the imaginary, dangerous cube you hold in your mind is a die. If it is, feel the pockmarks; count them. But don't roll it. This die is for gambling, all right, but not with money. It's for wagering with lives, maybe even yours. They don't call it a "die" for nothing.

Now put yourself, the imaginary you, atop that cube, and place your feet at an edge, so that your toes are just hanging over. If you're scared to get that close, creep up to the edge slowly, taking baby steps if you like, on your hands and knees, if that's better. Give yourself a safety harness, if that will get you closer, or a railing, something sturdy to grasp with your nervous hands. If you're brave enough to stand there on the edge unaided, with your toes hanging off, without even someone's hand to hold you up, or any net below, you may still wish to balance with your arms—whoa!—so you don't tumble accidentally over.

Look down. That's right, all at once if you can, but little by little if that's the only way you can manage. Sneak a peek through your eyelashes. Oh, God, it's a long way down there. You feel the pull, don't you? Is it merely gravity, that invisible hand that's got you by the front of your shirt and that threatens to jerk you off your feet so you go sailing over the ledge? Or is it a death wish? Maybe it's only an unbelievably intense desire to fly, to return to an archetypal, early evolutionary element you thought you'd forgotten. A life wish. What would the air feel like as you plunged through it, you pterosaur, you? Would it be thick and soft, so that you fell slowly, luxuriously, only bumping a bit, as if you were rolling down a hill of pillows? Or would it be as thin as watered soup so that you plummeted like a stone, a killer stone, a dead-heavy fossilized rock to the ground below, knowing only the terror of the fall and the fatal ending and never enjoying the ride? Is it the ride you long for (and fear), or is it the ending? There's another way, another route off the same ledge. This will take some extra imagination, if you're game for it.

Are you ready? All right, you're going _into_ the cube. That's right. Inside it, not off it. Jump down off the cube for a minute. Now turn around and look back up at it. Blow it up, make it big, huge, monstrous in size, make it dwarf you. Now its sides are sheer granite cliffs, now its ledges are precipices in the Himalayas. And you're going to scale one of those sleek, slick rock faces, you're going to climb it in order to stand backward at the top. And then you're going to leap into the depths of the apparently—perhaps deceptively—solid cube.

Want to go up?

You have to make the decision now.

No backing down once you've started the climb.

You'll ascend by your toenails and fingernails and teeth and knees and chin and elbows—no rope, no pickax, no footholds in the side of this elevation, just you going up like a fly on the face of a seamless, slippery moon. If you stop for one breath, if you hesitate for an instant, if so much as a microdot of one toenail slips, you're a goner. You'll start sliding backward and never stop, rocketing to a screeching, screaming, wailing, horrible, fabulous speed as you crash to the ground below. On this mountain, you only get one chance to make a good first impression.

So decide: going up?

Are you there yet, in your mind, in your imagination?

Let us know when you're safely on top of the cube, but don't move forward all the way onto it. Rest there, on your stomach, if you like, your legs hanging over the edge, your fingertips grabbing at the slickness at the top, and you, too exhausted for the moment to move another inch to further safety. But that safety's illusional anyway, because your epic journey's only half over.

Congratulations. You made it to the top. Here you are again.

Now, get to your feet. Careful, the edge is right behind you.

Stand there facing the center of the cube, with your heels—your high fashion heels—hanging off. How confident you look! What strength you've displayed, and stamina and courage. We're so proud of you! Pause now to catch your breath again, because you've earned it.

Oops, that slight respite was a mistake, wasn't it?

Should have plunged on into the cube, shouldn't have given yourself so much time to think about it. Now you see it, that solid field, and you're filled with awful doubts. It's *solid*, after all, so what is there to jump into? It looks *hard*. If you dive head-first you'll crack your skull open for sure and either kill yourself or be paralyzed from the neck down for the rest of your life. They'll arrest you for taking chances with life, or dun you for the cost of your rescue. Oh, God, what have you gotten yourself into this time?

Don't stop. Don't think about it anymore. Just do it.

Arms back, like a high diver.

Knees bent, ready to spring.

All right, okay, close your eyes if it helps . . .

Tense your thighs, your throat . . .

Now, leap! Over the edge into the top of the cube! Scream your bloody lungs out. *Aieee!* My God, you're going through . . . Oh, it's wonderful! No, it hurts! Can't stop to judge because the lights are getting brighter in front of your closed eyelids and you almost want to open them to see what there is to see . . .

You've gone over the edge.

Open your eyes.

Turn the page.

See what there is to see, read what there is to read, hear the stories that are told when someone goes over the edge.

The Case Of The Pietro Andromache

Sara Paretsky

"You only agreed to hire him because of his art collection. Of that I'm sure." Lotty Herschel bent down to adjust her stockings. "And don't waggle your eyebrows like that—it makes you look like an adolescent Groucho Marx."

Max Loewenthal obediently smoothed his eyebrows, but said, "It's your legs, Lotty; they remind me of my youth. You know, going into the Underground to wait out the air raids, looking at the ladies as they came down the escalators. The updraft always made their skirts billow."

"You're making this up, Max. I was in those Underground stations, too, and as I remember the ladies were always bundled in coats and children."

Max moved from the doorway to put an arm around Lotty. "That's what keeps us together, *Lottchen:* I am a romantic and you are severely logical. And you know we didn't hire Caudwell because of his collection. Although I admit I am eager to see it. The board wants Beth Israel to develop a transplant program. It's the only way we're going to become competitive—"

"Don't deliver your publicity lecture to me," Lotty

snapped. Her thick brows contracted to a solid black line across her forehead. "As far as I am concerned he is a cretin with the hands of a Caliban and the personality of Attila."

Lotty's intense commitment to medicine left no room for the mundane consideration of money. But as the hospital's executive director, Max was on the spot with the trustees to see that Beth Israel ran at a profit. Or at least a smaller loss than they'd achieved in recent years. They'd brought Caudwell in part to attract more paying patients— and to help screen out some of the indigent who made up twelve percent of Beth Israel's patient load. Max wondered how long the hospital could afford to support personalities as divergent as Lotty and Caudwell in their radically differing approaches to medicine.

He dropped his arm and smiled quizzically at her. "Why do you hate him so much, Lotty?"

"*I* am the person who has to justify the patients I admit to this—this troglodyte. Do you realize he tried to keep Mrs. Mendes from the operating room when he learned she had AIDS? He wasn't even being asked to sully his hands with her blood and he didn't want me performing surgery on her."

Lotty drew back from Max and pointed an accusing finger at him. "You may tell the board that if he keeps questioning my judgment they will find themselves looking for a new perinatologist. I am serious about this. You listen this afternoon, Max, you hear whether or not he calls me 'our little baby doctor.' I am fifty-eight years old, I am a Fellow of the Royal College of Surgeons besides having enough credentials in this country to support a whole hospital, and to him I am a 'little baby doctor.'"

Max sat on the daybed and pulled Lotty down next to him. "No, no, *Lottchen:* don't fight. Listen to me. Why haven't you told me any of this before?"

"Don't be an idiot, Max: you are the director of the hospital. I cannot use our special relationship to deal with problems I have with the staff. I said my piece when Caudwell came for his final interview. A number of the other physicians were not happy with his attitude. If you remember, we asked the board to bring him in as a cardiac surgeon first and promote him to chief of staff after a year if everyone was satisfied with his performance."

"We talked about doing it that way," Max admitted. "But he wouldn't take the appointment except as chief of staff. That was the only way we could offer him the kind of money he could get at one of the university hospitals or Humana. And, Lotty, even if you don't like his personality you must agree that he is a first-class surgeon."

"I agree to nothing." Red lights danced in her black eyes. "If he patronizes me, a fellow physician, how do you imagine he treats his patients? You cannot practice medicine if—"

"Now it's my turn to ask to be spared a lecture," Max interrupted gently. "But if you feel so strongly about him, maybe you shouldn't go to his party this afternoon."

"And admit that he can beat me? Never."

"Very well then." Max got up and placed a heavily brocaded wool shawl over Lotty's shoulders. "But you must promise to behave. This is a social function we are going to, remember, not a gladiator contest. Caudwell is trying to repay some hospitality this afternoon, not to belittle you."

"I don't need lessons in conduct from you: Herschels

were attending the emperors of Austria while the Loewen-thals were operating vegetable stalls on the Ring," Lotty said haughtily.

Max laughed and kissed her hand. "Then remember these regal Herschels and act like them, *Eure Hobeit.*"

II

Caudwell had bought an apartment sight unseen when he moved to Chicago. A divorced man whose children are in college only has to consult with his own taste in these matters. He asked the Beth Israel board to recommend a realtor, sent his requirements to them—twenties construction, near Lake Michigan, good security, modern plumbing—and dropped seven hundred and fifty thousand for an eight-room condo facing the lake at Scott Street.

Since Beth Israel paid handsomely for the privilege of retaining Dr. Charlotte Herschel as their perinatologist, nothing required her to live in a five-room walkup on the fringes of Uptown, so it was a bit unfair of her to mutter "Parvenu" to Max when they walked into the lobby.

Max relinquished Lotty gratefully when they got off the elevator. Being her lover was like trying to be companion to a Bengal tiger: you never knew when she'd take a lethal swipe at you. Still, if Caudwell were insulting her—and her judgment—maybe he needed to talk to the surgeon, explain how important Lotty was for the reputation of Beth Israel.

Caudwell's two children were making the obligatory Christmas visit. They were a boy and a girl, Deborah and Steve, within a year of the same age, both tall, both blond and poised, with a hearty sophistication born of a child-hood spent on expensive ski slopes. Max wasn't very big, and as one took his coat and the other performed brisk introductions, he felt himself shrinking, losing in self-assurance. He accepted a glass of special *cuvee* from one of them—was it the boy or the girl he wondered in confu-sion—and fled into the melee.

He landed next to one of Beth Israel's trustees, a woman in her sixties wearing a gray textured minidress whose black stripes were constructed of feathers. She commented brightly on Caudwell's art collection, but Max sensed an undercurrent of hostility: wealthy trustees don't like the idea that they can't out-buy the staff.

While he was frowning and nodding at appropriate inter-vals, it dawned on Max that Caudwell did know how much the hospital needed Lotty. Heart surgeons do not have the world's smallest egos: when you ask them to name the world's three leading practitioners, they never can remem-ber the names of the other two. Lotty was at the top of her field, and she, too, was used to having things her way. Since her confrontational style was reminiscent more of the Battle of the Bulge than the Imperial Court of Vienna, he didn't blame Caudwell for trying to force her out of the hospital.

Max moved away from Martha Gildersleeve to admire some of the paintings and figurines she'd be discussing. A collector himself of Chinese porcelains, Max raised his eyebrows and mouthed a soundless whistle at the pieces on display. A small Watteau and a Charles Demuth watercolor were worth as much as Beth Israel paid Caudwell in a year. No wonder Mrs. Gildersleeve had been so annoyed.

"Impressive, isn't it."

Max turned to see Arthur Gioia looming over him. Max was shorter than most of the Beth Israel staff, shorter than everyone but Lotty. But Gioia, a tall muscular immunologist, loomed over everyone. He had gone to the University of Arkansas on a football scholarship and had even spent a season playing tackle for Houston before starting medical school. It had been twenty years since he last lifted weights, but his neck still looked like a redwood stump.

Gioia had led the opposition to Caudwell's appointment. Max had suspected at the time that it was due more to a medicine man's not wanting a surgeon as his nominal boss than from any other cause, but after Lotty's outburst he wasn't so sure. He was debating whether to ask the doctor how he felt about Caudwell now that he'd worked with him for six months when their host surged over to him and shook his hand.

"Sorry I didn't see you when you came in, Loewenthal. You like the Watteau? It's one of my favorite pieces. Although a collector shouldn't play favorites any more than a father should, eh, sweetheart?" The last remark was addressed to the daughter, Deborah, who had come up behind Caudwell and slipped an arm around him.

Caudwell looked more like a Victorian sea dog than a surgeon. He had a round red face under a shock of yellow-white hair, a hearty Santa Claus laugh, and a bluff, direct manner. Despite Lotty's vituperations, he was immensely popular with his patients. In the short time he'd been at the hospital, referrals to cardiac surgery had increased fifteen percent.

His daughter squeezed his shoulder playfully. "I know you don't play favorites with us, Dad, but you're lying to

Mr. Loewenthal about your collection; come on, you know you are."

She turned to Max. "He has a piece he's so proud of he doesn't like to show it to people—he doesn't want them to see he's got vulnerable spots. But it's Christmas, Dad, relax, let people see how you feel for a change."

Max looked curiously at the surgeon, but Caudwell seemed pleased with his daughter's familiarity. The son came up and added his own jocular cajoling.

"This really is Dad's pride and joy. He stole it from Uncle Griffen when Grandfather died and kept Mother from getting her mitts on it when they split up."

Caudwell did bark out a mild reproof at that. "You'll be giving my colleagues the wrong impression of me, Steve. I didn't steal it from Grif. Told him he could have the rest of the estate if he'd leave me the Watteau and the Pietro."

"Of course he could've bought ten estates with what those two would fetch," Steve muttered to his sister over Max's head.

Deborah relinquished her father's arm to lean over Max and whisper back, "Mom, too."

Max moved away from the alarming pair to say to Caudwell, "A Pietro? You mean Pietro d'Alessandro? You have a model, or an actual sculpture?"

Caudwell gave his staccato admiral's laugh. "The real McCoy, Loewenthal. The real McCoy. An alabaster."

"An alabaster?" Max raised his eyebrows. "Surely not. I thought Pietro worked only in bronze and marble."

"Yes, yes," chuckled Caudwell, rubbing his hands together. "Everyone thinks so, but there were a few alabasters in private collections. I've had this one authenticated by experts. Come take a look at it—it'll knock your breath away. You come, too, Gioia,'' he barked at the immunologist. "You're Italian, you'll like to see what your ancestors were up to."

"A Pietro alabaster?" Lotty's clipped tones made Max start—he hadn't noticed her joining the little group. "I would very much like to see this piece."

"Then come along, Dr. Herschel, come along." Caudwell led them to a small hallway, exchanging genial greetings with his guests as he passed, pointing out a John William Hill miniature they might not have seen, picking up a few other people who for various reasons wanted to see his prize.

"By the way, Gioia, I was in New York last week, you know. Met an old friend of yours from Arkansas. Paul Nierman."

"Nierman?" Gioia seemed to be at a loss. "I'm afraid I don't remember him."

"Well, he remembered you pretty well. Sent you all kinds of messages—you'll have to stop by my office on Monday and get the full strength."

Caudwell opened a door on the right side of the hall and let them into his study. It was an octagonal room carved out of the corner of the building. Windows on two sides looked out on Lake Michigan. Caudwell drew salmon drapes as he talked about the room, why he'd chosen it for his study even though the view kept his mind from his work.

Lotty ignored him and walked over to a small pedestal which stood alone against the paneling on one of the far walls. Max followed her and gazed respectfully at the statue. He had seldom seen so fine a piece outside a museum. About a foot high, it depicted a woman in classical draperies hovering in anguish over the dead body of a soldier lying at her feet. The grief in her beautiful face was so poignant that it reminded you of every sorrow you had ever faced.

"Who is it meant to be?" Max asked curiously.

"Andromache," Lotty said in a strangled voice. "Andromache mourning Hector."

Max stared at Lotty, astonished equally by her emotion and her knowledge of the figure—Lotty was totally uninterested in sculpture.

Caudwell couldn't restrain the smug smile of a collector with a true coup. "Beautiful, isn't it? How do you know the subject?"

"I should know it." Lotty's voice was husky with emotion. "My grandmother had such a Pietro. An alabaster given her great-grandfather by the Emperor Joseph the Second himself for his help in consolidating imperial ties with Poland."

She swept the statue from its stand, ignoring a gasp from Max, and turned it over. "You can see the traces of the imperial stamp here still. And the chip on Hector's foot which made the Hapsburg wish to give the statue away to begin with. How came you to have this piece? Where did you find it?"

The small group that had joined Caudwell stood silent by the entrance, shocked at Lotty's outburst. Gioia looked more horrified than any of them, but he found Lotty overwhelming at the best of times—an elephant confronted by a hostile mouse.

"I think you're allowing your emotions to carry you away, doctor." Caudwell kept his tone light, making Lotty seem more gauche by contrast. "I inherited this piece from my father, who bought it—legitimately—in Europe. Perhaps from your—grandmother, was it? But I suspect you are confused about something you may have seen in a museum as a child."

Deborah gave a high-pitched laugh and called loudly to her brother, "Dad may have stolen it from Uncle Grif, but it looks like Grandfather snatched it to begin with anyway."

"Be quiet, Deborah," Caudwell barked sternly.

His daughter paid no attention to him. She laughed again and joined her brother to look at the imperial seal on the bottom of the statue.

Lotty brushed them aside. "*I* am confused about the seal of Joseph the Second?" she hissed at Caudwell. "Or about this chip on Hector's foot? You can see the line where some Philistine filled in the missing piece. Some person who thought his touch would add value to Pietro's work. Was that you, *doctor*? Or your father?"

"Lotty." Max was at her side, gently prising the statue from her shaking hands to restore it to its pedestal. "Lotty, this is not the place or the manner to discuss such things."

Angry tears sparked in her black eyes. "Are you doubting my word?"

Max shook his head. "I'm not doubting you. But I'm also not supporting you. I'm asking you not to talk about this matter in this way at this gathering."

"But, Max, either this man or his father is a thief!"

Caudwell strolled up to Lotty and pinched her chin. "You're working too hard, Dr. Herschel. You have too many things on your mind these days. I think the board would like to see you take a leave of absence for a few weeks, go someplace warm, get yourself relaxed. When you're this tense, you're no good to your patients. What do you say, Loewenthal?''

Max didn't say any of the things he wanted to—that Lotty was insufferable and Caudwell intolerable. He believed Lotty, believed that the piece had been her grandmother's. She knew too much about it, for one thing. And for another, a lot of artworks belonging to European Jews were now in museums or private collections around the world. It was only the most god-awful coincidence that the Pietro had ended up with Caudwell's father.

But how dare she raise the matter in the way most likely to alienate everyone present? He couldn't possibly support her in such a situation. And at the same time, Caudwell's pinching her chin in that condescending way made him wish he were not chained to a courtesy that would have kept him from knocking the surgeon out even if he'd been ten years younger and ten inches taller.

''I don't think this is the place or the time to discuss such matters,'' he reiterated as calmly as he could. ''Why don't we all cool down and get back together on Monday, eh?''

Lotty gasped involuntarily, then swept from the room without a backward glance.

Max refused to follow her. He was too angry with her to want to see her again that afternoon. When he got ready to leave the party an hour or so later, after a long conversation with Caudwell that taxed his sophisticated urbanity to the utmost, he heard with relief that Lotty was long gone. The tale of her outburst had of course spread through the gathering at something faster than the speed of sound; he wasn't up to defending her to Martha Gildersleeve who demanded an explanation of him in the elevator going down.

He went home for a solitary evening in his house in Evanston. Normally such time brought him pleasure, listening to music in his study, lying on the couch with his shoes off, reading history, letting the sounds of the lake wash over him.

Tonight, though, he could get no relief. Fury with Lotty merged into images of horror, the memories of his own disintegrated family, his search through Europe for his mother. He had never found anyone who was quite certain what became of her, although several people told him definitely of his father's suicide. And stamped over these wisps in his brain was the disturbing picture of Caudwell's children, their blond heads leaning backward at identical angles as they gleefully chanted, "Grandpa was a thief, Grandpa was a thief," while Caudwell edged his visitors out of the study.

By morning he would somehow have to reconstruct himself enough to face Lotty, to respond to the inevitable flood of calls from outraged trustees. He'd have to figure out a way of soothing Caudwell's vanity, bruised more by his children's behavior than anything Lotty had said. And find a way to keep both important doctors at Beth Israel.

Max rubbed his gray hair. Every week this job brought him less joy and more pain. Maybe it was time to step down, to let the board bring in a young MBA who would turn Beth Israel's finances around. Lotty would resign then, and it would be an end to the tension between her and Caudwell.

Max fell asleep on the couch. He awoke around five muttering, "By morning, by morning." His joints were stiff from cold, his eyes sticky with tears he'd shed unknowingly in his sleep.

But in the morning things changed. When Max got to his office he found the place buzzing, not with news of Lotty's outburst but word that Caudwell had missed his early morning surgery. Work came almost completely to a halt at noon when his children phoned to say they'd found the surgeon strangled in his own study and the Pietro Andromache missing. And on Tuesday, the police arrested Dr. Charlotte Herschel for Lewis Caudwell's murder.

III

Lotty would not speak to anyone. She was out on two hundred fifty thousand dollars' bail, the money raised by Max, but she had gone directly to her apartment on Sheffield after two nights in County Jail without stopping to thank him. She would not talk to reporters, she remained silent during all conversations with the police, and she emphatically refused to speak to the private investigator who had been her close friend for many years.

Max, too, stayed behind an impregnable shield of silence. While Lotty went on indefinite leave, turning her practice over to a series of colleagues, Max continued to go to the hospital every day. But he, too, would not speak to reporters; he wouldn't even say, "No comment." He talked to the police only after they threatened to lock him up as a material witness, and then every word had to be pried from him as if his mouth were stone and speech

Excalibur. For three days V.I. Warshawski left messages, which he refused to return.

On Friday, when no word came from the detective, when no reporter popped up from a nearby urinal in the men's room to try to trick him into speaking, when no more calls came from the state's attorney, Max felt a measure of relaxation as he drove home. As soon as the trial was over he would resign, retire to London. If he could only keep going until then, everything would be—not all right, but bearable.

He used the remote release for the garage door and eased his car into the small space. As he got out he realized bitterly he'd been too optimistic in thinking he'd be left in peace. He hadn't seen the woman sitting on the stoop leading from the garage to the kitchen when he drove in, only as she uncoiled herself at his approach.

"I'm glad you're home—I was beginning to freeze out here."

"How did you get into the garage, Victoria?"

The detective grinned in a way he usually found engaging. Now it seemed merely predatory. "Trade secret, Max. I know you don't want to see me, but I need to talk to you."

He unlocked the door into the kitchen. "Why not just let yourself into the house if you were cold? If your scruples permit you into the garage, why not into the house?"

She bit her lip in momentary discomfort but said lightly, "I couldn't manage my picklocks with my fingers this cold."

The detective followed him into the house. Another tall monster; five foot eight, athletic, light on her feet behind him. Maybe American mothers put growth hormones or steroids in their children's cornflakes. He'd have to ask Lotty. His mind winced at the thought.

"I've talked to the police, of course," the light alto continued behind him steadily, oblivious to his studied rudeness as he poured himself a cognac, took his shoes off, found his waiting slippers, and padded down the hall to the front door for his mail.

"I understand why they arrested Lotty—Caudwell had been doped with a whole bunch of Xanax and then strangled while he was sleeping it off. And, of course, she was back at the building Sunday night. She won't say why, but one of the tenants I.D.'d her as the woman who showed up around ten at the service entrance when he was walking his dog. She won't say if she talked to Caudwell, if he let her in, if he was still alive."

Max tried to ignore her clear voice. When that proved impossible he tried to read a journal which had come in the mail.

"And those kids, they're marvelous, aren't they? Like something out of the *Fabulous Furry Freak Brothers*. They won't talk to me but they gave a long interview to Murray Ryerson over at the *Star*.

"After Caudwell's guests left, they went to a flick at the Chestnut Street Station, had a pizza afterward, then took themselves dancing on Division Street. So they strolled in around two in the morning—confirmed by the doorman—saw the light on in the old man's study. But they were feeling no pain and he kind of overreacted—their term—if they were buzzed, so they didn't stop in to say good night. It was only when they got up around noon and went in that they found him."

V.I. had followed Max from the front hallway to the door

of his study as she spoke. He stood there irresolutely, not
wanting his private place desecrated with her insistent, air-
hammer speech, and finally went on down the hall to a
little-used living room. He sat stiffly on one of the brocade
armchairs and looked at her remotely when she perched
on the edge of its companion.

"The weak piece in the police story is the statue," V.I.
continued.

She eyed the Persian rug doubtfully and unzipped her
boots, sticking them on the bricks in front of the fireplace.

"Everyone who was at the party agrees that Lotty was
beside herself. By now the story has spread so far that
people who weren't even in the apartment when she
looked at the statue swear they heard her threaten to kill
him. But if that's the case, what happened to the statue?"

Max gave a slight shrug to indicate total lack of interest
in the topic.

V.I. ploughed on doggedly. "Now some people think
she might have given it to a friend or a relation to keep
for her until her name is cleared at the trial. And these
people think it would be either her Uncle Stefan here in
Chicago, her brother Hugo in Montreal, or you. So the
Mounties searched Hugo's place and are keeping an eye
on his mail. And the Chicago cops are doing the same for
Stefan. And I presume someone got a warrant and went
through here, right?"

Max said nothing, but he felt his heart beating faster.
Police in his house, searching his things? But wouldn't
they have to get his permission to enter? Or would they?
Victoria would know, but he couldn't bring himself to ask.
She waited for a few minutes, but when he still wouldn't

speak, she plunged on. He could see it was becoming an effort for her to talk, but he wouldn't help her.

"But I don't agree with those people. Because I know that Lotty is innocent. And that's why I'm here. Not like a bird of prey, as you think, using your misery for carrion. But to get you to help me. Lotty won't speak to me, and if she's that miserable I won't force her to. But surely, Max, you won't sit idly by and let her be railroaded for something she never did."

Max looked away from her. He was surprised to find himself holding the brandy snifter and set it carefully on a table beside him.

"Max!" Her voice was shot with astonishment. "I don't believe this. You actually think she killed Caudwell."

Max flushed a little, but she'd finally stung him into a response. "And you are God who sees all and knows she didn't?"

"I see more than you do," V.I. snapped. "I haven't known Lotty as long as you have, but I know when she's telling the truth."

"So you are God." Max bowed in heavy irony. "You see beyond the facts to the innermost souls of men and women."

He expected another outburst from the young woman, but she gazed at him steadily without speaking. It was a look sympathetic enough that Max felt embarrassed by his sarcasm and burst out with what was on his mind.

"What else am I to think? She hasn't said anything, but there's no doubt that she returned to his apartment Sunday night."

It was V.I.'s turn for sarcasm. "With a little vial of Xanax that she somehow induced him to swallow? And then strangled him for good measure? Come on, Max, you know Lotty: honesty follows her around like a cloud. If she'd killed Caudwell, she'd say something like, 'Yes, I bashed the little vermin's brains in.' Instead she's not speaking at all."

Suddenly the detective's eyes widened with incredulity. "Of course. She thinks you killed Caudwell. You're doing the only thing you can to protect her—standing mute. And she's doing the same thing. What an admirable pair of archaic knights."

"No!" Max said sharply. "It's not possible. How could she think such a thing? She carried on so wildly that it was embarrassing to be near her. I didn't want to see her or talk to her. That's why I've felt so terrible. If only I hadn't been so obstinate, if only I'd called her Sunday night. How could she think I would kill someone on her behalf when I was so angry with her?"

"Why else isn't she saying anything to anyone?" Warshawski demanded.

"Shame, maybe," Max offered. "You didn't see her on Sunday. I did. That is why I think she killed him, not because some man let her into the building."

His brown eyes screwed shut at the memory. "I have seen Lotty in the grip of anger many times, more than is pleasant to remember, really. But never, never have I seen her in this kind of—uncontrolled rage. You could not talk to her. It was impossible."

The detective didn't respond to that. Instead she said, "Tell me about the statue. I heard a couple of garbled versions from people who were at the party, but I haven't found anyone yet who was in the study when Caudwell showed it to you. Was it really her grandmother's, do you think? And how did Caudwell come to have it if it was?"

Max nodded mournfully. "Oh, yes. It was really her family's, I'm convinced of that. She could not have known in advance about the details, the flaw in the foot, the imperial seal on the bottom. As to how Caudwell got it, I did a little looking into that myself yesterday. His father was with the Army of Occupation in Germany after the war. A surgeon attached to Patton's staff. Men in such positions had endless opportunities to acquire artworks after the war."

V.I. shook her head questioningly.

"You must know something of this, Victoria. Well, maybe not. You know the Nazis helped themselves liberally to artwork belonging to Jews everywhere they occupied Europe. And not just Jews—they plundered Eastern Europe on a grand scale. The best guess is that they stole sixteen million pieces—statues, paintings, altarpieces, tapestries, rare books. The list is beyond reckoning, really."

The detective gave a little gasp. "Sixteen million! You're joking."

"Not a joke, Victoria. I wish it were so, but it is not. The U.S. Army of Occupation took charge of as many works of art as they found in the occupied territories. In theory, they were to find the rightful owners and try to restore them. But in practice few pieces were ever traced, and many of them ended up on the black market.

"You only had to say that such-and-such a piece was worth less than five thousand dollars and you were allowed to buy it. For an officer on Patton's staff, the opportunities for fabulous acquisitions would have been endless. Caudwell said he had the statue authenticated, but of course he never bothered to establish its provenance. Anyway, how could he?'' Max finished bitterly. ''Lotty's family had a deed of gift from the Emperor, but that would have disappeared long since with the dispersal of their possessions.''

''And you really think Lotty would have killed a man just to get this statue back? She couldn't have expected to keep it. Not if she'd killed someone to get it, I mean.''

''You are so practical, Victoria. You are too analytical, sometimes, to understand why people do what they do. That was not just a statue. True, it is a priceless artwork, but you know Lotty, you know she places no value on such possessions. No, it meant her family to her, her past, her history, everything that the war destroyed forever for her. You must not imagine that because she never discusses such matters that they do not weigh on her.''

V.I. flushed at Max's accusation. ''You should be glad I'm analytical. It convinces me that Lotty is innocent. And whether you believe it or not I'm going to prove it.''

Max lifted his shoulders slightly in a manner wholly European. ''We each support Lotty according to our lights. I saw that she met her bail, and I will see that she gets expert counsel. I am not convinced that she needs you making her innermost secrets public.''

V.I.'s gray eyes turned dark with a sudden flash of temper. ''You're dead wrong about Lotty. I'm sure the memory of the war is a pain that can never be cured, but Lotty lives in the present, she works in hope for the future. The past does not obsess and consume her as, perhaps, it does you.''

Max said nothing. His wide mouth turned in on itself in a narrow line. The detective laid a contrite hand on his arm.

"I'm sorry, Max. That was below the belt."

He forced the ghost of a smile to his mouth.

"Perhaps it's true. Perhaps it's why I love these ancient things so much. I wish I could believe you about Lotty. Ask me what you want to know. If you promise to leave as soon as I've answered and not to bother me again, I'll answer your questions."

IV

Max put in a dutiful appearance at the Michigan Avenue Presbyterian Church Monday afternoon for Lewis Caudwell's funeral. The surgeon's former wife came, flanked by her children and her ex-husband's brother Griffen. Even after three decades in America Max found himself puzzled sometimes by the natives' behavior: since she and Caudwell were divorced, why had his ex-wife draped herself in black? She was even wearing a veiled hat reminiscent of Queen Victoria.

The children behaved in a moderately subdued fashion, but the girl was wearing a white dress shot with black lightning forks which looked as though it belonged at a disco or a resort. Maybe it was her only dress or her only dress with black in it, Max thought, trying hard to look charitably at the blond Amazon—after all, she had been suddenly and horribly orphaned.

Even though she was a stranger both in the city and the church, Deborah had hired one of the church parlors and managed to find someone to cater coffee and light snacks. Max joined the rest of the congregation there after the service.

He felt absurd as he offered condolences to the divorced widow: did she really miss the dead man so much? She accepted his conventional words with graceful melancholy and leaned slightly against her son and daughter. They hovered near her with what struck Max as a stagey solicitude. Seen next to her daughter, Mrs. Caudwell looked so frail and undernourished that she seemed like a ghost. Or maybe it was just that her children had a hearty vitality that even a funeral couldn't quench.

Caudwell's brother Griffen stayed as close to the widow as the children would permit. The man was totally unlike the hearty sea dog surgeon. Max thought if he'd met the brothers standing side by side he would never have guessed their relationship. He was tall, like his niece and nephew, but without their robustness. Caudwell had had a thick mop of yellow-white hair; Griffen's domed head was covered by thin wisps of gray. He seemed weak and nervous, and lacked Caudwell's outgoing *bonhomie;* no wonder the surgeon had found it easy to decide the disposition of their father's estate in his favor. Max wondered what Griffen had gotten in return.

Mrs. Caudwell's vague, disoriented conversation indicated that she was heavily sedated. That, too, seemed strange. A man she hadn't lived with for four years and she was so upset at his death that she could only manage the funeral on drugs? Or maybe it was the shame of coming as the divorced woman, not a true widow? But then why come at all?

To his annoyance, Max found himself wishing he could ask Victoria about it. She would have some cynical explanation—Caudwell's death meant the end of the widow's alimony and she knew she wasn't remembered in the will.

Or she was having an affair with Griffen and was afraid she would betray herself without tranquilizers. Although it was hard to imagine the uncertain Griffen as the object of a strong passion.

Since he had told Victoria he didn't want to see her again when she left on Friday, it was ridiculous of him to wonder what she was doing, whether she was really uncovering evidence that would clear Lotty. Ever since she had gone he had felt a little flicker of hope in the bottom of his stomach. He kept trying to drown it, but it wouldn't quite go away.

Lotty, of course, had not come to the funeral, but most of the rest of the Beth Israel staff was there, along with the trustees. Arthur Gioia, his giant body filling the small parlor to the bursting point, tried to find a tactful balance between honesty and courtesy with the bereaved family; he made heavy going of it.

A sable-clad Martha Gildersleeve appeared under Gioia's elbow, rather like a furry football he might have tucked away. She made bright, unseemly remarks to the bereaved family about the disposal of Caudwell's artworks.

"Of course, the famous statue is gone now. What a pity. You could have endowed a chair in his honor with the proceeds from that piece alone." She gave a high, meaningless laugh.

Max sneaked a glance at his watch, wondering how long he had to stay before leaving would be rude. His sixth sense, the perfect courtesy that governed his movements, had deserted him, leaving him subject to the gaucheries of ordinary mortals. He never peeked at his watch at functions, and at any prior funeral he would have deftly pried Martha Gildersleeve from her victim. Instead he stood helplessly by while she tortured Mrs. Caudwell and other bystanders alike.

He glanced at his watch again. Only two minutes had passed since his last look. No wonder people kept their eyes on their watches at dull meetings: they couldn't believe the clock could move so slowly.

He inched stealthily toward the door, exchanging empty remarks with the staff members and trustees he passed. Nothing negative was said about Lotty to his face, but the comments cut off at his approach added to his misery.

He was almost at the exit when two newcomers appeared. Most of the group looked at them with indifferent curiosity, but Max suddenly felt an absurd stir of elation. Victoria, looking sane and modern in a navy suit, stood in the doorway, eyebrows raised, scanning the room. At her elbow was a police sergeant Max had met with her a few times. The man was in charge of Caudwell's death, too; it was that unpleasant association that kept the name momentarily from his mind.

Victoria finally spotted Max near the door and gave him a discreet sign. He went to her at once.

"I think we may have the goods," she murmured. "Can you get everyone to go? We just want the family, Mrs. Gildersleeve, and Gioia."

"*You* may have the goods," the police sergeant growled. "I'm here unofficially and reluctantly."

"But you're here." Victoria grinned, and Max wondered how he ever could have found the look predatory. His own spirits rose enormously at her smile. "You know in your heart of hearts that arresting Lotty was just plain dumb. And now I'm going to make you look real smart. In public, too."

Max felt his suave sophistication return with the rush of elation that an ailing diva must have when she finds her voice again. A touch here, a word there, and the guests disappeared like the hosts of Sennacherib. Meanwhile he solicitously escorted first Martha Gildersleeve, then Mrs. Caudwell to adjacent armchairs, got the brother to fetch coffee for Mrs. Gildersleeve, the daughter and son to look after the widow.

With Gioia he could be a bit more ruthless, telling him to wait because the police had something important to ask him. When the last guest had melted away, the immunologist stood nervously at the window rattling his change over and over in his pockets. The jingling suddenly was the only sound in the room. Gioia reddened and clasped his hands behind his back.

Victoria came into the room beaming like a governess with a delightful treat in store for her charges. She introduced herself to the Caudwells.

"You know Sergeant McGonnigal, I'm sure, after this last week. I'm a private investigator. Since I don't have any legal standing, you're not required to answer any questions I have. So I'm not going to ask you any questions. I'm just going to treat you to a travelogue. I wish I had slides, but you'll have to imagine the visuals while the audio track moves along."

"A private investigator!" Steve's mouth formed an exaggerated "O"; his eyes widened in amazement. "Just like Bogie."

He was speaking, as usual, to his sister. She gave her high-pitched laugh and said, "We'll win first prize in the 'How I Spent My Winter Vacation' contests. Our daddy was murdered. Zowie. Then his most valuable possession was snatched. Powie. But he'd already stolen it from the Jewish doctor who killed him. Yowie! And then a P.I. to wrap it all up. Yowie! Zowie! Powie!"

"Deborah, please," Mrs. Caudwell sighed. "I know you're excited, sweetie, but not right now, okay?"

"Your children keep you young, don't they, ma'am?" Victoria said. "How can you ever feel old when your kids stay seven all their lives?"

"Oo, ow, she bites. Debbie, watch out, she bites!" Steve cried.

McGonnigal made an involuntary movement, as though restraining himself from smacking the younger man. "Ms. Warshawski is right; you are under no obligation to answer any of her questions. But you're bright people, all of you; you know I wouldn't be here if the police didn't take her ideas very seriously. So let's have a little quiet and listen to what she's got on her mind."

Victoria seated herself in an armchair near Mrs. Caudwell. McGonnigal moved to the door and leaned against the jamb. Deborah and Steve whispered and poked each other until one or both of them shrieked. They then made their faces prim and sat with their hands folded on their laps, looking like bright-eyed choirboys.

Griffen hovered near Mrs. Caudwell. "You know you don't have to say anything, Vivian. In fact, I think you should return to your hotel and lie down. The stress of the funeral—then these strangers—"

Mrs. Caudwell's lips curled bravely below the bottom of her veil. "It's all right, Grif; if I managed to survive everything else, one more thing isn't going to do me in."

"Great." Victoria accepted a cup of coffee from Max. "Let me just sketch events for you as I saw them last week.

Like everyone else in Chicago, I read about Dr. Caudwell's murder and saw it on television. Since I know a number of people attached to Beth Israel, I may have paid more attention to it than the average viewer, but I didn't get personally involved until Dr. Herschel's arrest on Tuesday."

She swallowed some coffee and set the cup on the table next to her with a small snap. "I have known Dr. Herschel for close to twenty years. It is inconceivable that she would commit such a murder, as those who know her well should have realized at once. I don't fault the police, but others should have known better; she is hot-tempered. I'm not saying killing is beyond her—I don't think it's beyond any of us. She might have taken the statue and smashed Dr. Caudwell's head in the heat of rage. But it beggars belief to think she went home, brooded over her injustices, packed a dose of prescription tranquilizer, and headed back to the Gold Coast with murder in mind."

Max felt his cheeks turn hot at her words. He started to interject a protest but bit it back.

"Dr. Herschel refused to make a statement all week, but this afternoon, when I got back from my travels, she finally agreed to talk to me. Sergeant McGonnigal was with me. She doesn't deny that she returned to Dr. Caudwell's apartment at ten that night—she went back to apologize for her outburst and to try to plead with him to return the statue. He didn't answer when the doorman called up, and on impulse she went around to the back of the building, got in through the service entrance, and waited for some time outside the apartment door. When he neither answered the doorbell nor returned home himself, she finally went away around eleven o'clock. The children, of course, were having a night on the town."

"*She* says," Gioia interjected.

"Agreed." V.I. smiled. "I make no bones about being a partisan; I accept her version. The more so because the only reason she didn't give it a week ago was that she herself was protecting an old friend. She thought perhaps this friend had bestirred himself on her behalf and killed Caudwell to avenge deadly insults against her. It was only when I persuaded her that these suspicions were as un-merited as—well, as accusations against herself—that she agreed to talk."

Max bit his lip and busied himself with getting more coffee for the three women. Victoria waited for him to finish before continuing.

"When I finally got a detailed account of what took place at Caudwell's party, I heard about three people with an axe to grind. One always has to ask, what axe and how big a grindstone? That's what I've spent the weekend finding out. You might as well know that I've been to Little Rock and to Havelock, North Carolina."

Gioia began jingling the coins in his pockets again. Mrs. Caudwell said softly, "Grif, I am feeling a little faint. Per-haps—"

"Home you go, Mom," Steve cried out with alacrity.

"In a few minutes, Mrs. Caudwell," the sergeant said from the doorway. "Get her feet up, Warshawski."

For a moment Max was afraid that Steve or Deborah was going to attack Victoria, but McGonnigal moved over to the widow's chair and the children sat down again. Little drops of sweat dotted Griffen's balding head; Gioia's face had a greenish sheen, foliage on top of his redwood neck.

"The thing that leapt out at me," Victoria continued calmly, as though there had been no interruption, "was Caudwell's remark to Dr. Gioia. The doctor was clearly upset, but people were so focused on Lotty and the statue that they didn't pay any attention to that.

"So I went to Little Rock, Arkansas, on Saturday and found the Paul Nierman whose name Caudwell had mentioned to Gioia. Nierman lived in the same fraternity with Gioia when they were undergraduates together twenty-five years ago. And he took Dr. Gioia's anatomy and physiology exams his junior year when Gioia was in danger of academic probation, so he could stay on the football team.

"Well, that seemed unpleasant, perhaps disgraceful. But there's no question that Gioia did all his own work in medical school, passed his boards, and so on. So I didn't think the board would demand a resignation for this youthful indiscretion. The question was whether Gioia thought they would, and if he would have killed to prevent Caudwell making it public."

She paused, and the immunologist blurted out, "No. No. But Caudwell—Caudwell knew I'd opposed his appointment. He and I—our approaches to medicine were very opposite. And as soon as he said Nierman's name to me, I knew he'd found out and that he'd torment me with it forever. I—I went back to his place Sunday night to have it out with him. I was more determined than Dr. Herschel and got into his unit through the kitchen entrance; he hadn't locked that.

"I went to his study, but he was already dead. I couldn't believe it. It absolutely terrified me. I could see he'd been strangled and—well, it's no secret that I'm strong enough to have done it. I wasn't thinking straight. I just got clean away from there—I think I've been running ever since."

"You!" McGonnigal shouted. "How come we haven't heard about this before?"

"Because you insisted on focusing on Dr. Herschel," V.I. said nastily. "I knew he'd been there because the doorman told me. He would have told you if you'd asked."

"This is terrible," Mrs. Gildersleeve interjected. "I am going to talk to the board tomorrow and demand the resignations of Dr. Gioia and Dr. Herschel."

"Do," Victoria agreed cordially. "Tell them the reason you got to stay for this was because Murray Ryerson at the *Herald-Star* was doing a little checking for me here in Chicago. He found out that part of the reason you were so jealous of Caudwell's collection is that you're living terribly in debt. I won't humiliate you in public by telling people what your money has gone to, but you've had to sell your ex-husband's art collection and you have a third mortgage on your house. A valuable statue with no documented history would have taken care of everything."

Martha Gildersleeve shrank inside her sable. "You don't know anything about this."

"Well, Murray talked to Pablo and Eduardo. . . . Yes, I won't say anything else. So anyway, Murray checked whether either Gioia or Mrs. Gildersleeve had the statue. They didn't, so—"

"You've been in my house?" Mrs. Gildersleeve shrieked.

V.I. shook her head. "Not me. Murray Ryerson." She looked apologetically at the sergeant. "I knew you'd never get a warrant for me, since you'd made an arrest. And you'd never have got it in time, anyway."

She looked at her coffee cup, saw it was empty and put

it down again. Max took it from the table and filled it for her a third time. His fingertips were itching with nervous irritation; some of the coffee landed on his trouser leg.

"I talked to Murray Saturday night from Little Rock. When he came up empty here, I headed for North Carolina. To Havelock, where Griffen and Lewis Caudwell grew up and where Mrs. Caudwell still lives. And I saw the house where Griffen lives, and talked to the doctor who treats Mrs. Caudwell, and—"

"You really are a pooper snooper, aren't you," Steve said.

"Pooper snooper, pooper snooper," Deborah chanted. "Don't get enough thrills of your own so you have to live on other people's shit."

"Yeah, the neighbors talked to me about you two." Victoria looked at them with contemptuous indulgence. "You've been a two-person wolfpack terrifying most of the people around you since you were three. But the folks in Havelock admired how you always stuck up for your mother. You thought your father got her addicted to tranquilizers and then left her high and dry. So you brought her newest version with you and were all set—you just needed to decide when to give it to him. Dr. Herschel's outburst over the statue played right into your hands. You figured your father had stolen it from your uncle to begin with—why not send it back to him and let Dr. Herschel take the rap?"

"It wasn't like that," Steve said, red spots burning in his cheeks.

"What was it like, son?" McGonnigal had moved next to him.

"Don't talk to them—they're tricking you," Deborah shrieked. "The pooper snooper and her gopher gooper."

"She—Mommy used to love us before Daddy made her take all this shit. Then she went away. We just wanted him to see what it was like. We started putting Xanax in his coffee and stuff; we wanted to see if he'd fuck up during surgery, let his life get ruined. But then he was sleeping there in the study after his stupid-ass party, and we thought we'd just let him sleep through his morning surgery. Sleep forever, you know, it was so easy, we used his own Harvard necktie. I was so fucking sick of hearing 'Early to bed, early to rise' from him. And we sent the statue to Uncle Grif. I suppose the pooper snooper found it there. He can sell it and Mother can be all right again."

"Grandpa stole it from Jews and Daddy stole it from Grif, so we thought it worked out perfectly if we stole it from Daddy," Deborah cried. She leaned her blond head next to her brother's and shrieked with laughter.

V

Max watched the line of Lotty's legs change as she stood on tiptoe to reach a brandy snifter. Short, muscular from years of racing at top speed from one point to the next, maybe they weren't as svelte as the long legs of modern American girls, but he preferred them. He waited until her feet were securely planted before making his announcement.

"The board is bringing in Justin Hardwick for a final interview for chief of staff."

"Max!" She whirled, the Bengal fire sparkling in her eyes. "I know this Hardwick and he is another like Caudwell, looking for cost-cutting and no poverty patients. I won't have it."

"We've got you and Gioia and a dozen others bringing in so many nonpaying patients that we're not going to survive another five years at the present rate. I figure it's a balancing act. We need someone who can see that the hospital survives so that you and Art can practice medicine the way you want to. And when he knows what happened to his predecessor, he'll be very careful not to stir up our resident tigress."

"Max!" She was hurt and astonished at the same time. "Oh. You're joking, I see. It's not very funny to me, you know."

"My dear, we've got to learn to laugh about it; it's the only way we'll ever be able to forgive ourselves for our terrible misjudgments." He stepped over to put an arm around her. "Now where is this remarkable surprise you promised to show me?"

She shot him a look of pure mischief, Lotty on a dare as he first remembered meeting her at eighteen. His hold on her tightened and he followed her to her bedroom. In a glass case in the corner, complete with a humidity-control system, stood the Pietro Andromache.

Max looked at the beautiful, anguished face. I understand your sorrows, she seemed to say to him. I understand your grief for your mother, your family, your history, but it's all right to let go of them, to live in the present and hope for the future. It's not a betrayal.

Tears pricked his eyelids, but he demanded, "How did you get this? I was told the police had it under lock and key until lawyers decided on the disposition of Caudwell's estate."

"Victoria," Lotty said shortly. "I told her the problem and she got it for me. On the condition that I not ask how she did it. And Max, you know—*damned* well that it was not Caudwell's to dispose of."

It was Lotty's. Of course it was. Max wondered briefly how Joseph the Second had come by it to begin with. For that matter, what had Lotty's great-great-grandfather done to earn it from the emperor? Max looked into Lotty's tiger eyes and kept such reflections to himself. Instead he inspected Hector's foot where the filler had been carefully scraped away to reveal the old chip.

Betrayed

John D. MacDonald

It was an Indian summer afternoon in mid-October—Sunday afternoon. Francie had gone back to the lab, five miles from the lakeside cabin, but Dr. Blair Cudahy, the Administrator, had shooed her out, saying that he was committing enough perjury on the civil service hours-of-work reports without having her work Sundays, too.

And so Francie Aintrell had climbed back into her ten-year-old sedan and come rattling over the potholed highway back to the small cabin. She sat on the miniature porch, her back against a wooden upright, fingers laced around one blue-jeaned knee.

Work, she had learned, was one of the anesthetics. Work and time. They all talked about the healing wonder of time. As though each second could be another tiny layer of insulation between you and Bob. And one day, when enough seconds and minutes and years had gone by, you could look in your mirror and see a face old enough to be the mother of Bob, and his face would remain young and unchanged in memory.

But she could look in the wavery mirror in the little camp and touch her cheeks with her fingertips, touch the face that he had loved, see the blue eyes he had loved; the black hair.

And then she would forget the classic shape of the little tragedy. West Point, post–World War II class. Second Lieutenant Robert Aintrell. One of the expendable ones. And expended, of course, near a reservoir no one had ever heard of before.

KIA. A lot of them from that class became KIA on the record.

When he had been sent to Korea, she had gone from the West Coast back to the Pentagon and applied for reinstatement. Clerk-stenographer. CAF 6. Assigned to the District Control Section of the Industrial Service Branch of the Office of the Chief of Ordinance.

And then they send you a wire and you open it, and the whole world makes a convulsive twist and lands in a new pattern. It can't happen to you—and to Bob. But it has.

So after the first hurt, so sharp and wild that it was like a kind of insanity, Francie applied for work outside Washington, because they had been together in Washington, and that made it a place to escape from.

Everyone had been sweet. And then there had been the investigation. Very detailed, and very thorough. "Yes, Mrs. Aintrell is a loyal citizen. Class A security risk."

Promotion to CAF 7. "Report to Dr. Cudahy, please. Vanders, New York. Yes, that's in the Adirondacks—near Lake Arthur. Sorry the only name we have for that organization is Unit Thirty."

And three miles from Vanders, five miles from the lake, she had found a new gravel road, a shining wire fence at the end of it, a guard post, a cinder-block building, a power cable marching over the hills on towers, ending at the laboratory.

She had reported to Blair Cudahy, a fat little mild-eyed man. She could not tell, but she thought that he approved of her. "Mrs. Aintrell, you have been approved by Security. There is no need, I'm sure, to tell you not to discuss what we are doing here."

"No, sir," she had replied. "I quite understand."

"We are concerned with electronics, with radar. This is a research organization. The terminology will give you difficulty at first. If we accomplish our mission here, Mrs. Aintrell, we will be able to design a nose fuse for interceptor rockets which will make any air attack on this continent— too expensive to contemplate."

At that, Cudahy hitched in his chair and turned so that he could glance over his shoulder at an enlarged photograph of an illustration Francie remembered seeing in a magazine. It showed the fat red bloom of the atom god towering over the Manhattan skyline.

Cudahy turned back and smiled. "That is the threat that goads us on. Now come and meet the staff."

Most of them were young. The names and faces were a blur. Francie didn't mind. She knew that she would straighten them out soon enough. Ten scientists and engineers. About fifteen technicians. And then the guards and housekeeping personnel.

The bachelor staff lived behind the wire. The married staff rented cabins in the vicinity. Dr. Blair Cudahy's administrative assistant was a tall, youngish man with deep-set quiet eyes, a relaxed manner, a hint of stubbornness in the set of the jaw. His name was Clinton Reese.

After they were introduced, Cudahy said, "I believe Clint has found a place for you."

"Next best thing to a cave, Mrs. Aintrell," Clint Reese had said. "But you have lovely neighbors. Mostly bears. You have a car?"

"No, I haven't," she said. His casual banter seemed oddly out of place when she looked beyond his shoulder and saw that picture on Cudahy's office wall.

"I'll take you to the local car mart and we'll get you one."

Cudahy said, "Thanks, Clint. Show her where she'll work and give her a run-through on the duties, then take her out to that place you rented. We'll expect you at nine tomorrow morning, Mrs. Aintrell."

Clint took her to her desk. He said, "Those crazy people you met are scientists and engineers. They work in teams, attempting different avenues of approach to the same problem. Left to their own devices, they'd keep notes on the backs of match folders. Because even scientists sometimes drop dead, we have to keep progress reports up to date in case somebody else has to take over. There are three teams. You'll take notes, transcribe them, and keep the program files. Tomorrow I'll explain the problems involved in the care of madmen. Ready to go?"

They stopped at Vanders and picked up her luggage from the combination general store and bus depot. Clint Reese loaded it into the back of his late model sedan. He chattered amiably all the way out to the road that bordered the north shore of Lake Arthur.

He pulled off into a small clearing just off the road and said, "We'll leave the stuff here, in case it turns out to be a little too primitive."

The trail leading down the wooded slope toward the lake shore was hard-packed. At the steepest point there was a rustic handrail. When Francie first saw the small cabin, and the deep blue of the lake beyond it, her heart seemed to turn over. Bob had talked of just such a place. A porch overlooking the lake. A small wooden dock. And the perfect stillness of the woods in mid-September.

The interior was small. One fair-sized room with a wide, built-in bunk. A gray stone fireplace. A tiny kitchen and bath.

Clint Reese said, in the manner of a guide, "You will note that this little nest has modern conveniences. Running water, latest model lanterns for lights. Refrigerator, stove heater, and hot-water heater all run on bottled gas. We never get more than eight feet of snow, so I'm told, and you'll have to have a car. The unscrupulous landlord wants sixty a month. Like?"

She turned to him smiling. "Like very much."

"Now I'll claw my way up your hill and bring down your bags. You check the utensils and supplies. I laid in some food, on the gamble that you'd like it here."

He came down with the bags, making a mock show of exhaustion. He explained the intricacies of the lanterns and the heaters, then said that he'd pick her up in the morning at eight-fifteen.

"You've been very kind," she said.

"Dogs and children go wild about me. See you tomorrow."

After he had disappeared around the bend of the trail, she stood frowning. He was her immediate superior, and he had acted totally unlike any previous superior in the Civil Service hierarchy. Usually they were most reserved, most cautious. He seemed entirely too blithe and carefree to be able to do an administrative job of the type this Unit Thirty apparently demanded.

But she had to admit that he had been efficient about the cabin. And so, on a mid-September afternoon, she had unpacked. The first thing she took out of the large suitcase was Bob's picture. She could imagine him saying, "Baby, how do you *know* there aren't any bears in those woods? Fine life for a city gal."

"I'll get along, Bob," she told him. "I promise you, I'll get along."

And with his picture watching her, she unpacked and cooked, and ate, and went to bed in the deep bunk, surrounded by the pine smell, the leaf rustle, the lap of water against the small dock.

The work had been very hard at first, mostly because of the technical terms used in the reports, and also because of the backlog of data that had piled up since the illness of the previous girl. During the worst of it, Clint Reese found ways to make her smile. He helped her in her purchase of the ten-year-old car.

The names and faces straightened out quickly, with Clint's help. Gray chubby young Dr. Jonas McKay, with razor-sharp mind. Tom Blajoviak, with Slavic slanting merry eyes, heavy-handed joshing, big shoulders. Dr. Sherra, lost in a private fog of mental mathematics and conjecture.

Francie had pictured laboratories as being gleaming, spotless places full of stainless steel, sparkling glass, white smocks. Unit Thirty was a kind of orderly, chaotic jumble of dust and bits of wire and tubing and old technical journals stacked on the floor in wild disarray.

She soon caught the hang of their verbal shorthand, learned to put in the reports the complete terms to which they referred. McKay was orderly about summoning her. Tom Blajoviak found so much pleasure in dictating that he kept calling for her when he found nothing at all to report. Dr. Sherra had to be trapped before he would dictate to her. He considered progress reports to be a lot of nonsense.

With increasing knowledge of the personalities of the three team leaders came a new awareness of the strain under which they worked. The strain made them sometimes irritable, sometimes childish. Dr. Cudahy supervised and coordinated the technical aspects of the lines of research, treading very gently so as not to offend. And it was Clint's task to take the burden of all other routine matters off Cudahy's shoulders, so that he could function at maximum efficiency at the technical supervision at which he excelled.

It had been a very full month, with little time for relaxation. Francie sat on the porch of the cabin on the October Sunday afternoon, realizing how closely she had identified herself with the work of Unit Thirty during the past month.

With the Adirondack tour season over, most of the private camps were empty. There were only a few fishermen about. She heard the shrill keening of the reel long before the boat, following the shore line, came into view through the remaining lurid leaves of autumn.

A young girl, her hair pale and blond, rowed the boat very slowly. She wore a heavy cardigan and a wool skirt. A man stood in the boat, casting a black-and-white plug toward the shallows, and reeling it in with hopeful twitches of the rod tip. The sun was low, the lake still, the air sharp with the threat of coming winter. It made a very pretty picture. Francie wondered if they'd had any luck.

The boat moved slowly by, passing just ten feet or so from the end of the dock, not more than thirty feet from the small porch. The girl glanced up and smiled, and Francie instinctively waved. She remembered seeing them in Vanders in the store.

"Any luck?" Francie asked.

"One decent bass," the man said. He had a pleasant weather-burned face.

As he made the next cast Francie saw him slip. As the girl cried out he reached wildly at nothingness, and fell full-length into the lake, inadvertently pushing the boat away from him. He came up quickly, looked toward the boat, then paddled toward the end of Francie's dock. Francie ran down just as he climbed up onto the dock.

"That must have been graceful to watch," the man said ruefully, his teeth chattering.

The girl bumped the end of the dock with the boat. "Are you all right, dear?" she asked nervously.

"Oh, I'm just dandy," the man said, flapping his arms. "Row me home quick."

The blond girl looked appealingly at Francie. "If it wouldn't be too much trouble, I could row home and bring dry clothes here and—"

"Of course!" Francie said. "I was going to suggest that."

"I don't want to put you out," the man said. "Darn fool stunt, falling in the lake."

"Come on in before you freeze solid," Francie said.

The girl rowed quickly down the lake shore. The man followed Francie in. The fire was all laid. She touched a match to the exposed corner of paper, handed him a folded blanket from the foot of the bunk.

"That fireplace works fast," she said. "Get those clothes off and wrap yourself up in the blanket. I'll be on the porch. You holler when you're ready."

She sat on the porch and waited. When the man called she went in. She put three fingers of whiskey in the bottom of a water tumbler and handed it to him. "Drink your medicine."

"I ought to fall in the lake oftener! Hey, don't bother with those clothes!"

"I'll hang them out."

She put his shoes on the porch, hung the clothes on the line she had rigged from the porch corner to a small birch. Just as she finished she saw the girl coming back, rowing strongly. Francie went down and tied the bow line, and took the pile of clothes from her, so that she could get out of the boat more easily.

"How is he?" the girl asked in a worried tone.

"Warm on the inside and the outside, too."

"He wouldn't want me to tell you this. He likes to pretend it isn't so. But he isn't well. That's why I was so worried. You're being more than kind."

"When I fall out of a boat near your place I'll expect the same service."

"You'll get it," the girl said.

Francie saw that she was older than she had looked from a distance. There were fine lines near her eyes, a bit of gray in the blond temples. Late twenties, possibly.

The girl took the clothes, put out her free hand. "I'm Betty Jackson," she said. "And my husband's name is Stewart."

"I'm Francie Aintrell. I'm glad you—dropped in."

Francie waited on the porch again until Betty came out. "He's dressed now," Betty said. "If we could stay just a little longer—"

"Of course you can! Actually, I was sort of lonesome this afternoon."

They went in. Francie put another heavy piece of slab-wood on the fire. Stewart Jackson said, "I think I've stopped shivering. We certainly thank you, Miss Aintrell."

"It's Mrs. Aintrell. Francie Aintrell."

She saw Betty glance toward Bob's picture. "Is that your husband, Francie?"

"Yes, he—he was killed in Korea." Never before had she been able to say it so flatly, so factually.

Stewart Jackson looked down at his empty glass. "That's tough. Sorry I—"

"You couldn't have known. And I'm used to telling people." She went on quickly, in an effort to cover the awkwardness. "Are you on vacation? I think I've seen you over in town."

"No, we're not on vacation," Betty said. "Stewart sort of semiretired last year, and we bought a camp up here. It's—let me see—the seventh one down the shore from you. Stew has always been interested in fishing, and now we're making lures and trying to get a mail-order business started for them."

"I design 'em and test 'em and have a little firm down in Utica make up the wooden bodies of the plugs," Stewart said. "Then we put them together and put on the paint job. Are you working up here or vacationing?"

"I'm working for the Government," Francie said, "in the new weather station." That was the cover story which all employees were instructed to use—that Unit Thirty was doing meteorological research.

"We've heard about that place, of course," Betty said. "Sounds rather dull to me. Do you like it?"

"It's a job," Francie said. "I was working in Washington and after I heard about my husband, I asked for a transfer to some other place."

Jackson yawned. "Now I'm so comfortable, I'm getting sleepy. We better go."

"No," Francie said, meaning it. "Do stay. We're neighbors. How about hamburgers over the fire?"

She saw Betty and Stewart exchange glances. She liked them. There was something wholesome and comfortable about their relationship. And, because Stewart Jackson was obviously in his midforties, they did not give her the constant sense of loss that a younger couple might have caused.

"We'll stay if I can help," Betty said, "and if you'll return the visit. Soon."

"Signed and sealed," Francie said.

It was a pleasant evening. The Jacksons were relaxed, charming. Francie liked the faint wryness of Stew's humor. And both of them were perceptive enough to keep the conversation far away from any subject that might be related to Bob.

Francie lent them a flashlight for the boat trip back to their camp. She heard the oars as Betty rowed away, heard the night voices calling, "Night, Francie! Good night!"

Monday she came back from work too late to make the promised call. She found the flashlight on the porch near the door, along with a note that said, "Anytime at all, Francie. And we mean it. *Betty and Stew.*"

Tuesday was another late night. On Wednesday, Clint

Reese added up the hours she had worked and sent her home at three in the afternoon, saying, "Do you want us indicted by the Committee Investigating Abuses of Civil Service Secretaries?"

"I'm not abused."

"Out, now! Scat!"

At the cabin Francie Aintrell changed to jeans and a suede jacket and hiked down the trail by the empty camps to the one that the Jacksons had described. Stew was on the dock, casting with a spinning rod.

"Hi!" he said, grinning. "Thought the bears got you. Go on in. I'll be up soon as I find out why this little wooden monster won't wiggle like a fish."

Betty Jackson flushed with pleasure when she saw Francie. "It's nice of you to come. I'll show you the workshop before Stew does. He gets all wound up and takes hours."

The large glass-enclosed porch smelled of paint and glue. There were labels for the little glassine boxes, and rows of gay, shining lures.

"Here, it says in small print, is where we earn a living," Betty said. "But actually it's going pretty well." She held up a yellow lure with black spots. "This one," she said, "is called—believe it or not—the Jackson Higgledy-Piggledy. A pickerel on every cast. It's our latest achievement. Manufacturing costs twelve cents apiece, if you don't count labor. Mail-order price, one dollar."

"It's pretty," Francie said dubiously.

"Don't admire it or Stew will put you to work addressing the new catalogues to our sucker list."

Stew came in and said, "I'll bet if the sun was out it would be over the yardarm."

"Is a martini all right with you, Francie?" Betty asked.

Francie nodded, smiling. The martinis were good. The dinner much later was even better. Stew made her an ex-officio director of the Jackson Lure Company, in charge of color schemes on bass plugs. Many times during dinner Francie felt a pang of guilt as she heard her own laughter ring out. Yet it was ridiculous to feel guilty. Bob would have wanted her to learn how to laugh all over again.

She left at eleven, and as she had brought no flashlight, Betty walked home with her, carrying a gasoline lantern. They sat on the edge of Francie's porch for a time, smoking and watching the moonlight on the lake.

"It's a pretty good life for us," Betty said. "Quiet. Stew's supposed to avoid strenuous exercise. And he's really taking this business seriously. Probably a good thing. Our money won't last forever."

"I'm so glad you two people are going to be here all winter, Betty."

"And you don't know how glad I am to see you, Francie. I needed some girl talk. Say, how about a picnic soon?"

"I adore picnics."

"There's a place on the east shore where the afternoon sun keeps the rocks warm. But we can't do it until Sunday. Stew wants to take a run down to New York to wind up some business things. I do the driving. Sunday, okay then?" Betty stood up.

It was agreed and Francie stood on the small porch and watched the harsh lantern light bob along the trail until it finally disappeared beyond the trees.

Sunday dawned brisk and clear. It would be pleasant enough in the sun. Francie went down the trail with her basket. When she got to the Jackson camp, Betty was loading the boat. She looked cute and young in khaki trousers, a fuzzy white sweater, a peaked ballplayer's cap.

The girls took turns rowing against the wind as they went across the lake. Stewart trolled with a deep-running plug, without much success. He was grumbling about the lack of fish when they reached the far shore.

They unloaded the boat, carrying the food up to a small natural glade beyond the rocks. Stew settled down comfortably, finding a rock that fitted his back. Betty sat on another rock. Francie sprawled on her stomach on the grass, chin on the back of her hand.

Stew took a bit of soft pine out of his jacket pocket and a sharp-bladed knife. He began to carve carefully. He lifted the piece of pine up and squinted at it.

"Francie, if I'm clever enough, I can now carve myself something that a fish will snap at," he said. "A lure. A nice sparkly, dancy little thing that looks edible."

"With hooks in it," Francie said.

He looked down at her benignly. "Precisely. With hooks in it. You stop to think of it, an organization isn't very different from a fish. Now, I'm eventually going to catch a fish on this, because it will have precisely the appeal that fish are looking for. Now, you take an organization. You can always find one person in it, if you look hard enough, that can be attracted. But then, it's always better to use real bait instead of an artificial lure."

"Sounds cold-blooded," Francie said sleepily.

"I suppose it is. Now, let's take, for example, that super-secret organization you work for, Francie."

She stared at him. "What?"

"That so-called weather research outfit. Suppose we had to find bait to make somebody bite on a hook?"

Francie sat up and tried to smile. "You know, I don't like the way you're talking, Stew."

"You're among friends, honey. Betty and I are very friendly people."

Francie, confused, turned and looked at Betty. Her face had lost its usual animation. There was nothing there but a catlike watchfulness.

"What *is* this anyway?" Francie said, laughing. But her laughter sounded false.

"We came over here," Stew said, "because this is a nice, quiet place to settle down and make a deal. Now don't be alarmed, Francie. A lot of time and effort has gone into making exactly the right sort of contact with you. Of course, if it hadn't been you, it would have been somebody else in Unit Thirty. So this is the stroke of midnight at the fancy-dress ball. Everybody takes off their masks."

Slowly the incredible meaning behind his words penetrated to Francie's mind. She looked at them. They had been friends—friends quickly made and yet dear to her. Now suddenly they had become strangers. Stew's bland, open face seemed to hold all the guilelessness of the face of an evil child. And Betty's features had sharpened, had become almost feral.

"Is this some sort of a stupid test?" Francie demanded.

"I'll say it again. We are here to make a business deal. We give you something, you give us something. Everybody is satisfied." Stewart Jackson smiled at her.

Panic struck Francie Aintrell. She slipped as she scrambled to her feet. She ran as fast as she could toward the boat, heard the feet drumming behind her. As she bent to shove the boat off, Betty grabbed her, reached around her from behind, and with astonishing strength, twisted both of Francie's arms until her hands were pinned between her shoulder blades.

The pain doubled Francie over. "You're hurting me," she cried. There was an odd indignity in being hurt by another woman.

"Come on back," Betty said, her voice flat-calm.

Stew hadn't moved. He cut a long, paper-thin strip from the piece of pine. Betty shoved Francie toward him and released her.

"Sit down, honey," Stew said calmly. "No need to get all upset. You read the papers and magazines. I know that you're a well-informed, intelligent young woman. *Please* sit down. You make me nervous."

Francie sat on the grass, hugged her knees. She felt cold all the way through.

"I don't know what you expect me to do. But you might as well know that I'll never do it. You had better kill me or something, because just as fast as I can get to a phone I'm going to—"

"Please stop sounding like a suspense movie, Francie," Stewart said patiently. "We don't go around killing people. Just let me talk for a minute. Maybe you, as an intelligent young woman, have wondered why so many apparently loyal and responsible people have committed acts of treason against their country. To understand that, you have to have an appreciation of the painstaking care with which all trusted people are surveyed.

"Sooner or later, Mrs. Aintrell, we usually find an avenue of approach to at least one person in each secret setup in which we interest ourselves. And, in the case of Unit Thirty, the Fates seem to have elected you to provide us with complete transcripts of all current progress reports dictated by Dr. Sherra, Dr. McKay, and Mr. Blajoviak.''

Shock made Francie feel dull. She merely stared at him unbelievingly.

Stewart Jackson smiled blandly. ''I assure you our cover is perfect. And I believe you have helped us along by casually mentioning your nice neighbors, the Jacksons.''

''Yes, but—''

''We thought at first my boating accident might be too obvious, but then we remembered that there is nothing in your background to spoil your naiveté.''

''You're very clever and I've been very stupid. But I assure you that nothing you can say to me will make any difference.''

''Being hasty, isn't she?'' Stewart said.

With the warm, friendly manner of a man bestowing gifts, he reached into the inside pocket of his heavy tweed jacket and took out an envelope. He took a sheet of paper from the envelope, unfolded it, and handed it to her. It was the coarse, pulpy kind of paper.

In the top right hand corner were Chinese ideographs, crudely printed. In the top left hand corner was a symbol of the hammer and sickle. But it was the scrawled pencil writing that tore her heart in two as she read.

Baby, they say you will get this. Maybe it's like their other promises. Anyway I hope you do get it. This is a crumb-bum outfit. I keep telling them I'm sick, but nobody seems to be interested. The holes healed pretty good, but now they don't look so hot. Anything you can do to get me out of this, baby, do it. I can't last too long here, for sure. I love you, baby, and I keep thinking of us in front of a fireplace—it gets cold

here—and old Satchmo on the turntable and you in the
green housecoat, and Willy on the mantel.

Francie read it again and instinctively held it to her lips,
her eyes so misted that Stewart and the rock he leaned
against were merged in a gray-brown blur.

Bob was alive! There could be no doubt of it. No one
else would know about the green housecoat, about Bob's
delight in the zipper that went from throat to ankles. And
they had all been wrong. All of them! Happiness made
her feel dizzy, ill.

Stewart Jackson's voice came from remote distances:
". . . find it pretty interesting, at that. That piece of paper
crossed Siberia and Russia and came to Washington by air
in a diplomatic pouch—one that we don't have to identify.
When we reported your assignment to Unit Thirty, our
Central Intelligence ordered an immediate check of all
captive officer personnel. In that first retreat after the
Chinese came into it, they picked up quite a lot of wounded
American personnel.

"It was quite a break to find your husband reported as
killed in action instead of captured. If he'd been captured
they'd never have transferred you to Unit Thirty, you know.
So they told Lieutenant Aintrell the circumstances and he
wrote that letter you're holding. It got to you just as fast
as it could be managed."

"He says he's sick!" Francie exclaimed indignantly.
"Why isn't he being taken care of?"

"Not many doctors and not much medicine on the Chinese mainland, Francie. They use what they have for their
own troops."

"They've got to help him!"

Betty came over, put her arm around Francie's shoulders. "I guess, Francie, dear, that is going to be up to you."

Francie twisted away from her. "What do you mean?"

"It's out of our hands," Stew Jackson said. "You can think of us as just messengers from the boys who make the decisions. They say that when, as evidence of your good faith, they start to receive copies of Unit Thirty progress reports, they will see to it that your husband is made more comfortable. I understand that his wounds are not serious. You will get more letters from him, and he'll tell you in those letters that things are better. When your services are no longer needed they will make arrangements to have him turned over to some impartial agency—maybe to a Swedish hospital ship.

"He'll come home to you, and that will be your reward for services rendered. Now if you don't want to play ball, I'm supposed to pass the word along, and they'll see that he gets transferred from the military prison to a labor camp, where he may last a month or a year. Now, you better take time to think it all over."

"How can you stand yourselves or each other?" Francie asked. "How can two people like you get mixed up in such a filthy business?"

Stewart Jackson flushed. "You can skip that holier than thou attitude, Mrs. Aintrell. You believe in one thing. We believe in something else. Betty and I just happen to believe there's going to be a good spot for us when this capitalistic dictatorship goes bankrupt and collapses from its own weight."

Jackson leaned forward with a charming smile. "Come on, Francie. Cheer up. And you should know that, as an individual, you certainly are not going to affect the course of world affairs by the decisions you make. As a woman, you want your husband and your happiness. The odds are that Unit Thirty research will get nowhere anyway. So what harm can you do? And the people I work with are never afraid to show gratitude. Certainly your Bob won't thank you for selling him out, selling him into a labor camp."

"There's more than one way to sell Bob out."

"Sentimentality masquerading as patriotism, I'm afraid. Think it over. How about the food, Betty? Join us, Francie?"

Francie didn't answer. She stood up and walked down the shore of the lake. She sat huddled on a natural step in the rocks. There seemed to be no warmth in the sun. She looked at the letter. In two places the pencil had torn the cheap, coarse paper. His hand had held the pencil. She remembered the marriage vows. To honor and cherish. A sacred promise, made in front of man and God.

She felt as though she were being torn in half, slowly, surely. And she could not forget that he was in danger and frighteningly alone.

She walked slowly back to Stewart and Betty. "Is that promise any good?" she asked, in a voice which was not her own. "Would he really be returned to me?"

"Once a promise is made, Francie, it is kept. I can guarantee that."

"Like they've kept treaties?" Francie asked bitterly.

"The myth of national honor is part of the folklore of decadent capitalism, Francie," Betty said. "Don't be politically immature. This is a promise to an individual and on a different basis entirely."

Francie looked down at them. "Tell me what you want me to do," she asked.

"We have your pledge of cooperation?" Stewart Jackson asked.

"I—yes." Her mouth held a bitter dryness.

"Before we go into details, my dear Francie, I want you to understand that we appreciate the risk you are taking. If you ever get the urge to be a little tin heroine—at your husband's expense, of course—please understand that we shall take steps to protect ourselves. We would certainly make it quite impossible for you to testify against us."

Betty said quickly, "Francie wouldn't do that, Stew." She laughed shallowly.

"Now, Francie," Stewart said softly, "I will tell you what you will do."

When they rowed away from her dock they waved a cheerful good-bye to her. Francie went in and closed the door carefully behind her, knowing that doors and bolts and locks had become useless. Then she lay numbly on the bunk and pressed her forehead against the rough pine boards. Until at last the tears came. She cried herself out, and when she awakened from deep sleep the night was dark, the cabin cruelly cold.

She awakened to a changed world. The adjustment to Bob's death had been a precarious structure, moving in each emotional breeze. Now it collapsed utterly. She was again the bride, the Francie Aintrell of the day before the telegram arrived. And as she moved about, she began, in the back of her mind, to stage the scene and learn the lines for the moment of his return, for the moment when his arms would be around her again.

She pumped up the lantern and carried it over to the table. She set it down, and stood very still looking at the object. There, on the table, was one of the plugs manufactured by the Jacksons. It was a gay red lure, with two gang hooks, with yellow bead eyes.

The doors were still locked. She tried to tell herself it was purposeless melodrama, the sort of thing a small boy might do. She turned down slightly the harsh white light of the lantern and slowly walked into her bedroom.

Early next morning she parked her car behind the lab and walked in and sat at her desk. The smiling guards at the gate had a new look.

Clint Reese came out and gave her an impersonal good morning, and spun the dial on the locked file for her. She took the current Sherra folder from the drawer back to her desk, found her place, continued the transcription of notes that had been interrupted on Saturday.

They would want a full report, she told herself. Not just the final three or four pages. No one watched her closely. It would be easy to make one additional carbon. She planned how she would do it. Fold the additional carbons and stick them in the blue facial-tissue box. Then take the box with her to the lavatory. There she could fold them smaller and tuck them into her bra. But she would do it with the next report. Not this one, because it was only a portion of a report.

Sherra's report took twice as long as it should have. She made continual errors. Twice Clint Reese stopped by to pick up the completed report for checking by Cudahy and each time she told him it would be ready soon. When she took it to him at last she imagined that he gave her an odd look before he went on into Cudahy's office, the report in his hand.

Big Tom Blajoviak's note was on her spindle: *Come and get it, sweetheart.*

She took her book and went toward the cubicle in the

corner where there was barely room for Blajoviak and a desk.

The door was ajar a few inches. He glanced up at her and said, "Enter the place of the common people, Francie. Just because I'm not a doctor, it's no reason to—"

"Have you really got something this time, Tom? Or is it more repetition?"

"Child, your skepticism is on the uncomplimentary side. Open thy book and aim your little pointed ears in this direction. Hark to the Blajoviak."

"Honestly?"

His square strong face altered. The bantering look was gone. "At five o'clock yesterday, Francie, we began to get a little warm. Here we go." He held his copy of the last report in front of him. "This would be new main subject, Francie. I make it *Roman numeral nine*. Isolation of margin error in Berkhoff Effect. Sub A. Following the series of tests described in *Roman eight* above, one additional memory tube was added to circuit C. The rerunning of the tests was begun on October twenty-third—"

He dictated rapidly. Francie's pencil darted along the notebook lines with the automatic ease of long practice. It took nearly an hour for the dictation.

"So that's it," he said, leaning back, smiling with a certain pride.

"Not that it means anything to me, you know," she said.

"It just might, Francie. It just might mean that instead of getting fried into the asphalt, you might look out to sea and say, 'Ah' at the big white lights out there. Fireworks for the kiddies instead of a disintegration."

She glanced down at her whitened knuckles. "Is it that important, Tom?"

"Are you kidding?"

She shook her head. "No, I just don't understand—all this."

"There was a longbow, and some citizen comes up with body armor. And then the crossbow, and so they made heavier armor. And then gunpowder, which eventually put guys into tanks. Every time, it sounded like an ultimate weapon, and each time a defense just happened to come along in time. Now our ultimate weapon is the thermonuclear missile. Everybody is naked when that baby comes whining down out of the stratosphere. So we have to stop it up there where it won't do any harm."

He paused an instant, then went on earnestly. "We can't depend on the slow reaction time of a man. We've got to have a gizmo. And now, for the first time, I think we're getting close to the ultimate interceptor. If you-know-who could find out how close we are, I'll bet they'd risk everything to try to knock us out before we could get into production on the defensive end. Cudahy wants this one fast as you can get it out, honey."

She stood up. "All right, Tom. As soon as I can get it out."

Francie went to work. She watched her hands add the extra onionskin sheet to the copies required by office routine. At five o'clock Cudahy came out of his office to check the progress. He seemed to be concealing jubilation with great difficulty. He patted her shoulder.

"Take a food break at six, Mrs. Aintrell," he said, "and then get back to it. I'll be here, so you won't have to lock anything up."

"Yes, sir," she said in a thin voice.

Cudahy had not noticed the extra copy. But she could

not risk leaving the extra copy in sight while she went to the mess hall. At five of six she took the tissue box, containing the folded sheets into the lavatory. She tucked the sheets into her bra, molding the papers into an inconspicuous curve.

She looked at her face in the mirror, ran the fingertips of both hands down her cheeks. Bob had told her she would be lovely when she was seventy.

She looked into the barren depths of her own eyes and she could hear the voice of Tom Blajoviak: "Fireworks for the kiddies instead of disintegration. Knock us out before we could—"

Francie Aintrell squared her shoulders and walked out of the lavatory. She took her red shortcoat from the coat tree.

Clint Reese sat on the corner of a desk, one long leg swinging. He said, "Remind me to put all my black-haired women in red coats."

She found that she was glad to see him. His lighthearted manner made the lab work seem a little less important, made her own impending betrayal a more minor affair. And she sensed that during the past month Clint had grown more aware of her. A subtle game of awareness and flirtation would make her forget what she was about to do—or almost forget.

She said, "If you want to see a woman eat like a wolf, come on and join me."

He put on his wool jacket. "I'll take care of all the wolflike characteristics around here, lady."

They walked to the small mess hall. Wind whined around the corner of the building and they leaned into it.

"And after the dogs are gone, we can always boil up the harness," he said.

She heard the false note in her own laughter. They shut the mess-hall door against the wind, hung up their jackets. They filled their trays, carried them back from the service counter to a table for two by the wall. Clint Reese sat down and shut his eyes for a moment. She saw a weariness in his face that she had not noticed before.

Reese smiled at her. "Now make like a wolf," he said.

She had thought she was hungry, but found that she couldn't eat.

"Okay, Francie," he said. "Let's have it."

She gave him a startled look. For once there was no banter in his voice, no humor in his eyes.

"What do you mean?" she asked him.

"As official nursemaid to all personnel, I keep my eyes open. Something has been worrying you all day."

"Then make some jokes, and cheer me up, why don't you?"

He was grave. "Sometimes I get tired of jokes. Don't you?"

"Aren't you a little out of character, Mr. Reese? I thought you were the meringue on the local pie."

He looked through her and beyond her. "Perhaps I am. Tonight, my girl, I am lonesome and in a hair-taking down mood. Want to see my tresses fall?"

"Sure," she said.

He took a sip of his coffee, set his cup down. "Underneath this tattered shirt beats the heart of a missionary."

"No!"

"And perhaps a fool. I own a tidy little construction business. I was making myself useful, and discovering that I had a certain junior-executive-type flair for the commercial world, when the Army put its sticky finger in the back of my collar and yanked me off to the wars. I was flexing my obstacle-course muscles on Okinawa when they dropped those big boomers on the Nipponese.

"Now get the picture. There I was as intrigued by those big boomers as a kid at the country club on the night of the fourth. *Siss boom, ah!* A big child at heart. Still thinking I was living in a nice, cozy little world. I was in one of the first units to go to Japan. I wangled a pass and went to Hiroshima. It was unpretty. Very."

In the depths of his eyes she saw the ghosts that he had seen.

"Francie, you can't tell another person how it is to grow up in one day. I wandered around in a big daze, and at the end of the day I had made up my mind that this was a desperate world to live in, a frightening world. And it took me another month to decide that the only way I could live with myself was to try to do something about it.

"When they gave me a discharge I turned the management of the company over to my brother and went to school to learn something about nuclear physics. I learned that if I studied hard I'd know something about it by the time I was seventy-three, so I quit. What resource did I have? Just that little flair for administration, the knack for getting along with people and keeping them happy and getting work done.

"So I decided to be a dog-robber for the professional boys who really know what the score is. By being here I make Cudahy more effective. Cudahy in turn makes the teams more effective.

"And now, I understand, we're beginning to get someplace. Maybe because I'm here we get our solution a month sooner than otherwise. But if it were only twenty minutes sooner, I could say that I have made a contribution to something I believe in."

Francie felt a stinging in her eyes. She looked away from him, said huskily, "I'm just a little stupid I guess. You seemed so—casual, sort of."

He grinned. "With everybody going around grinding their teeth, you've got to have some relief. If I landed in a spot full of clowns I'd turn into the grimmest martinet you ever saw. Any administrative guy in a lab setup is a catalyst. So let's get back to the original question, now that you've made me prove my right to ask it. What's bothering you, Francie?"

She stood up so abruptly that her chair tilted and nearly fell over. She went through the door with her coat in her hand, put it on outside, walked into the night with long strides.

There was a small clump of pines within the compound. She headed blindly toward them. He caught her arm just as she reached them. He turned her around gently.

"Look. I didn't want to say the wrong thing. If this is just one of those days when you—remember too much, please forgive me, Francie. I'd never do anything to hurt you."

She held onto his wrist with both hands. "Clint, I'm so—terribly mixed up I don't know what to do."

"Let me help you if I can."

"Clint, what is the most important thing in the world to any individual? It's their own happiness, isn't it? Tell me it is?"

"Of course it is, but you don't need a definition of terms. Isn't happiness sort of a compound?"

"How do you mean?"

"Don't too many people confuse happiness with self-gratification? You can be happy if you have self-respect and also what an old-fashioned uncle of mine used to call the love of God."

She was crying soundlessly. "Honor, maybe?"

"That's a word, too. Little dog-eared through misuse, but still respectable."

"Suppose, Clint, that somebody saved your life and the only way they could do it was by violating all the things you believe in. Would you be grateful?"

"If someone saved me that way I think I'd begin to hate them, and hate myself, too, Francie. But don't think I'm a typical case. I'm a little top-heavy in the ethics department, they tell me."

"I married that sort of man, Clint. I understand."

"You still haven't told me how I can help you."

She turned half away from him, knowing that unless she did it quickly, she would be unable to do it at all. She unbuttoned the red coat, the jacket under it, the blouse under that. She found the folded packet of onionskin sheets and held it out where he could see it.

"You can help me by taking that, Clint. Before I change my mind."

He took it. "What is it?" he asked.

"A copy of what Tom dictated today," she said tonelessly.

"Why on earth are you carrying it around?" he demanded sharply.

"To give it to someone on the outside."

After a long silence he said, "Holy jumping Nellie!" His tone was husky.

"I was doing it to save Bob's life," she said.

"Your husband? But he's dead!"

"I found out yesterday that he's alive, Clint. Alive and in prison." She laughed, dangerously close to hysteria. "Not that it makes any difference. Now he *will* die."

He shook her hard but she could not stop laughing. He slapped her sharply, and she was able to stop. He walked her across the compound, unlocked a door, thrust her inside, turned on a light. The small room contained a chair, table, double bed, and bookshelf.

"Please wait here," he said gently. "I'll be back in a few minutes with Dr. Cudahy. Handkerchiefs in that top drawer."

Cudahy and Clint Reese were with her for over an hour. Clint sat beside her on the bed, holding her hand, luring her on with the story when she stumbled. Cudahy paced endlessly back and forth, white-lipped, grim. When he interrupted her now and then to ask a question his voice was harsh.

At last they knew all there was to know. Cudahy stopped in front of her. "And you, Mrs. Aintrell, were planning to give them the—"

"Please shut up, Doctor," Clint said tiredly.

Cudahy glared at him. "I'll require some explanation for that comment, Mr. Reese."

Clint lit two cigarettes and gave Francie one, while Cudahy waited for the explanation. Clint said, "I don't see how a tongue-lashing is going to help anything, Doctor. Forget your own motivations for a moment and think of hers. As far as this girl knows, she has just killed her husband—just as surely as if she had a gun to his head. I doubt, Dr. Cudahy, whether either you or I, under the same circumstances, would have that same quality of moral courage. I respect her for it. I respect her far too much to listen to you rant at her."

Cudahy let out a long breath. He turned a chair around and sat down. He gave Clint a sheepish glance and then said, "I'm sorry, Mrs. Aintrell. I got carried away with a sense of my own importance."

Francie said, tonelessly, "Bob told me once that they put him in a brown suit and made him expendable. I married him knowing that. And I guess my life can be as expendable as his. He said we had to be tough. I know they made him write that. He isn't the kind of man who begs. I almost—did what they wanted me to do. It isn't courage, I guess. I'm just—all mixed up."

"Francie," Clint said, "Dr. Cudahy and I are amateurs in the spy department. This is a job for the experts. But I'm in on this, and I'm going to stay in. I'm going to make it certain that the experts don't foul up your chances of getting your husband back. We're going to make the Jacksons believe that you are cooperating. The experts can't get here until tomorrow. Do you think you can handle it all right when they contact you tonight?"

He looked at her steadily.

"I—I think so. I can tell them that I didn't do any transcriptions today."

"Don't give them any reason to be suspicious."

"I'll try not to."

Clint Reese walked her to her car, stood with the door open after she had slid under the wheel. "Want me to come along?" he asked.

"I'm all right now."

"The best of luck, Francie."

He shut the door. The guard opened the gates. She drove down the gravel road toward Lake Arthur.

Betty Jackson, in ski pants and white cashmere sweater, was sitting on the bunk reading a magazine. The fire was burning. Her jacket was on a nearby chair.

Betty tossed the magazine aside and smiled up at her. "Hope you don't mind, hon. I nearly froze on the porch and I only had to make a tiny hole in the screen, just where the catch is."

Francie took off her coat, held her hands toward the flames. "It's all right."

"Got a little present for us, dear?"

"I couldn't manage it today. I took a lot of dictation and then I was put to work filing routine correspondence."

Betty leaned back, her blond head against the pine wall, fingers laced across her stomach. "Stew was pretty anxious. This might alarm him a little, hon. He might worry about whether you're cooperating or double-crossing. You know, he told me last night that lots of war widows got so depressed they killed themselves. I'm not threatening you. That's just the way his mind works sometimes."

"I dropped J. Edgar Hoover a personal note," Francie said bitterly. "It's so much simpler than getting a divorce."

"You don't have to be nasty, you know. This isn't personal with us, dear. We take orders just as you do."

"Tell your husband, if he is your husband, that I'll have something tomorrow."

After the woman left, Francie stood and bit at the inside of her lip until she tasted blood. "Forgive me, Bob," she said silently. "Forgive me." It had been done. Now nothing could save him.

She found the lure on the shelf over the sink, at eye level. The body carved to resemble a frog. After she stopped trembling she forced herself to pick it up and throw it on the fire.

The men arrived in midafternoon the very next day. Three of them. A slow-moving, dry-skinned sandy one with a farmer's cross-hatched neck. He was called Luke Osborne and he was in charge. The names of the other two were not given. They were dark, well-scrubbed young men in gleaming white shirts, dark-toned suits. Cudahy and Clint Reese were present for the conference.

Osborne looked to be half asleep as Francie told her story. He spoke only to bring out a more detailed description of the Jacksons.

"New blood," he said, "or some of the reserves. Go on."

She finished, produced the letter. Luke Osborne fingered it, and held it up to the light before reading it. He handed it to the nearest young man, who read it slowly and passed it on to the other young man.

Osborne said, "You're convinced your husband wrote that?"

"Of course!" Francie said wonderingly. "I know his writing. I know the way he says things. And then there are those references—the housecoat, Willy."

"Who is Willy?"

"We bought him in Kansas. He's in storage now. A little porcelain figure of an elf. We had him on the mantel. Bob used to say he was our good—"

Suddenly she couldn't go on. Osborne waited patiently until she had regained control.

"—our good luck charm," she said, her voice calm.

"It stinks," Osborne said.

They all looked at him.

"What do you mean?" Reese demanded.

"Oh, this girl is all right. I don't mean that. I mean, the whole thing implies an extent of organization that I personally don't believe they have. I just don't believe that in a little over thirty days they could fix it so Mrs. Aintrell, here, is balanced on the razor's edge. Three months, maybe. Not one."

"But Bob wrote that letter!" Francie said.

"And believing that he wrote it, you opened up for Reese here?" Osborne asked.

"I almost didn't," Francie told him.

"But you did. That's the point. You won't get any medals. There are a lot of people not getting any medals these days." Osborne's smile was an inverted U.

"What are your plans?" Dr. Cudahy demanded.

The office was very still. At last Luke Osborne looked over at Francie. "I'm going to go on the assumption that your husband is alive, Mrs. Aintrell, and that he wrote this letter. At least, until we can prove differently."

"Dr. Cudahy, have you got a file on some line of research that proved to be valueless? A nice, fat file?"

Cudahy frowned. "Things are so interrelated here that even data on unsuccessful experimentation might give us a line on the other stuff."

"Pardon me, sir," Clint Reese said. "How about that work Sherra was doing? And you couldn't make him stop. Wasn't that—?"

Cudahy thumped his palm with a chubby fist. "That should do it! I had to have progress files made to keep him happy. That work bore no relation to our other avenues of approach, Mr. Osborne."

"And if Mrs. Aintrell gives them Sherra's work, a bit at a time, as though it were brand-new stuff, it won't help them, eh?" He thought an instant, then asked, "But will it make them suspicious?"

"Only," said Cudahy, "if they know as much about what is going on here as I do."

"Reese, you turn that file over to Mrs. Aintrell. Mrs. Aintrell, copy enough each day to turn over to Jackson, so he won't get suspicious. Better make six copies or so and give him the last one. Fold it up as though you smuggled it out of here. Can do?"

"Yes," Francie said quickly.

"That should keep your husband alive, if he is alive. We have channels of communication into the likely areas where he'd be. It will take nearly two months to get any kind of a check on him, even if we started yesterday. The better way is to check through the Jacksons." Luke Osborne was regarding her steadily.

"What do you mean by that?" Francie demanded. "You can't go to him and—"

Osborne held up his hand and gave a rare smile. "Settle down, Mrs. Aintrell. Even if your husband weren't involved, we'd hardly go plunging through the shrubbery waving our credentials. They use their expendables on this sort of contact work, just the same as we do. We want the jokers who are buried three or four layers of communication back. I want Jackson to be given the dope, because I am anxious to see what he does with it, and who gets it."

"But—"

"Just trust us, Mrs. Aintrell."

Francie forced a smile. There was something about Luke Osborne that inspired trust. Yet she had no real confidence that he could match his cleverness with the Jacksons. Both Stewart and Betty seemed so supremely confident.

"I'll need your letters from your husband, Mrs. Aintrell. Every one of them."

Francie flushed. The overseas letters, since they had been subject to censorship, were written in a doubletalk understandable only to the two of them. But the letters he had sent her that had been mailed inside the country had been full of bold passages that had been meant for her eyes alone.

"Do you have to have them?"

"Please, Mrs. Aintrell. We will have them for a very short time. Just long enough to make photostats for study. When this case is over our photostats will be burned."

"But I can't imagine why—"

He smiled again. "Just call it a hunch. You have them at your cabin, I judge."

"Yes I do."

Clint Reese followed her home in his car at five-thirty that evening. They walked down the trail together. A fine, misty rain was falling and the rustic guard rail felt sodden under her hand.

Francie unlocked the door and went in. She looked on the porch and turned to Clint. "Nobody here," she said, relief in her voice.

She took the candy box full of letters out of the bureau drawer and handed it to him. "You'll be back at nine?"

"Thereabout," he said. He slipped the box into his

jacket pocket. Then he put both hands on her shoulders. "Take care," he whispered.

"I will," she said. She knew he wanted to kiss her, and also knew that he would not, that his sense of rightness would not permit him. He touched his lips lightly to her forehead, turned, and left.

She turned on the gas under the hot water heater, and when the water was ready she took a shower. While she was under the water she heard someone call her.

"In a minute," she called back. She dressed in tailored wool slacks, a plaid shirt cut like a man's. She walked out unsmiling. Betty sat on the bunk, one heel up, hands laced around her knee.

Francie said, "I brought something this time."

Betty smiled. "We knew you would. Stew is on his way over now."

Francie sat down across the room from her. "Did you get Stewart into this sort of thing, or did he get you in?"

"Clinical curiosity? We met while I was in college. We found out that we thought about things the same way. He had contacts and introduced me. After they started to trust me I kept needling Stew until he demanded a chance to do something active. They told us to stay under cover. No meetings. No cells. We did a little during the war, and a little bit last year in Canada. Satisfied?"

Stewart came in the door, shivering. "Going to be a long winter," he said.

"Here's what you want," Francie said, taking the folded sheets from the pocket of her slacks.

"Thank you, my dear," Stew said blandly. He sat down on the bunk beside Betty and they both read through the sheets, skimming them.

"Dr. Sherra's work, eh?" Stewart said. "Good man, Sherra. I think he was contacted once upon a time. Got stuffy about it though, and refused to play. He could have lived in Russia like a little tin king."

Jackson refolded the sheets, put them carefully in his wallet. "Did you have any trouble getting these out, Francie?"

"Not a bit."

"Good!" Stewart said. He still held the billfold in his hand. He dipped into it, took out some money, walked over, and dropped it into her lap.

Francie looked uncomprehendingly at the three twenty-dollar bills. "I'm not doing this for money."

He shrugged. "Keep it. It isn't important. Buy something pretty with it."

Francie fingered the bills. She folded them once, put them in the top left pocket of her plaid shirt.

"That's better," Stewart said. "Everybody gets paid for services rendered. Canada and London, Tennessee and Texas."

Francie remembered her instructions from Osborne. She leaned forward. "Please let them know right away that I'm cooperating. Bob's letter said he was sick. I want to know that he's being cared for."

Osborne had said to cry if she could. She found that it was no effort.

Stewart patted her shoulder. "Now don't fret, Francie. I was so certain of your cooperation that I already sent word that you're playing ball with us in every way that you can. I'd say that by the end of this week, no later, Bob ought to be getting all the attention he can use."

"Thank you," she said, meaning it completely. "Thank you so much."

Betty stood up, stretched like a plump kitten. "We'll see you tomorrow night, huh? Come on, Stew."

"I'll have more for you."

Francie stood up, too. She made herself stand quite still as Jackson patted her shoulder again. There was something about being touched by him that made her stomach turn over.

She stood at the side window and watched their flashlights bob down the trail through the trees. She made herself a light meal. Clint Reese arrived a little after nine. She took the box from him and put it back in the bureau drawer.

Clint gave an exaggerated sigh. "Osborne's orders. We got to go to the movies together. That gives me an excuse for coming down here, if they happen to be watching you. Ready to follow orders?"

She shivered. "I—I know they're watching me. I can feel it," she whispered. "I do want to be out of here for a little while." As they went out the door she stumbled on the wet boards. He caught her arm, held it tightly. They stood quite still for a few moments. It was a strange moment of tension between them, and she knew that he was as conscious of it as she was. The strain of the past few days, strain they had shared, had heightened an awareness of each other.

"Francie!" he said, his voice deeper than usual.

Shame was a rising red tide. Certainly her loyalty to Bob was sinking to a new low. To take the step that must lead to his death, and then take a silly pleasure in a strong male hand clasping her arm.

She pulled away, almost too violently, and said with false gaiety, "But I buy my own ticket, Mister."

"Sure," he said with no lift in his voice.

When they were in the car Clint said, "I'm always grabbing hold of females. Sort of a reflex. Hope you don't mind."

The car lights cut a bright tunnel through the wet night. "I didn't mind that. It was the sultry tone of voice that got me."

"Look. Slap me down when I get out of line. After the movies, to change the subject, we meet Osborne."

"It frightens me, having those people around. Suppose the Jacksons catch on."

"To everybody except you and me and Cudahy, they're new personnel on the project. And they're careful."

The movie was a dull musical. The crowd was very slim and no one sat within twenty feet of them.

"I can't help it, Francie," he said suddenly, blurting it out like a small boy. "I—"

"Clint, please listen to me. You told me once that you would never do anything to hurt me. This whole thing has torn me completely in half. I don't know who I am or where I am. I'm attracted to you, Clint, and I don't like that. I must ignore it, get over it. I have no other choice."

For a long time he did not answer. When he spoke again, the familiar light note had come back into his voice. "If you will permit me, madame, I shall finish my statement. Quote: I can't help it, Francie. I've got to have some popcorn. End quote."

She touched his arm. "Much better."

"What's better than popcorn?"

The movie ended and they filed out with the others. As

they walked toward the car, a match flared startlingly close, and the flame-light touched the high, hard cheekbones of the face of Stewart Jackson. Betty was a shadow beside him. Francie caught hard at Clint's arm, stumbling a little, her breathing suddenly shallow.

"Evening, Francie," Stewart said, a mild, sly triumph in his tone.

"Hello, Stewart. Hello, Betty," she forced herself to say, proud that her voice did not shake, knowing that the presence of Clint Reese had given her strength.

Once they were in the car and had turned out of the small parking lot, she said, "Oh, Clint, they were—"

"They just went to a movie. That's all. And found a chance to rattle you."

Clint turned off the main road onto a narrower one, and turned off lights and motor and waited for a time. No car followed them. He drove slowly up the hill and parked in a graveled space near some picnic tables. He gave Francie a cigarette, and she rolled her window down a few inches to let the smoke out.

When Osborne spoke, directly outside her window, he startled both of them. "Let me in before I freeze, kids."

She opened the door and slid over close to Clint. Osborne piled in and shut the door. "Let's have it, Mrs. Aintrell."

"They seemed pleased. Mr. Jackson told me that he'd already sent word to have Bob looked after, knowing in advance that I'd cooperate. And he gave me sixty dollars. He made me take it. Here it is."

"Keep it all together. He'll give you more. They love to pay off. They take some poor, idealistic fool who wants to help the Commies because he was nuts about *Das Kapital* when he was a college sophomore. When the fool finds out what kind of dictatorship he's dealing with and wants out, they sweetly remind him that he had accepted the money and he thereby established his own motive, and it is going to make him look very bad in court. So bad he'd better keep right on helping. By the way, thanks for the loan of the letters. The boys are tabulating them tonight."

"What do I—?"

"Just keep doing what you're doing. Feed them dope from the Sherra file."

"Oh, I forgot. Jackson mentioned that Sherra was contacted once. Is that important?"

"We know about it. Sherra reported it."

"Can I have that last letter back? The one from the prison camp?"

"You'll find it in the box with the others. I'll get a report from the handwriting experts soon."

"That's a waste of time. I know Bob wrote it. It sounds like him."

"Take her home Clint, before she convinces me," Osborne said, getting out of the car. "Night, people." The blackness of the night swallowed him at once.

On Wednesday and Thursday Francie turned more copies of the Sherra file over to the Jacksons, receiving each time an additional twenty-dollar bill, given to her with utmost casualness and good cheer by Stewart Jackson. On Friday afternoon Francie was called into Dr. Cudahy's office by Clint. Cudahy was not there. Just Luke Osborne. He looked weary.

As Clint paused uncertainly in the doorway Osborne said, "Sit in on this, Reese."

Clint pulled the door shut and sat down. Osborne was in Cudahy's chair.

"What have you found out?" Francie demanded.

"How long can you keep playing this little game of ours, Mrs. Aintrell?"

"Forever, if it will help Bob."

Osborne picked up a report sheet and looked at it, his expression remote. "Here's the report on the handwriting. They say it could be his handwriting, or it could be a clever forgery. There are certain changes, but they might be the result of fatigue or illness."

"I told you he wrote it."

Osborne studied her in silence. He looked more than ever like a prosperous Midwestern farmer worried about the Chicago grain market.

"Now can you take it on the chin?"

Francie looked down at her locked hands. "I—I guess so."

He picked up another sheet. "Tabulation report. It has a cross reference of the words in previous letters. We have numbered all his letters chronologically. Letter Four uses the term 'crumb-bum.' In Letter Sixteen there is a sentence as follows: 'Put old Satchmo on the turntable, baby, and when he sings "Blueberry Hill," make like I'm with you in front of a fireplace.' Letter Eighteen has a reference to Willy in it. And Letter Three mentions—uh—the green housecoat."

Osborne colored a bit, and Francie flushed violently as she remembered the passage to which he referred.

"What are you trying to tell me?" she asked, in a low voice.

"There are no new words or phrases or references in

that letter Stewart Jackson gave you. They can all be isolated in previous letters. We can assume that Jackson had access to those letters during the first few weeks you worked here."

"I don't see how that means anything," Francie said. "Of course, Bob would write as he always writes, and talk about the same things in letters that he always talked about. Wouldn't that be so?"

"Could be. But please let us consider it sufficient grounds—that and the handwriting report—to at least question the authenticity of the letter Jackson gave you. Remember, the handwriting report said that it *could* be a forgery."

Francie jumped up. "Why are you saying all this to me? I go through every day thinking every minute that if you slip up, just a little, Bob is going to die, and die in a horrible way. I'm doing the very best I can to keep him alive. If you keep trying to prove to me that he's been dead all the time, it takes away my reasons to go through all this—and I just can't see it like—"

She covered her eyes and sat down, not trying to fight against the harsh sobs.

Osborne said, "I'm telling you this, Mrs. Aintrell, because I want you to do something that may end all this, before you crack up under the strain. I never like to have anybody follow orders without knowing the reason behind the orders."

Francie uncovered her eyes, but she could not answer.

Osborne leaned forward and pointed a pencil at her. "I want you to reestablish friendly relations with these Jacksons. Talk about your husband, talk about him all the time. Bore them to death with talk about your husband.

Memorize the three items on this little slip of paper and give the slip back to me. I want those three items dropped into the conversation every chance you get."

Francie reached out and took the slip. There were three short statements on the paper: "Willy wears a green hat." . . . "Bob broke the Goodman recording of the 'Russian Lullaby' accidentally." . . . "You met in Boston."

It gave Francie a twisty, Alice-in-Wonderland feeling to read the nonsense phrases. She read them again and then stared wildly at Osborne, half expecting that it would be some monstrous joke. "Are you quite crazy?" she asked.

"Not exactly. And not all those words appear in the letters. We know you are clever, Mrs. Aintrell. We want you to tell the complete truth to the Jacksons, except for those three statements on that slip of paper. We assume they have a photostat of those letters, too. Nothing in the letters contradicts those three statements. You are not to repeat them so often that the Jacksons will become suspicious. Just often enough to implant them firmly in memory. Then we shall wait for one of those false statements to reappear either directly or by inference, in the next letter you get from your husband."

"And if they do, it will mean that—"

"That the army's report of your husband's death was correct. And that the Jacksons have been working one of the nastiest little deals I have ever heard of. Very clever, very brutal, and, except for your courage, Mrs. Aintrell, very effective."

With forced calmness Francie said, "You make it sound logical, and it might be easier for me if I could believe it. But I know Bob is alive."

"I merely ask you to keep in mind the possibility that

he may not be alive. Otherwise, should that second letter prove to be faked, you may break down in front of them."

"She won't break down," Clint said.

Francie gave him a quick smile. "Thank you."

"Just be patient," Osborne said. "Keep turning data over to them. Skip a day now and then to make it look better. We're trying to find their communication channel. When we find it we'll want you to demand the next letter from your husband. Maybe we can have you risk threatening to cut off the flow of data unless you get a letter. But get friendly with them now, and work in that information."

That night Francie walked down the shore path to the Jackson camp. She saw Stewart through the window in the living room. He let her in. Betty sat at the other end of the room, knitting.

"A little eager to deliver, this time, aren't you?" Stewart asked. He shut the door behind her and she gave him the folded packet. He glanced at it casually.

"Is something on your mind, Francie?"

"May I sit down?"

"Please do," Betty said.

Francie sat down, sensing their wariness at this deviation from routine. "This is something I have to talk to you about," she said. "I—I know I'd never have the nerve to consciously try to report you. But I am afraid of giving Dr. Cudahy or Mr. Reese a clue involuntarily."

"What do you mean?" Stewart demanded, leaning forward.

"It's just this: I think about Bob all the time. I think about how he is going to come home to me. It is the sort of thing a woman has to talk about, and there is no one to talk to. Sooner or later I may slip and mention Bob to either Dr. Cudahy or Mr. Reese. On my record it says that Bob is dead. They both know that. You see, I just don't like this chance I have to take every day, of my tongue slipping.''

"You haven't made a slip, have you?" Stewart asked.

"No. But today I—I almost—"

Betty came to her quickly, sat on the arm of the chair. "Stew, she's right. I know how it would be. Hon, could you talk to us, get it off your chest?"

"It might help, but—"

"But you don't particularly care for our company," Stewart said.

"It isn't that exactly. I don't like what you stand for. I hate it. But you are the only people I *can* talk to about Bob."

"And perhaps get into the habit of talking about him? So that you'd be more likely to make a slip?" Stewart asked.

"Oh no! Just to have *someone* listen."

Stewart stood up. "I want to impress on your mind just what a slip might mean, Francie. Not only would it mean you'd never see Bob again, but you wouldn't be around long enough to—"

"Leave her alone!" Betty said hotly. "A woman can understand this better than you, Stew. We'll be substitute friends for a while, Francie. You go ahead and talk your head off. Stew, it will be safer this way."

Stewart shrugged. Francie said, uncertainly, "I may bore you."

"You won't bore me," Betty said.

"I'm bursting with talk. Saving it up. I've been wondering what to do when he gets back. He'll be weak and sick, I suppose. I won't want to be here. I'll try to get a transfer back to Washington. I could rent a little apartment and get our things out of storage. I keep thinking of how I'm going to surprise him. Little ways, you know. He used to love our recording of 'Russian Lullaby.' The Benny Goodman one. And then he stepped on it. I could buy another one and have it all ready to play.

"And after I got the—the telegram, when I packed our things I was sort of shaky. I dropped Willy and chipped his green hat. I saved the piece, though, and I can have it glued on. You know, I can't even remember if I ever told him about saving the flowers. I pressed them—the ones I just happened to be wearing the day we first met in Boston. White flowers on a dark blue dress. I can get some flowers just like them. When he comes into the apartment, I'll have the record of 'Russian Lullaby' playing and Willy with his green hat fixed on the mantel and a blue dress and those flowers. Do you think he'd like that, Betty?"

"I'm sure he will, Francie."

"He isn't the sort of man who notices little things. I mean, I could get something new for the apartment and I'd always have to point it out to him. He used to—"

She seemed to be two people. One girl was talking on and on, talking in a soft, monotonous, lonely voice, and the other girl, the objective one, stood behind her, listening carefully. But the ice had been broken. Now she could talk about Bob and they would understand just why she had to. The words came in a soft torrent, unbroken.

After that, the days went by, and the constant strain was something she lived with, slept with, woke up with. The Sherra file was exhausted, and after careful consideration of the three team leaders, Cudahy brought Tom Blajoviak into the picture. Tom was enormously shocked at learning what was transpiring, and he was able to go into his personal files to find the basis for a new report on work that would in no way prejudice the current operations.

Stewart Jackson, although disappointed at the way the Sherra reports had reached negative conclusions, was pleased to begin to receive the Blajoviak reports.

Francie knew that she was becoming increasingly dependent on Clint Reese. No one else could make her smile, make her forget her precious moments. It was a quality of tenderness in him, of compassion, yet jaunty in its clown face.

And since that one night he never again put any part of his heart into his voice when he spoke to her. She thought that she could not bear it if he did.

During a frigid mid-November week Betty Jackson went away on an unexplained trip. Stewart collected the daily portions of the Blajoviak report. He smiled at Francie too much, and made clumsy, obvious passes which she pretended not to notice.

Betty left on a Tuesday night. She was back Friday night. Saturday morning Luke Osborne talked to Francie alone in Tom Blajoviak's tiny plywood office. Osborne was having difficulty concealing his jubilation behind a poker face.

"What have you found out?" Francie demanded, her voice rising.

"Nothing about Bob," he said quickly.

She sagged back into the chair and closed her eyes for a moment.

Osborne went on, "But we've gone places in another direction. Can't tell you too much, of course. But I thought you'd like to know. Evidently, they've been under orders to keep contacts at a minimum. I believe that Mrs. Jackson acted as a courier for everything accumulated up to date. She has good technical training for the job, but I don't think she has the feel for it. We put enough people on her so that even if she could push a button and make herself invisible, we'd still stay with her.

"Her contact is from one of the control groups we've been watching. She met him on a subway platform and went through a tired old transfer routine. He gave the stuff to a deluded young lady who works in Washington, taking a one-day vacation in New York. She took an inspirational walk when she got back to Washington. Visited national shrines by night and was picked up by the traditional black diplomatic sedan. By now those no good reports have cleared Gander, chained to the wrist of a courier from one of the cold war countries."

"Why are you telling me all this, Mr. Osborne?"

"It's time to get impatient. We know all we have to know. It has been a month since the first letter. How has it been going?"

"All right, I think. I don't think I've overworked those three things you told me to say. But it seems so pointless. I've been friendly. I help her with those lures they make, enameling them. And we talk a lot."

"Start tonight. No letter, no more reports. My guess is that they'll tell you one is on the way."

"One probably is."

"Please, Mrs. Aintrell, keep planning on the worst. Then if I'm wrong, it will be a pleasant surprise." Osborne smiled. "Young lady, you are doing fine, but, remember, give them a bad time tonight."

That evening fat, wet flakes of the first November snow

were coming down as she walked down the trail toward the Jackson camp. She walked slowly, rehearsing her lines.

She went up on their porch, knocked, and opened the door.

Betty put her knitting aside. "Well, hi!" she said. "Off early today."

Stewart was near the fire, reading. He put his book aside and said, "An afternoon nip to cut the ice?"

Francie stripped off her mittens, shoved them in her pocket. She unbuttoned the red coat, looking at them somberly. She saw the quick look Betty and Stew exchanged.

"I came over to tell you that I didn't bring you anything today. And I'm not going to bring you anything from now on."

Stewart Jackson took his time lighting a cigarette. "That's a pretty flat statement, Francie. What's behind it?"

"We made a bargain. I kept my end of it. A month is more than up. As far as I know, Bob may have died in that military prison. When I get the letter you promised me, the letter saying that he's better, then you get more data."

"Hon, we can understand your being impatient," Betty said, in an older sister tone. "But don't go off half-cocked."

"This isn't just an impulse," Francie said. "I've thought it over. Now I'm doing the bargaining. You must be reporting to somebody. They're probably pleased with what you've done. Well, until I get my letter they can stop being pleased, because you're going to have to explain to them why there aren't any more reports."

"Sit down, Francie," Stew said. "Let's be civilized about this."

Francie shook her head. "I have been civilized long enough. No letter, no reports. I can't make it any clearer."

Stewart smiled warmly. "Okay; there's no need of hiding this from you, Francie. We just didn't want to get you too excited. A letter is already on the way. I'm surprised we haven't gotten it already. Now, do you see how foolish your attitude is?"

It startled Francie to learn how accurate Luke Osborne's guess had been. And the rightness of his guess strengthened her determination. She turned from them, took a few steps toward the fire.

"No letter, no reports."

Stewart's smile grew a bit stiff. "You are being paid for those reports."

"I thought you'd bring that up. But it doesn't matter. I don't care what might happen to me. Here is step two in my ultimatum: Either I get my letter within a week or I consider it proof that Bob is dead. Then I'm going to go to Dr. Cudahy and tell him about you and what I've been doing."

She took pleasure in Stewart's look of concern, in Betty's muffled gasp.

"You wouldn't dare," Betty said.

"You're bluffing," Stewart said. "Sit down and we can talk it out."

Francie pulled her mittens on and turned toward the door.

Stewart barked, "I insist that you act more reasonably, Francie!"

"Look me up when you've got mail for me," Francie said crisply.

She slammed the door behind her and walked along

the lakeside trail. She felt neither strength nor weakness—just a gray, calm emptiness. When she got home the fire she had lit was blazing nicely. She sat on the floor in front of it, looking for Bob's face in the flames.

On Monday after listening to her report, Osborne said, "Now, understand this: You'll get a letter. If the letter proves by content to be a fake, it will be up to my superiors to make a policy decision. Either we take them into custody or we flush them and see which way they run. If the letter doesn't prove anything one way or another, then we go on as we are and wait for the report through Formosa. That may take until Christmas.

"If—and I am recognizing this possibility—the letter shows beyond any doubt that your husband is still alive, we'll continue to play along and use every resource to try to get him back for you. Just remember one thing: no matter what the letter shows you are to act as though you have no doubt. Can you do that?"

"I can try."

"We've asked a great deal of you, Francie. Just this little bit more."

The Jacksons came over to the cabin on Wednesday, minutes after Francie's arrival from the lab. They stamped the snow off their feet, and came in smiling.

"So you doubted me, eh?" Stew said cheerfully. "It came this morning."

As he fumbled for his pocket, Francie realized that Osborne's doubts had shaken her more than she knew. She was afraid of the letter—afraid to read it.

It seemed to take Stewart an impossibly long time to undo myriad buttons to get at the pocket that held the letter. Francie stood, looking beyond him, hand half out-stretched, and through the windows she saw the shale of new ice that reached tentatively out from the shore line into the lake. She heard Betty prodding the fire.

"Here you go!" Stewart said, holding out another folded sheet of the familiar cheap fibered paper.

Francie took it, her fingertips alive to the texture of it. Betty knelt in front of the fire, bulky in her ski suit, head turned, smiling. Stew stood in his shaggy winter clothes, beaming at her.

"Well go on!" Betty said. "You going to stand and hold it?"

Francie licked her lips, "Could I—read it alone please? It means so much."

"Read it now, honey," Stewart said. "We want to share your pleasure with you. It means a lot to us, too, you know."

She unfolded the letter. At first the pencil scrawl was blurred. She closed her eyes hard, turned her back to them, opened her eyes again.

Baby, now I know they weren't kidding when they said you'd get that other letter. I guess you're doing all you can for me. Anyway, I seem to be a guest of honor now. Sheets, even. Baby, don't feel bad about helping them. Maybe it's for the best. They've got something I've never understood before. For the first time I'm beginning to see the world as it really is. And now, darling, that fireplace seems closer than ever. And so do you. You still got those two freckles on the bridge of your nose? When I get my hands on you, baby, we'd better turn Willy's face to the wall.

Francie stopped reading for a moment and took a deep breath. A breath of joy and thanksgiving. He had to be alive. Nobody else could sound like that.

Remember that I love you and keep thinking that we'll be together again. That's what really counts, isn't it? Figure on me being back in the spring when all the world is turning as green as Willy's hat.

She stared at the last words. How could Bob have made such a grotesque and incredible mistake? The figurine wore no hat! How could he possibly—? And she read it again and saw the whole letter begin to go subtly false. This new letter and the one before it. False, contrived, artificial. It was all so clear to her now.

Bob, under the circumstances he described, would never have written in such a pseudo-gay way. His other letter had been like that because he had been trying to keep her from worrying about combat wounds or combat death. Now these letters, these fake letters, sounded absurdly lighthearted.

Still looking at the letter, her back turned toward them, Francie saw how they had taken the most precious part of her life and twisted it to their own ends. Bob was dead. He had died during the retreat. Had any doubt existed they would have labeled it *Missing in Action*. She had been the gullible fool. The stupid sentimental fool who clung to any hope, closing her eyes to its improbability.

Involuntarily she closed her hands on the letter, crumpling it, as though it were something evil.

Stewart Jackson had walked over to where he could see

her face. "Why are you doing that?" he asked, his voice oddly thin.

She fought for control, masking her anger. "I—I don't know. Excitement, I guess. To think that he'll be back in the spring and—we can—" But that was a spring that would never come.

In its own way this letter was far more ruthless than the original telegram. She couldn't pretend any longer, not with the two of them watching her so carefully.

She looked at them, hating them. Such a charming civilized couple. Stewart's face, which had seemed so bland and jolly, was now merely porcine and vicious. Betty, with features sharpening in the moment of strain, looked menacingly cruel.

"Filth!" Francie whispered, careless now of her own safety. "Filth! Both of you."

Stewart gave a grunt of surprise. "Now, now, after all we've done for—"

"Grab her, you fool!" Betty shouted. "It went wrong somewhere. Just look at her face!" Betty jumped to her feet.

Stewart hesitated a moment before lunging toward Francie, his arms outspread. In that moment of hesitation Francie started to move toward the door. His fingers brushed her shoulder, slid down her arm, clamped tightly on her wrist. The meaty touch of his hand on her bare wrist brought back all her fear.

His lunge had put him a bit off balance, and Francie's body contracted in a spasm of fright that threw her back. Stewart was pulled against the raised hearth of the fireplace. As he tripped, his hand slipped from her wrist and before she turned she saw him stumble forward, heard the thud his head made striking the edge of the fieldstone fireplace, saw both his hands slide toward the log fire.

As Betty cried out and ran toward Stewart, Francie found the knob and pulled the door open and ran in panic toward the trail. She went up the first slope, reached the handrail, caught it, used it to pull herself along faster.

She glanced back, gasping for breath, and saw Betty, her face set, her strong legs driving her rapidly up the hill.

Fear gave Francie renewed strength and for a few moments the distance between them remained the same. But soon she was fighting for air, mouth wide, while a sharp pain began to knot her left side.

Betty's feet were so close that she dared not look back. Her shoulder brushed a tree and then Betty's arms locked her thighs and they went down together, rolling across the sticky trail into the base of a small spruce.

Betty slapped her hard, using each hand alternately slapping until Francie's ears were full of a hard ringing and she could taste blood inside her mouth. But she could hear the ugly words with which Betty emphasized each blow.

"Stop!" Francie cried. "Oh stop!"

The hard slaps ceased and Francie knew that she had learned a great deal about Betty's motivations during those brutal moments.

"On your feet," Betty said.

Francie rolled painfully to her hands and knees. She reached up and grasped a limb of the small spruce to help herself to her feet. The limb she grasped was only a stub, two feet long. It broke off close to the trunk as she pulled herself up. She did not realize that, in effect, she held a club, until she saw Betty's eyes narrow, saw the woman take a step backward.

"Drop it, Francie," Betty said shrilly.

Francie felt her lips stretch in a meaningless smile. She stepped forward and swung the club with all her strength. It would have missed the blond woman entirely, but Betty, attempting to duck, moved directly into the path of the club. It shattered against the pale-gold head.

Betty stood for a moment bent forward from the waist, arms hanging, and then she went down with a boneless limpness. She hit on the slope, and momentum rolled her over onto her back.

Francie, laughing and crying, dropped to her knees beside the woman. She took what remained of the club in both hands and raised it high over her head, willing herself to smash it down against the unprotected face, her temples pounding.

For a long moment she held the club high, and then, just as she let it slip out of her hands to fall behind her, Clint Reese came down the wet path. He was half running, slipping on the wet snow, his overcoat fanning out behind him. When he saw Francie the tautness went out of his face. He took her arm and pulled her to her feet.

"Get off the path," he said roughly.

"They—"

He pulled her with him, forced her down, and crouched beside her. She heard the shots then. Two that were thin and bitter. Whipcracks across the snow. Then one heavy-throated shot, and after an interval, a second one.

She moved and Clint said, "Stay down! I came along to see if you were getting all the protection Osborne promised."

"Oh, Clint, they—"

"I know, darling. Hold it. Somebody's coming."

It was Luke Osborne, walking alone, coming up from the house. He walked slowly and the lines in his face were deeper. They came out to meet him. Osborne looked down at Betty Jackson. The woman moaned and stirred a little.

One of the young men, a stranger, came down the road.

Betty sat up. She looked vaguely at Osborne and the young man. Then she scrambled to her feet, her eyes wild. "Stewart," she screamed. "Stewart!"

Osborne blocked her as she started forward. "Your partner is dead, lady," he said. "Quite thoroughly dead."

Betty pressed the knuckles of both hands against her bared teeth. Instinctively Francie turned to Clint, and pressed her face against the rough topcoat texture. She heard Osborne saying, "Get her up to the car, Clint."

After giving Francie a shot, the doctor sent her to bed in the Cudahy guest room. As the drug took hold she let herself slip down and down, through endless layers of black velvet that folded over her, one after the other.

On the fourth day, Clint Reese took her from the Cudahy house back to her cabin. He helped her down the trail and pointed out where Osborne's men had been trying to protect her as much as possible without alarming the Jacksons.

He lit a fire, and tucked a blanket around her in the chair. And then he made coffee for them. He lounged on the bunk with coffee and cigarette. "Take tomorrow off," he said expansively.

"Yes, boss."

"Remember when I was going to say something in bad taste and you stopped me?"

"I remember."

"Oh, I'm not going to try to say it again, so don't look so worried. I'm going to say something else. Lines I memorized last night, in front of my mirror, trying to wear an appealing expression. The trouble is, they still happen to be sort of—well, previous. So I won't say them, either.

"But I'll keep practicing. You see, I've got to wait until you give me the go-ahead, then I'll say them someday. Old Reese, they always said, a very patient guy. Got a master's degree in waiting, that one has."

"It is too soon, Clint. Especially after all that's just happened."

"Well, I'll stick around and wait. The way we work it, you show up some morning one of these years with a lobster trap in your left hand and a hollyhock in your teeth, humming 'Hail to the chief.' That will be our little signal—just yours and mine. I'll catch on. Then I'll spout deathless lines you can scribble in your diary."

He stood up for a moment. His eyes were very grave.

"Is it a date?"

"It's a date, Clint."

"Thanks, Francie."

He left with an exaggerated casualness that touched her heart. She pushed the blanket aside and went to the window to watch Clinton Reese go up the trail.

Now the Adirondack winter was coming, and during the long months she would watch the frozen lake and let the snow fall gently on her heart. A time of whiteness and peace, a time of healing. By spring Bob's death would be a year old, and spring is a time of growth and change and renewal.

Francie recalled the look of gravity and warmth and wanting in Clint's eyes, the look that denied the casual smile.

Possibly with strength and luck and sanity, it might come sooner than either of them realized. For this might be the winter in which she could learn to say good-bye.

House Call

Howard Browne

At 8:15 on a heavily overcast morning in late October, Mr. Coombs awoke to the soft strains of a Bach fugue from the clock radio beside his bed. Because of his deep and abiding respect for the composer he waited until the selection ended before he threw back the blanket, slid blue-veined feet into a pair of slippers, and pattered into the bathroom.

After making sure there was no furry coating on his tongue and that his temperature was normal, he used some of the gargle strongly recommended by Mr. Latzos, the corner druggist who had suffered from a spastic colon for years. Next he brushed his teeth vigorously, then carefully shaved the graying stubble from his unlined cheeks, unaggressive chin, and narrow upper lip. Humming a slightly off-key accompaniment to a Mozart sonata from the bedroom radio, he adjusted the shower to lukewarm, shucked off his pajamas, and stepped under the needle spray.

This, Mr. Coombs told himself contentedly, showed definite promise of turning out to be a perfect day.

By the time he was dressed and had the bedroom and bath restored to their normal pristine neatness, it was a few minutes past nine. He polished the lenses of his horn-rimmed glasses, switched off the bedside radio, and entered the apartment's small kitchen, where he immediately turned on the radio over the sink. This time there was something from Grieg's *Lyric Suite*. Mr. Coombs always spoke very highly of Grieg.

Alert to the dangers of overeating, Mr. Coombs put together his customary breakfast of prune juice, a slice of whole-wheat toast, and one cup of decaffeinated coffee. Through the open window he could hear the young couple next door arguing about something or other.

Presently a door banged and quiet was restored. The coffee came to a boil and Mr. Coombs, an ear cocked to the soothing sound of strings in a Schubert serenade, got down a cup and saucer. He was reaching for the pot when two sharp sounds like pistol shots rang out from across the areaway, instantly followed by a high, hard voice lifted in song:

> *Go on baby, make it again;*
> *Right on baby, ain't no sin.*
> *Come on baby, lay it out,*
> *That's what lovin's all about . . .*

Dropping the cup, Mr. Coombs sprang to the window and slammed it shut with such force that the glass nearly shattered. He was trembling violently, his no longer gentle features twisted with fury, his breathing quick and hard. Faint but still insistent, the barbaric chant went on:

> *Rich folks, poor folks,*
> *They all shout . . .*

Mr. Coombs ground his teeth together and twisted the volume dial on his radio, bringing in Schubert loud enough to drown out that nerve-crippling wail. How any human could deliberately pour such acid into his ears defied comprehension. He placed the fingertips of his right hand on the pulse in his left wrist. A definite quickening.

Frowning, Mr. Coombs sat down to breakfast.

At 9:40 the doorbell rang. A deliveryman in an unmarked jumpsuit shoved a parcel into Mr. Coombs's hands, used a grimy forefinger to indicate the line on a clipboard pad reserved for his signature, and went off down the hallway. Mr. Coombs closed the door, put back the safety chain, and carried the package into the kitchen.

It was the size of a shoebox and the brown paper wrapping bore the self-adhesive label of an exclusive Northside bootery. Near an upper corner the word RUSH had been rubber-stamped in red.

Instead of immediately removing the wrapping, Mr. Coombs used a fingernail to loosen one corner of the label itself, then delicately stripped it free. On the reverse side, neatly printed in ink, were a name and address. These he committed to memory, then dug a book of matches from a drawer, touched a flame to the label, and flushed the ashes down the drain.

Humming a reprise of the Schubert piece, Mr. Coombs returned to the bedroom, pushed back the closet door, knelt, and turned back a corner of the carpeting. After lifting up a small section of floorboard, he reached into the cavity and brought out a small silk underarm holster and a short-barreled .32 Colt Police Special.

With the holstered gun in place and the jacket of his dark gray suit buttoned, Mr. Coombs eyed himself critically in the dresser mirror. Even a practiced eye, he assured himself, would fail to detect the slightest hint of a betraying bulge.

Patronizing the right tailor was essential to a man in Mr. Coombs's line of work.

At 2:55 that same afternoon a very pretty blond woman named Myra Selvin was setting out lunch for her husband in the kitchen of their tract home.

Selvin's Shack, as Bill Selvin called the house, was located in a still raw subdivision and a full block, thus far, from the nearest neighbor. This isolation was a constant source of worry to him since it meant sticking Myra and young Danny out there alone till one in the morning five nights a week. It had to be that way, for he normally worked the four-to-midnight shift on the copy desk at Universal News Service.

During the twelve years since Bill first found out there was a lot more to Myra than a pair of great legs and a superior superstructure, they had acquired an eleven-year-old son, an '84 Granada hardtop, and, four months ago, a staggering mortgage on an overpriced hunk of real estate.

It seemed they had something else, too—at least Myra did: a brand-new uncreased traffic ticket picked up three days ago for overtime parking. By this time she'd worked up enough courage to hand it to Bill, along with his second cup of coffee.

"Be a darling," she said, seeking the light touch, "and mail them a check when you get to the office. I'd do it myself but the household account is a little low. Like in zilch."

A single glance was all Bill needed. "Fifteen bucks! For Chrisake, Myra!"

"Could've been a lot worse," Myra said virtuously. "A smashed fender at least. If I hadn't been on my toes, that man in the blue sedan might've—"

"What man in *what* blue sedan?"

"The one parked in front of me. Scary-looking—the man, I mean. He comes tearing out of his apartment house next to the market and jumps into this blue sedan just as I was pulling out. Came right at me. If I hadn't cut the wheel—"

"Well, bully for you! Of course, if you'd parked in the lot instead of the street, there wouldn't've *been* a ticket and you wouldn't've *been* anywhere near this blue sedan and none—"

Myra put up her hands in surrender. "I might've known you'd get technical. Hurry it up or you'll miss your bus. And I have to be here when Danny gets home."

Bill was still sulking a little when Myra pulled up at the bus stop. "Fifteen bucks," he growled. "I could'a got me a new fly rod for—"

She kissed him fondly. "Not that I'm throwing you out, but here comes your bus."

She watched the bus pull away, then drove quickly back to the Shack. The school bus was due in twenty minutes; time enough for a cup of coffee and half a doughnut before Danny showed up.

It didn't work out that way. She'd barely filled her cup before the doorbell rang. Just her luck; some salesman, out canvassing the boondocks.

The caller turned out to be a neatly dressed middle-aged man of medium height and rather slight build. He had an unaggressive chin, a narrow upper lip, and a mildly apologetic manner. Not at all an impressive figure but his air of quiet authority was unmistakable.

He lifted his dark gray hat with a courtly gesture and bowed slightly. "Mrs. Myra Selvin?"

Myra nodded and fought back a smile. She couldn't recall the last time anyone had actually bowed to her. If ever.

"My name," the man said, "is Hayden. With the city Bureau of Urban Development."

He certainly looked harmless enough, Myra decided; but then you never know. "Could I see some identification, Mr. Hayden? If you don't mind."

Mr. Hayden didn't appear at all offended. "Very wise of you to ask, Mrs. Selvin." He got out his wallet and extracted a business card, handing it to her with something of a flourish.

Myra glanced at it, saw the wording bore out his statement. "I imagine it's my husband you'll want to see. He's at—"

Mr. Hayden's gentle smile and headshake stopped her there. "This is merely an inspection visit, Mrs. Selvin. No need to bother him. A few minor points about building-code requirements I have to check out. Should have been done long before this, of course, but city departments are notoriously slow."

Before Myra was quite sure how he managed it, the man was past her and moving along the short entrance hall leading to the living room. She closed the front door and followed him.

His eyes seemed to dart around the room. "Such lovely furnishings. You certainly have an eye for color coordination, Mrs. Selvin."

Myra warmed to the praise. This time she led the way, into the dining room and along the inner hall. He no longer seemed so much an intruder, she decided, as a guest being shown through the house.

In the kitchen, Mr. Hayden said, "I see you have only the two outer doors, side and front. Personally I approve of these modern layouts; somehow a back porch always seems to end up as a storeroom." There was a kind of shy warmth in his voice, and Myra was almost tempted to say, *You and Mrs. Hayden must drop in some evening.*

The inspection of the second floor was conducted in tactful silence. Mr. Hayden contented himself with merely glancing into the bedrooms and through the open door of the bath before returning to the living room. "Thank you, Mrs. Selvin," he said politely and slid a hand under the left lapel of his suit jacket.

The hand froze briefly, then came out again, empty. He said pleasantly, "Someone's at the front door, Mrs. Selvin."

Myra looked at him blankly. "Are you sure? I didn't hear—"

The doorbell rang.

"Excuse me," Myra said and went off down the hall. Such a strange little man, she was thinking. For all his gentlemanly manner, there was something . . . well, *chilling* about him.

But then Mr. Hayden was suddenly forgotten as she saw Miss Anderson, the school nurse, in the doorway holding Danny by the hand.

Myra reached quickly for the boy with quick concern. "What happened, Danny? Are you—"

Miss Anderson said, "No need to be upset, Mrs. Selvin." She edged Myra gently aside and led the boy into the hall. "Danny's fine. He seemed sort of listless in class and we found he was running a slight fever; probably a cold coming on. Not the least bit serious, but I thought I'd better bring him home instead of putting him on the school bus. You know how drafty they can be."

Myra turned away. "Come in, Miss Anderson. I'll call Dr. Evans."

The nurse shook her head, smiled reassuringly. "No need for that, really. Just put him to bed; if he's still running a temperature in the morning, then you might call the doctor."

"You're sure?"

"Of course. Youngsters Danny's age bounce back like a bad check."

They exchanged understanding smiles and Miss Anderson left. Myra hustled the protesting boy upstairs, gave him a hot bath, and put him to bed. Not until she was cleaning up the bathroom did she remember the man from the city housing bureau. Good Lord, what must he think of her.

But Mr. Hayden was not in the living room. Frowning Myra went through the entire house. Without result. It seemed Mr. Hayden had left without bothering to say good-bye.

Vaguely repentant, she looked out the front window. As usual the street was deserted, with nothing beyond that but open prairie. Apparently Mr. Hayden, not wanting to disturb her further, had simply left by the side door and driven away.

Myra returned to the kitchen, reheated the coffee, and was sipping at it over the morning paper when the doorbell rang. This time the caller was a tall, square-shouldered man in his early forties wearing a blue serge suit badly in need of pressing.

"Lieutenant Greer, ma'am. Police department." He flashed something shiny and official looking pinned to the inner flap of his wallet. "You Mrs. Myra Selvin?"

Myra stared at him incredulously. "I simply don't believe it."

The lieutenant lifted a shaggy eyebrow. "Ma'am?"

"Sending a policeman out here just to collect a measly fifteen dollars. I only got that parking ticket three days ago."

Lieutenant Greer gave her a one-sided smile. "That's not why I'm here. At least not directly." He looked past her shoulder. "May I come in?"

Seated in the living room lounge chair, Lieutenant Greer declined a cup of coffee and explained the chain of events that had brought him here. A notorious underworld figure, he said, had been shot dead three days ago in an apartment building near the Union Supermart.

"We understand the killer got away in a blue sedan," the lieutenant went on. "Nobody admitted getting a good look at him, leaving us at a dead end. Till this morning, that is, when Traffic came up with the information on your parking ticket. The officer who tagged you remembered seeing a blue sedan parked in front of your vehicle at the time." He spread his hands and looked at her hopefully. "We figured it was possible you got a look at the driver."

Myra leaned forward, her eyes sparkling with excitement. "I sure did. He was in such a big hurry he almost took my fender off."

The lieutenant's expression showed grim satisfaction. "Now we're getting somewhere. What'd he look like?"

Myra's forehead creased. "Well, he seemed kind of . . . big. His face was sort of . . . sort of ugly. And angry, you know? He had on a hat and a dark coat . . ."

Her voice ran down. Greer took a deep breath and managed to keep his disappointment from showing. "You think maybe you could recognize him from a mug shot? You know, a picture?"

"I'm positive I could," Myra said promptly.

"Fine." The lieutenant reached for his hat. "I'd like you to come down to Headquarters with me and go through some of them. I'm sure we can narrow down the number beforehand, so it won't take much of your time."

Regretfully, Myra shook her head. "I can't, Lieutenant. Not right now. My little boy's upstairs, sick, and my husband's at work. How about tomorrow morning? I could drive over then."

After a brief discussion, Lieutenant Greer arranged to meet her at the precinct station the following morning, bade her good-bye and drove off down the empty street.

That was at 4:25. At 4:40 a small gray Chevrolet coupe drew up at the curb a short distance from the Selvin residence and on the opposite side of the street.

Myra Selvin first noticed the gray car shortly after five o'clock. She was in the master bedroom straightening her bureau drawers when she caught a glimpse of it through the gathering darkness beyond the window.

Absently she wondered what a car was doing there at

all. The only house on the block was her own. Probably some salesman, she decided, filling out a report, or whatever salesmen did at the end of a day.

But when, twenty minutes later, she realized the Chevrolet was still there, a dim sense of alarm began to rise within her. Suddenly Lieutenant Greer's story of the killer in the blue sedan flooded back—and the sense of alarm was no longer dim.

She peered cautiously from behind the bedroom drapes, trying to learn if anyone was actually in the car. But at 5:30 in late October dusk had already filled the street, making it impossible to see into the car's interior.

It was then she remembered the field glasses hanging from a strap in Bill's closet. She got them out with unsteady hands, knelt at the open window, and focused the powerful lenses on the front seat of the small gray coupe.

Someone was sitting there.

Because of the downward angle she could not make out the upper half of the man's body, but she could see his upper thighs . . . and his hands. Something was in those hands; some small object she could not identify. If only there was more light . . .

As though in response to her silent plea, the street lamp almost directly above the car came on. In the yellow rays the magnified image of the object stood out sharply before Myra's straining eyes.

A gun.

The binoculars dropped from Myra's nerveless fingers. A wave of weakness washed over her and for a long moment she could not rise from her knees. Finally, trembling with mounting fear, she got to her feet, ran from the bedroom, and down the stairs.

The phone receiver came into her hand with the heartening feel of a life preserver to a drowning man. Thrusting a palsied finger into the last hole, she spun the dial and put the receiver to her ear.

No answering buzz, no faint crackling sound of an open wire. Just an empty silence that seemed slowly to spread and engulf her. Frantically she moved the bar up and down. *Please!* a voice screamed inside her. *Please answer!*

Nothing. Nothing at all. Slowly her eyes moved along the cord toward the wall. A dry sob tore at her throat and the receiver fell from her hand.

The cord had been ripped from the wall box.

Bill Selvin filled his cup from one of the office coffee carafes, took off his green eyeshade, and got up to stretch his legs. The wall clock put the time at 4:50. Why not, he thought, call Myra, tell her he really wasn't sore about that parking ticket. Hell, he'd paid off a few tickets himself that Myra didn't even know about. Not that she was sitting around crying her eyes out, but a guy ought to be understanding about such things.

After the tenth ring he slowly put back the receiver. Funny; she *had* to be home. If she'd gone out for any reason, she would have called him first. Unless she'd taken Danny to McDonald's for a burger . . . No; even then she'd have called to let him know.

He tried the number again. Still no answer. Scowling, he depressed the cutoff bar, released it, and dialed the operator.

Myra sat huddled on the floor at the downstairs front window, peering past a corner of the drawn drapes. The

burst of panic that had sent her flying to the telephone
had dissipated, leaving her limp with terror. *You're trapped,*
her mind shrilled; *there's nothing you can do!*

She closed her eyes, shivering, her fingers digging into
the carpet. She had seen the face of a murderer; for that
she must die. She knew now that when Mr. Hayden had
slipped a hand inside his jacket he was reaching for a gun.
Naturally he had been the first to hear Miss Anderson and
Danny at the front steps. He was a killer—a hired killer,
and would possess the sharpened senses of a stalking tiger.
The moment she had left him to answer the bell, he had
slipped out the side door. There had been no one to see
him arrive, no one to see him go.

And now he was back again. Sitting out there where he
could keep an eye on both outer doors, waiting till the
last trace of daylight was gone before forcing his way in
and doing what he had been hired to do.

Suddenly Myra was on her feet. There *was* a way! Yank
open the door and run. Run screaming into the night,
away from where he waited. If he dared shoot at all, there
was so little light that he *had* to miss a moving target. It
was worth trying. Anything was better than waiting to die
cowering in a corner like a helpless child . . .

Danny. My God—*Danny!*

Her knees seemed to melt and she leaned, shaking,
against the wall. Some strange alchemy of the mind had
managed to block Danny out, leaving only the thought of
her own danger. Briefly, she weighed the possibility of
getting him hurriedly dressed and, together, making a run
for it. But the thought of Danny out in the open as the
killer took slow and deliberate aim . . .

What if she simply left Danny upstairs in his room? If

he didn't *see* Mr. Hayden there would be no reason to harm him. The man wasn't a maniac; he was a cold, controlled executioner, killing only the person he was paid to kill.

A crazed kind of gratitude welled up within her toward the man outside. Her tormented mind became a twisted prism through which he was revealed as a good man, a kindly man, a man who would never senselessly harm a child . . .

She straightened as a sudden thought sent her spirits soaring. Hurrying to the living room desk, she found a thin plastic letter opener in one of the drawers, then sat down on the floor in front of the telephone box fastened low on the wall. Her fingers were steady as she removed the screws on either side and took off the black metal cover. Then her spirits plummeted as she stared helplessly at the maze of wires, their number and confusion magnified by fear as she poked at them with the double-pronged end of the loose cord.

He knew you couldn't fix it! her mind shrieked. *He doesn't make mistakes.*

She put her face in her hands. *This is the way he wants me to be,* she thought. Helpless, defeated, knowing that nothing could save her, that no door, no lock, would bar his way.

Her churning thoughts went back to Danny. At least he could be spared. She hurried up the stairs and found him propped up on the pillows leafing through one of his books in drowsy contentment. She forced a smile. "How do you feel, darling?"

Danny eyed her with open calculation. "Can I stay home tomorrow?"

"Of course you can. Tomorrow's Saturday."

His expression changed. "I'm not sick, Mom. It's just that ole Miss Anderson said so."

"But I want you to stay in bed. That's very important. Do you understand, Danny? No matter what, you must stay in bed!" She bit her lip, afraid she'd made too great a point of it, stirred his curiosity. He might . . .

"Can I play my radio, then?"

"After a while, darling." She bent and kissed him, careful to keep the caress from being the fiercely possessive act she yearned to make it. She straightened and looked down at her son for a long moment, then turned and went stiffly down the steps.

Mr. Hayden was waiting in the living room.

All during the timeless period of terror since she had first seen the gun, a corner of Myra Selvin's mind had dwelt on how the killer would act at the last moment. Would that narrow upper lip twist into a sneer? Would he strike her first? Or would he merely point the gun at her and pull the trigger?

There was no violence. He did not sneer. He stood there facing her, his expression serious, his hand holding the gun along his leg.

"I saw him," she said dully, the words forming without conscious volition. "I wish I hadn't, but he looked back, you see."

A flicker of interest stirred in the gray face. "Who was it you saw, Mrs. Selvin?"

"Why, the man. The man in the blue car. The man who killed somebody. Isn't that why you . . ."

The man who called himself Hayden, Coombs, or any of a dozen other names stared at her and said nothing.

"You mustn't k-kill me," Myra said in a small voice. Her nails were biting into her palms.

"I'm sorry, Mrs. Selvin. I'd much rather I didn't have to."

"Then go away," she whispered. "Just go away. Tell the man I won't say anything to the police."

"I'm afraid I wouldn't know how to do that," he said regretfully. "I never know the names of my . . . clients. It isn't at all necessary, you see."

He began slowly to bring up the muzzle of the gun. *Why don't I scream?* Myra wondered dazedly. *Why can't I turn and run? Or get down on my knees and beg?* She forced out a last whisper, a shattered prayer. "You won't hurt my boy—upstairs?"

The gun was level now, pointed at her heart. It seemed to swell, to grow in his hand. "Of course I won't, Mrs. Selvin."

"Thank you. Oh, thank . . ."

There were two very loud shots. But they came from upstairs, not from the gray man's gun. A blast of raucous sound followed; Danny had turned on his radio.

> *Go on baby, make it again;*
> *Right on baby, ain't no sin . . .*

Both Mr. Hayden and Myra reacted sharply; the former with a snarl, a visible shudder, a turning of his body toward the stairs. Myra, seeing only the snarl, knew that Danny was in danger. She threw herself at the man with instinctive and unreasoning ferocity, driving a shoulder into him at about the level of his belt buckle. Since Mr. Hayden was not a robust man it was not at all surprising that he toppled backward.

The gun fell from his hand as his head snapped back sharply on his thin neck, striking a leg of the couch with surprising force. His body seemed to contract convulsively, then go completely limp.

Myra crawled on hands and knees along the carpeting, her staring eyes glued to the gun. The blast of music from upstairs decreased sharply as the volume was adjusted. Myra's hand closed around the weapon's chill length and everything within her seemed to stop functioning. She sat there, one leg stretched out, and stared at the blued metal . . .

A bell was ringing. The doorbell. She wondered in a kind of detached way who it might be. She went on wondering, not moving, not calling out, and presently a cautious face appeared around the edge of the living-room archway. A young man's face under a shock of black unruly hair. Wondering eyes took in the scene. He stared at Myra. Myra stared at him.

"Telephone Company, lady. We got a rush out-of-order report on this number."

"The cord," Myra said. "It's been pulled out."

"I'll get it fixed right up, lady."

"Thank you."

It was completely mad. The way they spoke, the politely commonplace things they were saying. Like two friends witnessing something indecent while out for a stroll and hiding their embarrassment with casual conversation.

Ridiculous.

Then Myra fainted and the telephone man took over.

The Runaway

Barbara Michaels

The younger girl was fifteen. She told people she was sixteen when they asked, but usually they didn't even bother. They just looked at her narrow shoulders and flat chest and skinny legs, and shook their heads. Mary knew they probably thought she was about twelve or thirteen. Nobody would hire a kid that age, and she couldn't show any proof she was older. The problem was that she wasn't old enough.

Some of the men would have hired Angie. She was almost seventeen and she was pretty. "Angie is the pretty one," their mother always said. Angie's best feature was her hair, long and smooth and shiny as yellow silk. *Flat* and *skinny* were words nobody would apply to Angie. The cloth of her tight jeans was straining at every seam. That was where the men looked—at the seat of Angie's jeans and the lush curves that pushed out the front of her shirt. Angie couldn't understand why Mary wouldn't let her take jobs from the men who looked at her that way.

Though she was the younger of the two, Mary had always been the one who looked after Angie, instead of the other way around. Angie was . . . sensitive. Angie didn't understand some things. And when she was scared or unhappy, she stuck out her lip and made whimpering noises, like a homesick puppy.

She was whimpering now. Mary didn't blame her. She was scared, too, but she couldn't let Angie see that she was. One of them had to be tough.

It was so dark! Nights in town were never like this. There were always streetlights, lighted windows, cars passing by. They hadn't seen a car for a long time, not since they'd turned off the highway onto the narrow country road. The last house had been at least a mile back.

To make matters worse, there was a storm coming on. Heavy clouds obscured moon and stars. So far the rain had held off, but lightning and thunder were getting closer, louder. The wind made queer rustling noises in the bushes along the road. There were other noises that couldn't have been made by the wind, but Mary didn't mention them. Angie was upset enough already. She couldn't go much farther; she was scared to death of lightning. They had to find shelter soon.

As Mary looked anxiously around her, she tripped and fell. Gravel stung her palms, and something sharp, a stone or a piece of broken glass, ripped into her knee. She bit her lip and managed not to cry out.

Angie was the one who yelled, "Mary, what's the matter? Get up, get up, I can't—"

"I tripped, that's all." Mary staggered to her feet and reached for Angie's hand. "Shut up, Angie. Someone will hear you."

"I don't care if they do. I don't like this. We should have gone to that house back there."

"And have them call the cops?" Mary forced herself to

limp forward. Angie hung back, dragging at Mary's arm, and Mary lost her temper. "Damn it, Angie, this whole thing was your idea. You want to give up?"

"No, I won't go back. You know what he'll do. You promised! You said you'd take care of everything—"

"I've done all right so far, haven't I?" Mary demanded, stung by the note of criticism in her sister's voice.

"It was fun at first. But I told you we shouldn't've gone down this road."

"We wouldn't have had to if you hadn't come on to that sleazy character in the pizza place," Mary said. "He was following us—you, I mean."

"He was kind of cute," Angie said.

Mary was about to reply when a bolt of lightning split the sky and thunder rolled over them. Angie screamed.

"It's okay," Mary said, trying to steady her voice. "But we'd better walk faster. I don't want to be caught in the rain any more than you do. This damned road has to end up someplace."

Angie was genuinely terrified by lightning. She stumbled on, sobbing noisily, clutching Mary's hand till it ached.

Her distress softened Mary, as it always did. She got mad at Angie sometimes, but it was impossible to stay mad at her, she was so damned helpless. Giggling and grinning at that guy in the pizza place . . . Angie didn't know any better. She trusted everybody, even men whose eyes held that cold hunger when they looked at her. But she had a stubborn streak. When she had threatened to run away from home, Mary knew she meant it, and the thought of Angie out on her own, with no one to look after her, was too awful. She had had no choice but to go along. She wasn't all that crazy about what was happening at home, either.

Two hundred dollars—the savings of several years of baby-sitting—had seemed like a lot of money. But the bus fares had taken a big chunk; Mary wouldn't hitchhike, although Angie wanted to. And food cost a lot more than she had expected. Angie ate such a lot. As soon as they got jobs, everything would be all right, but so far they hadn't had any luck. Either people turned them down cold or the men looked at Angie in that hungry way.

And now, thanks to Angie's dumb stunt, they were lost on a dark country road with a storm about to cut loose. Mary wondered what time it was. It had been almost ten when they left the pizza place. It must be the middle of the night now. Her knee burned, and Angie kept dragging at her hand. She felt as if she weighed a ton.

Another flash of lightning won a squeal from Angie. Mary stopped. "There's a house over there. I saw it in the lightning. Come on, Angie."

But when they reached the gate, Angie's mulish streak surfaced. "The people who live here will ask questions," she whined. "I told you, Mary, I won't go back. You'll have to think of a story to tell them. Something smart."

"I won't have to be smart," Mary said wearily. "The house is empty, Angie. There're no lights, and everything is kind of falling down. Look."

Another flash of lightning proved her correct. The house was a farmhouse, of a type common in that part of the country—two stories high, with a steep-peaked roof. Children or tramps had broken most of the windows. The few remaining panes of glass reflected the livid flashes like blind white eyes.

Angie didn't like the look of the place, and said so in no uncertain terms. The first drops of rain spattering in the dust alongside the road ended her hesitation. Hands over her head, she ran with Mary. Before they reached the crumbling porch steps, the drops had thickened into a downpour.

Mary fell for the second time on the broken steps. She squatted on the porch, rocking back and forth in silent pain. Finally she got up, with Angie's help, and limped toward the door. It hung drunkenly on one hinge. It was so light, so rotted by time and weather, that they were able to push it back far enough to enter.

Angie took her comb from her purse. She started to run it through her damp hair. Soothed by the familiar gesture and by shelter, however poor, she spoke calmly.

"It smells funny."

"I guess it's been abandoned for a long time," Mary said, squinting into the darkness.

The house shuddered with every thunderclap. Rain trickled in through holes in the ceiling. Mary started as a chunk of wet plaster thudded to the floor. Anyhow, it was better than being outdoors.

The room was long and narrow. It was empty of furniture, but the floor was covered with debris. There was a fireplace on one wall.

"I'm hungry," Angie said.

"We've got those hamburgers. But I meant to save them for breakfast."

"We'll find a restaurant tomorrow. Let's eat now. But the hamburgers will be cold."

"I can't do anything about that," Mary said irritably.

"We could build a fire."

Mary looked at Angie in surprise. She came up with an idea so rarely that people tended to forget she could.

"Hey, yeah. There's lots of wood on the floor, and you have your lighter."

They cleared an area next to the fireplace and piled the scraps onto the hearth. Angie lit the heap. At first a lot of smoke billowed back into the room, making them cough, but finally the fire blazed up. The light was almost as welcome as the warmth, although it showed nothing but desolation—peeling wallpaper, rotted floorboards, and an ankle-deep layer of debris. Most of the latter burned nicely.

"It's funny," Mary said after dumping another load of scraps onto the fire.

"What is?" Angie was on her second hamburger. She was forced to eat it cold, after all, since her attempt to spit the first one on a stick had broken it apart.

"A lot of this wood looks like pieces of furniture," Mary said. "Like everything in the house has kind of fallen apart."

"I don't see what's so funny about that."

"Well, people don't leave their furniture when they move, do they? There's a table leg here, and enough pieces to make up a dozen chairs."

"Lucky for us," Angie said comfortably. "We can keep the fire going a long time."

"It's old wood," Mary said. "Dry. It burns fast."

It did burn fast, and it gave off a lot of heat. The part of the room near the fireplace was almost too warm. But a chill ran up Mary's back when she spoke those words. Dry . . . old . . . The syllables seemed to echo for a long time.

Angie finished her second hamburger and ate a candy

bar. She wanted another, but Mary wouldn't let her have it. That was their emergency supply. If the rain continued, they might have to depend on it for longer than she had expected.

Angie accepted the decree without too much grumbling. She combed her hair again. The silky strands shone in the firelight; she spread them out across her hands, ran her fingers through the shimmering web.

"Where are we going to sleep?" she asked, stretching like a cat in the warmth.

"Where else? Right here."

"Maybe there are beds upstairs."

"If the stairs are as rotten as everything else, I wouldn't trust them. Besides," she added craftily, as Angie started to object, "you wouldn't want to sleep on any old mattresses. Mice."

"Ugh," Angie said.

After finishing her hamburger, Mary stretched out her leg and rolled up her jeans. It was no wonder her knee hurt. Angie exclaimed sympathetically, "You've got a million splinters in there."

"Yeah." Mary pulled out a couple of the longer ones. She hated things sticking into her. Mother always said she was an absolute baby about shots. Pulling out the splinters made her skin crawl. But it had to be done, and the dirt ought to be washed off. She didn't want to risk infection.

"Oh, damn," she muttered.

"Want me to pull them out?" Angie asked cheerfully. "I don't mind."

"That's not why I said *damn*. All that rain outside and we don't have any way to catch the water."

"I'm thirsty," Angie said promptly.

"Me, too. And I'd like to wash my knee. Think of something."

"Who, me? You're the thinker in this family. 'Mary, she's the smart one,' " Angie mimicked their mother's voice.

"What about the cartons the hamburgers were in?"

"I threw them in the fire."

Mary said "Damn" again. "Go look in the kitchen, Angie. If the people who lived here left their furniture, maybe they left dishes, too."

"I'm not going in there alone," Angie said. "There are probably rats and everything."

Mary glowered at her sister with sudden dislike. Angie looked so *fat*, sprawled out on the floor. Her thighs filled her jeans like sausage stuffing. It seemed as if she could do something for somebody once in a while, instead of expecting to be waited on all the time.

There was no use arguing about it. Stiffly Mary got to her feet. She found a splintered chair leg and lit one end of it. It sputtered and smoked, but gave enough light to let her see where she was going. Angie trailed along. She said she was afraid to be alone, and in a way Mary didn't blame her.

The kitchen wasn't hard to find; there were only four rooms downstairs. It was in a state of ruin that made the living room look tidy by comparison. Part of the ceiling had fallen, half burying the massive bulk of an old cookstove. There was no refrigerator, unless a heap of rusty metal and rotting wood had once served that function. An icebox, Mary thought—the kind that had big chunks of real ice, instead of electricity, to keep things cold.

In the debris along the wall, where shelves had collapsed, spilling their contents onto the floor, she found one unbroken cup and a dish with a chip out of the edge. They were black with grime, but the rain would wash them out.

When they reached the porch, she threw the burning stick onto the soggy grass and licked her singed fingers. The storm was passing, but it was still raining heavily. Mary washed the dishes as well as she could, and let them fill with rainwater.

It felt rather cozy to stretch out in front of the fire again. Mary began working on her knee. She got the biggest splinters out, but some of the smaller ones, deeply imbedded, were hard to get hold of, even with Angie's eyebrow tweezers. Mary was concentrating, her eyes blurred with tears; Angie was half asleep. Neither of them heard the boy coming. He was simply there, as if he had materialized out of thin air.

When Mary saw him, she let out a yelp of surprise. Angie woke up. Mary expected she'd scream, too; but when she saw Angie's mouth curve in a smile, she realized that Angie wasn't afraid of anything young and male. That was part of her trouble.

Anyhow, this boy didn't look frightening. As her pounding heart slowed, Mary saw that he was as startled as she was. He was tall and thin; his ragged clothes hung in limp folds, as if he had lost a lot of weight, or as if they had originally belonged to somebody bigger. His shaggy hair was shoulder-length; his feet were bare. He had raised his arms in front of his face, as if to shield it.

"It's okay," Mary said. "I guess you came in to get out of the rain, like us, didn't you? Come over to the fire."

The boy obeyed. His bare feet, stepping lightly, made no sound on the dusty floor. His eyes were fixed on Mary. They were dark eyes—she saw that as he came closer, out of the shadows; saw that his face, exposed when he lowered his protecting arms, was long and thin, with cheekbones that stood out sharply under the sunken pits of the eye sockets. His mouth was a clown's mouth, too long for the framework of his hollow cheeks, curving down at the corners.

He stopped a little distance from Mary; his eyes narrowed as he continued to study her. Then, as if some silent message had passed from her to him, he smiled.

Mary caught her breath. That was why his face had looked wrong. The wide lips were generously cut, designed for laughter. When his mouth curved up, all his other features fell into their proper places and proportions. But he was awfully thin. . . .

"My name's Rob," he said. His voice was soft, with a queer little hesitation.

"I'm Mary. This is Angie."

But Angie, disconcerted by a boy who looked at Mary instead of at her, had turned her back.

"Hello," Rob said gravely.

"Sit down if you want to."

"Thank you." Rob sat, crossing his legs. The soles of his feet were covered by a thick, hardened layer of skin. He must have gone barefoot for months, maybe years, Mary thought.

"You hurt yourself," he said, looking at Mary's knee.

"I fell down." Mary laughed self-consciously. "I'm the clumsy one, always falling over my own feet."

Rob did not laugh. "I bet it hurts. Why don't you pull out them splinters?"

"I'm chicken," Mary admitted. "I got out as many as I could, but . . ."

He took the tweezers from her hand. It was the lightest, gentlest movement; she scarcely felt the touch of the metal tips as he plucked out the splinters.

"I think that's most of 'em," he said finally. "You better wash it off now. You got some cloth or something?"

"I guess I could tear up a shirt."

But her pack yielded nothing that would serve. The clothes were all knits, except for an extra pair of jeans. Rob exclaimed with admiration over the T-shirts.

"Say, that's pretty. 'Specially that one with the birds and flowers. You don't wanna spoil that. Maybe I can find some old thing around here."

With the same light, almost furtive movements, he slipped out of the room.

"Boy," Angie said. "Boy, you really are a hypocrite, you know that?"

Mary started. Crazy as it might sound, she had almost forgotten about Angie.

"What do you mean?"

"Always lecturing *me* about picking up men," Angie said. "You practically fell all over him."

"You're just mad because he didn't look at you," Mary said.

"Ha!" Angie registered amused contempt. "I wouldn't want him to look at me. He's weird. Ugly. He talks funny—"

"That's the way they talk around here," Mary said coldly. "You're so ignorant, you think everybody but you talks funny. He's nice. I like him."

"Mary." Angie reached out her hand. Her face had lost its healthy color. Even in the firelight she looked pale.

"Mary, he really is weird. There's something funny about him."

"Funny, weird—is that all you can say? You shut up, do you hear me? I don't want you hurting his feelings."

The warning was delivered just in time. Rob was back, carrying something. He held it out to Mary. It was an old calico shirt, faded so badly that the original print was almost gone.

"It's clean," he said anxiously. "I washed it myself. It's too small for me, anyways. You go on, tear it up."

Mary would have objected, but it was obvious that the garment was far too small for Rob. It must have been bought for him when he was thirteen or fourteen, before he had shot up to his present height.

"You been carrying this around with you?" she asked as she began to tear the cloth. "I wouldn't have bothered packing anything this old."

"No, it was upstairs," Rob said calmly.

Angie made a small sound, deep in her throat. Mary stared, a strip of cloth dangling from her fingers.

"Upstairs? You mean, you—"

"I useta live here," Rob said. "I was away for a long time, but I come back. They—they was all gone when I come. Musta moved away. . . ." His forehead wrinkled; for a moment the dark eyes went blank, like those of a sleepwalker. Then he smiled. "Sure is nice to have company. It's been lonesome."

That radiant smile dispelled Mary's uneasiness. She started dabbing at her knee.

"We ran away, too," she said. "But we aren't going back."

"How come you run away?" Rob asked.

"Well, see, our father died . . ." Mary began.

She paused, waiting for the sympathetic comment that should have followed. She was a little taken aback when Rob nodded and said, "Mine, too."

"Really?"

"He was killed in the war."

"Vietnam? Ours died of a heart attack." Mary realized it sounded kind of flat. A heart attack wasn't nearly as romantic or tragic as death in battle. She went on, "Then Mother got married again. We have a stepfather."

"Me, too."

"You're kidding."

"I guess they ain't that scarce," Rob said. "Stepfathers, I mean."

He smiled tentatively, to indicate he wasn't making fun of her, just joking. Mary's suspicions dissolved. He was right, stepfathers weren't uncommon.

"He was Pa's friend, in the war," Rob explained. "He brung Pa's things home, after it was over. Then he just . . . stayed. Ma had to have a man around. Woman can't run a farm by herself. I was too small to help." He paused, scraping at a frayed spot on his faded pants. Then he asked, "Was he mean to you? Your stepfather?"

"George? He was nice at first," Mary said darkly. "To lull our suspicions. Lately he's been on our backs all the time. Discipline, discipline, that's all we heard. Last week was the last straw. He said Angie should be sent away to school. Some awful boarding school where they make you get up at seven o'clock and have room checks and study hall every night, and no dates unless the boy has a certified letter from the President of the United States. . . ."

Rob was listening sympathetically, his flexible mouth

reflecting her indignation; but somehow the description of the horrors of boarding school lacked drama, even to Mary. She added, with genuine distress, "We've always been together. You'd think that would make them happy, that we like each other. Most sisters fight all the time. We never . . . Well, we don't fight much. But George said we weren't good for each other. He said Angie depended on me too much, and I wasn't making friends of my own because I was always with her. . . ." Rob was looking bewildered. Mary gave it up. "You wouldn't understand," she said. "I guess girls have different problems from boys. What was the matter with your stepfather?"

"He useta lick me a lot. But it wasn't that so much, it was—"

Angie giggled.

"Lick you?" she repeated.

"Shut up," Mary snapped.

"You shouldn't talk mean to your little sister," Rob said reproachfully.

It was Mary's turn to laugh.

"She's not my little sister, she's my big sister. But she doesn't understand a lot of things. You mean, your stepfather actually hit you? You didn't have to put up with that. There are laws."

"Laws?"

"To protect kids from being beaten," Mary said impatiently. "Even back here in the boonies you must have heard of them. If he really hurt you—"

"Oh, he useta lay it on pretty good," Rob said matter-of-factly. And then, before Mary had any inkling of what he meant to do, he swung around and flipped up his shirt.

For a moment there was no sound in the room except

the drip of rain and the crackle of the flames. Then Angie let out a gasp of hysterical laughter.

They were old scars, long healed; but it was obvious that the ridged patterns were not the product of a single beating but of systematic, long-range abuse. The play of firelight and shadow on Rob's back made them look even worse than they were.

Rob let his shirt fall, and turned. At the sight of Mary's face his mouth dropped miserably.

"Say, I didn't mean to make you feel bad. It don't hurt, honest. I'd almost forgot about it till you started talking about—"

"Forgot *that?*"

"Well, it's my head," Rob said apologetically. "It got hurt. . . . I don't remember so good since then. Seems like I forget a lot of things."

"Did your stepfather hit you on the head, too?"

"He didn't much care where he hit me," Rob said with a touch of wry humor. "He was usually likkered up when he done it."

"Let me see," Mary said.

"Not if it makes you feel bad."

"It won't make me feel bad." Mary could not have explained why she felt the need to see for herself. Her reasons had nothing in common with the ghoulish interest that had drawn Angie closer.

"Okay," Rob said obediently. He bowed his head and parted his untidy brown hair. The raised scar stood up like a ridge of splintered bone.

Mary knew she mustn't upset him by any further expressions of distress, but as he sat patiently awaiting her comment, his head bowed and his long, dirty fingers passive in his tumbled hair, her eyes filled with tears. She put out her hand.

Suddenly Rob was on his feet, some distance away. His eyes were narrowed, and his thin chest rose and fell with his agitated breathing.

"Don't touch me," he whispered. "You mustn't touch me."

"I didn't mean any harm," Mary said. Two tears spilled over and left muddy tracks through the grime on her cheeks. "I only wanted—"

"I know." The boy's taut body relaxed. "I thank you. But you mustn't . . . ."

Slowly, step by step, he began to back away.

Mary rose to her knees, ignoring the pain.

"Don't go away!"

"I'll come right back." He smiled at her but continued to retreat. He faded into the shadows in the open doorway.

As soon as he was gone, Angie flung herself at her sister, her fingers clawing at Mary's arm.

"Let's get out of here, Mary. Hurry. Quick, before he comes back—"

"Are you crazy?" Mary tried to free her arm, but Angie hung on.

"I'm not crazy, he is! Can't you see he's some kind of psycho? The way he talks . . . All that about forgetting things, and those awful scars . . . He's a homicidal maniac, like on TV. He'll kill us—"

"No," Mary said. "No, he wouldn't hurt anybody."

"How do you know?"

"I know. Look, Angie, you stop that kind of talk. You haven't got any sense about people. Some of the guys you used to go out with—"

"Oh, so that's it," Angie said. "You think you've got yourself a boyfriend. First time anybody looks at you . . . That shows he's crazy." She tossed her head so that the long, shining locks flared out. "Just don't try anything. Even if you think I'm asleep, you can't get away with any funny business."

Mary stared at her sister. As the meaning of Angie's speech penetrated, she felt a deep flush warm her face.

"You're disgusting, Angie, you know that?"

Angie began to cry. "That's an awful thing to say," she sobbed. "I'm scared, and hungry, and cold, and all you can say—" The rest of the words were lost in gulping sobs.

"All right, all right," Mary said. "Stop bawling. We can't leave here; it's still raining, and it's pitch-dark, and I don't know where we are. I'll sit up all night and protect you from that fierce, dangerous boy. Go to sleep and stop worrying."

It took the last of the hamburgers to stop Angie's moans. When she had eaten it, she curled up by the fire, and after an interval her sobs smoothed out into soft snores. Mary didn't feel sleepy. She looked at her sister's huddled form and felt as if she were looking at a stranger.

It wasn't the first time Angie had made cracks about her not having boyfriends or dates, but never before had she expressed her malice so openly. And to suggest that Rob would . . . Mary felt her face get hot again, this time with anger. Nobody but a stupid fool could think of Rob that way. He was too pathetic. All he wanted was kindness and companionship, and some response to the gentleness that had miraculously survived the terrible treatment he had received.

He had been gone a long time. Maybe he had gone for

good. The idea left Mary feeling a little sick. Had their unthinking cruelty driven him out into the rain and darkness, away from even the poor refuge he had found? But when she looked at the doorway, he was there, watching her.

"I thought you weren't coming back," she said.

"I said I would." Rob came forward, stepping softly. He jerked his head toward Angie. "She asleep?"

"Yes."

"I tried to find some blankets, or something to keep you warm. I guess everything around here is just too old or too dirty. I'm sorry."

"It's warm enough, with the fire." Mary tossed another handful of wood on it. The flames leapt. "But thanks for trying. Where do you sleep?"

"Upstairs. But I don't sleep much." Rob sat down a little distance from her. "If you want to go to sleep, I'll sort of keep an eye on things."

"What's there to watch out for?"

"Well, there's rats," Rob said calmly. "They wouldn't hurt you, but I know girls is scared of rats."

"Ugh." Mary shivered. "I hate them."

"They ain't so bad. They only bite people when they're scared or hungry. Right smart animals, rats are. I had one for a pet once."

"Really? I knew a boy who had a pet rat. It was a white one."

"Mine was brown. I called him Horatius, after that fella in the poem."

Mary didn't know what poem he was talking about, and she didn't want to admit her ignorance, so she changed the subject.

"What are you going to do, Rob? You can't stay here."

"I have to."

"No, you don't. You could—you could come with us."

"With you?"

"Yes." Mary felt herself blushing again. She lowered her eyes, cursing Angie; if Angie hadn't put ideas into her head, she wouldn't be embarrassed. Tracing patterns in the dust of the floor with her forefinger, she went on rapidly, "We're going to get jobs. You could work, too. We could have an apartment—maybe even a little house. . . ."

"I sure would like to," Rob said. "I'd like to be with you. I never knew a girl like you before. I didn't know you, did I? Seems as if I did somehow. I forget so much . . ."

Mary looked up sharply. Her cheeks were still flaming; as her eyes met Rob's she forgot to be self-conscious. He was speaking the simple, literal truth, as he felt it.

"No," she said, just as simply. "I never met you. But it's funny, I feel that way, too. As if we had known each other someplace . . . sometime. . . ."

For a long, suspended moment, they looked at each other, not speaking, because there was no need to speak. Then Rob's mobile, expressive face lengthened. He bowed his head.

"No," he muttered. "I can't do it. I been telling you lies. Not lies, exactly, but not the truth, neither. I—I didn't run away from here. I was took from here. It was some other place I run away from, some place a long, long ways from here."

Mary felt as if a giant hand had clamped over her ribs, squeezing the breath out of her lungs. She stared at Rob's drooping head. His long, curved lashes cast delicate shadows across his bony cheeks.

So Angie had been right—for once.

Rob's stumbling, reluctant confession was like the missing piece in a jigsaw puzzle. The pattern was clear now. But then, it had been pretty obvious all along. Angie had seen it, and she herself would have recognized it if she had not refused to do so.

Rob was . . . different. Not crazy, not any of those ugly words Angie had used. He was sick; and no wonder, after what had been done to him. The place he had run away from was probably an institution, a kind of hospital. Some of those places were pretty bad; she had seen stories about them on TV. He must have been in—that place—for years, long enough for the house to fall into ruin after his family had moved away, abandoning him. But he had returned, like a sick animal, to the only place he knew, and his hurt mind couldn't understand what had happened.

Rob's head sank lower, till she could see only a mop of tumbled brown hair. In a sudden, final flash of insight Mary knew that Angie had been wrong, after all—Angie and those others who had locked Rob up. Rob's mind had been damaged, like his bruised body, but its essential quality had not been changed. He was still gentle, considerate of others, oddly innocent. He wouldn't hurt anybody; he was too vulnerable himself.

She wanted to touch him, to reassure him. But she remembered his reaction the first time she had reached out.

"It's okay," she said softly. "I understand. It's all right."

Rob looked up.

"No," he said. He spoke with difficulty. There were long pauses between phrases as he went on. "I guess it ain't all right. It's all wrong. I don't suppose I can explain it. I don't understand so good myself. But I understand better than I did. Having somebody to talk to—somebody like you, who listens, and don't yell or get mad . . . All I know is, I can't come with you. I gotta go back there. It's no good running away from things."

He saw her face change and was quick to reassure her. "Say, now, I didn't mean you. You were right to run away when they treated you so bad. Guess you wouldn't do anything wrong, you're too smart. But I'm kind of mixed up. Seems like I'm always doing the wrong thing; seems like running away was another wrong thing. It wasn't a bad place, you know. They wanted to help me. If I go back and let them do what it was they wanted . . . Maybe later you and I could . . . You aren't mad, are you? Mary?"

It was the first time he had said her name. Mary couldn't speak, but she shook her head and managed to shape a watery smile. Rob smiled back at her.

"You look awful tired," he said, with a new note of gentle authority in his voice. "You lay down and get some sleep. I'll keep watch."

Suddenly she was tired—tired and strangely cold, as if she had worked hard through a long day and night of winter. She gathered up all the loose scraps that lay within reach, and heaped them on the fire. As it blazed up, she stretched out with her back to its warmth. She wanted to watch Rob; she was afraid he might try to sneak away while she slept. She was too tired to argue, but she hadn't given up. In the morning, when she wasn't so sleepy, she would try again to convince him.

Maybe he needed help, but the place he had run away from couldn't be the right place. George would find a place. George was a lawyer; he knew about things like that. George would help.

She was too drowsy to realize that she had reached a decision until after it was irrevocably fixed in her mind. Yes, she would go home—crawl back in disgrace. It wouldn't be pleasant. She'd be grounded for weeks; probably she would have to have boring sessions with a dumb psychologist or counselor. Mother would cry, and Angie . . . Angie would have to take care of herself. Anything, so long as Rob got the help he needed. Anything, so she didn't lose him.

He was still there. Her eyes closed and her breathing slowed. The last thing she saw before exhaustion claimed her was the play of firelight on Rob's thin, thoughtful face.

She awoke to a nightmare—a swirling, smoky blackness shot with tongues of flame; air she couldn't breathe; and a hoarse, wordless shouting. The voice was unrecognizable; it might even have been her own. She knew she must be dreaming, because she couldn't move. It was a relief when the blackness overcame the fiery light and swallowed her.

She came fully awake much later, with hard hands shaking her and a face close to hers.

"Rob," she croaked, but it wasn't Rob; the face was that of a man she had never seen before—brown and weather-wrinkled, with parallel scarlike lines framing his thin-lipped mouth.

"This one's all right," he said. His voice sounded angry. "What about the other one?"

If there was an answer, Mary didn't hear it. Feeling dizzy and slightly sick to her stomach, she closed her eyes. When she opened them again, the man was gone. She raised herself on one elbow and looked around.

She was lying in the long, wet grass in front of the house. Her clothes were soaked, and she was shivering in a sharp breeze—a dawn breeze. The sky was streaked with light beyond the chimneys of the house. The house was burning.

There was a horrifying beauty about the way it burned. Long veils of fire rose like creatures trying to break free of earth. Rosy flame spouted from the empty windows and wreathed crimson blossoms around the chimneys. Then the roof fell in with a giant gush of flame and sparks, and her dazed senses came fully to life.

"Angie." She gasped and staggered to her feet.

Before she had time to panic, she saw her sister, flat on the grass a few feet away. A man was bending over her. As Mary stumbled toward them, the man looked up. He was not the man she had seen before; he was older. A stubble of white beard frosted his jaws, and when he spoke, she saw that his teeth were brown, with gaps in their rows.

"Friend o' yours?"

"My sister."

"She'll do," the old man said cheerfully. "Swallowed some smoke, but I reckon she'll be all right."

Then Mary remembered.

"Rob. Rob! Where—"

She spun around. The old man straightened, one hand clutching the small of his back.

"Was there somebody else with you, girl?"

"Yes. Rob. Didn't you find him? Oh, please . . ."

The old man's silence was answer enough.

Mary ran toward the incandescent bed of coals that had once been a house. The daylight had strengthened; against the dawn, the blackened chimney stood up like a gaunt sentinel. She heard the old man shout but did not stop running till someone grabbed her. She had forgotten the other man. When she tried to struggle, he slapped her hard. The older man came up, panting.

"Don't hit her, Frank."

"Too bad her folks didn't tan her hide a long time ago," Frank said angrily. "Damned spoiled brats. Wouldn't a been no fire if they hadn't set it. Lucky they didn't kill themselves."

"Frank, she says there was another youngster with them. A boy."

The hands that held Mary did not relax their grip, but when Frank spoke again, his voice had lost its hard edge.

"Didn't find anybody else. If he was in there . . ."

The three stared silently at the fiery grave of the house. Then the old man said gently, "Maybe he got out, child. Maybe he drug you out. Frank saw the smoke when he went to feed the stock, but we didn't get here till the place was blazing. Found you gals outside on the grass. Reckon your friend ran and hid when he saw us. Sure, that's what must of happened."

The words should have consoled Mary, because they made sense. She knew she hadn't dragged Angie out of the house; she couldn't even remember walking out herself. Strangely, she felt no emotion, neither horror nor loss of hope. She looked at the old man through the lank locks of hair that hung over her face, and his eyes shifted away.

"Better take 'em home, Frank. You wanna go fetch the car?"

"Why can't they walk?" Frank demanded.

"Other one's still snoring," the old man said with a faint grin. "You kin carry her if you want; she's too fat for me to hoist."

"All right," Frank said grudgingly. "Damned spoiled runaway brats, burning down a house. . . ."

"Maybe it's just as well," the old man said. The eyes of the two men met in a long, meaningful glance. Then Frank shrugged and set off across the lawn. When Mary looked in that direction, she saw chimneys beyond the trees. They had been close to shelter and human help. . . . Not that they would have sought it out.

The old man bent stiffly over Angie's recumbent form.

"She's all right," he said. "Sleeping it off."

"I'm sorry," Mary said. "About the house. It was raining so hard, I never thought it could catch fire."

"Don't suppose you thought at all," the old man said sarcastically. "Inside of the place was bone-dry and rotten."

"Why did you say that—about it being just as well the house was burned?"

The old man shrugged and looked away.

"Been falling for years. No good to anybody."

"Why wasn't it any good to anybody? Why did the people who owned it let it fall apart? Who lived there? What— what happened to them?"

"Full of questions, ain't you?" The old man grinned, but the glance he gave her from under his shaggy white brows was oblique and sly. Suddenly, though she could not have explained why, she had to know the answers to the questions she had asked.

"Why?" she demanded, her voice loud and shrill. "What was wrong with the house?"

The old man licked his lips. He glanced over his shoulder at the blackened ruins.

"Folks said it was haunted," he mumbled. "I seen lights there myself. Mighta been tramps, but . . ."

"Haunted," Mary repeated. She shivered. The early morning air was cold, and she was wet to the bone.

As if the word had been a plug in his mind that held back speech, the old man became garrulous. After all, it was a good story and she was a fresh audience.

"There was a murder there one time. Years ago, it was. The widow moved away afterward, took the other kids with her. Place changed hands a couple of times; but nobody could live in that house for long. State took it over for taxes finally. Couldn't even rent it, people knew the story—"

He broke off, eyeing her uneasily. Mary had stopped listening. Now she repeated the phrase that had twisted into her mind like a knife.

"Other kids," she said in a strangled voice. "She took the other . . . Who was it who was killed?"

"The father," the old man said reluctantly. "Stepfather, he was, really. Say, you look kind of peaked. Maybe I better not—"

"Who killed him?"

"Here's Frank with the car," the old man said, looking relieved. "Come on."

The car had stopped by the tumbledown fence. Frank got out, holding a blanket.

"Mother says bring 'em right to the house," he said, looking at Angie. "Think you can take her feet, Granddad, if I—"

"Who was it?" Mary begged. "Who killed him?"

Frank gave the old man a disapproving look.

"You been telling her that story? Shame on you, Granddad. That's what's wrong with kids today; they hear too many stories about killing and stuff." He turned on Mary. "Just you forget all that. You oughta be thinking about this gal here—and your folks, bet they're worried sick about you. Get in the car."

Angie was coming out of her stupor, but she was always a good sleeper. Once in the car, she snuggled into the blanket, muttered something, and closed her eyes.

The two men stood staring at the remains of the house.

"So it's gone," the old man said. "Yep. Just as well. They say fire's a cleaning thing. If ever a place needed cleaning, that one did. And if ever a man deserved killing . . ."

"You never even knew him," Frank said.

"I heard Pop talk about him. Drunken brute he was, used to beat that poor woman to a pulp, and the kids . . . Nowadays they'd say the boy wasn't in his right mind. Not responsible."

"That's the trouble with nowadays. Nobody's ever responsible."

"Maybe so. But when you keep beating on a kid, stands to reason his brain isn't gonna be right. And seeing his ma knocked around . . . Pop said it was a cruel thing, the way she turned on the boy. Wouldn't see him or say anything in his defense, even at the trial. And the way he died . . . Suicide, it was supposed to be, but the guard at the county jail was one of the Weavers, and the Weavers has always had a mean streak. . . ."

Frank shook himself like a dog coming out of the water.

"What're we standing around talking for?" he demanded grumpily. "It's over and done with, years ago, and I'm late with the chores, thanks to these fool girls. Get in the car, Granddad."

The old man obeyed, giving Mary a strange sidelong look. She had a feeling that he had remembered the name of the boy who had died in prison so many years before.

He wouldn't say anything, though. He knew, as she did, how the reasonable, everyday world would react to such a story.

A story decades old, older than Granddad himself. How many years had it been since a certain man returned from a war—not Vietnam, she should have realized the dates were wrong. Maybe the horrors of that war had turned him into a drunkard and a sadist. She would never know. All she knew was that Rob had been a victim, not a killer. Just once, after years of abuse and misery, he had struck back. He hadn't meant to kill, only to defend himself and the others. She knew that as certainly as if she had been present when it happened.

As the car started forward, Mary pressed her face against the window for a last look. The sun was up and the damp grass glowed like a field of emeralds. From the dying embers trails of pale smoke rose and broke in the breeze.

When the ashes were cold, weeds and wildflowers would rise to cover the ruins. Animals would burrow and raise their young. But Rob would not come again. He had gone back, as she was going, but to a much more distant place. In her mind a voice said softly, "Maybe later. You and I . . ."

I'm In The Book

Loren D. Estleman

When I got in to see Alec Wynn of Reiner, Switz, Gals-
worthy, & Wynn, the sun was high over Lake St. Clair
outside the window behind his desk and striking sparks
off the choppy steel-blue surface with sailboats gliding
around on it cutting white foam, their sharkfin sails striped
in broad bright bikini colors. Wynn sat with his back to
the view and never turned to look at it. He didn't need
to. On the wall across from him hung a big framed color
photograph of bright-striped sailboats cutting white foam
on the steel-blue surface of Lake St. Clair.

Wynn was a big neat man with a black widow's peak
trimmed tight to his skull and the soft gray hair at his
temples worn long over the tops of his ears. He had on
aviator's glasses with clear plastic rims and a suit the color
and approximate weight of ground fog, that fit him like
no suit will ever fit me if I hit the Michigan Lottery tomorrow. He had deep lines in his Miami-brown face and a
mouth that turned down like a shark's to show a bottom
row of caps as white and even as military monuments. It
was a predator's face. I liked it fine. It belonged to a lawyer,

and in my business lawyers mean a warm feeling in the pit of the bank account.

"Walker, Amos," he said, as if he were reading roll call. "I like the name. It has a certain smoky strength."

"I've had it a long time."

He looked at me with his strong white hands folded on top of his absolutely clean desk. His palms didn't leave marks on the glossy surface the way mine would have. "I keep seeing your name on reports. The Reliance people employ your services often."

"Only when the job involves people," I said. "Those big investigation agencies are good with computers and diamonds and those teeny little cameras you can hide in your left ear. But when it comes to stroking old ladies who see things and leaning on supermarket stock boys who smuggle sides of beef out the back door, they remember us little shows."

"How big is your agency?"

"You're looking at it. I have an answering service," I added quickly.

"Better and better. It means you can keep a secret. You have a reputation for that, too."

"Who told?"

"The humor I can take or let alone." He refolded his hands the other way. "I don't like going behind Reliance's back like this. We've worked together for years and the director's an old friend. But this is a personal matter, and there are some things you would prefer to have a stranger know than someone you play poker with every Saturday night."

"I don't play poker," I said. "Whoops, sorry." I got out

a cigarette and smoothed it between my fingers. "Who's missing, your wife or your daughter?"

He shot me a look he probably would have kept hooded in court. Then he sat back, nodding slightly. "I guess it's not all that uncommon."

"I do other work but my main specialty is tracing missing persons. You get so you smell it coming." I waited.

"It's my wife. She's left me again."

"Again?"

"Last time it was with one of the apprentices here, a man named Lloyd Debner. But they came back after three days. I fired him, naturally."

"Naturally."

A thin smile played around with his shark's mouth, gave it up and went away. "Seems awfully Old Testament, I know. I tried to be modern about it. There's really no sense in blaming the other man. But I saw myself hiding out in here to avoid meeting him in the hall, and that would be grotesque. I gave him excellent references. One of our competitors snapped him up right away."

"What about this time?"

"She left the usual note saying she was going away and I was not to look for her. I called Debner but he assured me he hadn't seen Cecelia since their first—fling. I believe him. But it's been almost a week now and I'm concerned for her safety."

"What about the police?"

"I believe we covered that when we were discussing keeping secrets," he said acidly.

"You've been married how long?"

"Six years. And, yes, she's younger than I, by fourteen years. That was your next question, wasn't it?"

"It was in there. Do you think that had anything to do with her leaving?"

"I think it had everything to do with it. She has appetites that I've been increasingly unable to fulfill. But I never thought it was a problem until she left the first time."

"You quarreled?"

"The normal amount. Never about that. Which I suppose is revealing. I rather think she's found a new boy-friend, but I'm damned if I can say who it is."

"May I see the note?"

He extracted a fold of paper from an inside breast pocket and passed it across the desk. "I'm afraid I got my finger-prints all over it before I thought over all the angles."

"That's okay. I never have worked on anything where prints were any use."

It was written on common drugstore stationery, tinted blue with a spray of flowers in the upper right-hand corner. A hasty hand full of sharp points and closed loops. It said what he'd reported it had said and nothing else. Signed with a C.

"There's no date."

"She knew I'd read it the day she wrote it. It was last Tuesday."

"Uh-huh."

"That means what?" he demanded.

"Just uh-huh. It's something I say when I can't think of anything to say." I gave back the note. "Any ideas where she might go to be alone? Favorite vacation spot, her home-town, a summer house, anything like that? I don't mean to insult you. Sometimes the hardest place to find your hat is on your head."

"We sublet our Florida home in the off-season. She grew

up in this area and has universally disliked every place we've visited on vacation. Really, I was expecting something more from a professional.''

"I'm just groping for a handle. Does she have any hobbies?"

"Spending my money."

I watched my cigarette smoke drifting toward the window. "It seems to me you don't know your wife too well after six years, Mr. Wynn. When I find her, if I find her, I can tell you where she is, but I can't make her come back, and from the sound of things she may not want to come back. I wouldn't be representing your best interests if I didn't advise you to save your money and set the cops loose on it. I can't give guarantees they won't give."

"Are you saying you don't want the job?"

"Not me. I don't have any practice at that. Just being straight with a client I'd prefer keeping."

"Don't do me any favors, Walker."

"Okay. I'll need a picture. And what's her maiden name? She may go back to it."

"Collier." He spelled it. "And here." He got a wallet-size color photograph out of the top drawer of the desk and skidded it across the glossy top like someone dealing a card.

She was a redhead, and the top of that line. She looked like someone who would wind up married to a full partner in a weighty law firm with gray temples and an office overlooking Lake St. Clair. It would be in her high school yearbook under Predictions.

I put the picture in my breast pocket. "Where do I find this Debner?"

"He's with Paxton and Ring on West Michigan. But I told you he doesn't know where Cecelia is."

"Maybe he should be asked a different way." I killed my stub in the smoking stand next to the chair and rose. "You'll be hearing from me."

His eyes followed me up. All eight of his fingers were lined up on the near edge of his desk, the nails pink and perfect. "Can you be reached if I want to hear from you sooner?"

"My service will page me. I'm in the book."

II

A Japanese accent at Paxton & Ring told me over the telephone that Lloyd Debner would be tied up all afternoon in Detroit Recorder's Court. Lawyers are always in court the way executives are always in meetings. At the Frank Murphy Hall of Justice a bailiff stopped spitting on his handkerchief and rubbing at a spot on his uniform to point out a bearded man in his early thirties with a mane of black hair, smoking a pipe and talking to a gray-headed man in the corridor outside one of the courtrooms. I went over there and introduced myself.

"Second," he said, without taking his eyes off the other man. "Tim, we're talking a lousy twenty bucks over the fifteen hundred. Even if you win, the judge will order probation. The kid'll get that anyway if we plead Larceny Under, and there's no percentage in mucking up his record for life just to fatten your win column. And there's nothing saying you'll win."

I said, "This won't take long."

"Make an appointment. Listen, Tim—"

"It's about Cecelia Wynn," I said. "We can talk about it out here in the hall if you like. Tim won't mind."

He looked at me then for the first time. "Tim, I'll catch you later."

"After the sentencing." The gray-headed man went into the courtroom, chuckling.

"Who'd you say you were?" Debner demanded.

"Amos Walker. I still am, but a little older. I'm a P.I. Alec Wynn hired me to look for his wife."

"You came to the wrong place. That's all over."

"I'm interested in when it wasn't."

He glanced up and down the hall. There were a few people in it, lawyers and fixers and the bailiff with the stain that wouldn't go away from his crisp blue uniform shirt. "Come on. I can give you a couple of minutes."

I followed him into a men's room two doors down. We stared at a guy combing his hair in front of the long mirror over the sinks until he put away his comb and picked up a brown leather briefcase and left. Debner bent down to see if there were any feet in the stalls, straightened, and knocked out his pipe into a sink. He laid it on a soap canister to cool and moved his necktie a centimeter to the right.

"I don't see Cecelia when we pass on the street," he said, inspecting the results in the mirror. "I had my phone number changed after we got back from Jamaica so she couldn't call me."

"That where you went?"

"I rented a bungalow outside Kingston. Worst mistake I ever made. I was headed for a junior partnership at Reiner when this happened. Now I'm back to dealing school board presidents' sons out of jams they wouldn't be in if five guys ahead of me hadn't dealt them out of jams just like them starting when they were in junior high."

"How'd you and Cecelia get on?"

"Oh, swell. So good we crammed a two-week reservation into three days and came back home."

"What went wrong?"

"Different drummers." He picked up his pipe and blew through it.

"Not good enough," I said.

He grinned boyishly. "I didn't think so. To begin with, she's a health nut. I run and take a little wheat germ myself sometimes—you don't even have to point a gun at me—but I draw the line at dropping vitamins and herb pills at every meal. She must've taken sixteen capsules every time we sat down to eat. It can drive you blinkers. People in restaurants must've figured her for a drug addict."

"Sure she wasn't?"

"She was pretty open about taking them if she was. She filled the capsules herself from plastic bags. Her purse rattled like a used car."

A fat party in a gray suit and pink shirt came in and smiled and nodded at both of us and used the urinal and washed his hands. Debner used the time to recharge his pipe.

"Still not good enough," I said, when the fat party had gone. "You don't cut a vacation short just because your bedpartner does wild garlic."

"It just didn't work out. Look, I'm due back in court."

"Not at half-past noon." I waited.

He finished lighting his pipe, dropped the match into the sink where he'd knocked his ashes, grinned around the stem. I bet that melted the women jurors. "If this gets around I'm washed up with every pretty legal secretary in the building."

"Nothing has to get around. I'm just looking for Cecelia Wynn."

"Yeah. You said." He puffed on the pipe, took it out, smoothed his beard, and looked at it in the mirror. "Yeah. Well, she said she wasn't satisfied."

"Uh-huh."

"No one's ever told me that before. I'm not used to complaints."

"Uh-*huh.*"

He turned back toward me. His eyes flicked up and down. "We never had this conversation, okay?"

"What conversation?"

"Yeah." He put the pipe back between his teeth, puffed. "Yeah."

We shook hands. He squeezed a little harder than I figured he did normally.

III

I dropped two dimes into a pay telephone in the downstairs lobby and fought my way through two secretaries before Alec Wynn came on the line. His voice was a full octave deeper than it had been in person. I figured it was that way in court, too.

"Just checking back, Mr. Wynn. How come when I asked you about hobbies you didn't tell me your wife was into herbs?"

"Into *what?*"

I told him what Debner had said about the capsules. He said, "I haven't dined with my wife in months. Most legal business is conducted in restaurants."

"I guess you wouldn't know who her herbalist is, then."

"Herbalist?"

"Sort of an oregano guru. They tell their customers which herbs to take in the never-ending American quest for a healthy body. Not a few of the runaways I've traced take their restlessness to them first."

"Well, I wouldn't know anything about that. Trina might. Our maid. She's at the house now."

"Would you call her and tell her I'm coming?"

He said he would and broke the connection.

IV

It was a nice place if you like windows. There must have been fifty on the street side alone, with ivy or something just as green crawling up the brick wall around them and a courtyard with a marble fountain in the center and a black chauffeur with no shirt on washing a blue Mercedes in front. They are always washing cars. A white-haired Puerto Rican woman with muddy eyes and a faint mustache answered my ring.

"Trina?"

"Yes. You are Mr. Walker? Mr. Wynn told me to expect you."

I followed her through a room twice the size of my living room, but that was designed just for following maids through, and down a hall with dark paintings on the walls to a glassed-in porch at the back of the house containing ferns in pots and lawn chairs upholstered in floral print. The sliding glass door leading outside was ajar and a strong chlorine stench floated in from an outdoor crescent-shaped swimming pool. She slid the door shut.

"The pool man says alkali is leaking into the water from an underground spring," she said. "The chlorine controls the smell."

"The rich suffer, too." I told her what I wanted.

"Capsules? Yes, Mrs. Wynn has many bottles of capsules in her room. There is a name on the bottles. I will get one."

"No hurry. What sort of woman is Mrs. Wynn to work for?"

"I don't know that that is a good question to answer."

"You're a good maid, Trina." I wound a five-dollar bill around my right index finger.

She slid the tube off the finger and flattened it and folded it over and tucked it inside her apron pocket. "She is a good employer. She says please and does not run her fingers over the furniture after I have dusted, like the last woman I worked for."

"Is that all you can tell me?"

"I have not worked here long, sir. Only five weeks."

"Who was maid before that?"

"A girl named Ann Foster, at my agency. Multi-Urban Services. She was fired." Her voice sank to a whisper on the last part. We were alone.

"Fired why?"

"William the chauffeur told me she was fired. I didn't ask why. I have been a maid long enough to learn that the less you know the more you work. I will get one of the bottles."

She left me, returning a few minutes later carrying a glass container the size of an aspirin bottle, with a cork in the top. It was half full of gelatin capsules filled with fine brown powder. I pulled the cork and sniffed. A sharp, spicy scent. The name of a health foods store on Livernois was typewritten on the label.

"How many of these does Mrs. Wynn have in her bedroom?" I asked.

"Many. Ten or twelve bottles."

"As full as this?"

"More, some of them."

"That's a lot of capsules to fill and then leave behind. Did she take many clothes with her?"

"No, sir. Her closets and drawers are full."

I thanked her and gave her back the bottle. It was getting to be the damnedest disappearing act I had covered in a long, long time.

The black chauffeur was hosing off the Mercedes when I came out. He was tall, almost my height, and the bluish skin of his torso was stretched taut over lumpy muscle. I asked him if he was William.

He twisted shut the nozzle of the hose, watching me from under his brows with his head down, like a boxer. Scar tissue shone around his eyes. "Depends on who you might be."

I sighed. When you can't even get their name out of them, the rest is like pulling nails with your toes. I stood a folded ten-spot on the Mercedes' hood. He watched the bottom edge darken as it soaked up water. "Ann Foster," I said.

"What about her?"

"How close was she to Cecelia Wynn?"

"I wouldn't know. I work outside."

"Who fired her, Mr. or Mrs. Wynn?"

He thought about it. Watched the bill getting wetter. Then he snatched it up and waved it dry. "She did. Mrs. Wynn."

"Why?"

He shrugged. I reached up and plucked the bill out of his fingers. He grabbed for it but I drew it back out of his reach. He shrugged again, wringing the hose in his hands to make his muscles bulge. "They had a fight of some kind the day Ann left. I could hear them screaming at each other out here. I don't know what it was about."

"Where'd she go after she left here?"

He started to shrug a third time, stopped. "Back to the agency, maybe. I don't ask questions. In this line—"

"Yeah. The less you know the more you work." I gave him the ten and split.

V

The health foods place was standard, plank floor and hanging plants and stuff you can buy in any supermarket for a fraction of what they were asking. The herbalist was a small, pretty woman of about 30, in a gypsy blouse and floor-length denim skirt with bare feet poking out underneath and a bandana tied around her head. She also owned the place. She hadn't seen Mrs. Wynn since before she'd turned up missing. I bought a package of unsalted nuts for her trouble and ate them on the way to the office. They needed salt.

I found Multi-Urban Services in the Detroit metropolitan

directory and dialed the number. A woman whose voice reminded me of the way cool green mints taste answered.

"We're not at liberty to give out information about our clients."

"I'm sorry to hear that," I said. "I went to a party at the Wynn place in Grosse Pointe about six weeks ago and was very impressed with Miss Foster's efficiency. I'd heard she was free and was thinking of engaging her services on a full-time basis."

The mints melted. "I'm sorry, Miss Foster is no longer with this agency. But I can recommend another girl just as efficient. Multi-Urban prides itself—"

"I'm sure it does. Can you tell me where Miss Foster is currently working?"

"Stormy Heat Productions. But not as a maid."

I thanked her and hung up, thinking about how little it takes to turn mint to acid. Stormy Heat was listed on Mt. Elliott. Its line was busy. Before leaving the office, I broke the Smith & Wesson out of the desk drawer and snapped the holster onto my belt under my jacket. It was that kind of neighborhood.

VI

The outfit worked out of an old gymnasium across from Mt. Elliott Cemetery, a scorched brick building as old as the eight-hour day with a hand-lettered sign over the door and a concrete stoop deep in the process of going back to the land. The door was locked. I pushed a sunken button that grated in its socket. No sound issued from within. I was about to knock when a square panel opened in the door at head level and a mean black face with a beard that grew to a point looked into mine.

"You've got to be kidding," I said.

"What do you want?" demanded the face.

"Ann Foster."

"What for?"

"Talk."

"Sorry." The panel slid shut.

I was smoking a cigarette. I dropped it to the stoop and crushed it out and used the button again. When the panel shot back I reached up and grasped the beard in my fist and yanked. His chest banged the door.

"You white—!"

I twisted the beard in my fist. He gasped and tears sprang to his eyes. "Joe sent me," I said. "The goose flies high. May the Force be with you. Pick the password you like, but open the door."

"Who—?"

"Jerk Root, the Painless Barber. Open."

"Okay, okay." Metal snapped on his side. Still hanging on to his whiskers, I reached down with my free hand and tried the knob. It turned. I let go and opened the door. He was standing just inside the threshold, a big man in threadbare jeans and a white shirt open to the navel Byron-fashion, smoothing his beard with thick fingers. He had a Colt magnum in his other hand pointed at my belt buckle.

"Nice," I said. "The nickel plating goes with your eyes. You got a permit for that?"

He smiled crookedly. His eyes were still watering. "Why didn't you say you was cop?" He reached back and jammed the revolver into a hip pocket. "You got paper?"

"Not today. I'm not raiding the place. I just want to talk to Ann Foster."

"Okay," he said. "Okay. I don't need no beef with the laws. You don't see nothing on the way, deal?"

I spread my hands. "I'm blind. This isn't an election year."

There was a lot not to see. Films produced by Stormy Heat were not interested in the Academy Award or even feature billing at the all-night grindhouses on Woodward Avenue. Its actors were thin and ferretlike and its actresses used powder to fill the cavities in their faces and cover their stretch marks. The lights and cameras were strictly surplus, their cables frayed and patched all over like old garden hoses. We walked past carnal scenes, unnoticed by the grunting performers or the sweat-stained crews, to a scuffed steel door at the rear that had originally led into a locker room. My escort went through it without pausing. I followed.

"Don't they teach you to knock in the jungle?"

I'd had a flash of a naked youthful brown body, and then it was covered by a red silk kimono that left a pair of long legs bare to the tops of the thighs. She had her hair cut very short and her face, with its upturned nose and lower lip thrust out in a belligerent pout, was boyish. I had seen enough to know she wasn't a boy.

"What's to see that I ain't already seen out on the floor?" asked the Beard. "Man to see you. From the Machine."

Ann Foster looked at me quickly. The whites of her eyes had a bluish tinge against her dark skin. "Since when they picking matinee idols for cops?"

"Thanks," I said. "But I've got a job."

We stared at the guy with the beard until he left us,

letting the door drift shut behind him. The room had been converted into a community dressing room, but without much conviction. A library table littered with combs and brushes and pots of industrial strength makeup stood before a long mirror, but the bench on this side had come with the place and the air smelled of mildew and old sweat. She said, "Show me you're a cop."

I flashed my photostat and honorary sheriff's star. "I'm private. I let Lothar out there think different. It saved time."

"Well, you wasted it all here. I don't like rental heat any more than the other kind. I don't even like men."

"You picked a swell business not to like them."

She smiled, not unpleasantly. "I work with an all-girl cast."

"Does it pay better than being a maid?"

"About as much. But when I get on my knees it's not to scrub floors."

"Cecelia Wynn," I said.

Her face moved as if I'd slapped her. "What about her?" she barked.

"She's missing. Her husband wants her back. You had a fight with her just before you got fired. What started it?"

"What happens if I don't answer?"

"Nothing. Now. But if it turns out she doesn't want to be missing, the cops get it. I could save you a trip downtown."

She said, "Hell, she's probably off someplace with her lawyer boyfriend like last time."

"No, he's accounted for. Also she left almost all her clothes behind, along with the herbs she spent a small country buying and a lot of time stuffing into capsules. It's starting to look like leaving wasn't her idea, or that where she was going she wouldn't need those things. What was the fight about?''

"I wouldn't do windows."

I slapped her for real. It made a loud flat noise off the echoing walls and she yelled. The door swung open. Beard stuck his face inside. Farther down the magnum glittered. "What."

I looked at him, looked at the woman. She stroked her burning cheek. My revolver was behind my right hipbone, a thousand miles away. Finally she said, "Nothing."

"Sure?"

She nodded. The man with the beard left his eyes on me a moment longer, then withdrew. The door closed.

"It was weird," she told me. "Serving dinner this one night I spilled salad oil down the front of my uniform. I went to my room to change. Mrs. Wynn stepped inside to ask for something, just like you walked in on me just now. She caught me naked."

"So?"

"So she excused herself and got out. Half an hour later I was canned. For spilling the salad oil. I yelled about it, as who wouldn't? But it wasn't the reason."

"What was?"

She smoothed the kimono across her pelvis. "You think I don't know that look on another woman's face when I see it?"

We talked some more, but none of it was for me. On my way out I laid a twenty on the dressing table and stood a pot of mascara on top of it. I hesitated, then added one of my cards to the stack. "In case something happens to change your mind about rental heat," I said. "If you lose the card, I'm in the book."

Back in civilization I gassed up and used the telephone in the service station to call Alec Wynn at his office. I asked him to meet me at his home in Grosse Pointe in twenty minutes.

"I can't," he said. "I'm meeting a client at four."

"He'll keep. If you don't show you may be one yourself." We stopped talking to each other.

VII

Both William the chauffeur and the Mercedes were gone from the courtyard, leaving only a puddle on the asphalt to reflect the window-studded façade of the big house. Trina let me in and listened to me and escorted me back to the enclosed porch. When she left I slid open the glass door and stepped outside to the pool area. I was there when Wynn came out five minutes later. His gray suit looked right even in those surroundings. It always would.

"You've caused me to place an important case in the hands of an apprentice," he announced. "I hope this means you've found Cecelia."

"I've found her. I think."

"What's that supposed to signify? Or is this the famous Walker sense of humor at work?"

"Save it for your next jury, Mr. Wynn. We're just two guys talking. How long have you been hanging on to your wife's good-bye note? Since the first time she walked out?"

"You're babbling."

"It worried me that it wasn't dated," I said. "A thing

like that comes in handy too often. Being in corporate law, you might not know that the cops have ways now to treat writing in ink with chemicals that can prove within a number of weeks when it was written."

His face was starting to match his suit. I went on.

"Someone else knew you hadn't been able to satisfy Cecelia sexually, or you wouldn't have been so quick to tell me. Masculine pride is a strong motive for murder, and in case something had happened to her, you wanted to be sure you were covered. That's why you hired me, and that's why you dusted off the old note. She didn't leave one this time, did she?"

"You have found her."

I said nothing. Suddenly he was an old man. He shuffled blindly to a marble bench near the pool and sank down onto it. His hands worked on his knees.

"When I didn't hear from her after several days I became frightened," he said. "The servants knew we argued. She'd told Debner of my—shortcomings. Before I left criminal law, I saw several convictions obtained on flimsier evidence. Can you understand that I had to protect myself?"

I said, "It wasn't necessary. Debner was just as unsuccessful keeping her happy. Any man would have been. Your wife was a lesbian, Mr. Wynn."

"That's a damn lie!" He started to rise. Halfway up, his knees gave out and he sat back down with a thud.

"Not a practicing one. It's possible she didn't even realize what her problem was until about five weeks ago, when she accidentally saw your former maid naked. The maid is a lesbian and recognized the reaction. Was Cecelia a proud woman?"

"Intensely."

"A lot of smoke gets blown about the male fear of loss of masculinity," I said. "No one gives much thought to women's fears for their femininity. They can drive a woman to fire a servant out of hand, but she would just be removing temptation from her path for the moment. After a time, when the full force of her situation struck home, she might do something more desperate.

"She would be too proud to leave a note."

Wynn had his elbows on his knees and his face in his hands. I peeled cellophane off a fresh pack of Winstons.

"The cops can't really tell when a note was written, Mr. Wynn. I just said that to hear what you'd say."

"Where is she, Walker?"

I watched my reflection in the pool's turquoise-colored surface, squinting against the chlorine fumes. The water was clear enough to see through to the bottom, but there was a recessed area along the north edge with a shelf obscuring it from above, a design flaw that would trap leaves and twigs and other debris that would normally be exposed when the pool was drained. Shadows swirled in the pocket, thick and dark and full of secrets.

The Reason Why

Ed Gorman

"I'm scared."

"This was your idea, Karen."

"You scared?"

"No."

"You bastard."

"Because I'm not scared I'm a bastard?"

"You not being scared means you don't believe me."

"Well."

"See. I knew it."

"What?"

"Just the way you said 'Well.' You bastard."

I sighed and looked out at the big red brick building that sprawled over a quarter mile of spring grass turned silver by a fat June moon. Twenty-five years ago a 1950 Ford fastback had sat in the adjacent parking lot. Mine for two summers of grocery store work.

We were sitting in her car, a Volvo she'd cadged from her last marriage settlement, number four if you're interested, and sharing a pint of bourbon the way we used to in high school when we'd been more than friends but never quite lovers.

The occasion tonight was our twenty-fifth class reunion.
But there was another occasion, too. In our senior year a
boy named Michael Brandon had jumped off a steep clay
cliff called Pierce Point to his death on the winding river
road below. Suicide. That, anyway, had been the official
version.

A month ago Karen Lane (she had gone back to her
maiden name these days, the Karen Lane-Cummings-
Todd-Browne-LeMay getting a tad too long) had called to
see if I wanted to go to dinner and I said yes, if I could
bring Donna along, but then Donna surprised me by saying
she didn't care to go along, that by now we should be at
the point in our relationship where we trusted each other
("God, Dwyer, I don't even look at other men, not for
very long anyway, you know?"), and Karen and I had had
dinner and she'd had many drinks, enough that I saw she
had a problem, and then she'd told me about something
that had troubled her for a long time . . .

In senior year she'd gone to a party and gotten sick on
wine and stumbled out to somebody's backyard to throw
up and it was there she'd overheard the three boys talking.
They were earnestly discussing what had happened to
Michael Brandon the previous week and they were even
more earnestly discussing what would happen to them if
"anybody ever really found out the truth."

"It's bothered me all these years," she'd said over dinner
a month earlier. "They murdered him and they got away
with it."

"Why didn't you tell the police?"

"I didn't think they'd believe me."

"Why not?"

She shrugged and put her lovely little face down, dark

hair covering her features. Whenever she put her face down that way it meant that she didn't want to tell you a lie so she'd just as soon talk about something else.

"Why not, Karen?"

"Because of where we came from. The Highlands."

The Highlands is an area that used to ring the iron foundries and factories of this city. Way before pollution became a fashionable concern, you could stand on your front porch and see a peculiarly beautiful orange haze on the sky every dusk. The Highlands had bars where men lost ears, eyes, and fingers in just garden-variety fights, and streets where nobody sane ever walked after dark, not even cops unless they were in pairs. But it wasn't the physical violence you remembered so much as the emotional violence of poverty. You get tired of hearing your mother scream because there isn't enough money for food and hearing your father scream back because there's nothing he can do about it. Nothing.

Karen Lane and I had come from the Highlands, but we were smarter and, in her case, better looking than most of the people from the area, so when we went to Wilson High School—one of those nightmare conglomerates that shoves the poorest kids in a city in with the richest—we didn't do badly for ourselves. By senior year we found ourselves hanging out with the sons and daughters of bankers and doctors and city officials and lawyers and riding around in new Impala convertibles and attending an occasional party where you saw an actual maid. But wherever we went, we'd manage for at least a few minutes to get away from our dates and talk to each other. What we were doing, of course, was trying to comfort ourselves. We shared terrible and confusing feelings—pride that we were acceptable to those we saw as glamorous, shame that we felt disgrace for being from the Highlands and having fathers who worked in factories and mothers who went to Mass as often as nuns and brothers and sisters who were doomed to punching the clock and yelling at ragged kids in the cold factory dusk. (You never realize what a toll such shame takes till you see your father's waxen face there in the years-later casket.)

That was the big secret we shared, of course, Karen and I, that we were going to get out, leave the place once and for all. And her brown eyes never sparkled more Christmas-morning bright than at those moments when it all was ahead of us, money, sex, endless thrills, immortality. She had the kind of clean good looks brought out best by a blue cardigan with a line of white button-down shirt at the top and a brown suede car coat over her slender shoulders and moderately tight jeans displaying her quietly artful ass. Nothing splashy about her. She had the sort of face that snuck up on you. You had the impression you were talking to a pretty but in no way spectacular girl, and then all of a sudden you saw how the eyes burned with sad humor and how wry the mouth got at certain times and how absolutely perfect that straight little nose was and how the freckles enhanced rather than detracted from her beauty and by then of course you were hopelessly entangled. Hopelessly.

This wasn't just my opinion, either. I mentioned four divorce settlements. True facts. Karen was one of those prizes that powerful and rich men like to collect with the understanding that it's only something you hold in trust, like a yachting cup. So, in her time, she'd been an ornament for a professional football player (her college beau), an orthodontist ("I think he used to have sexual fantasies about Barry Goldwater"), the owner of a large commuter airline ("I slept with half his pilots; it was kind of a company benefit"), and a sixty-nine-year-old millionaire who was dying of heart disease ("He used to have me sit next to his bedside and just hold his hand—the weird thing was that of all of them, I loved him, I really did—and his eyes would be closed and then every once in a while tears would start streaming down his cheeks as if he was remembering something that really filled him with remorse; he was really a sweetie, but then cancer got him before the heart disease and I never did find out what he regretted so much, I mean if it was about his son or his wife or what"), and now she was comfortably fixed for the rest of her life and if the crow's feet were a little more pronounced around eyes and mouth and if the slenderness was just a trifle too slender (she weighed, at five-three, maybe ninety pounds and kept a variety of diet books in her big sunny kitchen), she was a damn good-looking woman nonetheless, the world's absurdity catalogued and evaluated in a gaze that managed to be both weary and impish, with a laugh that was knowing without being cynical.

So now she wanted to play detective.

I had some more bourbon from the pint—it burned beautifully—and said, "If I had your money, you know what I'd do?"

"Buy yourself a new shirt?"

"You don't like my shirt?"

"I didn't know you had this thing about Hawaii."

"If I had your money, I'd just forget about all this."

"I thought cops were sworn to uphold the right and the true."

"I'm an ex-cop."

"You wear a uniform."

"That's for the American Security Agency."

She sighed. "So I shouldn't have sent the letters?"

"No."

"Well, if they're guilty, they'll show up at Pierce Point tonight."

"Not necessarily."

"Why?"

"Maybe they'll know it's a trap. And not do anything."

She nodded to the school. "You hear that?"

"What?"

"The song."

It was Bobby Vinton's "Roses Are Red."

"I remember one party when we both hated our dates and we ended up dancing to that over and over again. Somebody's basement. You remember?"

"Sort of, I guess," I said.

"Good. Let's go in the gym and then we can dance to it again."

Donna, my lady friend, was out of town attending an advertising convention. I hoped she wasn't going to dance with anybody else because it would sure make me mad.

I started to open the door and she said, "I want to ask you a question."

"What?" I sensed what it was going to be so I kept my eyes on the parking lot.

"Turn around and look at me."

I turned around and looked at her. "Okay."

"Since the time we had dinner a month or so ago I've started receiving brochures from Alcoholics Anonymous

in the mail. If you were having them sent to me, would
you be honest enough to tell me?"

"Yes, I would."

"Are you having them sent to me?"

"Yes, I am."

"You think I'm a lush?"

"Don't you?"

"I asked you first."

So we went into the gym and danced.

Crepe of red and white, the school colors, draped the
ceiling; the stage was a cave of white light on which stood
four balding fat guys with spit curls and shimmery gold
lamé dinner jackets (could these be the illegitimate sons
of Bill Haley?) playing guitars, drum, and saxophone; on
the dance floor couples who'd lost hair, teeth, jawlines,
courage, and energy (everything, it seemed, but weight)
danced to lame cover versions of "Breaking Up Is Hard
To Do" and "Sheila," "Runaround Sue" and "Running
Scared" (tonight's lead singer sensibly not even trying Roy
Orbison's beautiful falsetto) and then, while I got Karen
and myself some no-alcohol punch, they broke into a medley of dance tunes—everything from "Locomotion" to
"The Peppermint Twist"—and the place went a little
crazy, and I went right along with it.

"Come on," I said.

"Great."

We went out there and we burned ass. We'd both agreed
not to dress up for the occasion so we were ready for this.
I wore the Hawaiian shirt she found so despicable plus a
blue blazer, white socks and cordovan penny-loafers. She
wore a salmon-colored Merikani shirt belted at the waist

and tan cotton fatigue pants and, sweet Christ, she was so adorable half the guys in the place did the kind of doubletakes usually reserved for somebody outrageous or famous.

Over the blasting music, I shouted, "Everybody's watching you!"

She shouted right back, "I know! Isn't it wonderful?"

The medley went twenty minutes and could easily have been confused with an aerobics session. By the end I was sopping and wishing I was carrying ten or fifteen pounds less and sometimes feeling guilty because I was having too much fun (I just hoped Donna, probably having too much fun, too, was feeling equally guilty), and then finally it ended and mate fell into the arms of mate, hanging on to stave off sheer collapse.

Then the head Bill Haley clone said, "Okay, now we're going to do a ballad medley," so then we got everybody from Johnny Mathis to Connie Francis and we couldn't resist that, so I moved her around the floor with clumsy pleasure and she moved me right back with equally clumsy pleasure. "You know something?" I said.

"We're both shitty dancers?"

"Right."

But we kept on, of course, laughing and whirling a few times, and then coming tighter together and just holding each other silently for a time, two human beings getting older and scared about getting older, remembering some things and trying to forget others and trying to make sense of an existence that ultimately made sense to nobody, and then she said, "There's one of them."

I didn't have to ask her what "them" referred to. Until

now she'd refused to identify any of the three people she'd sent the letters to.

At first I didn't recognize him. He had almost white hair and a tan so dark it looked fake. He wore a black dinner jacket with a lacy shirt and a black bow tie. He didn't seem to have put on a pound in the quarter century since I'd last seen him.

"Ted Forester?"

"Forester," she said. "He's president of the same savings and loan his father was president of."

"Who are the other two?"

"Why don't we get some punch?"

"The kiddie kind?"

"You could really make me mad with all this lecturing about alcoholism."

"If you're not really a lush then you won't mind getting the kiddie kind."

"My friend, Sigmund Fraud."

We had a couple of pink punches and caught our respective breaths and squinted in the gloom at name tags to see who we were saying hello to and realized all the terrible things you realize at high school reunions, namely that people who thought they were better than you still think that way, and that all the sad little people you feared for— the ones with blackheads and low IQs and lame left legs and walleyes and lisps and every other sort of unfair infirmity people get stuck with—generally turned out to be deserving of your fear, for there was a sadness in their eyes tonight that spoke of failures of every sort, and you wanted to go up and say something to them (I wanted to go up to nervous Karl Carberry, who used to twitch—his whole body twitched—and throw my arm around him and tell him

what a neat guy he was, tell him there was no reason
whatsoever for his twitching, grant him peace and self-
esteem and at least a modicum of hope; if he needed a
woman, get him a woman, too), but of course you didn'
do that, you didn't go up, you just made edgy jokes and
nodded a lot and drifted on to the next piece of human
carnage.

"There's number two," Karen whispered.

This one I remembered. And despised. The six-three
blond movie-star looks had grown only slightly older. His
blue dinner jacket just seemed to enhance his air of mali-
cious superiority. Larry Price. His wife Sally was still perfect
too, though you could see in the lacquered blond hair and
maybe a hint of face lift that she'd had to work at it a little
harder. A year out of high school, at a bar that took teenage
IDs checked by a guy who must have been legally blind
I'd gotten drunk and told Larry that he was essentially an
asshole for beating up a friend of mine who hadn't had a
chance against him. I had the street boy's secret belief that
I could take anybody whose father was a surgeon and whose
house included a swimming pool. I had hatred, bitterness
and rage going, right? Well, Larry and I went out into the
parking lot, ringed by a lot of drunken spectators, and
before I got off a single punch, Larry hit me with a shot
that stood me straight up, giving him a great opportunity
to hit me again. He hit me three times before I found his
face and sent him a shot hard enough to push him back
for a time. Before we could go at it again, the guy who
checked IDs got himself between us. He was madder than
either Larry or me. He ended the fight by taking us both
by the ears (he must have trained with nuns) and dragging
us out to the curb and telling neither of us to come back

"You remember the night you fought him?"

"Yeah."

"You could have taken him, Dwyer. Those three punches he got in were just lucky."

"Yeah, that was my impression, too. Lucky."

She laughed. "I was afraid he was going to kill you."

I was going to say something smart, but then a new group of people came up and we gushed through a little social dance of nostalgia and lies and self-justifications. We talked success (at high school reunions, everybody sounds like Amway representatives at a pep rally) and the old days (nobody seems to remember all the kids who got treated like shit for reasons they had no control over) and didn't so-and-so look great (usually this meant they'd managed to keep their toupees on straight) and introducing new spouses (we all had to explain what happened to our original mates; I said mine had been eaten by alligators in the Amazon, but nobody seemed to find that especially believable) and in the midst of all this, Karen tugged my sleeve and said, "There's the third one."

Him I recognized, too. David Haskins. He didn't look any happier than he ever had. Parent trouble was always the explanation you got for his grief back in high school. His parents had been rich, truly so, his father an importer of some kind, and their arguments so violent that they were as eagerly discussed as who was or who was not pregnant. Apparently David's parents weren't getting along any better today because although the features of his face were open and friendly enough, there was still the sense of some terrible secret stooping his shoulders and keeping his smiles to furtive wretched imitations. He was a paunchy

balding little man who might have been a church usher
with a sour stomach.

"The Duke of Earl" started up then and there was no
way we were going to let that pass so we got out on the
floor; but by now, of course, we both watched the three
people she'd sent letters to. Her instructions had been to
meet the anonymous letter writer at nine-thirty at Pierce
Point. If they were going to be there on time, they'd be
leaving soon.

"You think they're going to go?"

"I doubt it, Karen."

"You still don't believe that's what I heard them say that
night?"

"It was a long time ago and you were drunk."

"It's a good thing I like you because otherwise you'd be
a distinct pain in the ass."

Which is when I saw all three of them go stand under
one of the glowing red EXIT signs and open a fire door
that led to the parking lot.

"They're going!" she said.

"Maybe they're just having a cigarette."

"You know better, Dwyer. You know better."

Her car was in the lot on the opposite side of the gym.
"Well, it's worth a drive even if they don't show up. Pierce
Point should be nice tonight."

She squeezed against me and said, "Thanks, Dwyer.
Really."

So we went and got her Volvo and went out to Pierce
Point where twenty-five years ago a shy kid named Michael
Brandon had fallen or been pushed to his death.

Apparently we were about to find out which.

* * *

The river road wound along a high wall of clay cliffs on the left and a wide expanse of water on the right. The spring night was impossibly beautiful, one of those moments so rich with sweet odor and even sweeter sight you wanted to take your clothes off and run around in some kind of crazed animal circles out of sheer joy.

"You still like jazz," she said, nodding to the radio.

"I hope you didn't mind my turning the station."

"I'm kind of into Country."

"I didn't get the impression you were listening."

She looked over at me. "Actually, I wasn't. I was thinking about you sending me all those AA pamphlets."

"It was arrogant and presumptuous and I apologize."

"No, it wasn't. It was sweet and I appreciate it."

The rest of the ride, I leaned my head back and smelled flowers and grass and river water and watched moonglow through the elms and oaks and birches of this new spring. There was a Dakota Staton song, "Street of Dreams," and I wondered as always where she was and what she was doing, she'd been so fine, maybe the most underappreciated jazz singer of the entire fifties.

Then we were going up a long, twisting gravel road. We pulled up next to a big park pavilion and got out and stood in the wet grass, and she came over and slid her arm around my waist and sort of hugged me in a half-serious way. "This is all probably crazy, isn't it?"

I sort of hugged her back in a half-serious way. "Yeah, but it's a nice night for a walk so what the hell."

"You ready?"

"Yep."

"Let's go then."

So we went up the hill to the Point itself, and first we looked out at the far side of the river where white birches glowed in the gloom and where beyond you could see the horseshoe shape of the city lights. Then we looked down, straight down the drop of two hundred feet, to the road where Michael Brandon had died.

When I heard the car starting up the road to the east, I said, "Let's get in those bushes over there."

A thick line of shrubs and second-growth timber would give us a place to hide, to watch them.

By the time we were in place, ducked down behind a wide elm and a mulberry bush, a new yellow Mercedes sedan swung into sight and stopped several yards from the edge of the Point.

A car radio played loud in the night. A Top 40 song. Three men got out. Dignified Forester, matinee-idol Price, anxiety-tight Haskins.

Forester leaned back into the car and snapped the radio off. But he left the headlights on. Forester and Price each had cans of beer. Haskins bit his nails.

They looked around in the gloom. The headlights made the darkness beyond seem much darker and the grass in its illumination much greener. Price said harshly, "I told you this was just some goddamn prank. Nobody knows squat."

"He's right, he's probably right," Haskins said to Forester. Obviously he was hoping that was the case.

Forester said, "If somebody didn't know something, we would never have gotten those letters."

She moved then and I hadn't expected her to move at all. I'd been under the impression we would just sit there and listen and let them ramble and maybe in so doing reveal something useful.

But she had other ideas.

She pushed through the undergrowth and stumbled a little and got to her feet again and then walked right up to them.

"Karen!" Haskins said.

"So you did kill Michael," she said.

Price moved toward her abruptly, his hand raised. He was drunk and apparently hitting women was something he did without much trouble.

Then I stepped out from our hiding place and said, "Put your hand down, Price."

Forester said, "Dwyer."

"So," Price said, lowering his hand, "I was right, wasn't I?" He was speaking to Forester.

Forester shook his silver head. He seemed genuinely saddened. "Yes, Price, for once your cynicism is justified."

Price said, "Well, you two aren't getting a goddamned penny, do you know that?"

He lunged toward me, still a bully. But I was ready for him, wanted it. I also had the advantage of being sober. When he was two steps away, I hit him just once and very hard in his solar plexus. He backed away, eyes startled, and then he turned abruptly away.

We all stood looking at one another, pretending not to hear the sounds of violent vomiting on the other side of the splendid new Mercedes.

Forester said, "When I saw you there, Karen, I wondered if you could do it alone."

"Do what?"

"What?" Forester said. "What? Let's at least stop the games. You two want money."

"Christ," I said to Karen, who looked perplexed, "they think we're trying to shake them down."

"Shake them down?"

"Blackmail them."

"Exactly," Forester said.

Price had come back around. He was wiping his mouth with the back of his hand. In his other hand he carried a silver-plated .45, the sort of weapon professional gamblers favor.

Haskins said, "Larry, Jesus, what is that?"

"What does it look like?"

"Larry, that's how people get killed." Haskins sounded like Price's mother.

Price's eyes were on me. "Yeah, it would be terrible if Dwyer here got killed, wouldn't it?" He waved the gun at me. I didn't really think he'd shoot, but I sure was afraid he'd trip and the damn thing would go off accidentally. "You've been waiting since senior year to do that to me, haven't you, Dwyer?"

I shrugged. "I guess so, yeah."

"Well, why don't I give Forester here the gun and then you and I can try it again."

"Fine with me."

He handed Forester the .45. Forester took it all right, but what he did was toss it somewhere into the gloom surrounding the car. "Larry, if you don't straighten up here, I'll fight you myself. Do you understand me?" Forester had a certain dignity and when he spoke, his voice carried an easy authority. "There will be no more fighting, do you both understand that?"

"I agree with Ted," Karen said.

Forester, like a teacher tired of naughty children, decided to get on with the real business. "You wrote those letters, Dwyer?"

"No."

"No?"

"No. Karen wrote them."

A curious glance was exchanged by Forester and Karen. "I guess I should have known that," Forester said.

"Jesus, Ted," Karen said, "I'm not trying to blackmail you, no matter what you think."

"Then just what exactly are you trying to do?"

She shook her lovely little head. I sensed she regretted ever writing the letters, stirring it all up again. "I just want the truth to come out about what really happened to Michael Brandon that night."

"The truth," Price said. "Isn't that goddamn touching?"

"Shut up, Larry," Haskins said.

Forester said, "You know what happened to Michael Brandon?"

"I've got a good idea," Karen said. "I overheard you three talking at a party one night."

"What did we say?"

"What?"

"What did you overhear us say?"

Karen said, "You said that you hoped nobody looked into what really happened to Michael that night."

A smile touched Forester's lips. "So on that basis you concluded that we murdered him?"

"There wasn't much else to conclude."

Price said, weaving still, leaning on the fender for support, "I don't goddamn believe this."

Forester nodded to me. "Dwyer, I'd like to have a talk with Price and Haskins here, if you don't mind. Just a few minutes." He pointed to the darkness beyond the car. "We'll walk over there. You know we won't try to get away because you'll have our car. All right?"

I looked at Karen.

She shrugged.

They left, back into the gloom, voices receding and fading into the sounds of crickets and a barn owl and a distant roaring train.

"You think they're up to something?"

"I don't know," I said.

We stood with our shoes getting soaked and looked at the green, green grass in the headlights.

"What do you think they're doing?" Karen asked.

"Deciding what they want to tell us."

"You're used to this kind of thing, aren't you?"

"I guess."

"It's sort of sad, isn't it?"

"Yeah. It is."

"Except for you getting the chance to punch out Larry Price after all these years."

"Christ, you really think I'm that petty?"

"I know you are. I know you are."

Then we both turned to look back to where they were. There'd been a cry and Forester shouted, "You hit him again, Larry, and I'll break your goddamn jaw." They were arguing about something and it had turned vicious.

I leaned back against the car. She leaned back against me. "You think we'll ever go to bed?"

"I'd sure like to, Karen, but I can't."

"Donna?"

"Yeah. I'm really trying to learn how to be faithful."

"That been a problem?"

"It cost me a marriage."

"Maybe I'll learn how someday, too."

Then they were back. Somebody, presumably Forester, had torn Price's nice lacy shirt into shreds. Haskins looked miserable.

Forester said, "I'm going to tell you what happened that night."

I nodded.

"I've got some beer in the backseat. Would either of you like one?"

Karen said, "Yes, we would."

So he went and got a six pack of Michelob and we all had a beer and just before he started talking he and Karen shared another one of those peculiar glances and then he said, "The four of us—myself, Price, Haskins, and Michael Brandon—had done something we were very ashamed of."

"Afraid of," Haskins said.

"Afraid that, if it came out, our lives would be ruined. Forever," Forester said.

Price said, "Just say it, Forester." He glared at me. "We raped a girl, the four of us."

"Brandon spent two months afterward seeing the girl, bringing her flowers, apologizing to her over and over again, telling her how sorry we were, that we'd been drunk and it wasn't like us to do that and—" Forester sighed, put his eyes to the ground. "In fact we had been drunk; in fact it wasn't like us to do such a thing—"

Haskins said, "It really wasn't. It really wasn't."

For a time there was just the barn owl and the crickets again, no talk, and then gently I said, "What happened to Brandon that night?"

"We were out as we usually were, drinking beer, talking about it, afraid the girl would finally turn us in to the police, still trying to figure out why we'd ever done such a thing—"

The hatred was gone from Price's eyes. For the first time the matinee idol looked as melancholy as his friends. "No matter what you think of me, Dwyer, I don't rape women. But that night—" He shrugged, looked away.

"Brandon," I said. "You were going to tell me about Brandon."

"We came up here, had a case of beer or something, and talked about it some more, and that night," Forester said, "that night Brandon just snapped. He couldn't handle how ashamed he was or how afraid he was of being turned in. Right in the middle of talking—"

Haskins took over. "Right in the middle, he just got up and ran out to the Point." He indicated the cliff behind us. "And before we could stop him, he jumped."

"Jesus," Price said, "I can't forget his screaming on the way down. I can't ever forget it."

I looked at Karen. "So what she heard you three talking about outside the party that night was not that you'd killed Brandon but that you were afraid a serious investigation into his suicide might turn up the rape?"

Forester said, "Exactly." He stared at Karen. "We didn't kill Michael, Karen. We loved him. He was our friend."

But by then, completely without warning, she had started to cry and then she began literally sobbing, her entire body shaking with some grief I could neither understand nor assuage.

I nodded to Forester to get back in his car and leave. They stood and watched us a moment and then they got into the Mercedes and went away, taking the burden of years and guilt with them.

This time I drove. I went far out the river road, miles out, where you pick up the piney hills and the deer standing by the side of the road.

From the glove compartment she took a pint of J&B, and I knew better than to try and stop her.

I said, "You were the girl they raped, weren't you?"

"Yes."

"Why didn't you tell the police?"

She smiled at me. "The police weren't exactly going to believe a girl from the Highlands about the sons of rich men."

I sighed. She was right.

"Then Michael started coming around to see me. I can't say I ever forgave him, but I started to feel sorry for him. His fear—" She shook her head, looked out the window. She said, almost to herself, "But I had to write those letters, get them there tonight, know for sure if they killed him." She paused. "You believe them?"

"That they didn't kill him?"

"Right."

"Yes, I believe them."

"So do I."

Then she went back to staring out the window, her small

face childlike there in silhouette against the moonsilver river. "Can I ask you a question, Dwyer?"

"Sure."

"You think we're ever going to get out of the Highlands?"

"No," I said, and drove on faster in her fine new expensive car. "No, I don't."

Seeing Red

Barbara Collins

It seemed to Deborah that every cell in her bloated body was about to burst. If her period didn't start soon, she was going to *kill* somebody!

She sat back in the leather chair and tugged viciously through her red silk dress at the tight elastic waistband on her pantyhose. Then she leaned forward and opened the top right drawer of her mahogany desk and pulled out a pair of long silver scissors, which she dropped into her open purse on the floor by her feet. She got up from the desk, taking the purse, and walked briskly, tensely, to the closed office door. But as soon as she opened it, she forced her body to relax, and changed her cross expression to one of pleasantry.

"I'll be back in a minute, Shirley," she said sweetly to the secretary who sat behind a desk in the outer room.

The secretary, a rather homely woman with short hair and big, round glasses, looked up briefly from what she was doing. "Yes, Ms. Nova," she said, then returned to her work.

Deborah walked down the plushly carpeted corridor toward the executive washroom, nodding and smiling at a few people along the way . . . but once inside the bathroom, behind its thick bronze-colored door, her expression changed back to one of annoyance as she marched across the marble floor, her high-heeled shoes click, click, clicking.

She threw open a stall, entered, then slammed it shut.

She got out the scissors and yanked up her dress.

"I'd like to get my hands on the son of a bitch that designed these pantyhose," she snarled, sliding one of the silver blades down between her stomach and the hose, cutting away savagely at the binding band. "You can *bet* it wasn't a *woman!*"

Her discomfort somewhat relieved, she held up the scissors in front of her face. Snip! snip! went the blades, glinting in the overhead light. "I'd take *this* to his . . ."

Water ran in a sink.

Composing herself, Deborah exited the stall.

A younger woman in a dark tailored suit stood at one of the shell-shaped basins washing her hands. Her blond hair was pulled back from an attractive face and held at the nape of her neck by an ornate barrette. Expensive earrings clung to delicate ears.

"Hello, Deborah," the woman said.

"Heather," Deborah responded, noncommittally. She moved to an adjacent basin and turned the crystal knobs on the faucet. The two women, standing side by side, eyed each other in the mirror. They looked similar, despite their difference in age, which was almost a decade.

Deborah thought she herself looked better.

"I need your help," Heather said, breaking the silence.

Deborah, wiping her hands on a paper towel, turned to face the woman. "Oh?" she smiled.

"I understand the second chair hasn't been filled yet for the Owens case. I'd like a shot at it."

Deborah continued to smile.

"I would do a good job," the woman said confidently.

"Yes, I believe you could."

"Then you'll recommend me?"

Deborah, finished with the towel, wadded it up. "Certainly I will," she said.

Heather smiled and thanked Deborah, and left the bathroom.

Deborah stared after the woman, nerves strung out as tight as pantyhose in a strangler's hands.

"Certainly I will," she repeated. *"Not!"*

She reared back and threw the wadded-up paper towel angrily at the wastebasket. "I didn't claw my way up this good-old-boy network just to hand *you* a plum position on a silver platter!"

Deborah turned back to the mirror and got lipstick out of her purse and applied the blood-red color to her collagen-injected lips.

"You'd better go home," she warned her reflection, "before you blow it. Remember Laura."

The thought of that woman and what happened to her brought a new rush of heat to Deborah's already flushed cheeks.

It was fifteen years ago that Deborah, fresh out of law school and new to the firm, was an associate to Laura. The woman was her idol, a Harvard graduate of distinction, a talented and brilliant lawyer . . . and the first female certain to become a partner in this all-boys' club.

But it never came to pass. Because Laura made a fatal mistake one day: she showed some emotion.

Mr. Laroma, a senior partner in a pin-striped suit, looked at Laura from across the conference table and smirked, "Maybe we should discuss this later . . . *after* you've had your period."

Though a stunned silence hung in the air, Deborah would never forget the collective look on the men's faces: one of masked approval. Laura fled the room and, a short time later, the company.

The incident was a turning point for Deborah; after that, she told herself, she would be a man in drag.

And now, with partnership so close she could almost reach out and touch it, she'd better not show *any* female weakness. Especially hormonal.

Deborah walked back to her office.

"If Mr. Laroma should need me," Deborah informed her secretary, "he can reach me at home."

Deborah packed up her briefcase, then took the elevator down to an underground garage where she got into her gray BMW and drove out to the street. After a few blocks she pulled into a No Parking zone in front of a dry cleaner, got out of the car and entered the store.

A thin young man with a bad case of acne stood behind the counter. She stepped up and set her purse down, then rummaged around in the bag for her dry-cleaning ticket. She stopped, realizing she'd left it at home.

"Damn," she said irritably. "I don't have the ticket . . . but it's a white silk blouse and blue suit."

"Sorry," the kid said flatly, "I need the ticket."

Deborah softened her expression and voice. "Can't you make an exception?" she asked sweetly.

"Nope. Those are the rules."

Deborah studied him for a moment, then sighed deeply.

"And I *so* wanted to wear them to the AIDS benefit tonight."

For a moment the kid seemed to reconsider. But then he said, again, "I need the ticket."

Deborah slammed both fists on the counter making her purse jump. "Listen, you pimply faced faggot," she growled, "give me my clothes or I'll . . ."

"*I'll* call the cops," he said firmly, and moved toward a nearby phone to make good on his threat.

Deborah turned in a huff and stomped out to the curb where she found a different kind of ticket on the windshield of her car.

She grabbed the pink parking violation, nearly dislocating the wiper, and looked up and down the street. She spotted the policewoman who had given her the ticket.

"I was *just* in there a *minute!*" Deborah shouted at her.

The cop ignored Deborah.

So Deborah screamed, "Why don't you get a *real* job!" and tore the ticket into tiny pieces, scattering them to the wind.

She got in her car and, without looking, pulled out from the curb, nearly causing an accident. Brakes squealed as the other motorist honked his horn.

She gave him the finger.

Weaving recklessly in and out of the downtown traffic, Deborah caught the northbound expressway that would take her out to her home in the suburbs. But before long the expressway slowed, congested with commuters, and Deborah, behind the wheel, fumed, then found some classical music on the radio to calm herself down. But after a while, the violin concerto sounded like fingernails on a blackboard, and Deborah shut off the radio with a *click*.

Now the traffic was at a near standstill, and Deborah, crawling past an exit, got off. She'd wait out the rush hour at a nearby mall, and besides, she thought, shopping always made her feel better. And she could use the time to find a present for her mother's birthday—though it didn't matter how carefully Deborah picked out the gift or how expensive it was . . . nothing ever pleased her mother.

It seemed to Deborah that she spent her entire life looking for affection, though she got it, briefly, from her father—until she was eight years old. That's when he left her. He didn't have the decency to wait until she had gone off to school that morning. She stood crying at the window—just a little girl—watching him get in the car with his suitcases. He didn't even look back.

She didn't see or hear from him again until a few years ago. He called her at the office, out of the blue . . . said he was sorry he had dropped out of sight. He'd like to make it up to her.

She wanted—so badly—to reach out to him, to know him, to love him. But the little girl wouldn't let her.

She told him to go fuck himself.

Deborah pulled her car into the parking lot of the mall, which was full. She drove around and around looking for a place to park. The third time she passed the empty handicapped spaces up at the front, she complained, "How *many* do they *need*? They get all the breaks!"

Then two heavy-set women in jogging clothes—obviously on their way to use the mall as a track, a trend Deborah hated—stepped out into the crosswalk, and she had to slam on her brakes and let them pass.

She watched the women disdainfully, envisioning elephants, and rolled down her window and hollered, "It's not working!"

Around she drove again, when suddenly, up at the front and very close to the mall, brake lights went on.

"There *is* a God!" Deborah cried, and zoomed ahead, putting on her turn signal to lay claim to the spot.

Impatiently she tapped her red nails on the steering wheel, waiting for the Chevy truck to back out, its body perched precariously up on big wheels.

"Come on, come *on,*" she muttered. "Show me a jacked-up truck and I'll show you a man who wishes his *dick* were bigger."

Slowly the Chevy backed out and started to leave, but as soon as it did, a black Porsche roared around the corner and stole the parking space.

Behind the wheel of the Porsche was a businessman in a suit. And a smirk on his face.

Shouting a string of obscenities, Deborah exploded, slammed her accelerator to the floor and aimed the front of her car for the back of his ass!

Steve was depressed. Up until six months ago—that's when it started—the feeling had been foreign to him.

An outgoing, upbeat, aggressive man, he'd enjoyed a damn near perfect life. Nurturing and supportive parents, attending the best schools, more friends than he knew what to do with . . . Steve seemed blessed from birth. After graduating from college, he had married the prettiest woman on campus and landed a good job with an insurance company.

Now, fifteen years later, walking out of that company into a cold, gray, overcast day, Steve felt the jaws of depression tighten their grip, pulling him down, down, into a dark abyss out of which he could see no possible escape.

He got into his black Porsche, kicking a small handgun that had slid out from under the front seat; he had bought the weapon last year when there was a rash of smash-and-grab car thieves terrorizing the city.

That's all he needed, he thought, was to shoot himself in the goddamn foot. Shaking his head, he tucked the gun back under the seat, started the car and roared off, catching the southbound freeway that would head him toward the city to an apartment where he lived alone.

But traffic was snarled, at a near standstill, giving Steve nothing to do but think. And finally, he allowed something that had been eating away inside of him to gnaw its way out . . .

It was last May when Steve went back to his hometown for his twenty-fifth high-school class reunion. His wife, Kathleen, decided not to go; their three kids were busy with their own activities, and she would be needed. And besides, Kathleen had said with a smile, he'd have more fun by himself.

Steve hadn't been back to Iowa since graduating from high school. Over the years, the tenth, fifteenth, then twentieth class reunion forms found their way to him as he moved around the country for his company. And each time he sat down at his desk and filled out the paper—until he came to the part that asked his occupation. Insurance salesman. Not very befitting to the boy voted most likely to succeed. No, he told himself, until he could write that he was president of the company, he wouldn't attend.

But this time Steve made an exception. He was now a vice-president, with the presidency certain to be his.

The night before he left, he dug out his old high-school yearbook and pored over it so he would remember his classmates. Then he got out the booklet that came with his banquet ticket; it told what everyone was presently doing. He studied it, as if there would be an exam, smiling as he did so until he reached the last page. Fifteen names filled a memorial page. It upset him to know that these people were dead. . . .

Yet it would be *great* to see old friends. Especially Rob. He grinned, thinking of all the rebellious scrapes he and his best friend had gotten into.

Steve shook his head, his smile fading. How could he have lost touch with Rob? They were like brothers, for Christ's sake! He made a promise to himself that at the reunion he would renew that friendship. After all, he thought, looking again at the memorial page, life was just too damn short.

Steve thumbed back through the booklet, and noticed that his old girlfriend, Melissa, listed no spouse . . .

Okay, so he envisioned making it with Melissa. So what. Like no married *woman* ever had thoughts about another man. It was just a harmless fantasy that helped pass the time on his long drive back to Iowa. Yes, he knew he had a great job, a wonderful wife, and three terrific kids. He wasn't *stupid*. And yet, memories of Melissa—a love almost consummated—seemed more and more like unfinished business in his mind.

After arriving in town, Steve checked into a hotel, taking a suite in case anyone might want to come back and party. Then he showered and shaved, and carefully combed his recently dyed hair. He put on tight, white bermuda shorts and a pale yellow polo shirt that showed off his spa-tanned skin. A leather Rolex was strapped to his wrist.

He stood at the mirror—looking more like thirty-three than a forty-three-year-old man—and, satisfied with his appearance, he left the room, and went out to his Porsche.

Indianola was a small town in a rural community with a population of about fifteen thousand. Driving around the downtown, which was built in a square around a quaint little park, Steve thought things hadn't changed much in twenty-five years. Oh, sure, there were some new shops, but the old Gothic theater with its great marquee, and Pasquale's Pizzeria—where *everyone* hung out—took him zooming back in time.

Steve felt a lump in his throat.

He turned down a side street and pulled his Porsche into a parking lot next to a big, three-story brown brick building that was the old YMCA where they used to have sock-hops. Vacant for some time, it was reopened for this Friday night dance—for old times' sake.

Steve parked his car and got out.

As he opened the door to the building, loud talking and laughter floated down from the second-floor parlor. He smiled as he climbed the short flight of steps, nervous in a way he hadn't felt since high school.

But when he entered the parlor he became confused and disoriented, like a kid who'd wandered into the wrong classroom. Looking out over the sea of faces he recognized no one. He must be at the wrong reunion; these people were *old*. And yet, some reached out and grabbed at him and called his name.

With a frozen smile he moved through the crowd, as if in a slow motion picture.

Then behind him he heard a low, soft voice.

Melissa.

He sighed, relieved to know someone, and grinning, he turned.

But the grin collapsed like a fat lady in a folding chair, for Melissa was short and dumpy. Beneath curly gray hair lay a wrinkled face where here and there skin-tags clung like tiny particles of forgotten food. The bright orange dress she wore (Christ on a crutch, why would she want to draw attention to herself?) was shaped like a tent.

Steve's thoughts must have registered on his face, because Melissa had a hurt look on hers. Quickly he turned on the charm and told her how nice it was to see her again and how pretty she looked.

She perked up, and latched onto him, and launched into her life's history since high school . . . which was a *nightmare*. Listening to her babble on and on, Steve never realized it before, but the woman had the I.Q. of a gerbil! When she started to show him pictures of ugly grandchildren, he got away from her and moved to the other side of the room.

What *happened?* he thought. Was *this* the generation that was going to change the world? It didn't seem possible! Had they just given the fuck up? Turned into their parents but *worse?*

Was this *old man* in plaid polyester pants, now boring him to death with talk of aluminum siding, the same Rob from high school? Steve stared at his old friend.

Hello! Hello! Is anybody in there?

Steve fled the parlor, hurrying up a flight of wide, wooden steps that creaked and moaned with their age, and went into the gymnasium where the dance was being held.

It was dark in there, mercifully the only source of light coming from the band on stage and a large glittering ball that revolved on the ceiling. The ball sent a million white spots swirling around, making it look like the room had some contagious disease. The gym itself was small, just the size of a basketball court with no room for bleachers. Crepe paper hung from corner to corner, while a hundred balloons clung to the walls.

Steve took a chair at one of the long banquet tables, and watched the couples out on the floor, holding each other, dancing to a slow song, seemingly content with their lives . . .

He felt miserable.

Then the band—five guys who were also no spring chickens—began to play a song by the Association he hadn't heard since high school.

Enter the young, yeah!

Slowly Steve rose to his feet.

Here they come, yeah!

He started to weep.

And when they got to the words, "Not only learn to think but to dare," he bolted from the room and down the wooden steps and out the front door to his car, where he drove to an all-night liquor store, bought a bottle of bourbon, went back to his hotel room and drank it, until he passed out, on the floor, in his own vomit.

And now, crawling along the expressway, it occurred to Steve—in a revelation—that it was just a few weeks after returning from that class reunion that the anxiety attacks began.

The first one sent him rushing to the emergency room in the middle of the night, certain he was having heart failure. But an EKG and follow-up tests showed nothing was wrong. After that, he suffered them in silence.

The next indignity was Kathleen accusing him of being obsessed with sex. He'd always felt he had a satisfying love life—hell, *better* than satisfying. He was damn lucky to have such a sexy and obliging wife and with three kids in the house! He supposed he *had* been hornier than usual—as if the mass production of his sperm somehow held the promise of immortality—but he never foresaw the night when, in a tearful confrontation, Kathleen told him she had had enough and to get it someplace else.

So he did.

Kathleen kicked him out, of course. He couldn't blame her. His life was out of control, like a child's top spinning wildly on a table, heading straight for the edge . . . and he had neither the ability nor the desire to stop it.

Then came the *coup de grace*. Somebody else got to be president of the company. A younger man. Suddenly, as if overnight, Steve was perceived—or so he thought—as "too old." What depressed him more than anything else was knowing the finality of what lay before him: too late to start over with another company, he would go no further up the ladder of success.

Steve needed a fix . . . in the form of Jennifer who worked at an Orange Julius at a mall. She was dumb as a post, but young and pretty. And between her creamy white thighs was the only place he could get away from his demons.

He left the crowded expressway, and drove to the mall. He'd treat Jennifer to an expensive dinner, he thought, then she would make him feel better ... sad pathetic excuse of a man that he was. . . .

He smirked, hating himself, and pulled into a parking place. He turned off the engine and was undoing the seat belt when a tremendous force from behind drove him into the windshield, cracking his head up against the glass. While he didn't lose consciousness, Steve was so stunned he remained motionless for a moment, slumped over the steering wheel.

Then dazed, his head throbbing, he leaned back against the seat, and saw, in his rearview mirror, the car that hit him roar off. Suddenly he sat up straight, given a jolt of electricity in the form of vengeance, and started his car and took off after the BMW.

He caught up to it after the fourth stop light, but there was another car between them. He wheeled into a corner gas station, came out the other end and went into the intersection, in front of the BMW, to cut it off; he could not see inside the car's tinted windows.

When the light changed, car horns blared at him for blocking the way and the BMW accelerated, slamming his left backside, spinning him around, leaving him in the dust.

Now nothing mattered to Steve—not his life nor the life of anyone else—in his pursuit of the bastard in the BMW, over curbs and through red lights on their mad race out of the suburbs and into the country.

After a while the BMW swerved off the highway onto a secondary road. On a straightaway, Steve tried to overtake it, but the BMW was just too powerful. He pulled back a bit, saving his engine for the upgrade just ahead as the road began to wind up a steep hill that led to a quarry.

Was this maniac luring him to some desolate place in order to kill him? Steve wasn't about to wait and find out; he reached under his seat for the gun.

On a curve up the hill he buried his accelerator on the floor and sped up as close as he could to the other car, rolled down his window and fired. *Blam!* The back window of the BMW exploded, glass shards flying back onto his windshield and hand.

The BMW careened violently to the left and then to the right, skittering along a metal guardrail that bowed out as if it were a rubber band, straining to keep the car from going over the edge of the cliff.

The BMW spun around and came to a halt, hung up on the rail.

Steve pulled his Porsche off to the side and waited.

Operating on adrenaline, legs feeling weak, Steve shielded his eyes from the sun that peered out from the clouds like an interested spectator as he carefully approached the BMW. He yanked open the car door on the driver's side, gun ready to use.

But it didn't seem necessary. A woman in a red dress was slumped over the wheel, blond hair covering her face.

Steve didn't know what to think; he'd expected a man.

Carefully he pushed the woman back against the seat, revealing her face, which he did not recognize. She didn't appear to be badly hurt; the only sign of blood was a thin trickle down her left leg.

Steve relaxed his grip on the gun. Was she someone he had picked up in a bar for a one-night stand? he wondered. Was that what this was? Some kind of fatal attraction?

On the front seat, next to the woman, lay a purse,

opened. He leaned in over her to look for some identification.

His fingers were on a wallet when he felt a burning in his side that made him scream out with pain. He pulled back, out of the car, and saw scissors sticking out of his side.

Now the woman came at him, with a wild look in her eyes, and he brought up his hand with the gun and shot her. The force threw her back on the seat, but after a second she sat up like some superwoman and threw herself on him and they stumbled backward, doing an awkward little dance like a pair of marionettes, and tripped on the mangled guardrail and went over the cliff's edge together in a stunned embrace.

Below, a pair of frightened eyes watched.

He'd been out in the stream, fishing, looking for food to feed his family, when the violence erupted. It forced him back to the bank where he hid in the brush, fearful of repercussions, shivering in his brown fur coat.

After a while, when the sun began to set behind the cliff, its long rays winking good-bye, he ventured out. Cautiously he slid into the stream and swam toward the humans that lay twisted on the rocks, their limbs entwined like the briar bush he had just crawled out of.

Halfway across he stopped, sniffing, his head bobbing on the water's surface. He need not go any further: death hung in the air.

He turned and swam downstream a ways, then dove under and entered a hole in the bottom of the bank that then led upward to his house.

Inside the dark, dank chamber, lined with grass, the

female muskrat waited; nestled against her warm body were four tiny babies.

He lay protectively next to her and she snuggled up to him.

Tomorrow, he would hunt for tadpoles—but further downstream, away from the vile humans. And she would clean the house and take care of the babies . . .

Yes, tomorrow would be another glorious day.

Black Wind

Bill Pronzini

It was one of those freezing late-November nights, just before the winter snows, when a funny east wind comes howling down out of the mountains and across Woodbine Lake a quarter mile from the village. The sound that wind makes is something hellish, full of screams and wailings that can raise the hackles on your neck if you're not used to it. In the old days the Indians who used to live around here called it a "black wind"; they believed that it carried the voices of evil spirits, and that if you listened to it long enough it could drive you mad.

Well, there are a lot of superstitions in our part of upstate New York; nobody pays much mind to them in this modern age. Or if they do, they won't admit it even to themselves. The fact is, though, that when the black wind blows the local folks stay pretty close to home and the village, like as not, is deserted after dusk.

That was the way it was on this night. I hadn't had a customer in my diner in more than an hour, since just before seven o'clock, and I had about decided to close up early and go on home. To a glass of brandy and a good hot fire.

I was pouring myself a last cup of coffee when the head-lights swung into the diner's parking lot.

They whipped in fast, off the county highway, and I heard the squeal of brakes on the gravel just out front. Kids, I thought, because that was the way a lot of them drove, even around here—fast and a little reckless. But it wasn't kids. It turned out instead to be a man and a woman in their late thirties, strangers, both of them bundled up in winter coats and mufflers, the woman carrying a big fancy alligator purse.

The wind came in with them, shrieking and swirling. I could feel the numbing chill of it even in the few seconds the door was open; it cuts through you like the blade of a knife, that wind, right straight to the bone.

The man clumped immediately to where I was behind the counter, letting the woman close the door. He was handsome in a suave, barbered city way; but his face was closed up into a mask of controlled rage.

"Coffee," he said. The word came out in a voice that matched his expression—hard and angry, like a threat.

"Sure thing. Two coffees."

"One coffee," he said. "Let her order her own."

The woman had come up on his left, but not close to him—one stool between them. She was nice-looking in the same kind of made-up, city way. Or she would have been if her face wasn't pinched up worse than his; the skin across her cheekbones was stretched so tight it seemed ready to split. Her eyes glistened like a pair of wet stones and didn't blink at all.

"Black coffee," she said to me.

I looked at her, at him, and I started to feel a little uneasy. There was a kind of savage tension between them, thick and crackling; I could feel it like static electricity. I wet my lips, not saying anything, and reached behind me for the coffeepot and two mugs.

The man said, "I'll have a ham-and-cheese sandwich on rye bread. No mustard, no mayonnaise; just butter. Make it to go."

"Yes, sir. How about you, ma'am?"

"Tuna fish on white," she said thinly. She had close-cropped blond hair, wind-tangled under a loose scarf; she kept brushing at it with an agitated hand. "I'll eat it here."

"No, she won't," the man said to me. "Make it to go, just like mine."

She threw him an ugly look. "I want to eat here."

"Fine," he said—to me again; it was as if she wasn't there. "But I'm leaving in five minutes; as soon as I drink my coffee. I want that ham-and-cheese ready by then."

"Yes, sir."

I finished pouring out the coffee and set the two mugs on the counter. The man took his, swung around, and stomped over to one of the tables. He sat down and stared at the door, blowing into the mug, using it to warm his hands.

"All right," the woman said, "all right, all right. All right." Four times like that, all to herself. Her eyes had cold little lights in them now, like spots of foxfire.

I said hesitantly, "Ma'am? You still want the tuna sandwich to eat here?"

She blinked then, for the first time, and focused on me. "No. To hell with it. I don't want anything to eat." She caught up her mug and took it to another of the tables, two away from the one he was sitting at.

I went down to the sandwich board and got out two

pieces of rye bread and spread them with butter. The stillness in there had a strained feel, made almost eerie by the constant wailing outside. I could feel myself getting more jittery as the seconds passed.

While I sliced ham I watched the two of them at the tables—him still staring at the door, drinking his coffee in quick angry sips; her facing the other way, her hands fisted in her lap, the steam from her cup spiraling up around her face. Well-off married couple from New York City, I thought: they were both wearing the same type of expensive wedding ring. On their way to a weekend in the mountains, maybe, or up to Canada for a few days. And they'd had a hell of a fight over something, the way married people do on long tiring drives; that was all there was to it.

Except that that *wasn't* all there was to it.

I've owned this diner thirty years and I've seen a lot of folks come and go in that time; a lot of tourists from the city, with all sorts of marital problems. But I'd never seen any like these two. That tension between them wasn't anything fresh-born, wasn't just the brief and meaningless aftermath of a squabble. No, there was real hatred on both sides—the kind that builds and builds, seething, over long bitter weeks or months or even years. The kind that's liable to explode some day.

Well, it wasn't really any of my business. Not unless the blowup happened in here, it wasn't, and that wasn't likely. Or so I kept telling myself. But I was a little worried just the same. On a night like this, with that damned black wind blowing and playing hell with people's nerves, anything could happen. Anything at all.

I finished making the sandwich, cut it in half, and plastic-bagged it. Just as I slid it into a paper sack, there was a loud banging noise from across the room that made me jump half a foot; it sounded like a pistol shot. But it had only been the man slamming his empty mug down on the table.

I took a breath, let it out silently. He scraped back his chair as I did that, stood up, and jammed his hands into his coat pockets. Without looking at her, he said to the woman, "You pay for the food," and started past her table toward the rest rooms in the rear.

She said, "Why the hell should I pay for it?"

He paused and glared back at her. "You've got all the money."

"I've got all the money? Oh, that's a laugh. *I've* got all the money!"

"Go on, keep it up." Then in a louder voice, as if he wanted to make sure I heard, he said, "Bitch." And stalked away from her.

She watched him until he was gone inside the corridor leading to the rest rooms; she was as rigid as a chunk of wood. She sat that way for another five or six seconds, until the wind gusted outside, thudded against the door and the window like something trying to break in. Jerkily she got to her feet and came over to where I was at the sandwich board. Those cold lights still glowed in her eyes.

"Is his sandwich ready?"

I nodded and made myself smile. "Will that be all, ma'am?"

"No. I've changed my mind. I want something to eat, too." She leaned forward and stared at the glass pastry container on the back counter. "What kind of pie is that?"

"Cinnamon apple."

"I'll have a piece of it."

"Okay—sure. Just one?"

"Yes. Just one."

I turned back there, got the pie out, cut a slice, and wrapped it in waxed paper. When I came around with it she was rummaging in her purse, getting her wallet out. Back in the rest room area, I heard the man's hard, heavy steps; in the next second he appeared. And headed straight for the door.

The woman said, "How much do I owe you?"

I put the pie into the paper sack with the sandwich, and the sack on the counter. "That'll be three-eighty."

The man opened the door; the wind came shrieking in, eddying drafts of icy air. He went right on out, not even glancing at the woman or me, and slammed the door shut behind him.

She laid a five-dollar bill on the counter. Caught up the sack, pivoted, and started for the door.

"Ma'am?" I said. "You've got change coming."

She must have heard me, but she didn't look back and she didn't slow up. The pair of headlights came on out front, slicing pale wedges from the darkness; through the front window I could see the evergreens at the far edge of the lot, thick swaying shadows bent almost double by the wind. The shrieking rose again for two or three seconds, then fell back to a muted whine; she was gone.

I had never been gladder or more relieved to see customers go. I let out another breath, picked up the fiver, and moved over to the cash register. Outside, above the thrumming and wailing, the car engine revved up to a roar and there was the ratcheting noise of tires spinning on gravel.

The headlights shot around and probed out toward the county highway.

Time now to close up and go home, all right; I wanted a glass of brandy and a good hot fire more than ever. I went around to the tables they'd used, to gather up the coffee cups. But as much as I wanted to forget the two of them, I couldn't seem to get them out of my mind. Especially the woman.

I kept seeing those eyes of hers, cold and hateful like the wind, as if there was a black wind blowing inside her, too, and she'd been listening to it too long. I kept seeing her lean forward across the counter and stare at the pastry container. And I kept seeing her rummage in that big alligator purse when I turned around with the slice of pie. Something funny about the way she'd been doing that. As if she hadn't just been getting her wallet out to pay me. As if she'd been—

Oh my God, I thought.

I ran back behind the counter. Then I ran out again to the door, threw it open, and stumbled onto the gravel lot. But they were long gone; the night was a solid ebony wall.

I didn't know what to do. What could I do? Maybe she'd done what I suspicioned, and maybe she hadn't; I couldn't be sure because I don't keep an inventory on the slots of utensils behind the sandwich board. And I didn't know who they were or where they were going. I didn't even know what kind of car they were riding in.

I kept on standing there, chills racing up and down my back, listening to that black wind scream and scream around me. Feeling the cold sharp edge of it cut into my bare flesh, cut straight to the bone.

Just like the blade of a knife . . .

Death's Brother

Bill Crider

O soft embalmer of the still midnight,
Shutting with careful fingers and benign,
Our gloom-pleas'd eyes, embower'd from the light,
Enshaded in forgetfulness divine . . .

Jon Cline closed the leatherbound book on Keats's poem
"To Sleep" and thought about the words. He especially
liked the part about the "soft embalmer of the still midnight," with its suggestions of the undertaker's parlor and
cool marble slabs, but he also liked the "careful fingers
and benign."

He looked at his own fingers, wondering how benign
they were, put the book on the end table by his leather-
upholstered recliner, and took the glass of Wild Turkey
that was sitting there. Sipping the smooth, fiery liquid, he
thought about the time he had first heard about Sleep,
Death's brother.

It had been in high school, in an English class where
the teacher was discussing Greek mythology. Even then

Cline had been interested in literature, and he remembered most of what the teacher had said, though of course he had read the story again later on.

It seems there were two gods that most of the other gods didn't like at all. The two who proved to be so unpopular were the sons of Night—Death and his brother, Sleep. The other gods had so little regard for those two that they wouldn't even let them reside up on Mount Olympus, where all the rest of the immortals were living—and having a high old time of it to boot. Sleep had to live in a cave quite some distance away and was hardly even mentioned in any myths at all.

The gods apparently didn't even like to think about him—not until they needed him, anyway.

The story Cline remembered best about Sleep concerned a man who had to die for some reason or another. Cline couldn't quite remember why. The man was the helmsman on one of the ships of Aeneas, and the gods sent Sleep to do him in. Sleep pulled all the tricks he knew, but the man—Palinurus was his name, Cline suddenly recalled—was too devoted to his duty; he just wouldn't let go of the helm and fall into the sea.

Sleep must have learned a few things from his brother, though, because he finally just pushed Palinurus over the side.

The man slipped into the sea, still clinging to the helm. In fact, he took it right along with him, but Sleep got the job done, all right.

Cline had always admired him for that.

* * *

The old man's room stank. It smelled like someone had puked in there, and Cline would have bet the toilet in the little adjoining bathroom hadn't been cleaned in a month.

There was a lamp on the nightstand next to the old man's bed, but it had maybe a twenty-watt bulb in it. It mostly made a lot of shadows and gave the room a kind of yellow glow.

That was good enough for Cline, though. He could see just fine.

There was a big chair over in one corner with what looked like a week's laundry in it, sheets, pajamas, things like that. Maybe some of the stink was coming from there.

There was a TV set sitting on top of a chest of drawers, but Cline doubted if the old man had watched it in a long time. He didn't look to be in much of a condition to watch anything, from what Cline could see of him.

What Cline could see of him in the dim light was just his head, which was sticking out from under the dingy sheets of the bed he was lying in. It looked like one of those heads Cline used to see as a kid in the old movies when they unwrapped The Mummy, or when Dracula had been in the sun about a minute too long, dried and shriveled and covered with lines like a road map.

The rest of him probably wasn't in much better shape. Cline could see sort of an outline of him under the sheet and lightweight thermal blanket that covered him. Hell, he probably looked *worse* than The Mummy. Out from under those covers, the old guy would probably make The Mummy look like he'd just gotten back from a visit to a health spa.

The covers hardly moved with the old man's shallow

breathing. A clear bubble of spit formed in his mouth as Cline watched him.

The man had been like that for months, more than a year. He should have died long ago, but for some reason he kept clinging to a life that had nothing of dignity left in it.

There was dirt in the corners of the smelly room where he lay. He had to wear diapers and be changed like a baby. He was unable to identify his own daughter when she appeared in the room.

He needed someone to push him over the side.

That was Cline's job. He hadn't taken it on voluntarily, not exactly, but he hadn't run from it, either.

"I don't know what I'm going to do, Jon," Dana Randall had said to him. "I need the money so much, and I'll never get it as long as he's alive."

They had been sitting in deck chairs, looking out beyond the pool and the tennis courts at the woods that bordered the Randall estate. The sun dappled the wooden redwood deck, and the leaves of a huge pecan tree speckled it with shadows.

"Surely there's enough to run the estate," Cline said, sneaking a look at Dana's long, tanned legs. They were just about the best legs Cline had ever seen. Movie actresses like the ones in the 1950s, the ones who were always going and having what they referred to as their "gams" insured for a million dollars, would have killed for legs like that.

Dana raised a languid hand and let it drop. "There's enough for *that,* of course. But not for anything else."

"Anything else" in Dana's terms covered all the things

that really mattered to her—cars, parties, clothes, jewelry—the necessities of life.

"He can't last forever," Cline said. He'd known Dana for almost a year, ever since she had signed up for his class in Romantic poetry at the university as a way to ease her boredom and kill a little time while she waited to come into her inheritance.

Cline had soon found himself doing more than was required of him as a professor to help her do both those things. He spent extra time tutoring her in his office and then at her home.

Before long, she was tutoring him. In the bedroom.

It was the kind of tutoring Cline had often longed for. He was single and lonely. And while he had heard stories of other professors who got involved with nubile young women, it had certainly never happened to him. That it finally had seemed like a minor miracle.

Dana tossed her long black hair and looked at Cline. "There was something you said in class one time, something Byron said when he was hoping for an inheritance."

Cline remembered. "It had to do with the fact that old women never die."

"That's right. They just hang on to life forever. Just like my father. He'll never die, Jon. He'll hang on for ten more years just to spite me, so I'll be too old to enjoy the money. It isn't fair."

Cline figured that Dana would be around thirty-six in ten years. He was ten years past that already.

Dana turned in her chair and looked at Cline with intense blue eyes, the eyes that were so startling with her dark hair and tanned skin.

"You could help me," she said. "I'll give you ten thousand dollars if you do."

The old man stirred slightly in the bed. Not much. He didn't seem capable of much.

Cline walked over and looked down at him. He wondered what it would be like to be so near to dying, and he thought about a line from Keats: "Many a time I have been half in love with easeful Death."

Maybe the old man felt that way. Maybe he wanted to die and just couldn't say so. Cline was pretty sure he would want to die if he were in that situation.

Well, there was no use in putting it off any longer. It was time to help the old man cease upon the midnight with no pain.

Cline took one of the flimsy pillows from the bed and prepared to press it to the old man's face.

Dana had assured him that it would be all right. "People die in places like that all the time. And I can guarantee you there won't be an autopsy. I won't allow it."

That was one reason she had put him in the Happy Hills Nursing Home. The old man's money would have bought him much better, but with more care and watchfulness on the part of the staff it would have been harder to do him in. Dana admitted to Cline that she'd planned it that way from the beginning.

Cline leaned down and the lamp threw a long shadow across the old man's bed, darkening his face.

Cline brought the pillow down.

The old man's eyes popped open. He stared wildly at Cline, at the descending pillow. He might have had difficulty recognizing Dana on her infrequent visits, but he

had no trouble at all recognizing what was about to happen
to him. He struggled with the covers and managed to get
one spidery hand out, raising it as if to protect his face.

Cline hesitated, stopping the pillow's descent. He didn't
know what to do. Dana had told him that her father wasn't
aware of anything, didn't even know where he was or what
was going on around him.

The old man's hand reached up and his scrawny fingers
tangled in the pillow case as he tried to force it away from
him. He had almost no strength.

Cline moved the pillow and leaned down. He could
smell the old man's breath, foul and hot.

"Wha . . . ?" the old man said. "Wh . . . why?"

Cline looked behind him, though the voice was lower
than a whisper. The door was securely closed. Cline looked
back at the man on the bed.

"Because," Cline said. He suddenly realized that he was
sweating profusely. "Because it's past your time. You have
to die. You should *want* to die." He brought the pillow
down again, feeling the almost intangible pressure of the
old man's hand.

"No." The word wheezed out of the old man's mouth.
"I don't want to die. I want to *live.*"

Why? Cline wondered. Why would anyone want to live
in that dark room with that rank smell, with that body that
was nothing but a husk?

He held his breath and pressed down hard on the pillow.

Cline needed the ten thousand. His salary at the university wasn't that bad, but he'd made a few terrible investments right before the oil bust and his retirement plans
had been set back five years. Worse, in need of some cash

in a hurry to cover one of the investments, he'd borrowed heavily and was now in danger of losing both his house and his car.

"It wouldn't be like you were killing him," Dana had said. They were at a seafood restaurant, a place known for the bounty of its buffet supper, and they had eaten crab and shrimp and gumbo until they couldn't eat any more. "He's practically dead already."

"But he's *not* dead," Cline pointed out. "There's a big difference."

"He doesn't even know me when I visit," Dana said, spearing one more shrimp on her cocktail fork and popping it into her red mouth. "He doesn't move, he doesn't talk, and he even smells dead."

Cline didn't give in that easily, but later that night, in the rumpled sheets of her bed, he capitulated.

"It would be almost like you were doing him a favor," Dana said. "After all, he doesn't have anything to live for."

The trouble was, no one had explained that to the old man. He clung to his life with a tenacity that surprised and frightened Cline, writhing under the thin covers and clawing at Cline's hands with amazing vigor and seeming almost to grow stronger the closer he got to death.

But Cline persisted, and finally the struggling stopped.

Cline took the pillow away from the ravaged face and put it on the bed. There would certainly be an investigation if he left things as they were. The old man had kicked the covers loose from both sides of the bed and the foot, and even the rubber sheet over the mattress pad had twisted beneath him.

The old man's bulging eyes stared blankly at the ceiling.

Cline straightened everything as best he could. He wanted it to look as if the old man had died peacefully in his sleep. The last thing he did was close the staring eyes.

Getting out of Happy Hills was easy. He had never been there before, and he had come in wearing a heavy tweed sports jacket, a beret, and very dark, very big sunglasses. He had walked right past the reception desk as if he knew exactly where he was going, because he did. Dana had given him explicit directions. Leaving, he had the jacket draped over his arm, the beret in one of its pockets. He was still wearing the sunglasses.

His precautions didn't really seem to matter much. The woman at the desk never looked up.

The sun slanted in through a gap in the curtains and fell across the table as Cline scanned his newspaper at the breakfast table the next day.

Cline had expected to see headlines about Randall's death; after all, at one time Randall had been a big name, a well-known man in financial circles.

But there was nothing. Cline stared at the obituaries, wondering if Randall's body had even been discovered yet. Happy Hills had seemed pretty lax, but not that lax.

Then the name Happy Hills caught his eye and he found himself reading an article about the suspicious circumstances of the death of one Gregory McCarthy.

"Jesus wept," Cline said.

He kept reading and discovered that McCarthy's son Thomas had gone to visit his father at Happy Hills late in the afternoon and found the old man's body. He had called for a supervisor, who had called the police. The police were investigating the receptionist's story of a mysterious visitor to McCarthy's room. The visitor was described in detail, right down to the color of his eyes, and the description fit Cline like a thousand-dollar suit. There was no mention of the sunglasses, the tweedy coat, the beret. An autopsy of the body had been ordered.

"Son of a bitch," Cline said, and he knew he'd been screwed.

Thomas McCarthy had been a student in the same class with Dana Randall. McCarthy was an athlete, and he had not performed well in class, but Cline had to admit that the young man was certainly handsome. He had broad shoulders, crisp and curly blond hair, green eyes, and a killer smile.

Cline, on the other hand, was balding, skinny, and prone to dandruff. He'd sometimes wondered how Dana Randall had been attracted to him, but he'd attributed it to his brains.

Now he knew it was something else. And it certainly hadn't been his goddamned brains.

He put the paper down on the breakfast table. It lay there between the cup of cooling coffee and the plate of half-eaten bacon and eggs while Cline tried to figure things out.

Why would Dana have tricked him into killing someone else's father?

Probably for the same reason he had been willing to kill hers.

Money.

She had set Cline up and played him for a sap. He had walked right into it. He remembered the way it had developed now, with her gradually allowing him more and more intimacy with her and finally mentioning her father's condition.

It had never occurred to him to check out the truth of things. He had simply believed her.

"Idiot!" he said aloud. What a fool he had been. Old man Randall was probably alive and well on a tropical island somewhere, or maybe he was living on a ranch in Colorado or in a condo in San Francisco. It didn't much matter. It was certain that he still controlled all the finances in the family. Dana had no doubt told the truth about one thing. She had no money of her own.

But Thomas McCarthy did. Or would, as soon as his father's will was probated. That part of the story had probably been true as well, except that it was Thomas rather than Dana who needed someone out of the way.

So Thomas and Dana had met in class, hit it off, and wondered how to get the money. They needed someone else. A patsy. That was the term, and Cline certainly fit the definition.

He could never go to the police, of course. How could he tell them that he was innocent of McCarthy's death, that it had all been a simple misunderstanding? They would get quite a laugh out of something like that.

There was no way out, even if he did go to the police. He had believed Dana when she said that there would be no investigation. His fingerprints were probably all over the old man's room, and he didn't doubt that the receptionist could pick him out of any lineup. She would have been coached carefully and provided with a good clear photo. All Dana had to do was deny everything.

But what about motive? What motive did he have for

killing Gregory McCarthy? None at all. Wouldn't the police
see that?

They might, he thought, but the fingerprints, the
description, the identification by the receptionist—those
would outweigh the lack of motive. The police wouldn't
give a damn, and the jury probably wouldn't either.

Cline was suddenly sweating as much as he had in the
old man's room. He stood up and walked to the telephone.
Maybe he was completely wrong. Maybe his imagination
was getting the better of him. He had to find out.

He reached for the phone.

Dana knew who the caller was before she picked up the
phone. She had been expecting the call.

"Hello?" she said.

"Dana?" Cline's voice was uncharacteristically weak.

"Who is this?" she asked. She held the phone in her
right hand and examined the fingernails of her left as she
talked. The polish was chipped on the index finger.

"You know who it is. It's Jon."

"Jon?"

"Jon Cline, goddammit."

"Oh, yes, the professor at the university. What can I do
for you, Dr. Cline?"

Her voice was cool and impersonal. Cline knew he
didn't have a chance against her. He hung up without
saying another word.

He knew there was no use in asking for his ten thousand
dollars.

Cline didn't go to the campus that day. He called his
department head and told her that he was coming down

with something. He spent most of the morning wondering how in the hell he had gotten himself into such a mess and what he was going to do about it.

Cline's problem was that he didn't think of himself as a murderer, but then he had never thought of himself as being someone who could be transformed into a total ass by a beautiful woman, either.

As far as the murder went, he was probably in the clear as long as he kept quiet. His description was like that of a lot of other men his age, and his fingerprints would be meaningless to the police. He had never been in the military, never been arrested.

It was the situation that was intolerable. He thought of himself as an intellectual, one who liked and appreciated the things of the mind and soul. Now he was a killer.

In a way, he knew that he was kidding himself about the intellectual bit. The material things of life were of great interest to him, and so were the luxuries. His interest in the ten thousand was evidence of the first, and his passion for Dana spoke amply of the second.

Another part of the problem, however, was that now Dana would always have him in her power. She didn't need him at the moment, but there might be an occasion when she would.

"Yes, Jon," she might say. "I want you to kill someone else for me. . . . What's that? You don't want to? But what if that receptionist from Happy Hills were to accidentally pass you on the street and recognize you? You wouldn't want that, would you, Jon?"

No, he wouldn't want that.

He went into his study, pulled a volume of Keats from

the loaded bookshelves, opened a bottle of Wild Turkey, and started to drink and read.

The liquor made everything clear.

He had done nothing really wrong. He had ended an old man's life, but the old man would not have lived long anyway. What did it matter that there was still some life in him? Couldn't he appreciate the fact that Cline had relieved him of the burdens of existence?

Look at Keats. There was a man who would have appreciated a little relief, someone like Cline who could deliver him from the weariness, the fever, and the fret, where men sit and hear each other groan.

It had been a mission worthy of Sleep, Death's brother. The old man was clinging to the tiller, and all Cline had done was push him over the side, nothing more.

It was all Dana's fault, anyway. She had asked him to do it, taken advantage of his weakness and his feelings for her. She was the one who should be punished. Along with her stud, Thomas McCarthy.

Cline couldn't go to the police. That would just be playing into Dana's hands.

He would have to take care of things himself. He took a last drink of the whiskey and got unsteadily to his feet. He tried to remember how much he had drunk. Too much, probably. It was already late afternoon. He had been sitting in the study all day. The bottle was nearly empty.

He went into the bedroom and began rummaging through the closet. After a while he found the pistol, a .38 revolver that he had bought five or six years before because of a rash of burglaries in the neighborhood. He had even learned how to use the pistol by taking a course at the firing range of a nearby community college, though he didn't remember much of what he had learned. He had kept the pistol in his nightstand for several weeks, then put it in a box in the closet where it had remained ever since.

The gun was not loaded. Cline had prudently removed the shells, but he found them in their green-and-yellow box. He extracted five of them and awkwardly thumbed them into the chambers.

He struggled clumsily into a sports coat, slipped the pistol into the pocket, and left the house.

There was a red Mazda Miata parked in front of Dana's house.

Cline had known somehow they would be there, but he was surprised that McCarthy was already wasting his inheritance by spending two or three thousand dollars over list for a toy car.

Cline parked his own car, a three-year-old Chevy Malibu that wasn't sporty but was at least made in America. When he got out, the pistol sagged against his hip.

He walked around to the back of the house. He was sure they would be taking a swim or maybe sitting on the deck, sipping white wine before dinner, which they would probably eat at one of the town's trendy restaurants.

They were there, all right, sitting in the same chairs where he and Dana had sat when she brought up the subject of her father's murder. They were both in bathing suits, Dana looking as if she'd just walked out of the *Sports Illustrated* swimsuit issue, McCarthy looking like something carved from a block of marble. The low sun slanted across their perfect bodies.

Cline reached for the pistol. The sight caught on the lining of the pocket, but he got it out after making only a minor tear in the fabric.

Then he found that he couldn't hold the weapon steady. His hand refused to stop shaking. *Too much Wild Turkey,* he thought.

His foot scraped on the wooden steps of the deck, and McCarthy heard him.

"Jesus Christ," he said, looking casually around. "It's the fucking masked avenger."

Cline thought the comment was unnecessarily crude as well as inaccurate. He wasn't wearing a mask.

Dana turned her blue eyes on him. "Don't be silly, Jon," she said.

Silly. That was what she thought of him. That was what they both thought of him. Well, they were wrong.

"Bitch," he said. He'd thought he could say it clearly, but it came out sounding like "Bish."

McCarthy laughed. "The old fart's drunk."

"Go home, Jon," Dana said. "There's nothing for you here."

"Used me," Cline said, muttering. "Used me."

"Of course I did," Dana told him. "What did you expect? Thomas and I needed a little help, and you seemed like just the person to provide it."

"Damn right," McCarthy said. "You don't think she fucked you because she liked it, do you?" He stood up and ran a hand over his completely hairless chest. "Not when she had something like this around."

Cline wanted to shoot McCarthy more than anything in the world, but the alcohol had not quite short-circuited his brain. He knew now that he wasn't going to kill anyone.

"Told me you usually couldn't get it up," he said to McCarthy. "Told me when you did, it wasn't any bigger than her little toe."

"Asshole," McCarthy said. He started across the deck toward Cline.

"Don't, Thomas," Dana said. "He's just trying to upset you."

"It worked," McCarthy said. He was reaching for the pistol. "I'm gonna take that thing and make you eat it, Cline."

Cline was trying to pull the trigger, but he couldn't hold the gun steady and his finger didn't seem to have any strength in it.

McCarthy's big hand closed over Cline's smaller one and crunched. Cline's fingers felt like chicken bones about to splinter and pop through his skin.

"Gimme that gun," McCarthy said.

Cline stubbornly held on, and McCarthy reached out to swat him in the face with a palm the size of a tennis racquet.

The palm connected, snapping Cline's head back, and the pistol went off though Cline wasn't conscious of having pulled the trigger. He staggered back into the yard and fell down.

When he looked up he saw McCarthy staring at his right shoulder. Bright red blood was running down over his chest.

"Are you all right, Thomas?" Dana said. She still hadn't gotten up.

"I'm gonna kill that sumbitch," McCarthy answered, coming down off the deck after Cline.

Cline's head seemed to be vibrating, and he couldn't get to his feet. He looked around him for the pistol, which he had dropped, but he couldn't see it. The whiskey he had drunk was burning in his stomach, and he felt it about to come up. He didn't try to stop it.

"Gross!" McCarthy said when Cline spewed the Wild Turkey on the lawn. McCarthy was obviously repulsed, but he didn't slow down. He kicked Cline in the chest with a right foot that could have propelled a field goal attempt through the posts at fifty-five yards.

Cline felt something in his chest crack as he tumbled backward. He didn't even try to get up this time, and McCarthy kicked him again, this time in the face. Cline's nose flattened with a grinding sound and he felt teeth break.

McCarthy reached down and grabbed a handful of Cline's thinning hair and hauled the older man to his feet. He held him up as he punched him repeatedly in the stomach and chest.

As the fist smashed into his ribs, Cline felt as if someone were stabbing his insides with a sharp knife. He opened his mouth to scream, and McCarthy unhinged his jaw with another blow from his open palm.

"Mine's bigger than yours, goddammit," McCarthy said.

In a frenzy of desperation, Cline yanked his head back as hard as he could, leaving McCarthy with a handful of hair and a bit of scalp to go with it. Blood trickled into Cline's eyes.

Cline's knees were wobbly, but not because he was drunk. He had never been more sober. The pain had done that for him. God, he wished he *were* drunk, now.

He stumbled backward, trying to escape McCarthy. Through foggy eyes he saw Dana calmly watching them from the porch. She didn't seem to be disturbed or excited in the least.

McCarthy was both. It was as if the blood had inflamed him. He caught up with Cline and grabbed his left arm. Cline slumped, and McCarthy brought the arm down sharply over his bent leg, snapping Cline's radius and ulna like dry cane.

Cline shrieked and nearly fainted, but McCarthy wasn't through.

He pulled Cline up and rammed his knee into Cline's testicles, raising Cline up a foot off the ground. Cline's mouth opened in the rictus of a scream, but only a dry cawing sound came out.

"Don't matter how big it is if you can't use it," McCarthy said.

Then he kicked Cline twice more. The toe of his shoe hit Cline's stomach and then nearly touched his backbone.

Cline lay on the ground, gagging. McCarthy was hardly winded. He spat on Cline's upturned face.

"Asshole," he said, turning to go back up on the deck.

Cline felt something hard and metallic under his right hand. It was the pistol. He got his fingers around it, lifted it, pushed himself up on one elbow.

"McCarthy," he tried to say. It came out of his ruined mouth sounding more like *Muhguthy*, but the boy turned around.

Cline wasn't sure he even had the strength to pull the trigger, but he did. He pulled it three times.

The first shot missed and zinged by Dana. She rolled out of the chair and fell to the deck. Cline might have laughed had he been able, but he wasn't. He was pulling the trigger again, and this time, as much by accident as by design, he hit McCarthy in the stomach, bringing a look of shocked surprise to McCarthy's face, a look that was obliterated by the next bullet, which hit McCarthy right in the mouth and punched out the back of his head, taking a surprisingly neat square of skull right along with it, as well as some other stuff of red and gray that was not nearly so neat.

McCarthy stood there for a second, and then something told him he was dead.

He fell like a stone.

The pistol dropped from Cline's fingers and he lay back on the grass.

Dana stood up and walked across the deck and onto the lawn. She stood for a second looking down at McCarthy's body without any noticeable regret.

Then she walked over to Cline. "I knew I could count on you, Jon," she said.

He looked at her pleadingly. He didn't understand.

"Daddy's never let me have enough money," she said. "That was the truth. But he's as healthy as a horse. The doctors are always amazed at his checkups. He'll live to be a hundred."

"Buh-buh . . ."

"I decided to get Thomas's money. We've been engaged for ten months. Time enough for Thomas to make a will leaving everything to me. I saw to that. His father was in the way, of course, but you took care of that for me yesterday."

Dana looked off into the distance. The sun was going down now, and her black hair looked even blacker in the dying light.

"Then Thomas was in the way. I didn't want him any

more than I wanted you, Jon. But you took care of that, too, didn't you?"

Cline looked at her in wonder. All he could feel was pain in his arm, his chest, his stomach, his head. It had all blended into one gigantic pain that threatened to tear him apart.

"Jealousy is a terrible thing, isn't it?" she said. "You killed Thomas's father, God knows why. And then you came over here to kill him." She looked back over her shoulder at Thomas's body. "You did it, too. But you didn't survive, did you?"

Cline realized that he was crying. The hot tears were rolling down his face.

"I was in the house when I heard the fighting," Dana said. "But by the time I could get here it was too late. I saw you shoot Thomas, and then you turned the gun on me, but you were weak and I wrestled it away from you."

She bent down and picked up the pistol. "Four shots. There should be at least one more bullet, shouldn't there, Jon?"

She pointed the pistol at Cline's face.

His broken mouth worked as he tried to speak, but no words came out.

"What is it that you want, Jon?" Dana asked.

The pain ran through him like a living flame, searing him inside and out. His head rang like a cathedral bell. He had never known that pain could be like that. He thought he might shudder to pieces, or maybe explode, if he just let himself go.

I want to die, he thought.

But then the words came, and with them a sudden understanding. "I . . . want to live," he managed to say.

Dana threw back her head and laughed. She had a beautiful laugh.

Then she bent down over Cline like a ministering angel and shot him between the eyes.

She dropped the pistol in the grass and walked back to the house, thinking of all the ways she would spend the money that would soon be hers.

Marble Mildred

Max Allan Collins

In June 1936, Chicago was in the midst of the Great Depression and a sweltering summer, and I was in the midst of Chicago. Specifically, on this Tuesday afternoon, the ninth to be exact, I was sitting on a sofa in the minuscule lobby of the Van Buren Hotel. The sofa had seen better days, and so had the hotel. The Van Buren was no flophouse, merely a moderately rundown residential hotel just west of the El tracks, near the LaSalle Street Station.

Divorce work wasn't the bread and butter of the A-1 Detective Agency, but we didn't turn it away. I use the editorial "we," but actually there was only one of us, me, Nathan Heller, "president" of the firm. And despite my high-flown title, I was just a down-at-the-heels dick reading a racing form in a seedy hotel's seedy lobby, waiting to see if a certain husband showed up in the company of another woman.

An other woman, that is, than the one he was married to, the dumpy, dusky dame who'd come to my office yesterday.

"I'm not as good-looking as I was fourteen years ago," she'd said, coyly, her voice honeyed by a southern drawl, "but I'm a darn sight younger looking than *some* women I know."

"You're a very handsome woman, Mrs. Bolton," I said, smiling, figuring she was fifty if she was a day, "and I'm sure there's nothing to your suspicions."

She had been a looker once, but she'd run to fat, and her badly hennaed hair and overdone makeup were no help; nor was the raccoon stole she wore over a faded floral-print housedress. The stole looked a bit ratty and in any case was hardly called for in this weather.

"Mr. Heller, they are more than suspicions. My husband is a successful businessman, with an office in the financial district. He is easy prey to gold diggers."

The strained formality of her tone made the raccoon stole make sense, somehow.

"This isn't the first time you've suspected him of infidelity."

"Unfortunately, no."

"Are you hoping for reconciliation, or has a lawyer advised you to establish grounds for divorce?"

"At this point," she said, calmly, the southern drawl making her words seem more casual than they were, "I wish only to know. Can you understand that, Mr. Heller?"

"Certainly. I'm afraid I'll need some details . . ."

She had them. Though they lived in Hyde Park, a quiet, quietly well-off residential area, Bolton was keeping a room at the Van Buren Hotel, a few blocks down the street from the very office in which we sat. Mrs. Bolton believed that he went to the hotel on assignations while pretending to leave town on business trips.

"How did you happen to find that out?" I asked her.

"His secretary told me," she said, with a crinkly little smile, proud of herself.

"Are you sure you need a detective? You seem to be doing pretty well on your own . . ."

The smile disappeared and she seemed quite serious now, digging into her big black purse and coming back with a folded wad of cash. She thrust it across the desk toward me, as if daring me to take it.

I don't take dares, but I do take money. And there was plenty of it: a hundred in tens and fives.

"My rate's ten dollars a day and expenses," I said, reluctantly, the notion of refusing money going against the grain. "A thirty-dollar retainer would be plenty . . ."

She nodded curtly. "I'd prefer you accept that. But it's all I can afford, remember; when it's gone, it's gone."

I wrote her out a receipt and told her I hoped to refund some of the money, though of course I hoped the opposite, and that I hoped to be able to dispel her fears about her husband's fidelity, though there was little hope of that, either. Hope was in short supply in Chicago, these days.

Right now, she said, Joe was supposedly on a business trip; but the secretary had called to confide in Mrs. Bolton that her husband had been in the office all day.

I had to ask the usual questions. She gave me a complete description (and a photo she'd had the foresight to bring), his business address, working hours, a list of places he was known to frequent.

And, so, I had staked out the hotel yesterday, starting late afternoon. I didn't start in the lobby. The hotel was a walk-up, the lobby on the second floor, the first floor leased out to a saloon, in the window of which I sat nursing beers and watching people stroll by. One of them, finally, was Joseph Bolton, a tall, nattily attired businessman about ten years his wife's junior; he was pleasant looking, but with his wire-rimmed glasses and receding brown hair was no Robert Taylor.

Nor was he enjoying feminine company, unless said company was already up in the hotel room before I'd arrived on the scene. I followed him up the stairs across the glorified landing of a lobby, where I paused at the desk while he went on up the next flight of stairs to his room—there were no elevators in the Van Buren—and, after buying a newspaper from the desk clerk, went up to Bolton's floor, the third of the four-story hotel, and watched from around a corner as he entered his room.

Back down in the lobby, I approached the desk clerk, an older guy with rheumy eyes and a blue bow tie. I offered him a buck for the name of the guest in room 3C.

"Bolton," he said.

"You're kidding," I said. "Let me see the register." I hadn't bothered coming in earlier to bribe a look because I figured Bolton would be here under an assumed name.

"What's it worth to you?" he asked.

"I already paid," I said, and turned his register around and looked in it. Joseph Bolton it was. Using his own goddamn name. That was a first.

"Any women?" I asked.

"Not that I know of," he said.

"Regular customer?"

"He's been living here a couple months."

"Living here? He's here every night?"

"I dunno. He pays his six bits a day, is all I know. I don't tuck him in."

I gave the guy half a buck to let me rent his threadbare

sofa. Sat for another couple of hours and followed two women upstairs. Both seemed to be hookers; neither stopped at Bolton's room.

At a little after eight, Bolton left the hotel and I followed him over to Adams Street, to the Berghoff, the best German restaurant for the money in the loop. What the hell—I hadn't eaten yet either. We both dined alone.

That night I phoned Mrs. Bolton with my report, such as it was.

"He has a woman in his room," she insisted.

"It's possible," I allowed.

"Stay on the job," she said, and hung up.

I stayed on the job. That is, the next afternoon I returned to the Van Buren Hotel, or anyway to the saloon underneath it, and drank beers and watched the world go by. Now and then the world would go up the hotel stairs. Men I ignored; women that looked like hookers I ignored. One woman, who showed up around four-thirty, I did not ignore.

She was as slender and attractive a woman as Mildred Bolton was not, though she was only a few years younger. And her wardrobe was considerably more stylish than my client's—high-collared white dress with a bright, colorful figured print, white gloves, white shoes, a felt hat with a wide turned-down brim.

She did not look like the sort of woman who would be stopping in at the Van Buren Hotel; but stop in she did.

So did I. I trailed her up to the third floor, where she was met at the door of Bolton's room by a male figure. I just got a glimpse of the guy, but he didn't seem to be Bolton. She went inside.

I used a pay phone in the saloon downstairs and called Mrs. Bolton in Hyde Park.

"I can be there in forty minutes," she said.

"What are you talking about?"

"I want to catch them together. I'm going to claw that hussy's eyes out."

"Mrs. Bolton, you don't want to do that . . ."

"I most certainly do. You can go home, Mr. Heller. You've done your job, and nicely."

And she had hung up.

I had mentioned to her that the man in her husband's room did not seem to be her husband; but that apparently didn't matter. Now I had a choice: I could walk back up to my office and write Mrs. Bolton out a check refunding seventy of her hundred dollars, goddamn it (ten bucks a day, ten bucks expenses—she'd pay for my bribes and beers).

Or I could do the Christian thing and wait around and try to defuse this thing before it got even uglier.

I decided to do the latter. Not because it was the Christian thing—I wasn't a Christian, after all—but because I might be able to convince Mrs. Bolton she needed a few more days' work out of me, to figure out what was really going on here. It seemed to me she could use a little more substantial information, if a divorce was to come out of this. It also seemed to me I could use the money.

I don't know how she arrived—whether by El or streetcar or bus or auto—but as fast as she was walking, it could've been on foot. She was red in the face, eyes hard and round as marbles, fists churning as she strode, her head floating above the incongruous raccoon stole.

I hopped off my bar stool and caught her at the sidewalk.

"Don't go in there, Mrs. Bolton," I said, taking her arm gently.

She swung it away from me, held her head back and, short as she was, looked down at me, nostrils flared. I felt like a matador who dropped his cape.

"You've been discharged for the day, Mr. Heller," she said.

"You still need my help. You're not going about this the right way."

With indignation she began, "My husband . . ."

"Your husband isn't in there. He doesn't even get off work till six."

She swallowed. The redness of her face seemed to fade some; I was quieting her down.

Then fucking fate stepped in, in the form of that swanky dame in the felt hat, who picked that very moment to come strolling out of the Van Buren Hotel, like it was the goddamn Palmer House. On her arm was a young man, perhaps eighteen, perhaps twenty, in a cream-color seer-sucker suit and a gold tie with a pale complexion and sky blue eyes and corn-silk blond hair; he and the woman on his arm shared the same sensitive mouth.

"Whore!" somebody shouted.

Who else? My client.

I put my hand over my face and shook my head and wished I was dead, or at least in my office.

"Degenerate!" Mrs. Bolton sang out. She rushed toward the slender woman, who reared back, properly horrified. The young man gripped the woman's arm tightly; whether to protect her or himself, it wasn't quite clear.

Well, the sidewalks were filled with people who'd gotten

off work, heading for the El or the LaSalle Street Station, so we had an audience. Yes we did.

And Mrs. Bolton was standing nose to nose with the startled woman, saying defiantly, "I am *Mrs.* Bolton—you've been up to see my husband!"

"Why, Mrs. Bolton," the woman said, backing away as best she could. "Your husband is not in his room."

"Liar!"

"If he were in the room, I wouldn't have been in there myself, I assure you."

"Lying whore . . ."

"Okay," I said, wading in, taking Mrs. Bolton by the arm, less gently this time, "that's enough."

"Don't talk to my mother that way," the young man said to Mrs. Bolton.

"I'll talk to her any way I like, you little degenerate."

And the young man slapped my client. It was a loud, ringing slap and drew blood from one corner of her wide mouth.

I pointed a finger at the kid's nose. "That wasn't nice. Back away."

My client's eyes were glittering; she was smiling, a blood-flecked smile that wasn't the sanest thing I ever saw. Despite the gleeful expression, she began to scream things at the couple: "Whore! Degenerate!"

"Oh Christ," I said, wishing I'd listened to my old man and finished college.

We were encircled by a crowd who watched all this with bemused interest, some people smiling, others frowning, others frankly amazed. In the street the clop-clop of an approaching mounted police officer, interrupted in the pursuit of parking violators, cut through the din. A tall, lanky officer, he climbed off his mount and pushed through the crowd.

"What's going on here?" he asked.

"This little degenerate hit me," my client said, wearing her bloody mouth and her righteous indignation like medals, and she grabbed the kid by the tie and yanked the poor son of a bitch by it, jerking him silly.

It made me laugh. It was amusing only in a sick way, but I was sick enough to appreciate it.

"That'll be all of that," the officer said. "Now what happened here?"

I filled him in, in a general way, while my client interrupted with occasional non sequiturs; the mother and son just stood there looking chagrined about being the center of attention for perhaps a score of onlookers.

"I want that dirty little brute arrested," Mrs. Bolton said, through an off-white picket fence of clenched teeth. "I'm a victim of assault!"

The poor shaken kid was hardly a brute, and he was cleaner than most, but he admitted having struck her, when the officer asked him.

"I'm going to have to take you in, son," the officer said.

The boy looked like he might cry. Head bowed, he shrugged and his mother, eyes brimming with tears herself, hugged him.

The officer went to a call box and summoned a squad car and soon the boy was sent away, the mother waiting pitifully at the curb as the car pulled off, the boy's pale face looking back, a sad cameo in the window.

I was at my client's side.

"Let me help you get home, Mrs. Bolton," I said, taking her arm again.

She smiled tightly, patronizingly, withdrew her arm. "I'm fine, Mr. Heller. I can take care of myself. I thank you for your assistance."

And she rolled like a tank through what remained of the crowd, toward the El station.

I stood there a while, trying to gather my wits; it would have taken a better detective than yours truly to find them, however, so, finally, I approached the shattered woman who still stood at the curb. The crowd was gone. So was the mounted officer. All that remained were a few horse apples and me.

"I'm sorry about all that," I told her.

She looked at me, her face smooth, her eyes sad; they were a darker blue than her son's. "What's your role in this?"

"I'm an investigator. Mrs. Bolton suspects her husband of infidelity."

She laughed harshly—a very harsh laugh for such a refined woman. "My understanding is that Mrs. Bolton has suspected that for some fourteen years—and without foundation. But at this point, it would seem moot, one would think."

"Moot? What are you talking about?"

"The Boltons have been separated for months. Mr. Bolton is suing her for divorce."

"What? Since when?"

"Why, since January."

"Then Bolton *does* live at the Van Buren Hotel, here?"

"Yes. My brother and I have known Mr. Bolton for years. My son Charles came up to Chicago recently, to find work, and Joe—Mr. Bolton—is helping him find a job."

"You're, uh, not from Chicago?"

"I live in Woodstock. I'm a widow. Have you any other questions?"

"Excuse me, ma'am. I'm sorry about this. Really. My client misled me about a few things." I tipped my hat to her.

She warmed up a bit; gave me a smile. Tentative, but a smile. "Your apology is accepted, mister . . . ?"

"Heller," I said. "Nathan. And your name?"

"Marie Winston," she said, and extended her gloved hand.

I grasped it, smiled.

"Well," I said, shrugged, smiled, tipped my hat again and headed back for my office.

It wasn't the first time a client had lied to me, and it sure wouldn't be the last. But I'd never been lied to in quite this way. For one thing, I wasn't sure Mildred Bolton knew she *was* lying. This lady clearly did not have all her marbles.

I put the hundred bucks in the bank and the matter out of my mind, until I received a phone call, on the afternoon of June 14.

"This is Marie Winston, Mr. Heller. Do you remember me?"

At first, frankly, I didn't; but said, "Certainly. What can I do for you, Mrs. Winston?"

"That . . . incident out in front of the Van Buren Hotel last Wednesday, which you witnessed . . ."

"Oh yes. What about it?"

"Mrs. Bolton has insisted on pressing charges. I wonder if you could appear in police court tomorrow morning and explain what happened?"

"Well . . ."

"Mr. Heller, I would greatly appreciate it."

I don't like turning down attractive women, even on the telephone; but there was more to it than that: the emotion in her voice got to me.

"Well, sure," I said.

So the next morning I headed over to the south Loop police court and spoke my piece. I kept to the facts, which I felt would pretty much exonerate all concerned. The circumstances were, as they say, extenuating.

Mildred Bolton, who glared at me as if I'd betrayed her, approached the bench and spoke of the young man's "unprovoked assault." She claimed to be suffering physically and mentally from the blow she'd received. The latter, at least, was believable. Her eyes were round and wild as she answered the judge's questions.

When the judge fined young Winston one hundred dollars, Mrs. Bolton stood in her place in the gallery and began to clap. The judge looked at her, too startled to rap his gavel and demand order; then she flounced out of the courtroom, very girlishly, tossing her raccoon stole over her shoulder, exulting in her victory.

An embarrassed silence fell across the room. And it's hard to embarrass hookers, a brace of which were awaiting their turn at the docket.

Then the judge pounded his gavel and said, "The court vacates this young man's fine."

Winston, who'd been hangdog throughout the proceedings, brightened like his switch had been turned on; he pumped his lawyer's hand and turned to his mother, seated behind him just beyond the railing, and they hugged.

On the way out Marie Winston, smiling gently, touched my arm and said, "Thank you very much, Mr. Heller."

"I don't think I made much difference."

"I think you did. The judge vacated the fine, after all."

"Hell, I had nothing to do with that. Mildred was your star witness."

"In a way I guess she was."

"I notice her husband wasn't here."

Son Charles spoke up. "No, he's at work. He . . . well, he thought it was better he not be here. We figured *that woman* would be here, after all."

" 'That woman' is sick."

"In the head," Charles said bitterly.

"That's right. You or I could be sick that way, too. Somebody ought to help her."

Marie Winston, straining to find some compassion for Mildred Bolton, said, "Who would you suggest?"

"Damn it," I said, "the husband. He's been with her fourteen years. She didn't get this way overnight. The way I see it, he's got a responsibility to get her some goddamn *help* before he dumps her by the side of the road."

Mrs. Winston smiled at that, some compassion coming through after all. "You have a very modern point of view, Mr. Heller."

"Not really. I'm not even used to talkies yet. Anyway, I'll see you, Mrs. Winston. Charles."

And I left the graystone building and climbed in my '32 Auburn and drove back to my office. I parked in the alley in my space, and walked over to the Berghoff for lunch. I think I hoped to find Bolton there. But he wasn't.

I went back to the office and puttered a while; I had a pile of retail credit-risk checks to whittle away at.

Hell with it, I thought, and walked over to Bolton's office building, a narrow, fifteen-story white granite structure just behind the Federal Reserve on West Jackson, next to the El. Bolton was doing all right—better than me, certainly—but as a broker he was in the financial district only by a hair. No doubt he was a relatively small-time insurance broker, making twenty or twenty-five grand a year.

Big money by my standards, but a lot of guys over at the Board of Trade spilled more than that.

There was no lobby really, just a wide hall between facing rows of shops, travel agency, cigar store. A uniformed elevator operator, a skinny, pockmarked guy about my age, was waiting for a passenger; I was it.

"Tenth floor," I told him, and he took me up.

He was pulling open the cage doors when we heard the air crack, three times.

"What the hell was that?" he said.

"It wasn't a car backfiring," I said. "You better stay here."

I moved cautiously out into the hall. The elevators came up a central shaft, with a squared-off C of offices all about. I glanced at the names on the pebbled glass in the wood-partition walls, and finally lit upon BOLTON AND SCHMIDT, INSURANCE BROKERS. I swallowed and moved cautiously in that direction as the door flew open and a young woman flew out, a dark-haired dish of maybe twenty with wide eyes and a face drained of blood, her silk stockings flashing as she rushed my way.

She fell into my arms and I said, "Are you wounded?"

"No," she swallowed, "but somebody is."

The poor kid was gasping for air; I hauled her toward the bank of elevators. Even under the strain, I was enjoying the feel and smell of her.

"You wouldn't be Joseph Bolton's secretary, by any chance?" I asked, helping her onto the elevator.

She nodded, eyes still huge.

"Take her down," I told the operator.

And I headed back for that office. It was barely in sight when the door opened again and Joseph Bolton lurched out. He had a gun in his hand. His light brown suitcoat was splotched with blood in several places; so was his right arm. He wasn't wearing his eyeglasses, which made his face seem naked somehow. His expression seemed at once frightened, pained and sorrowful.

He staggered toward me like a child taking its first steps, and I held my arms out to him like daddy. But they were more likely his last steps: he fell to the marble floor and began to writhe, tracing abstract designs in his own blood on the smooth surface.

I moved toward him and he pointed the gun at me, a little .32 revolver. "Stay away! Stay away!"

"Okay, bud, okay," I said.

I heard someone laughing.

A woman.

I looked up and in the doorway, feet planted like a giant surveying a puny world, was dumpy little Mildred, in her floral housedress and raccoon stole. Her mug was split in a big, goofy smile.

"Don't pay any attention to him, Mr. Heller," she said, lightly. "He's just faking."

"He's shot to shit, lady!" I said.

Keeping their distance out of respect and fear were various tenth-floor tenants, standing near their various offices, as if witnessing some strange performance.

"Keep her away from me!" Bolton managed to shout.

His mouth was bubbling with blood. His body moved slowly across the marble floor, like a slug, leaving a slimy red trail.

I moved to Mrs. Bolton, stood between her and Bolton. "You just take it easy . . ."

Mrs. Bolton, giggling, peeked out from in back of me. "Look at him, fooling everybody."

"You behave," I told her. Then I called out to a businessman of about fifty near the elevators. I asked him if there were any doctors in the building, and he said yes, and I said then for Christsake go get one.

"Why don't you get up and stop faking?" she said teasingly to her fallen husband, the southern drawl dripping off her words, as she craned her neck around me to see him, like she couldn't bear to miss a moment of the show.

"Keep her away! Keep her away!"

Bolton continued to writhe like a wounded snake, but he kept clutching that gun, and wouldn't let anyone near him. He would cry out that he couldn't breathe, beating his legs against the floor; but he seemed always conscious of his wife's presence. He would move his head so as to keep my body between him and her round, cold, glittering eyes.

"Don't you mind Joe, Mr. Heller. He's just putting on an act."

If so, I had a hunch it was his final performance.

And now he began to scream in pain.

I approached him and he looked at me with tears in his eyes, eyes that bore the confusion of a child in pain, and he relented, allowed me to come close, handed me the gun, like he was offering a gift. I accepted it, by the nose of the thing, and dropped it in my pocket.

"Did you shoot yourself, Mr. Bolton?" I asked him.

"Keep that woman away from me," he managed, lips bloody.

"He's not really hurt," his wife said, mincingly, from the office doorway.

"Did your wife shoot you?"

"Just keep her away . . ."

Two people in white came rushing toward us—a doctor and a nurse—and I stepped aside, but the doctor, a middle-aged, rather heavyset man with glasses, asked if I'd give him a hand. I said sure and pitched in.

Bolton was a big man, nearly two hundred pounds I'd say, and pretty much dead weight; we staggered toward the elevator like drunks. Like Bolton himself had staggered toward me, actually. The nurse tagged along.

So did Mrs. Bolton.

The nurse, young, blond, slender, did her best to keep Mrs. Bolton out of the elevator; but Mrs. Bolton pushed her way through like a fullback. The doctor and I, bracing Bolton, couldn't help out the young nurse.

Bolton, barely conscious, said, "Please . . . please, keep her away."

"Now, now," Mrs. Bolton said, the violence of her entry into the elevator forgotten (by her), standing almost primly now, hands folded over the big black purse, "everything will be all right, dear. You'll see."

Bolton began to moan; the pain it suggested wasn't entirely physical.

On the thirteenth floor, a second doctor met us and took my place hauling Bolton, and I went ahead and opened the door onto a waiting room where patients, having witnessed the doctor and nurse race madly out of the office, were milling about expectantly. The nurse guided the doctors and their burden down a hall into an X-ray room. The nurse shut the door on them and faced Mrs. Bolton with a firm look.

"I'm sorry, Mrs. Bolton, you'll have to wait."

"Is that so?" she said.

"Mrs. Bolton," I said, touching her arm.

She glared at me. "Who invited you?"

I resisted the urge to say, *you did, you fucking cow,* and just stood back while she moved up and down the narrow corridor between the offices and examining rooms, searching for a door that would lead her to her beloved husband. She trundled up and down, grunting, talking to herself and the nurse looked at me helplessly.

"She *is* the wife," I said, with a facial shrug.

The nurse sighed heavily and went to a door adjacent to the X-ray room and called out to Mrs. Bolton; Mrs. Bolton whirled and looked at her fiercely.

"You can view your husband's treatment from in here," the nurse said.

Mrs. Bolton smiled in tight triumph and drove her taxi cab of a body into the room. I followed her. Don't ask me why.

A wide glass panel looked in on the X-ray room. Mrs. Bolton climbed onto an examination table and got up on her knees and watched the flurry of activity beyond the glass, as her husband lay on a table being attended by the pair of frantic doctors.

"Did you shoot him, Mrs. Bolton?" I asked her.

She frowned but did not look at me. "Are *you* still here?"

"You lied to me, Mrs. Bolton."

"No I didn't. And I didn't shoot him, either."

"What happened in there?"

"I never touched that gun." She was moving her head side to side, like somebody in the bleachers trying to see past the person sitting in front.

"Did your husband shoot himself?"

She made a childishly smug face. "Joe's just faking to get everybody's sympathy. He's not really hurt."

The door opened behind me and I turned to see a police officer step in.

The officer frowned at us, and shook his head as if to say, "Oh no." It was an understandable response: it was the same cop, the mounted officer, who'd come upon the disturbance outside the Van Buren Hotel. Not surprising, really—this part of the Loop was his beat, or anyway his horse's.

He crooked his finger for me to step out in the hall and did.

"I heard a murder was being committed up on the tenth floor of one-sixty-six," he explained, meaning 166 West Jackson. "Do you know what happened? Did you see it?"

I told him what I knew, which for being on the scene was damned little.

"Did she do it?" the officer asked.

"The gun was in the husband's hand," I shrugged. "Speaking of which . . ."

And I took the little revolver out of my pocket, holding the gun by its nose again.

"What make is this?" the officer said, taking it.

"I don't recognize it."

He read off the side: "Narizmande Eibar Spair. Thirty-two caliber."

"It got the job done."

He held the gun so that his hand avoided the grip; tried to break it open, but couldn't.

"What's wrong with this thing?" he said.

"The trigger's been snapped on empty shells, I'd say."

"What does that mean?"

"It means that after six slugs were gone, the shooter kept shooting. Just once around wouldn't drive the shells into the barrel like that."

"Judas," the officer said.

The X-ray room's door opened and the doctor I'd shared the elevator and Bolton's dead weight with stepped into the hall, bloody and bowed.

"He's dead," the doctor said, wearily. "Choked to death on his own blood, poor bastard."

I said nothing; just glanced at the cop, who shrugged.

"The wife's in there," I said, pointing.

But I was pointing to Mrs. Bolton, who had stepped out into the hall. She was smiling pleasantly.

She said, "You're not going to frighten me about Joe. He's a great big man and as strong as a horse. Of course I begin to think he ought to go to the hospital this time— for a while."

"Mrs. Bolton," the doctor said, flatly, with no sympathy whatsoever, "your husband is dead."

Like a spiteful child, she stuck out her tongue. "Liar," she said.

The doctor sighed, turned to the cop. "Shall I call the morgue, or would you like the honor?"

"You should make the call, doctor," the officer said.

Mrs. Bolton moved slowly toward the door to the X ray room, from which the other doctor, his smock blood spattered, emerged. She seemed to lose her footing, then

and I took her arm yet again. This time she accepted the
help. I walked her into the room and she approached the
body, stroked its brow with stubby fingers.

"I can't believe he'd go," she said.

From behind me, the doctor said, "He's dead, Mrs.
Bolton. Please leave the room."

Still stroking her late husband's brow, she said, "He
feels cold. So cold."

She kissed his cheek.

Then she smiled down at the body and patted its head, as
one might a sleeping child, and said, "He's got a beautiful
head, hasn't he?"

The officer stepped into the room and said, "You'd
better come along with me, Mrs. Bolton. Captain Stege
wants to talk to you."

"You're making a terrible mistake. I didn't shoot him."

He took her arm; she assumed a regal posture. He asked
her if she would like him to notify any relatives or friends.

"I have no relatives or friends," she said, proudly. "I
never had anybody or wanted anybody except Joe."

A crowd was waiting on the street. Damn near a mob,
and at the forefront were the newshounds, legmen and
cameramen alike. Cameras were clicking away as Davis of
the *News* and a couple of others blocked the car waiting
at the curb to take Mrs. Bolton to the Homicide Bureau.
The mounted cop, with her in tow, brushed them and
their questions aside and soon the car, with her in it, was
inching into the late afternoon traffic. The reporters and
photogs began flagging cabs to take quick pursuit, but
snide, boyish Davis lingered to ask me a question.

"What were you doing here, Heller?"

"Getting a hangnail looked at up at the doctor's office."

"Fuck, Heller, you got blood all over you!"

I shrugged, lifted my middle finger. "Hell of a hang-nail."

He smirked and I smirked and pushed through the crowd and hoofed it back to my office.

I was sitting at my desk, about an hour later, when the phone rang.

"Get your ass over here!"

"Captain Stege?"

"No, Walter Winchell. You were an eyewitness to a homicide, Heller! Get your ass over here!"

The phone clicked in my ear and I shrugged to nobody and got my hat and went over to the First District Station, entering off 11th. It was a new, modern, nondescript high rise; if this was the future, who needed it.

In Stege's clean little office, the clean little cop looked out his black-rimmed, round-lensed, glasses at me from behind his desk and said, "Did you see her do it?"

"I told the officer at the scene all about it, Captain."

"You didn't make a statement."

"Get a stenographer in here and I will."

He did and I did.

That seemed to cool the stocky little cop down. He and I had been adversaries once, and were getting along better these days. But there was still a strain.

Thought gripped his doughy, owlish countenance. "How do you read it, Heller?"

"I don't know. He had the gun. Maybe it was suicide."

"Everybody in that building agrees with you. Bolton's been having a lot of trouble with his better half. They think she drove him to suicide, finally. But there's a hitch."

"Yeah?"

"Suicides don't usually shoot themselves five times, two of 'em in the back."

I had to give him that.

"You think she's nuts?" Stege asked.

"Nuttier than a fruitcake."

"Maybe. But that was murder—premeditated."

"Oh, I doubt that, Captain. Don't you know a crime of passion when you see it? Doesn't the unwritten law apply to women as well as men?"

"The answer to your question is yes to the first, and no to the second. You want to see something?"

"Sure."

From his desk he handed me a small slip of paper.

It was a receipt for a gun sold on June 11 by the Hammond Loan Company, Hammond, Indiana, to a Mrs. Sarah Weston.

"That was in her purse," Stege said, smugly. "Along with a powder puff, a hanky and some prayer leaflets."

"And you think Sarah Weston is just a name Mrs. Bolton used to buy the .32 from this pawn shop?"

"Certainly. And that slip—found in a narrow side pocket in the lining of her purse—proves premeditation."

"Does it, Captain?" I said, smiling, standing, hat in hand. "It seems to me premeditation would have warned her to get *rid* of that receipt. But then, what do I know? I'm no cop." From the doorway I said, "Just a detective."

And I left him there to mull that over.

In the corridor, on my way out, Sam Backus buttonholed me.

"Got a minute for a pal, Nate?"

"Sam, if we were pals, I'd see you someplace but in court."

Sam was with the Public Defender's office, and I'd bumped into him from time to time, dating back to my cop days. He was a conscientious and skillful attorney who, in better times, might have had a lucrative private practice; in times like these, he was glad to have a job. Sam's sharp features and receding hairline gave the smallish man a ferretlike appearance; he was similarly intense, too.

"My client says she employed you to do some work for her," he said, in a rush. "She'd like you to continue . . ."

"Wait a minute, wait a minute—your client? Not Mrs. Mildred Bolton?"

"Yes."

"She's poison. You're on your own."

"She tells me you were given a hundred-dollar retainer."

"Well, that's true, but I figure I earned it."

"She figures you owe her some work, or some dough."

"Sam, she lied to me. She misrepresented herself and her intentions." I was walking out of the building and he was staying right with me.

"She's a disturbed individual. And she's maintaining she didn't kill her husband."

"They got her cold." I told him about Stege's evidence.

"It could've been planted," he said, meaning the receipt. "Look, Bolton's secretary was up there, and Mrs. Bolton says he and the girl—an Angela something, sounds like 'who-you'—were having an affair."

"I thought the affair was supposed to be with Marie Winston."

"Her, too. Bolton must've been a real ladies' man. And the Winston woman was up there at that office this afternoon, too, before the shooting."

"Was she there during the shooting, though?"

"I don't know. I need to find out. The Public Defender's office doesn't have an investigative staff, you know that, Nate. And I can't afford to hire anybody, and I don't have the time to do the legwork myself. You owe her some days. Deliver."

He had a point.

I gathered some names from Sam, and the next morning I began to interview the participants.

"An affair with Joe?" Angela Houyoux said. "Why, that's nonsense."

We were in the outer office of BOLTON AND SCHMIDT. She'd given me the nickel tour of the place, one outer office, and two inner ones, the one to the south having been Bolton's. The crime scene told me nothing. Angela, the pretty, twentyish, sweet-smelling dark-haired beauty who'd tumbled into my arms and the elevator yesterday, did.

"I was rather shaken by Mrs. Bolton's behavior at first— and his. But then it became rather matter-of-fact to come to the office and find the glass in the door broken, or Mr. Bolton with his hands cut from taking a knife away from Mrs. Bolton. After a few weeks, I grew quite accustomed to having dictation interrupted while Mr. and Mrs. Bolton scuffled and fought and yelled. Lately they argued about Mrs. Winston a lot."

"How was your relationship with Mrs. Bolton?"

"Spotty, I guess you'd call it. Sometimes she'd seem to think I was interested in her husband. Other times she'd confide in me like a sister. I never said much to her. I'd just jerk my shoulders or just look at her kind of sympathetic. I had the feeling she didn't have anybody else to talk to about this. She'd cry and say her husband was unfaithful—

I didn't dare point out they'd been separated for a year and that Mr. Bolton had filed for divorce and all. One time . . . well, maybe I shouldn't say it."

"Say it."

"One time she said she 'just might kill' her husband. She said they never convict a woman for murder in Cook County."

Others in the building at West Jackson told similar tales. Bolton's business partner Schmidt wondered why Bolton bothered to get an injunction to keep his wife out of the office, but then refused to mail her her temporary alimony, giving her a reason to come to the office all the time.

"He would dole out the money, two or three dollars at a time," Schmidt said. "He could have paid her what she had coming for a month, or at least a week—Joe made decent money. It would've got rid of her. Why dole it out?"

The elevator operator I'd met yesterday had a particularly wild yarn.

"Yesterday, early afternoon, Mr. Bolton got on at the ninth floor; he seemed in an awful hurry and said, 'Shoot me up to eleven.' I had a signal to stop at ten, so I made the stop and Mrs. Bolton came charging aboard. Mr. Bolton was right next to me. He kind of hid behind me and said, 'For God's sake, she'll kill us both!' I sort of forced the door closed on her, and she stood there in the corridor and raised her fist and said, 'Goddamnit, I'll fix you!' I guess she meant Bolton, not me."

"Apparently."

"Anyway, I took him up to eleven and he kind of sighed and as he got off he said, 'It's just hell, isn't it?' I said it was a damn shame he couldn't do anything about it."

"This was yesterday."

"Yes, sir. Not long before he was killed."

"Did it occur to you, at the time, it might lead to that?"

"No, sir. It was pretty typical, actually. I helped him escape from her before. And I kept her from getting on the elevator downstairs, sometimes. After all, he had an injunction to keep her from 'molesting him at his place of business,' he said."

Even the heavyset doctor up on thirteen found time for me.

"I think they were *both* sick," he said, rather bitterly I thought.

"What do you mean, doctor?"

"I mean that I've administered more first aid to that man than a battlefield physician. That woman has beaten her husband, cut him with a knife, with a razor, created such commotions and scenes with such regularity that the patrol wagon coming for Mildred is a commonplace occurrence on West Jackson."

"How well did you know Bolton?"

"We were friendly. God knows I spent enough time with him, patching him up. He should've been a much more successful man than he was, you know. She drove him out of one job and another. I never understood him."

"Oh?"

"Well, they live, or lived, in Hyde Park. That's a university neighborhood. Fairly refined, very intellectual, really."

"Was Bolton a scholar?"

"He had bookish interests. He liked having the University of Chicago handy. Now why would a man of his sensibilities endure a violent harridan like Mildred Bolton?"

"In my trade, Doc," I said, "we call that a mystery."

I talked to more people. I talked to a pretty, blond legal

secretary named Peggy O'Reilly who, in 1933, had been employed by Ocean Accident and Guarantee Company where Joseph Bolton Jr. was a business associate.

"His desk was four feet from mine," she said. "But I never went out to dinner with him. There was no social contact whatsoever, but Mrs. Bolton didn't believe that. She came into the office and accused me of—well, called me a 'dirty hussy,' if you must know. I asked her to step out into the hall where we wouldn't attract so much attention, and she did—and proceeded to tear my clothes off me. She tore the clothes off my body, scratched my neck, my face, kicked me, it was horrible. The attention it attracted, oh, oh—several hundred people witnessed the sight; two nice men pulled her off of me. I was badly bruised and out of the office a week. When I came back, Mr. Bolton had been discharged."

A pattern was forming here, one I'd seen before; but usually it was the wife who was battered and yet who somehow endured and even encouraged the twisted union. Only Bolton was a battered husband, a strapping man who never turned physically on his abusing wife; his only punishment had been to withhold that money from her, dole it out a few bucks at a time. That was the only satisfaction, the only revenge, he'd been able to extract.

At the Van Buren Hotel I knocked on the door of what had been Bolton's room. 3C.

Young Charles Winston answered. He looked terrible. Pale as milk, only not near as healthy. Eyes bloodshot. He was in a T-shirt and boxer shorts. The other times I'd seen him he'd been fully and even nattily attired.

"Put some clothes on," I said. "We have to talk."

In the saloon below the hotel we did that very thing.

"Joe was a great guy," he said, eyes brimming with tears. He would have cried into his beer, only he was having a mixed drink. I was picking up the tab, so Mildred Bolton was buying it.

"Is your mother still in town?"

He looked up with sharp curiosity. "No. She's back in Woodstock. Why?"

"She was up at the office shortly before Bolton was killed."

"I know. I was there, too."

"Oh?" Now, that was news.

"We went right over, after the hearing."

"To tell him how it came out?"

"Yes, and to thank him. You see, after that incident out in front, last Wednesday, when they took me off to jail, Mother went to see Joe. They met at the Twelfth Street Bus Depot. She asked him if he would take care of my bail—she could have had her brother do it, but I'd have had to spend the night in jail first." He smiled fondly. "Joe went right over to the police station with the money and got me out."

"That was white of him."

"Sure was. Then we met Mother over at the taproom of the Auditorium Hotel."

Very posh digs; interesting place for folks who lived at the Van Buren to be hanging out.

"Unfortunately, I'd taken time to stop back at the hotel to pick up some packages my mother had left behind. Mrs. Bolton must've been waiting here for me, and she followed me to the Auditorium taproom, where she attacked me with her fists, and told the crowd in no uncertain terms, and in a voice to wake the dead, that my mother was"—

he shook his head—" 'nothing but a whore' and such. Finally the management ejected her."

"Was your mother in love with Joe?"

He looked at me sharply. "Of course not. They were friendly. That's the extent of it."

"When did you and your mother leave Bolton's office?"

"Yesterday? About one-thirty. Mrs. Bolton was announced as being in the outer office, and we just got the hell out."

"Neither of you lingered."

"No. Are you going to talk to my mother?"

"Probably."

"I wish you wouldn't," he said glumly.

I drank my beer, studying the kid.

"Maybe I won't have to," I said, smiled at him, patted his shoulder, and left.

I met with Public Defender Backus in a small interrogation room at the First District Station.

"Your client is guilty," I said.

I was sitting. He was standing. Pacing.

"The secretary was in the outer office at all times," I said. "In view of other witnesses. The Winstons left around one-thirty. They were seen leaving by the elevator operator on duty."

"One of them could have sneaked back up the stairs . . ."

"I don't think so. Anyway, this meeting ends my participation, other than a report I'll type up for you. I've used up the hundred."

From my notes I read off summaries of the various interviews I'd conducted. He finally sat, sweat beading his brow, eyes slitted behind the glasses.

"She says she didn't do it," he said.

"She says a lot of things. I think you can get her off, anyway."

He smirked. "Are you a lawyer now?"

"No. Just a guy who's been in the thick of this bizarre fucking case since day one."

"I bow to your experience if not expertise."

"You can plead her insane, Sam."

"A very tough defense to pull off, and besides, she won't hear of it. She wants no psychiatrists, no alienists involved."

"You can still get her off."

"How in hell?"

I let some air out. "I'm going to have to talk to her before I say any more. It's going to have to be up to her."

"You can't tell me?"

"You're not my client."

Mildred Bolton was.

And she was ushered into the interrogation room by a matron who then waited outside the door. She wore the same floral-print dress, but the raccoon stole was gone. She smiled faintly upon seeing me, sat across from me.

"You been having fun with the press, Mildred, haven't you?"

"I sure have. They call me 'Marble Mildred.' They think I'm cold."

"They think it's unusual for a widow to joke about her dead husband."

"They're silly people. They asked me the name of my attorney and I said, 'Horsefeathers.'" She laughed. That struck her very funny; she was proud of herself over that witty remark.

"I'm glad you can find something to smile about."

"I'm getting hundreds of letters, you know. Fan mail!

They say, you should have killed him whether you did or not. I'm not the only woman wronged in Chicago, you know."

"They've got you dead to rights, Mildred. I've seen some of the evidence. I've talked to the witnesses."

"Did you talk to Mrs. Winston? It was her fault, you know. Her and that . . . that boy."

"You went to see Joe after the boy was fined in court."

"Yes! I called him and told him that the little degenerate had been convicted and fined. Then I asked Joe, did he have any money, because I didn't have anything to eat, and he said yes. So I went to the office and when I got there he tried to give me a check for ten dollars. I said, 'I guess you're going to pay that boy's fine and that's why you haven't any money for me?' He said, 'That's all you're going to get.' And I said, 'Do you mean for a whole *week*? To pay rent out of and eat on?' He said, 'Yes, that's all you get.' "

"He was punishing you."

"I suppose. We argued for about an hour and then he said he had business on another floor—that boy's lawyer is on the ninth floor, you know—and I followed him, chased him to the elevator but he got away. I went back and said to Miss Houyoux, 'He ran away from me.' I waited in his office and in about an hour he came back. I said, 'Joe, I have been your wife for fourteen years and I think I deserve more respect and better treatment than that.' He just leaned back in his chair so cocky and said, 'You know what you are?' And then he said it."

"Said it?"

She swallowed; for the first time, those marble eyes filled with tears. "He said, 'You're just a dirty old bitch.' Then he said it again. Then I said, 'Just a dirty old bitch after fourteen years?' And I pointed the gun at him."

"Where was it?"

"It was on his desk where I put it. It was in a blue box I carried in with me."

"What did you do with it, Mildred?"

"The box?"

"The gun."

"Oh. That. I fired it at him."

I gave her a handkerchief and she dabbed her eyes with it.

"How many times did you fire the gun, Mildred?"

"I don't know. He fell over in his chair and then he got up and came toward me and he said, 'Give me that gun, give me that gun.' I said, 'No, I'm going to finish myself now. Let go of me because my hand is on the trigger!'" Her teeth were clenched. "He struggled with me, and his glasses got knocked off, but he got the gun from my hand and he went out in the hall with it. I followed him, but then I turned and went back in his office. I was going to jump out of the window, but I heard him scream in the hall and I ran to him. The gun was lying beside him and I reached for it but he reached and got it first. I went back in the office."

"Why?"

"To jump out the window, I told you. But I just couldn't leave him. I started to go back out and when I opened the door some people were around. You were one of them, Mr. Heller."

"Where did you get that gun, Mildred?"

"At a pawn shop in Hammond, Indiana."

"To kill Joe?"

"To kill myself."

"But you didn't."

"I'm sorry I didn't. I had plenty of time to do it at home, but I wanted to do it in his office. I wanted to embarrass him that way."

"He was shot in the back, Mildred, twice."

"I don't know about that. Maybe his body turned when I was firing. I don't know. I don't remember."

"You know that the prosecution will not buy your suicide claims."

"They are *not* claims!"

"I know they aren't. But they won't buy them. They'll tell the judge and the jury that your talk of suicide is a clever excuse to get around planning Joe's murder. In other words, that you premeditated the killing and supplied yourself with a gun—and a reason for having a gun."

"I don't know about those things."

"Would you like to walk away from this?"

"Well, of course. I'm not crazy."

Right.

"You can, I think. But it's going to be hard on you. They're going to paint you as a shrew. As a brutal woman who battered her husband. They'll suggest that Bolton was too much of a gentleman for his own good, that he should have struck back at you, physically."

She giggled. "He wasn't such a gentleman."

"Really?"

"He wasn't what you think at all. Not at all."

"What do you mean, Mildred?"

"We were married for fourteen years before he tried to get rid of me. That's a long time."

"It sure is. What is it about your husband that we're getting wrong?"

"I haven't said."

"I know that. Tell me."

"I won't tell you. I've never told a living soul. I never will."

"I think you should. I think you need to."

"I won't. I won't now. I won't ever."

"There were no other women, were there, Mildred?"

"There were countless women, countless!"

"Like Marie Winston."

"She was the worst!"

"What about her son?"

"That little . . ." She stopped herself.

"That little degenerate? That's what you seem to always call . . ."

She nodded, pursing her thin wide lips.

"Joe was living in a fleabag hotel," I said. "A guy with *his* money. Why?"

"It was close to his work."

"Relatively. I think it had to do with who he was living with. A young man."

"A lot of men room together."

"There were no other women, were there, Mildred? Your husband used you to hide behind, didn't he, for many years."

She was crying now. The marble woman was crying now. "I loved him. I loved him."

"I know you did. And I don't know when you discovered it. Maybe you never did, really. Maybe you just suspected, and couldn't bring yourself to admit it. Then, after he left you, after he moved out of the house, you finally decided to find out, really find out, hiring me, springing for a hundred precious bucks you'd scrimped and saved, knowing I might find things out you'd want kept quiet. Knowing I might confirm the suspicions that drove you bughouse for years."

"Stop it . . . please stop it . . ."

"Your refined husband who liked to be near a college campus. You knew there were affairs. And there were. But not with women."

She stood, squeezing my hanky in one fist. "I don't have to listen to this!"

"You do if you want to be a free woman. The unwritten law doesn't seem to apply for women as equally as it does for men. But if you tell the truth about your husband— about just who it was he was seeing behind your back—I guarantee you no jury will convict you."

Her mouth was trembling.

I stood. "It's up to you, Mildred."

"Are you going to tell Mr. Backus?"

"No. You're my client. I'll respect your wishes."

"I wish you would just go. Just go, Mr. Heller."

I went.

I told Backus nothing except that I would suggest he introduce expert testimony from an alienist. He didn't. His client wouldn't hear of it.

The papers continued to have a great time with Marble Mildred. She got to know the boys of the press, became bosom buddies with the sob sisters, warned cameramen not to take a profile pic or she'd break their lens, shouted greetings and wisecracks to one and all. She laughed and talked; being on trial for murder was a lark for her.

Of course as the trial wore on, she grew less boisterous,

even became sullen at times; on the stand she told her story more or less straight, but minus any hint her husband was bent. The prosecution, as I had told her they would, ridiculed her statement that she'd bought the .32 to do herself in. The prosecutor extolled "motherhood and wifehood," but expressed "the utmost contempt for Mildred Bolton." She was described as "dirt," "filth," "vicious," and more. She was sentenced to die in the electric chair.

She didn't want an appeal, a new trial.

"As far as I am concerned," she told the stunned judge, "I am perfectly satisfied with things as they now stand."

But Cook County was squeamish about electrocuting a woman; just half an hour before the execution was to take place, hair shaved above one ear, wearing special femalesonly electrocution shorts, Mildred was spared by Governor Horner.

Mildred, who'd been strangely blissful in contemplation of her electrocution, was less pleased with her new sentence of 199 years. Nonetheless she was a model prisoner, until August 29, 1943, when she was found slumped in her cell, wrists slashed. She had managed to smuggle some scissors in. It took her hours to die. Sitting in the darkness, waiting for the blood to empty out of her.

She left a note, stuck to one wall: "To whom it may concern. In the event of my death do not notify anybody or try to get in touch with family or friends. I wish to die as I have lived, completely alone."

What she said was true, but I wondered if I was the only person alive who knew that it hadn't been by choice.

Afraid All The Time

Nancy Pickard

"Ribbon a darkness over me . . ."

Mel Brown, known variously as Pell Mell and Animel, sang the line from the song over and over behind his windshield as he flew from Missouri into Kansas on his old black Harley-Davidson motorcycle.

Already he loved Kansas, because the highway that stretched ahead of him was like a long, flat, dark ribbon unfurled just for him.

"Ribbon a darkness over me . . ."

He flew full throttle into the late-afternoon glare, feeling as if he were soaring gloriously drunk and blind on a skyway to the sun. The clouds in the far distance looked as if they'd rain on him that night, but he didn't worry about it. He'd heard there were plenty of empty farm and ranch houses in Kansas where a man could break in to spend the night. He'd heard it was like having your choice of free motels, Kansas was.

"Ribbon a darkness over me . . ."

Three hundred miles to the southwest, Jane Baum suddenly stopped what she was doing. The fear had hit her again. It was always like that, striking out of nowhere, like a fist against her heart. She dropped her clothes basket from rigid fingers and stood as if paralyzed between the two clotheslines in her yard. There was a wet sheet to her right, another to her left. For once the wind had died down, so the sheets hung as still and silent as walls. She felt enclosed in a narrow, white, sterile room of cloth, and she never wanted to leave it.

Outside of it was danger.

On either side of the sheets lay the endless prairie where she felt like a tiny mouse exposed to every hawk in the sky.

It took all of her willpower not to scream.

She hugged her own shoulders to comfort herself. It didn't help. Within a few moments she was crying, and then shaking with a palsy of terror.

She hadn't known she'd be so afraid.

Eight months ago, before she had moved to this small farm she'd inherited, she'd had romantic notions about it, even about such simple things as hanging clothes on a line. It would feel so good, she had imagined, they would smell so sweet. Instead, everything had seemed strange and threatening to her from the start, and it was getting worse. Now she didn't even feel protected by the house. She was beginning to feel as if it were fear instead of electricity that lighted her lamps, filled her tub, lined her cupboards and covered her bed—fear that she breathed instead of air.

She hated the prairie and everything on it.

The city had never frightened her, not like this. She knew the city, she understood it, she knew how to avoid its dangers and its troubles. In the city there were buildings everywhere, and now she knew why—it was to blot out the true and terrible openness of the earth on which all of the inhabitants were so horribly exposed to danger.

The wind picked up again. It snapped the wet sheets against her body. Janie bolted from her shelter. Like a mouse with a hawk circling overhead, she ran as if she were being chased. She ran out of her yard and then down the highway, racing frantically, breathlessly, for the only other shelter she knew.

When she reached Cissy Johnson's house, she pulled open the side door and flung herself inside without knocking.

"*Cissy?*"

"I'm afraid all the time."

"I know, Janie."

Cissy Johnson stood at her kitchen sink peeling potatoes for supper while she listened to Jane Baum's familiar litany of fear. By now Cissy knew it by heart. Janie was afraid of: being alone in the house she had inherited from her aunt; the dark; the crack of every twig in the night; the storm cellar; the horses that might step on her, the cows that might trample her, the chickens that might peck her, the cats that might bite her and have rabies, the coyotes that might attack her; the truckers who drove by her house, especially the flirtatious ones who blasted their horns when they saw her in the yard; tornadoes, blizzards, electrical storms; having to drive so far just to get simple groceries and supplies.

At first Cissy had been sympathetic, offering daily doses of coffee and friendship. But it was getting harder all the time to remain patient with somebody who just burst in without knocking and who complained all the time about imaginary problems and who—

"You've lived here all your life," Jane said, as if the woman at the sink had not previously been alert to that fact. She sat in a kitchen chair, huddled into herself like a child being punished. Her voice was low, as if she were talking more to herself than to Cissy. "You're used to it, that's why it doesn't scare you."

"Um," Cissy murmured, as if agreeing. But out of her neighbor's sight, she dug viciously at the eye of a potato. She rooted it out—leaving behind a white, moist, open wound in the vegetable—and flicked the dead black skin into the sink where the water running from the faucet washed it down the garbage disposal. She thought how she'd like to pour Janie's fears down the sink and similarly grind them up and flush them away. She held the potato to her nose and sniffed, inhaling the crisp, raw smell.

Then, as if having gained strength from that private moment, she glanced back over her shoulder at her visitor. Cissy was ashamed of the fact that the mere sight of Jane Baum now repelled her. It was a crime, really, how she'd let herself go. She wished Jane would comb her hair, pull her shoulders back, paint a little coloring onto her pale face, and wear something else besides that ugly denim jumper that came nearly to her heels. Cissy's husband, Bob, called Janie "Cissy's pup," and he called that jumper the "pup tent." He was right, Cissy thought, the woman did look like an insecure, spotty adolescent, and not at all like a grown woman of thirty-five-plus years. And darn it, Janie did follow Cissy around like a neurotic nuisance of a puppy.

"Is Bob coming back tonight?" Jane asked.

Now she's even invading my mind, Cissy thought. She whacked resentfully at the potato, peeling off more meat than skin. "Tomorrow." Her shoulders tensed.

"Then can I sleep over here tonight?"

"No." Cissy surprised herself with the shortness of her reply. She could practically feel Janie radiating hurt, and so she tried to make up for it by softening her tone. "I'm sorry, Janie, but I've got too much book work to do, and it's hard to concentrate with people in the house. I've even told the girls they can take their sleeping bags to the barn tonight to give me some peace." The girls were her daughters, Tessie, thirteen, and Mandy, eleven. "They want to spend the night out there 'cause we've got that new little blind calf we're nursing. His mother won't have anything to do with him, poor little thing. Tessie has named him Flopper, because he tries to stand up but he just flops back down. So the girls are bottle-feeding him, and they want to sleep near . . ."

"Oh." It was heavy with reproach.

Cissy stepped away from the sink to turn her oven on to 350°. Her own internal temperature was rising, too. God forbid she should talk about her life! God forbid they should ever talk about anything but Janie and all the damned things she was scared of! She could write a book about it: *How Jane Baum Made a Big Mistake by Leaving Kansas City and How Everything About the Country Just Scared Her to Death.*

"Aren't you afraid of anything, Cissy?"

The implied admiration came with a bit of a whine to it—*anything*—like a curve on a fastball.

"Yes." Cissy drew out the word reluctantly.

"You *are?* What?"

Cissy turned around at the sink and laughed self-consciously.

"It's so silly . . . I'm even afraid to mention it."

"Tell me! I'll feel better if I know you're afraid of things, too."

There! Cissy thought. *Even my fears come down to how they affect you!*

"All right." She sighed. "Well, I'm afraid of something happening to Bobby, a wreck on the highway or something, or to one of the girls, or my folks, things like that. I mean, like leukemia or a heart attack or something I can't control. I'm always afraid there won't be enough money and we might have to sell this place. We're so happy here. I guess I'm afraid that might change." She paused, dismayed by the sudden realization that she had not been as happy since Jane Baum moved in down the road. For a moment, she stared accusingly at her neighbor. "I guess that's what I'm afraid of." Then Cissy added deliberately, "But I don't think about it all the time."

"I think about mine all the time," Jane whispered.

"I know."

"I hate it here!"

"You could move back."

Janie stared reproachfully. "You know I can't afford that!"

Cissy closed her eyes momentarily. The idea of having to listen to *this* for who knew how many years . . .

"I love coming over here," Janie said wistfully, as if reading Cissy's mind again. "It always makes me feel so much better. This is the only place I feel safe anymore. I just hate going home to the big old house all by myself."

I will not *invite you to supper,* Cissy thought.

Janie sighed.

Cissy gazed out the big square window behind Janie. It was October, her favorite month, when the grass turned as red as the curly hair on a Hereford's back and the sky turned a steel gray like the highway that ran between their houses. It was as if the whole world blended into itself— the grass into the cattle, the roads into the sky, and she into all of it. There was an electricity in the air, as if something more important than winter were about to happen, as if all the world were one and about to burst apart into something brand-new. Cissy loved the prairie, and it hurt her feelings a little that Janie didn't. How could anyone live in the middle of so much beauty, she puzzled, and be frightened of it?

"We'll never get a better chance." Tess ticked off the rationale for the adventure by holding up the fingers of her right hand, one at a time, an inch from her sister's scared face. "Dad's gone. We're in the barn. Mom'll be asleep. It's a new moon." She ran out of fingers on that hand and lifted her left thumb. "And the dogs know us."

"They'll find out!" Mandy wailed.

"*Who'll* find out?"

"Mom and Daddy will!"

"They won't! Who's gonna tell 'em? The gas-station owner? You think we left a trail of toilet paper he's going to follow from his station to here? And he's gonna call the sheriff and say lock up those Johnson girls, boys, they stole my toilet paper!"

"Yes!"

Together they turned to gaze—one of them with pride and cunning, the other with pride and trepidation—at the small hill of hay that was piled, for no apparent reason, in the shadows of a far corner of the barn. Underneath that pile lay their collection of six rolls of toilet paper—a new one filched from their own linen closet, and five partly used ones (stolen one trip at a time and hidden in their school jackets) from the ladies' bathroom at the gas station in town. Tess's plan was for the two of them to "t.p." their neighbor's house that night, after dark. Tess had lovely visions of how it would look—all ghostly and spooky, with streamers of white hanging down from the tree limbs and waving eerily in the breeze.

"They do it all the time in Kansas City, jerk," Tess proclaimed. "And I'll bet they don't make any big crybaby deal out of it." She wanted to be the first one in her class to do it, and she wasn't about to let her little sister chicken out on her. This plan would, Tess was sure, make her famous in at least a four-county area. No grown-up would ever figure out who had done it, but all the kids would know, even if she had to tell them.

"Mom'll kill us!"

"Nobody'll know!"

"It's gonna rain!"

"It's not gonna rain."

"We shouldn't leave Flopper!"

Now they looked, together, at the baby bull calf in one of the stalls. It stared blindly in the direction of their voices, tried to rise, but was too frail to do it.

"Don't be a dope. We leave him all the time."

Mandy sighed.

Tess, who recognized the sound of surrender when she heard it, smiled magnanimously at her sister.

"You can throw the first roll," she offered.

* * *

In a truck stop in Emporia, Mel Brown slopped up his supper gravy with the last third of a cloverleaf roll. He had a table by a window. As he ate, he stared with pleasure at his bike outside. If he moved his head just so, the rays from the setting sun flashed off the handlebars. He thought about how the leather seat and grips would feel soft and warm and supple, the way a woman in leather felt, when he got back on. At the thought he got a warm feeling in his crotch, too, and he smiled.

God, he loved living like this.

When he was hungry, he ate. When he was tired, he slept. When he was horny, he found a woman. When he was thirsty, he stopped at a bar.

Right now Mel felt like not paying the entire $5.46 for this lousy chicken-fried steak dinner and coffee. He pulled four dollar bills out of his wallet and a couple of quarters out of his right front pocket and set it all out on the table, with the money sticking out from under the check.

Mel got up and walked past the waitress.

"It's on the table," he told her.

"No cherry pie?" she asked him.

It sounded like a proposition, so he grinned as he said, "Nah." *If you weren't so ugly,* he thought, *I just might stay for dessert.*

"Come again," she said.

You wish, he thought.

If they called him back, he'd say he couldn't read her handwriting. Her fault. No wonder she didn't get a tip. Smiling, he lifted a toothpick off the cashier's counter and used it to salute the man behind the cash register.

"Thanks," the man said.

"You bet."

Outside, Mel stood in the parking lot and stretched, shoving his arms high in the air, letting anybody who was watching get a good look at him. Nothin' to hide. Eat your heart out, baby. Then he strolled over to his bike and kicked up the stand with his heel. He poked around his mouth with the toothpick, spat out a sliver of meat, then flipped the toothpick onto the ground. He climbed back on his bike, letting out a breath of satisfaction when his butt hit the warm leather seat.

Mel accelerated slowly, savoring the surge of power building between his legs.

Jane Baum was in bed by 10:30 that night, exhausted once again by her own fear. Lying there in her late aunt's double bed, she obsessed on the mistake she had made in moving to this dreadful, empty place in the middle of nowhere. She had expected to feel nervous for a while, as any other city dweller might who moved to the country. But she hadn't counted on being actually phobic about it—of being possessed by a fear so strong that it seemed to inhabit every cell of her body until at night, every night, she felt she could die from it. She hadn't known—how could she have known?—she would be one of those people who is terrified by the vastness of the prairie. She had visited the farm only a few times as a child, and from those visits she had remembered only warm and fuzzy things like caterpillars and chicks. She had only dimly remembered how antlike a human being feels on the prairie.

Her aunt's house had been broken into twice during the period between her aunt's death and her own occupancy. That fact cemented her fantasies in a foundation of terrifying reality. When Cissy said, "It's your imagination," Janie retorted, "But it happened twice before! Twice!" She wasn't making it up! There were strange, brutal men— that's how she imagined them, they were never caught by the police—who broke in and took whatever they wanted—cans in the cupboard, the radio in the kitchen. It could happen again, Janie thought obsessively as she lay in the bed; it could happen over and over. *To me, to me, to me.*

On the prairie, the darkness seemed absolute to her. There were millions of stars but no streetlights. Coyotes howled, or cattle bawled. Occasionally the big night-riding semis whirred by out front. Their tire and engine sounds seemed to come out of nowhere, build to an intolerable whine and then disappear in an uncanny way. She pictured the drivers as big, rough, intense men hopped up on amphetamines; she worried that one night she would hear truck tires turning into her gravel drive, that an engine would switch off, that a truck door would quietly open and then close, that careful footsteps would slur across her gravel.

Her fear had grown so huge, so bad, that she was even frightened of it. It was like a monstrous balloon that inflated every time she breathed. Every night the fear got worse. The balloon got bigger. It nearly filled the bedroom now.

The upstairs bedroom where she lay was hot because she had the windows pulled down and latched, and the curtains drawn. She could have cooled it with a fan on the dressing table, but she was afraid the fan's noise might cover the sound of whatever might break into the first floor and climb the stairs to attack her. She lay with a sheet and a blanket pulled up over her arms and shoulders, to just under her chin. She was sweating, as if her fear-frozen body were melting, but it felt warm and almost comfortable to her. She always wore pajamas and thin wool socks to bed because she felt safer when she was completely dressed. She especially felt more secure in pajama pants, which no dirty hand could shove up onto her belly as it could a nightgown.

Lying in bed like a quadriplegic, unmoving, eyes open, Janie reviewed her precautions. Every door was locked; every window was permanently shut and locked, so that she didn't have to check them every night; all the curtains were drawn; the porch lights were off; and her car was locked in the barn so no trucker would think she was home.

Lately she had taken to sleeping with her aunt's loaded pistol on the pillow beside her head.

Cissy crawled into bed just before midnight, tired from hours of accounting. She had been out to the barn to check on her giggling girls and the blind calf. She had talked to her husband when he called from Oklahoma City. Now she was thinking about how she would try to start easing Janie Baum out of their lives.

"I'm sorry, Janie, but I'm awfully busy today. I don't think you ought to come over . . ."

Oh, but there would be that meek, martyred little voice, just like a baby mouse needing somebody to mother it. How would she deny that need? She was already feeling guilty about refusing Janie's request to sleep over.

"Well, I will. I just will do it, that's all. If I could say no to the FHA girls when they were selling fruitcakes, I can

start saying no more often to Janie Baum. Anyway, she's
never going to get over her fears if I indulge them."

Bob had said as much when she'd complained to him
long-distance. "Cissy, you're not helping her," he'd said.
"You're just letting her get worse." And then he'd said
something new that had disturbed her. "Anyway, I don't
like the girls being around her so much. She's getting too
weird, Cissy."

She thought of her daughters—of fearless Tess and dear
little Mandy—and of how *safe* and *nice* it was for children
in the country. . . .

"Besides," Bob had said, "she's got to do more of her
own chores. We need Tess and Mandy to help out around
our place more; we can't be having them always running
off to mow her grass and plant her flowers and feed her
cows and water her horse and get her eggs, just because
she's scared to stick her silly hand under a damned
hen. . . ."

Counting the chores put Cissy to sleep.

"Tess!" Mandy hissed desperately. "Wait!"

The older girl slowed, to give Mandy time to catch up
to her, and then to touch Tess for reassurance. They
paused for a moment to catch their breath and to crouch
in the shadow of Jane Baum's porch. Tess carried three
rolls of toilet paper in a makeshift pouch she'd formed in
the belly of her black sweatshirt. ("We gotta wear black,
remember!") and Mandy was similarly equipped. Tess
decided that now was the right moment to drop her bomb.

"I've been thinking," she whispered.

Mandy was struck cold to her heart by that familiar and
dreaded phrase. She moaned quietly. "What?"

"It might rain."

"I told you!"

"So I think we better do it inside."

"Inside?"

"Shh! It'll scare her to death, it'll be great! Nobody else'll ever have the guts to do anything as neat as this! We'll do the kitchen, and if we have time, maybe the dining room."

"Ohhh, noooo."

"She thinks she's got all the doors and windows locked, but she doesn't!" Tess giggled. She had it all figured out that when Jane Baum came downstairs in the morning, she'd take one look, scream, faint, and then, when she woke up, call everybody in town. The fact that Jane might also call the sheriff had occurred to her, but since Tess didn't have any faith in the ability of adults to figure out anything important, she wasn't worried about getting caught. "When I took in her eggs, I unlocked the downstairs bathroom window! Come on! This'll be great!"

The ribbon of darkness ahead of Mel Brown was no longer straight. It was now bunched into long, steep hills. He hadn't expected hills. Nobody had told him there was any part of Kansas that wasn't flat. So he wasn't making as good time, and he couldn't run full-bore. But then, he wasn't in a hurry, except for the hell of it. And this was more interesting, more dangerous, and he liked the thrill of that. He started edging closer to the centerline every time he roared up a hill, playing a game of highway roulette in which he was the winner as long as whatever coming from the other direction had its headlights on.

When that got boring, he turned his own headlights off.

Now he roared past cars and trucks like a dark demon.

Mel laughed every time, thinking how surprised they must be, and how frightened. They'd think, *Crazy fool, I could have hit him.* . . .

He supposed he wasn't afraid of anything, except maybe going back to prison, and he didn't think they'd send him down on a speeding ticket. Besides, if Kansas was like most states, it was long on roads and short on highway patrolmen. . . .

Roaring downhill was even more fun, because of the way his stomach dropped out. He felt like a kid, yelling "Fuuuuck," all the way down the other side. What a goddamned roller coaster of a state this was turning out to be.

The rain still looked miles away.

Mel felt as if he could ride all night. Except that his eyes were gritty, the first sign that he'd better start looking for a likely place to spend the night. He wasn't one to sleep under the stars, not if he could find a ceiling.

Tess directed her sister to stack the rolls of toilet paper underneath the bathroom window on the first floor of Jane Baum's house. The six rolls, all white, stacked three in a row, two high, gave Tess the little bit of height and leverage she needed to push up the glass with her palms. She stuck her fingers under the bottom edge and laboriously attempted to raise the window. It was stiff in its coats of paint.

"Damn!" she exclaimed, and let her arms slump. Beneath her feet, the toilet paper was getting squashed.

She tried again, and this time she showed her strength from lifting calves and tossing hay. With a crack of paint and a thump of wood on wood, the window slid all the way up.

"Shhh!" Mandy held her fists in front of her face and knocked her knuckles against each other in excitement and agitation. Her ears picked up the sound of a roaring engine on the highway, and she was immediately sure it was the sheriff, coming to arrest her and Tess. She tugged frantically at the calf of her sister's right leg.

Tess jerked her leg out of Mandy's grasp and disappeared through the open window.

The crack of the window and the thunder of the approaching motorcycle confused themselves in Jane's sleeping consciousness, so that when she awoke from dreams full of anxiety—her eyes flying open, the rest of her body frozen—she imagined in a confused, hallucinatory kind of way that somebody was both coming to get her and already there in the house.

Jane then did as she had trained herself to do. She had practiced over and over every night, so that her actions would be instinctive. She turned her face to the pistol on the other pillow and placed her thumb on the trigger.

Her fear—of rape, of torture, of kidnapping, of agony, of death—was a balloon, and she floated horribly in the center of it. There were thumps and other sounds downstairs, and they joined her in the balloon. There was an engine roaring, and then suddenly it was silent, and a slurring of wheels in her gravel drive, and these sounds joined her in her balloon. When she couldn't bear it any longer, she popped the balloon by shooting herself in the forehead.

* * *

In the driveway, Mel Brown heard the gun go off.

He slung his leg back onto his motorcycle and roared back out onto the highway. So the place had looked empty. So he'd been wrong. So he'd find someplace else. But holy shit. Get the fuck outta here.

Inside the house, in the bathroom, Tess also heard the shot and, being a ranch child, recognized it instantly for what it was, although she wasn't exactly sure where it had come from. Cussing and sobbing, she clambered over the sink and back out the window, falling onto her head and shoulders on the rolls of toilet paper.

"It's the sheriff!" Mandy was hysterical. "He's shooting at us!"

Tess grabbed her little sister by a wrist and pulled her away from the house. They were both crying and stumbling. They ran in the drainage ditch all the way home and flung themselves into the barn.

Mandy ran to lie beside the little blind bull calf. She lay her head on Flopper's side. When he didn't respond, she jerked to her feet. She glared at her sister.

"He's dead!"

"Shut up!"

Cissy Johnson had awakened, too, although she hadn't known why. Something, some noise, had stirred her. And now she sat up in bed, breathing hard, frightened for no good reason she could fathom. If Bob had been home, she'd have sent him out to the barn to check on the girls. But why? The girls were all right, they must be, this was just the result of a bad dream. But she didn't remember having any such dream.

Cissy got out of bed and ran to the window.

No, it wasn't a storm, the rain hadn't come.

A motorcycle!

That's what she'd heard, that's what had awakened her!

Quickly, with nervous fingers, Cissy put on a robe and tennis shoes. Darn you, Janie Baum, she thought, your fears are contagious, that's what they are. The thought popped into her head: If you don't have fears, they can't come true.

Cissy raced out to the barn.

Body Count

Wayne D. Dundee

"I want to warn you right up front," Myra Caine said after I'd settled into the booth across from her, "that getting involved with me may expose you to grave danger."

I grinned. "You're beautiful enough to take a man's breath away," I conceded, "but I hardly think that could prove fatal."

She gave a quick, impatient shake of her head. "It's no joking matter, Mr. Hannibal. This maniac may have me on the brink of hysteria, but I'm not overreacting. He's crazy and he's dangerous and he's already responsible for three deaths."

"You're certain of that?"

"If you mean did I actually see him do it, of course not. But he told me he did, and I believe him. Three men are dead, there's no denying that."

"But the police failed to see any connection in those deaths, and two of them remain on the books as accidents."

"Yeah, well I know better. *I'm* the connection. And the first two killings were only made to *look* like accidents."

A buxom young barmaid appeared at that point to take our drink orders. In the rather tense silence that followed her interruption, I hung a cigarette from the corner of my mouth, set fire to it, and studied my prospective client through the curling smoke.

She was a beauty all right. Early thirties, medium height, heart-shaped face highlighted by almond eyes and a sensual, full-lipped mouth above a terrific body well displayed in a pantsuit of clinging blue silk. All topped off with thick chestnut hair and wrapped in some exotic, unfamiliar, but doubtless very expensive scent.

"Let's do it this way," I said after the drinks had arrived. "I'll tell you everything the judge has already told me, and then you can fill in the holes. Fair enough?"

She reached for her highball glass. "Fair enough," she said.

"You're a call girl. Five hundred a night. Very exclusive. You've been operating here in Rockford for approximately six years, and you regularly entertain some of the most prominent men in northern Illinois. Everything was going great for you until a couple weeks ago when one of your johns—"

"I hate that term."

"—until one of your customers started getting too possessive. He claimed he loved you and even went so far as to propose marriage. When you laughed it off, he went a little crazy. Said he wouldn't allow other men to touch you and if any did he swore he'd kill them. You refused to see him anymore, naturally enough, but you failed to take his threat seriously. And then came the night one Albert Renman died shortly after spending some time with you. From all appearances, it was one of those freak accidents; he fell going up the back steps of his house, fell and broke his neck. But the next day you got a phone call from your loony admirer—"

"His name is Earl Mardix."

"—and this Mardix claimed he was the one responsible for Renman's death. You hung up on him when he tried to give you all the gory details. It shook you up plenty, but you managed to convince yourself that he was just trying to take advantage of a grisly coincidence. Only a couple nights later the same thing happened all over again. A man named Edward Traver left your bed and turned up dead within the hour. This time it was what appeared to be a single-vehicle car wreck. But you knew better, even before the phone call from Mardix came just as it had the first time. You tried to threaten him with the cops, but he called your bluff because he knew the last thing a girl in your position wanted was a police investigation coming down around her. What you did instead was to contact Judge Hugh Farrow, one of your regular customers of some years' standing. You told him you had some nut harassing you without bothering to tell him that this nut had already killed two men. The judge agreed to help you by calling on the services of an ex-con who owed him some favors, an aging strongarm specialist named Max Cobb. Cobb was to track down Mardix and rough him up enough to scare him off you. But things didn't go according to that plan at all. This time there was no attempt to make it look like an accident. Max Cobb was found in an alley yesterday morning with his throat slit from ear to ear."

Myra Caine closed her eyes and exhaled a ragged breath.

I went on. "You had no choice but to tell the judge the whole story then. I'll bet he gave you a royal chewing out, but he was no more anxious to go to the cops now than you were. Because of his involvement in hiring Cobb, he was in it up to his ears. So he got in touch with me. Gave me the rundown as he knew it and set up this meeting with you."

"He filled you in very thoroughly," the Caine woman observed. "He must trust you a great deal."

"Yeah," I said. "Too bad you didn't have some of that trust when you decided to turn to him for help. You should have leveled with him right off the bat."

"You don't like me very much, do you?"

I shrugged. "I don't know you well enough to like or dislike you. But I do have a high regard for Hugh Farrow. He's a decent man. I'd hate to see his career and reputation go down the tubes because of some . . ."

"Because of some what? Tart? Tramp? Whore? Go ahead and say it, if it will make you feel better. I've been called a lot worse by a lot better than you."

"Look, I don't have to like you to do my job. You ought to be able to relate to that."

Bright red color flared high on each cheek, and suddenly those lovely almond eyes were leaking tears.

She started to get to her feet, but I put out a hand to stop her. "Hey," I said. "Come on, no need for that."

She settled back down after a minute and began digging for a handkerchief. I stabbed out my cigarette and gave myself a mental kick in the pants. I'm no good at handling bawling females, especially when I'm the one who triggered the tears.

"Look," I said, "you've got enough troubles without me pointing an accusing finger and spouting off at the mouth. I don't usually do things like that. I'm sorry, all right?"

She was busy with the hanky and made no reply. I left

her sniffling and honking, got up and walked to the bar to get our drinks refilled. When I returned, she seemed to have regained her composure.

Without looking at me she said, "I don't make a habit of wearing my emotions on my sleeve and I never *ever* cry in front of anyone."

"So we're even," I said. "We both acted out of character. Now we can get on with the business at hand."

Her gaze lifted. "Then you'll do it? You'll help me?"

"I'd pretty much decided that when I agreed to meet with you."

"You're doing it because of Hugh, right?"

"Probably."

"At least you're honest."

"Then let me be honest about something else, too. I'll do everything I can to nail Mardix and keep you and the judge out of it. But you have to understand it may not be possible to do both. I won't jeopardize my P.I. license or any more lives just to keep you two in the clear. Stopping Mardix is priority one. If I can't see any other way, I'll have to bring the cops in on it."

She studied the contents of her glass for a long moment, then nodded and said, "All right, I accept that. You have my leave to do whatever you feel is necessary."

A light rain was falling by the time we emerged from the out-of-the-way little bar. It had taken the better part of an hour to hash over the remaining details of the case. I'd scribbled notes and sipped good bourbon, and all the while her perfume and the nearness of her had been working on me. When it comes right down to it, beautiful women are a dime a dozen. But in addition to her great looks, this one had the most stunningly powerful aura of sexuality I'd ever encountered. Before I knew it, it had penetrated my shell of animosity and was stirring yearnings in my gut that were hard to ignore. I could almost understand why a man would pay five hundred dollars for a night of her favors.

Meeting Myra Caine at a public establishment—rather than at my office or her apartment—had been my idea. It had been evident from what the judge had told me that Mardix had her under some sort of surveillance, and I wasn't about to make it that easy for him to spot me and possibly mark me as his next target. This way I'd been able to stake out the bar ahead of time and make sure no one was following her.

The next move seemed obvious enough: I planned on taking advantage of the fact that Mardix, for whatever reason, had relaxed his vigil. I had to do some fast talking to dissuade Myra from returning to her place, but I won out in the end by reminding her of what she'd said about going along with whatever I felt was necessary.

The ride to the St. George Hotel was made in sullen silence on her part. I parked near the side entrance and hustled her in through the worsening rain. The St. George was on Seventh Street, not far from my Broadway office. I chose it for that reason, and also because I knew the house dick there, a crusty old retired cop named Bill Grissom. The place had seen better days and was undoubtedly a far cry from what a five-hundred-dollar-a-night call girl was used to, but it was clean and relatively free of riffraff, and a twenty in Grissom's palm got me a promise he'd keep an eye on my brand-new client until I returned.

Back outside, the March rain was being kicked into stinging sheets by a cold, gusting wind. As I threaded my old Mustang through the tail end of the lunch-hour traffic, I had to flip on the defogger as well as the wipers to keep the windshield clear enough to prevent my crawling into somebody's trunk.

Hugh Farrow was waiting for me in the study of his sprawling North Park home. Bottin, his chauffeur/manservant for as many years as anyone could remember, showed me in.

"Had lunch yet?" the judge wanted to know.

I shook my head. "As a matter of fact, no."

"Bottin, how about a tray of sandwiches and some cold beer?"

The tall, painfully thin manservant gave an almost imperceptible nod, spun on his heel, and glided from the room.

In sharp contrast to his faithful employee, the judge was built considerably thicker and closer to the ground. He moved with the bulky grace of a former athlete who wasn't exactly winning his battle of the bulge but hadn't thrown in the towel yet, either. I look in the mirror a time or two each day and see another guy, twenty years younger and a little taller, you could describe pretty much the same way.

"Well?"

The question was abrupt, almost demanding. It irritated me.

"Well what?" I said.

"Did you meet with her?"

"Yeah, I met with her."

"And?"

"And I agreed to look into the mess. To try and help her. And you. You damn fool."

His facial muscles pulled tight, and his eyes narrowed for an instant. Then the quick anger was past, and his mouth curved in a rueful smile. "Yeah, I guess I am at that. No fool like an old fool, right?"

"No fool like a guy who makes a chump of himself over a dame."

"Ah, there's where you're wrong, Joe. You're still a relatively young man, still have some of the fire and cockiness of youth left in you. When you're a little older, then you'll know, too. There is nothing—absolutely nothing on this earth, my friend—*better* to make a fool of yourself over than a woman."

"Christ," I growled. "Are you drunk?"

"Drunk? Naw, I've got the flu, that's all. Why else would I not be at the courthouse performing my judicial duties? Home sick with the flu, that's me. The fact that I can't quite bring myself to put on those grand old robes and pretend to dispense wisdom and justice while there's a killer running loose—a killer I fed a victim to—hasn't a goddamn thing to do with it!"

He was standing near a massive fireplace. Suddenly he pivoted and smacked his right fist against the flat stone face of the hearth. The sound of the impact made me wince.

Bottin entered at that moment, carrying a tray of sandwiches stacked around a silver bucket of ice in which a half dozen bottles of Michelob were nestled. If he'd seen or heard the punch, he made no indication.

"Your food and drink, sir," he said calmly.

Hugh Farrow stood facing the hearth with his fist still pressed against the gunmetal gray stone. Without turning, he said, "That'll be all for now, Bottin. Thanks."

When Bottin had withdrawn, I sat down before the tray of eats and twisted open a bottle of Michelob. I drained a third of it, then tried one of the sandwiches. Turkey. Delicious. Over my shoulder I said, "If you need help pulling your fist out of that stone, you'll have to wait until I'm finished here."

After a minute or so, the judge came over and sat down across from me. The knuckles of his right hand were scraped and bleeding. We both pretended not to notice.

Halfway through our second bottles of beer, he was ready to talk about it.

"You've met her," he said. "Unless you're made of wood, you certainly felt the impact she can have on a man. What can I say? She's been a great comfort to me over the past few years, ever since Margaret passed away. Even some before that, to be perfectly frank about it. I was almost grateful for the chance to do something for her in return." He paused, watching the carbon bubbles rise behind the dark glass of one of the bottles. When he spoke again, it was in a slightly quieter, huskier voice. "Even if I'd known the truth about Mardix when she first came to me, I think I still would have been willing to do what I did."

I let that lie there.

"Tell me about Max Cobb," I said.

He shrugged. "What's to tell? You knew him."

"Knew of him," I corrected.

"He was a strong-arm artist, a leg-breaker from way back. No spring chicken anymore, middle fifties but still rough as a cob, just like his name. That was his boast, and he could back it up. He would have been damned hard to take, Joe. That makes this Mardix a very dangerous character."

"What do you know about him? Anything?"

"Zip so far. A man of mystery. I ran some checks that yielded nothing, and I've got some more going now. I know people in all the right places and I know how to pull their strings, but it takes time to get it done with discretion. As soon as I turn up anything, I'll let you know."

"That leaves me with only one possible lead on him."

"What's that?"

"Myra only saw new customers on recommendation. Who do you think originally recommended Earl Mardix?"

"I give. Who?"

"Albert Renman, his first victim."

"Ironic."

"Yeah. Or is it more than that? At any rate, wives tend to know their husband's friends, right? I'm going to pay Renman's widow a visit this afternoon. Maybe she can point me toward Mardix."

We talked until the beer and sandwiches were polished off. I told him about stashing Myra at the St. George. I also gave him my spiel about going to the cops if I had to.

When I stood to leave, I said, "One more thing."

"What's that?"

"What you said before about those grand old judicial robes? They'll still fit if you give them half a chance. One mistake shouldn't cancel out a lifetime of making the right moves. You're a judge, not God. You're human, just like the rest of us. Give yourself the same break you'd give any first-time offender."

Roberta Renman turned out to be a frail-looking woman of about forty, with stringy blond hair and nervous, birdlike movements. To give her her due, she was probably pretty enough under normal circumstances, but right now she was going through the worst period of widowhood, the hollow, empty time that hits a couple weeks after the funeral, when the relatives and friends have quit dropping by and all that's left is the sense of loss.

I fed her a line about working for some big security outfit and checking out the employment application of one Earl Mardix.

"His previous job record looks good," I explained. "But my company places a good deal of importance on character references. Unfortunately, this Mardix seems to be a bit of a loner, and one of the few personal references he provided was your late husband. I really hate to bother you at a time like this, but I thought you might also be acquainted with Mr. Mardix and could help me out."

"Mardix ... Mardix ..." She tried the name out loud a couple times to jog her memory.

"First name Earl," I said, then offered the description Myra had provided me with. "About thirty, medium height and build, straw-colored hair worn on the longish side."

She frowned over it a minute or so more and then gave an apologetic little smile. "I'm sorry, but Albert met so darn many people at the auto dealership ... I couldn't begin to remember them all."

I thanked her for her time and went back out into the rain. My mood was as gray as the overcast sky.

I returned to the city, remembering to swing by my bank and deposit Myra Caine's retainer check, then decided it was time to pay a visit to my office. I hadn't bothered to check in that morning, so I had to wade through a pile of mail (eighty percent bills, twenty percent circulars, zero percent anything important) that had been shoved through the mail slot. I wadded the whole works into a ball and slam-dunked it into the wastebasket on the way by. Eat your heart out, Darryl Dawkins.

While a pot of day-old coffee was reheating, I punched the playback on the phone answering machine. Some little old lady wanted me to find her pet parakeet that had flown out the window of her tenth-floor apartment; a horseplayer I knew wanted to borrow some money to bet on a "sure thing"; and a lavender-voiced individual named Floyd wanted me to find his dear friend Marcus and convince him that all was forgiven and he should come home. I mentally took care of all three requests in the same manner as the day's mail.

The coffee was just this side of unbearable, but I managed to down a couple cups as I went over my notes on the Caine case and wrapped up the loose ends on a few other matters. It was dusk by the time I finished.

Before leaving the office, I took care of one more piece of business. The well-oiled old .45 came out of its resting place in the desk drawer and the shoulder rig came off its hook in the closet and, together, they ended up on my person. The .22 magnum derringer I wear clipped inside the rim of my right boot is adequate for emergencies and everyday walk-around business, but when I recognize in advance that a situation could turn hairy—like this one— then it's time to strap on the heavy artillery.

I picked Myra up around seven and took her out for supper at a little steak house I frequent. Over two of the best sirloins in Rockford, I reported on my afternoon's activities and then worked my way into some other things I had on my mind.

"A couple things have been bugging me," I said. "For

one, it's obvious Mardix has had you under pretty close surveillance ever since he swore he wouldn't allow another man to touch you. Any idea why you were able to give him the slip this morning?"

She shook her head. "No. I never really thought about it."

"Then it wasn't anything you did intentionally. Did you change your regular routine in some way?"

"Well, sure. I went to meet you. Otherwise, I'm almost never up before noon."

I nodded. "Okay, it's probably as simple as that. He has to sleep and eat just like everybody else, and he'd have been doing it to fit your schedule. You changed your routine and threw him off."

"What else? You said a couple things."

"Any idea what made him fall so hard for you, become so possessive in the first place?"

She shrugged. "Because I helped him over his sexual hang-ups, I guess. When he first came to me, he had a lot of problems. It's not uncommon for guys like that to fall in love with a hooker who has the patience and expertise to help them in ways a straight chick wouldn't—or couldn't."

"Sort of like falling in love with your psychiatrist or a doctor who's saved your life."

"You make it sound corny but, yeah, something like that."

"Was he over his hang-ups completely, or just with you?"

"I'm not sure. If I had to guess, I'd say just with me." Her mouth curved in a dubious little smile. "Is all this really necessary, or are you being a teeny bit voyeuristic?"

I shook my head. "I'm just trying to get a feel for the guy, that's all. We know so damn little about him. Where does he live? What does he do? Hell, Earl Mardix apparently isn't even his real name. There's no phone listing, published or private, for anyone by that name. And from what Mrs. Renman said it sounds as if her husband met him at a car dealership, yet there's no vehicle registration or city sticker issued to a Mardix. The judge sure as hell hit it on the head when he called him a man of mystery.''

"There's one thing that might help."

"What's that?"

"I think he was in the war. You know, Vietnam. He had a bad dream one night, and he called out some things in his sleep. I couldn't make sense of what he said, but there were a lot of Asian-sounding names and phrases, you know? When I tried to ask him about it later, he got really uptight."

I made a mental note to pass that bit of info along to the judge. It could be another angle for him to have checked.

"I'll take you back to the St. George when we're finished here," I told Myra, "and then I'm going to spend the night at your place."

"What on earth for?"

"If we're right, if your change-up maneuver is what gave Mardix the slip this morning, then by now he's got to know he lost you. It's a safe bet that that will have him riled. With any luck it could rattle him enough to make him do something dumb. Like maybe break into your apartment and try to find some clue as to where you went."

"And you'll be there waiting for him?"

"Exactly."

"Won't that be dangerous for you?"

"Could be. But if I play it right, it'll be a lot more dangerous for him."

We finished our meal, passed on dessert, and I drove her back to the St. George. On the way she asked me to stop somewhere so she could pick up some overnight things. When I turned into a Kmart, she commented dryly, "Gee, Hannibal, you take me to all the finest places." I saw her to her room, and as we stood facing each other in the doorway, I was again acutely aware of her raw sexuality. I fantasized briefly about saying to hell with Earl Mardix, sweeping her up in my arms, carrying her into the room, and hanging out the "Do Not Disturb" sign for the rest of the week.

Instead I settled for a quick peck on the cheek from her and a huskily whispered, "For luck."

Myra Caine's apartment was on the third floor of a luxury condo just off East State. I went up the back way from the parking garage and used every trick I know to make sure I wasn't observed. It was a little before nine when I let myself in.

I locked the door behind me and left the lights off. Guided by the thin beam of a pencil flash, I made a tour of the apartment, familiarizing myself with the layout. She lived very well. Elegance without extravagance.

By half past nine I was ready to take up my post. Early in my tour I'd noted the doors to a large walk-in closet just off the living room and had decided on that as a likely spot. It was centrally located without being readily visible to anyone entering the apartment. I plucked a couple sofa pillows from the couch and carried them over along with the thermos of coffee I'd brought. I slid the doors open.

He exploded out of the closet with a nerve-freezing combat cry. He threw three lightning kicks to my chest, knocking me back, then a fourth wiped my legs out from under me. I crashed down across the end of the couch. I rolled, trying to escape his stamping feet. An end table got in the way, and I turned it into splinters. His face was just a blur in the darkness, but I knew it had to be Mardix. The sneaky sonofabitch had gotten in ahead of me somehow and had lain in hiding all the while I was prowling. I could hear his grunts of effort and feel the breeze as his heels whistled past my face in near misses.

I managed to get my knees under me, then my feet, and lunged up into him. We bounced off the wall in a clinch. I tried to throw a knee into his groin, but he blocked it with his hip. He head-butted me in the face and jerked away. I swung a roundhouse right that hit nothing but air.

I lost him in the dark. I stood in the center of the room with fists bailed and eyes watering from the head butt, and the only thing I could hear was the puff of my own labored breathing. I felt as if I were fighting a goddamn shadow.

And then he was behind me. The bloodcurdling cry again, and in the same instant a length of piano wire slipped down over my face and bit into my throat. He slammed a foot against the nape of my neck and pulled into it. I bridged and thrust back like a man hit by high voltage, but he moved expertly with me, never lessening the pressure. I sank to my knees with a strange sound filling my ears. I realized it was a roar of pain and rage and panic trying to escape from deep inside me.

I had only seconds before the piano wire did its trick. It was already embedded so deeply in my flesh that I could barely feel it with my clawing fingertips. I reached for the .45, but my hand found nothing but an empty holster. The big gun had fallen out sometime during the struggle. And the derringer was out of reach now with my legs pinned under Mardix as he rode me down. I sagged forward. My head felt ready to explode, and my throat burned like fire as the wire bit deeper and deeper.

On the carpet just ahead of me something glinted dully in the almost nonexistent light. My thermos. The one I'd brought along, filled with coffee to keep me awake through what might have turned out to be a long, uneventful night. I reached out and gripped it with rubbery fingers, slipping my right hand through the plastic handle. I had time enough and strength enough for one attempt. If it failed, I'd never get another chance.

I whipped the metal-cased cylinder up over my head, then back and down. I heard the sharp crack of metal striking flesh and bone and felt the shock of the impact vibrate through my wrist. Mardix emitted a different kind of cry this time as he released his grip on the wire ends and toppled off my back. I fell forward, flames flooding down through my chest as I sucked in great mouthfuls of air. I tore away the wire and spun to face him. We were both on our hands and knees. Dark blood ran down over his left eye, and he was poised catlike, as if ready to pounce on me. I lashed out with the thermos again. His reflexes were still good, and I managed only to graze the top of his head. I belly-flopped with the effort. He rolled away, scrambled to his feet, fumbled for a moment with the door lock, then ran out. Bright light poured in from the hallway, stinging my eyes as I lay there and listened to the sound of his retreat.

I hauled myself up, relocked the door, turned on every light I could get my hands on. I found the .45 amidst the rubble of the destroyed end table. I sat for a long time with it resting in my lap while I caught my breath and gently rubbed my scraped, bleeding throat.

It was well past ten when I killed the lights and quit the apartment. I walked down to the parking garage with my hands thrust deep in my jacket pockets, the right one firmly gripping the .45. I felt restless and angry. Angry with myself. I'd had Mardix right in my hands and let him get away. Damn it all. But at the same time a part of me was in no hurry to meet up with him again. Twice I jumped at shadows and silently cursed my skittishness.

The city was a kaleidoscope of rain-blurred neon, with cars hissing across the shiny pavement like darting reptiles. I drove without knowing exactly where I wanted to go, until, abruptly it seemed, I found myself in front of the St. George. I parked and went in with my collar flipped up to hide my bloodied throat. I called Myra's room from the lobby to let her know I was coming up.

She was waiting for me in her doorway, wrapped in a powder-blue quilted robe. She hadn't been to sleep yet, but her hair was pinned up and her only makeup was a touch of fresh lipstick. She looked more gorgeous than ever. I told her what had happened, coloring my narrative with plenty of four-lettered adjectives. When she saw my throat, she called down to the desk for a first-aid kit and, at my insistence, a bottle of bourbon.

When they arrived, I belted down some of the whiskey while Myra played Florence Nightingale. I don't know exactly how what happened next came about, or even who made the first move. It wasn't what I had gone there for. Or maybe, on some subconscious level, it was. I don't know. But suddenly I had her in my arms. The robe slipped away, and beneath it she was even more splendid than I'd imagined. We fell back across the bed and, for a frenzied span of time, lost ourselves in each other and the immediate needs of our flesh.

"What was that?" Myra said afterward. "Reaffirmation of life after nearly dying in that dark apartment?"

"It was just sex," I replied. "No need to read anything more into it."

"Well, it doesn't seem to have cheered you up a whole hell of a lot."

I sat on the edge of the bed and reached for a cigarette. "That sonofabitch is still out there somewhere," I said. "I know next to nothing about him, and the one chance I had to get my hands on him, I blew. I'm not likely to get real cheery until I rectify some of that."

"That reminds me," Myra said, sitting up behind me. "The judge called just after you left. He said he'd learned some things about Mardix that you should know. I explained to him that you'd be at my apartment with the phone switched off, so he said if I heard from you before he did, to have you get in touch with him right away."

I smoked my cigarette. The restlessness and anger hadn't abated much, not even with the help of booze and sex. The latter, in fact, had added a twinge of guilt to my already tangled emotions. I knew I wasn't ready for sleep.

I got up and walked over to the phone, dialed Hugh Farrow's number. A busy signal burped in my ear. I tried four more times in the next twenty minutes with the same results. A nagging fear crawled through me. It was past midnight, hardly the hour for lengthy phone conversations. I began pulling on my clothes.

"Where are you going?" Myra wanted to know.

"Out," I told her. "Keep the lights low and stay away from the windows. Lock the door when I leave, and don't open it for anyone but me."

I pulled the derringer from my boot and handed it to her. Her eyes flicked down to the weapon, then back up, wide with uncertainty and a trace of fear.

I said, "Mardix is running scared now, maybe completely out of control. At best, there's a fine line between love and hate. There's a good chance he's crossed that line, and that means his obsession for you may have changed from lust to fury."

"You mean he blames me for the trouble he's in?"

"I've seen it happen that way."

"Jesus."

"I'll wake Grissom and put him right outside the door. I'll be back as quick as I can. Try to relax, but remember everything I said."

It was a twenty-minute drive from the St. George to North Park. I spotted the Farrow house from six blocks away. Every light in it was on.

I slammed the old Mustang to a halt in the middle of the driveway, left it rocking back and forth on worn springs with headlights still on and the door hanging open as I raced through the stinging rain up to the front door. I went in with the .45 in my fist.

There was blood on the walls of the front hall, and Bottin lay at the foot of the open stairway with his throat slit open like a second mouth. He was beyond help. I leaped over him and went bounding up the stairs.

I found the judge in his bedroom, on the bed, feet and hands lashed to the cornerposts with torn strips of sheeting.

His chest was a crisscross of black and red welts, and I could smell the burned flesh. A poker from the smoldering fireplace lay nearby on a patch of singed carpet.

He rolled his head and looked up at me through pain-dulled eyes. "Jesus Christ, Joe," he said hoarsely. "Jesus . . Christ."

I knelt at the edge of the bed and began untying his hands. "Easy, old buddy," I said. "Everything's going to be okay. Don't try to talk."

But he had things he wanted me to know. "His real name is Evan Maddox," he said. "He was a Special Forces war hero in Vietnam. He was part of an elite penetration team that specialized in assassination and subversive tactics behind enemy lines. He became an artist with silent weapons—garrote, knife, bow and arrow, bare hands, you name it. They thought they had him deprogrammed after the war and sent him home to his family in Michigan. Everything went okay for a few years, but then something snapped in the winter of 1980. He killed his parents and wife of six months and three neighbors before fleeing in a stolen car. The Army formed a special team to track him down. They came close a few times but never could close the lid. They learned he hired out for mercenary work, using aliases such as Earl Mardix. Nine months ago they lost all track of him. My inquiries came to their attention, and the team is on its way here now."

"Swell," I said. "They can take over this whole mess. Nobody's better than those military boys when it comes to smoothing things over."

The judge grabbed my sleeve. "You don't understand. We can't wait for them now."

"Why not?"

"Don't you see? Why do you think Mardix came here tonight and did this? He must have been following Myra when she first contacted me. After you spooked him at her place, he returned here and forced me to tell him where she is."

"Damn!" I exploded.

"I tried to hold out, but I . . . I couldn't."

"Nobody can blame you for that. How long ago did he leave here?"

"I'm not sure. I think he left me for dead. I sort of . . . drifted in and out."

"Listen, can you hang on long enough to make a phone call?"

"Damn right I can."

"Call Bill Grissom at the St. George; he's the house dick there. Tell him what's coming down. Tell him to get Myra out of there if he can. Then call the cops and anybody else you can think of. I'm on my way, and I'll take all the help I can get!"

On the return trip, I cut my previous time in half. The Mustang's half-bald tires wouldn't grip the rain-slick pavement, and the front end jumped the curb in front of the St. George before the brakes held. I bailed out, repeating my door-left-open-and-lights-on routine, plunged into the lobby with the .45 drawn and ready.

The desk clerk was sprawled half in, half out of his chair, with his neck twisted in an impossible way. Déjà vu. I pounded up the stairs and down the second-floor hall toward Myra's room. Grissom lay on the floor outside the shattered door. An old revolver lay beside him and I could smell the stink of cordite, so at least he'd gotten off a shot.

But it hadn't done him much good. He was as dead as the plaster on the walls.

I went into the room with my heart thumping up in my throat. I was half afraid of what I would find and half afraid of what I wouldn't.

Nothing. The room in shambles but nobody there.

And then I spotted the open window.

They were out there, on the flat, tar-papered roof that stretched out over the hotel's single-storied dining and kitchen unit. Myra, naked except for satiny briefs, was backing up with the derringer, gripped in both hands, held at arm's length in front of her. I could hear the repeated snap of the firing pin falling on an empty chamber. Mardix was moving slowly but relentlessly toward her. He seemed slightly unsteady on his feet. I guessed that at least one of those bullets—either from the derringer or from Grissom's old revolver—had found its mark.

I went over the windowsill and cat-footed across the roof, moving to a point where Myra was out of my line of fire.

Mardix was talking. The wind caught his words and tossed them around, but I could hear most of what he was saying.

"All I wanted was to love you," he told Myra. "Do you know how long it's been since I felt love? Why couldn't you try to return it? . . . Why make me do those things?"

"Mardix!" I called out.

He spun to face me. I could see the crimson stains on the front of him now. He'd taken two slugs and was losing a lot of blood.

"She's not the one who made you do those things," I said. "You're sick, you need help. It has to end right here. One way or another."

"I shouldn't have left you alive," he snarled.

"Maybe not," I replied evenly. "But I won't make the same mistake. This is a .45 in my fist. Take a good look at it. One wrong move and it will blow you in half."

I could hear the whine of sirens now, not far off. Mardix heard them, too. His eyes flicked around, scanning the rooftop.

"You don't have a prayer," I warned.

The eyes came back to me. And then he did a strange thing. He smiled. And in a flat, emotionless voice he said "Yeah, I know."

Even with two bullets in him, his speed and reflexes were incredible. His right hand blurred up, reaching behind his neck, and the arm snapped down in a throwing motion I caught the glint of the blade as it whirled from his finger tips, and in the same instant I fired. I saw his body jerk and hurtle backward as if yanked by invisible wires before the knife thunked into my shoulder and spun me around

I went to one knee with fiery pain boiling down across my back and through my left arm. My head swam, and for a minute I thought I was going to black out. Myra's scream gave me something else to focus on, helped me cling to consciousness. When my head cleared, I stood up.

Mardix lay in a heap near the edge of the roof. I walked toward him with the knife handle jutting out ahead of me like the jib boom of a listing schooner. The .45 was still in my hand, and I kept it trained on him every step of the way. He'd nearly killed me twice this night; I half expected him to leap up and try again. But the gaping hole over his heart convinced me I had nothing more to fear from him. No one did.

Myra's screams had deteriorated to ragged sobs. I put my good arm around her. "It's okay," I said. "It's over."

We stood there leaning on each other until the cops arrived.

A Crime Of Passion

Richard T. Chizmar

Past midnight. A dark cabin nestled in the wilderness. Night sounds . . . invaded by the whisper of heavy tires. Doors slamming. The crunch of gravel under footsteps.

Many footsteps.

Instantly awake, Drake lifted the .38 from the nightstand and slipped out from beneath the bedsheet. He crouched to a knee, listening, staring out the open curtains at the front yard below. He glimpsed a flicker of sparks in the darkness, then the orange tint of flames, and thought: *My God, they're going to burn down the cabin.*

II

Thomas Drake sold his first novel, *Nightlife,* on his thirtieth birthday. He celebrated both events with a carry-out pizza and a solo trip to the movies. The book—an urban crime thriller—sold well in hardcover and the paperback edition snuck onto the *New York Times* list for three weeks. The resulting four-book contract allowed him to quit his job as a social worker and write full time.

Despite the lucrative deal, Drake continued to live a comfortable, rather conservative life in the suburbs outside Baltimore. He was a bachelor by choice, rarely dated, and had never dated the same woman twice. Whose fault that was, he claimed he didn't know.

Drake did admit—and too often, his few friends scolded—that except for his bank account, he didn't offer a very attractive or exciting package. He was barely of average height, and at least ten pounds underweight. Receding hairline. Pale skin. A face of little character.

And he was far from daring or spontaneous, writing in an upstairs office six days a week, eight hours a day, preferring mornings and early afternoons, walking his two-year-old Labrador retriever several times a day, playing poker on odd Monday nights (more out of habit than actual enjoyment) and golf twice a week. And, no matter what the day had been like or what the next had to offer, he always read himself to sleep.

III

Drake scrambled closer to the second-floor window, his heart pounding at his bare chest. Their van was parked at the bottom of the cabin's gravel driveway, parking lights still on. Cocky bastards. Surprised they didn't toot the damn horn to announce their arrival. A small fire burned to the side of the van, a safe distance from the cabin. The flames threw distorted shadows across the lawn, and Drake watched as the figures took form. He counted all four of them, and found a hint of relief in knowing that no one was lurking beyond his view. They didn't appear to carry weapons, but Drake knew the firepower was there.

For just a moment, he contemplated opening fire on them from the window, but ruled against it. Despite an extensive book knowledge of weapons, he'd never actually fired a gun until a week ago. And a week's practice hadn't helped much; six bottles out of ten remained his best score. He knew his only chance was at close range.

The woman remained by the fire—it was now waist high and growing—while the others returned to the van. The back doors stood open and Drake could see several stacks of boxes inside. The men waited in turn, then carried armloads of what he immediately recognized as books— his own novel *The Prey,* he knew—and took turns dropping them onto the fire. With a flush of surprise and anger, he realized that they were replaying the book burnings from New York and Chicago and the other cities they'd followed him to.

None of them made a move toward the cabin, content for the moment with the destruction of his books. He could hear them mumbling through the slightly open window. Nothing loud or clear enough to understand, but he guessed that they were congratulating themselves for finding him again, for destroying more of his evil work. Crazy fuckers. Probably thought he was cowering in fear. *Let them think it,* Drake thought. *It'll make my job that much easier.*

He remained at the window and watched, recognizing each of their faces in the glow of the fire. The woman named Jessie. Strikingly beautiful and clearly insane. She was their leader. And the three men. All large and equally crazy.

Six days. It'd taken almost a week, but they'd somehow

tracked him across hundreds of miles. Drake had known they'd eventually find him—in fact, he'd spent most of the six days at the cabin trying to prepare for this moment—but he couldn't help but wonder how they'd done it. He'd told no one where he was going. *No one,* because, quite simply, there'd been no one left. Drake shifted his weight and flexed the fingers holding the pistol. *Let 'em come,* he thought.

Outside, the fire spat gray smoke, and Drake imagined he could feel its warmth wash his face. He touched a finger to his cheek. It was hot, but only from anticipation . . . and yes, he admitted, from fear. As the three men returned to the van for another load, Drake pushed the curtains aside and thought: *That damn* Times *critic was right: I never should've sold it to the movies . . .*

IV

Despite his mounting insecurities, the follow-up novels did well and continued Drake's success. His main character, Robert Steele, was an aggressive New York City attorney (by day); a street-smart vigilante with a penchant for breaking the law and serving his own brand of justice (by night). A rather trite theme, Drake admitted, but he'd added what proved to be an irresistible quality to his character. He had made the lawyer a hopeless romantic; a puppy-eyed tough guy with a heart of gold and a body to match. Steele chased criminals while women chased him. Steele's audience grew into a wide and loyal one, and it showed in Drake's royalty statements.

By his fourth novel, Drake was a major force in the crime

and mystery fields. A regular on the best-seller lists. Guest-of-honor at conventions. Major awards winner. Book club selections. Frequent appearances in the media: television, radio, newspaper.

Foreign sales from his first four novels had even allowed him to buy a lakeside cabin in the hills of Western Maryland. A place to escape the creeping closeness of suburbia, a place to really be alone. No neighbors. No telephone. No mail. Just a two-story cabin with spacious rooms, a double fireplace, and an office with a view of the lake.

Then . . . came trouble.

The Prey, Drake's fifth and most daring novel, drew more attention than all of his previous books combined. Part of the reason was that, for the first time, a Thomas Drake novel had debuted in the top five on both the *Times* and the *Publisher's Weekly* lists. The other, more publicized reason, however, was the novel's controversial theme.

The Prey was darker—and more ambitious—than the typical Steele novel. Less romance and more drama. The book followed Steele as he infiltrated the seedy New York underworld of child prostitution and pornography to search for the killer of his lover's teenage sister. The world Drake described was ugly and dark and violent; his characters breathed hate and perversion. The writing, itself, was grim and graphically violent, and the ending was not a happy one.

Drake, his agent, and his editor all agreed that it was a risk, moving away from the popular Steele formula, but when the book debuted so high on the best-seller lists and stayed there, and when the critics lauded it as "chilling and thought-provoking" and "disturbingly real," their concern changed to delight.

So when Warner offered close to seven figures for the motion picture rights to *The Prey,* no one was particularly surprised; despite his reservations about the book's graphic nature, the offer proved too much for Drake to resist. He signed the contracts, kept his fingers crossed . . . and waited anxiously for the movie's premiere.

The film was a disaster, bearing little, if any, semblance to its source material. Warner's final creation was a tasteless 98-minute, new-wave-director-on-speed's version of hell on earth, a thumbnail away from an NC-17 rating. The film was overly violent and obscene and grossly erotic. *Pornography for a mass audience,* the angry reviews shouted.

Concerned citizens protested the movie's showing in dozens of cities. The critics hated it, the public hated it, and Drake hated it.

And an underground group of fanatics who called themselves Mother Earth branded the movie "filthy" and "evil" and hated it enough to kill.

V

One of them was gone.

Drake leaned closer to the window and frantically scanned the yard. *Christ, he could only see three of them.* They were standing next to the van, watching the cabin, talking low. Drake squinted, trying to focus on their features. Too dark.

The fire had eventually weakened, thanks to a limited supply of books. *They must've bought out a dozen stores,* he'd thought, watching them dump the last load. Drake had suspected that, with the book burning nearly complete, they'd make a move for the cabin soon. So he'd left the window momentarily and hurried back to the nightstand, grabbed a full box of ammunition, then returned. The process couldn't have taken more than five or six seconds but they must've known all along where he was watching from and taken advantage of his mistake.

He finger-tipped a flannel shirt from the chair near the window and slipped it on. Then he emptied the box of bullets into the pocket over his heart. Again, he considered opening fire from the window, surprising them, and hopefully taking advantage of the confusion. He tensed. It just might work . . . *no! Damn it!* Drake thought. It would just force their hand that much quicker, show them that he wasn't going to surrender easily. *Damn it!* He thought he'd be ready for this. Ready for anything after what had happened back at home.

The roof creaked and Drake flinched, almost dropping the gun. He imagined one of them standing directly above him, motioning to the others and laughing. Then, lowering his weapon and drilling machine gun fire through the roof.

The second-floor windows were unprotected, but the doors and windows downstairs were heavily boarded from the inside. They wouldn't withstand constant battering, but they'd prevent a quick and easy entrance and allow Drake the time to defend the breach. He'd begun transforming the cabin into a fortress during the second day, feeling, at times, both paranoid and silly. Now, he knew he'd been right.

Suddenly, he heard a crack of breaking glass and wood

downstairs. Den window. Side of the house. Another crack followed.

Drake glanced out the window again, a chill tracking his spine. Only one of them remained by the van now; the others had disappeared. Another board cracked. Louder this time. Closer. He sprinted for the stairs.

VI

Mother Earth's reign of terror over Drake had started two months earlier with a two-page letter to Warner Studios. The group had determined that *The Prey* was an "evil movie; a deranged portrayal of America's youth," and condemned the movie studio for making the film and blamed the book's author for producing such trash.

Over the course of several weeks, Warner and Putnam forwarded a total of twenty-three letters to Drake from the organization. None of the letters listed a return address, and the postmarks on the envelopes were of various states.

Shortly after, similar letters began arriving at Drake's post office box, an address he'd been certain only business associates were aware of. Finally, they began showing up at the house.

All the letters were written in the same handwriting and all carried essentially the same warning: *If you don't stop the paperback release of* The Prey, *withdraw from your upcoming signing tour, and seek redemption for your sins we will have no choice but to punish you.*

And each letter was always signed the same: *The faithful disciples of Mother Earth. Jessie. Carl. Randy. Willie.*

No one Drake spoke with had ever heard of the group

and considering the apparent size of its membership, he wasn't surprised. His publisher ran a check through the research department and even checked with the F.B.I., but nothing turned up on either's computer files. The postal service tried but couldn't help, and the police claimed that they needed more to go on than a stack of crazy letters. Their only advice: *just ignore the freaks and they'll eventually forget all about you.*

But they didn't forget him.

They sent more letters. Then packages. Cardboard boxes full of black ash and charred copies of *The Prey;* burned, they claimed, to symbolize their contempt for the novel's author.

Mutilated publicity photos of Drake.

Mangled baby dolls, signifying the author's ill effect on the country's youth.

Then, during the signing tour that Putnam had arranged, he'd begun noticing the same face in the crowd in different cities. A tall, raven-haired woman. Thin and very attractive. Well-dressed. Intense. Always watching him.

He initially spotted her during a book signing, staring at him through the store window. Then ... sitting alone at a corner table in a Detroit restaurant, walking in a Houston airport terminal, and in the passing crowd at several other signings. Only her professional appearance had kept Drake's suspicions to a minimum. *Perhaps she's a stewardess,* he thought. Curious and strangely attracted, he tried to follow her twice, and both times, she'd vanished.

The woman finally confronted him during a signing at a midwest Kroch's & Brentano's. She waited her turn in line *unnoticed by the author,* then while Drake scribbled a signature, she leaned over and quietly introduced herself as Jessie from the organization Mother Earth.

The words froze Drake and instead of grabbing the woman—as he would later wish he had—he was too terrified to even look up. After a moment, he dropped the pen and slowly lifted his head. The tall woman's red lips spread into a smile and he immediately recognized her as the woman he'd seen in the crowd.

Before he could react, she doused the book-covered table with a container of clear fluid and set it afire. The crowd panicked and scrambled, and Drake knocked over two rows of paperback racks trying to escape the small fire. The woman disappeared in the ensuing commotion.

The woman did not appear again, but there were six more book burnings. Each time hundreds of copies of *The Prey* were set afire on the sidewalk in front of the bookstore in which Drake was appearing. And each time the culprits escaped without a trace. Witnesses in each city claimed that there were four persons involved: three men and a woman.

Finally, after a bomb threat was phoned into a Washington D.C. mall bookstore, the tour was cut short and Drake was granted an early vacation.

He returned to Baltimore, where the county sheriff's office agreed to give him protection outside his home. But after a week passed uneventfully, the police left.

Then, the phone calls began . . .

The first call came late on a Sunday night, during the local weather broadcast on the eleven o'clock news. Drake had called it an early night and was reading an old Dean Koontz paperback in bed—half-listening to the news—

when the phone rang. He picked it up after the first ring, startled and annoyed by the shrill interruption.

"Hello."

"Is this Thomas Drake?" A woman's voice.

He immediately knew who it was on the other end. He shivered and stared at the closed bedroom door, the drape-shrouded windows. His number was unlisted. Always had been. Only his agent, two editors at Putnam, and a few relatives and friends had the number. He couldn't believe that they'd found it. He went to hang up the receiver, then changed his mind. Just play it cool. Play their game.

"Yes, this is Thomas Drake. And who is this?"

"I think you know who this is. And I suggest that you listen very carefully to what I have to say."

"And if I don't?" He got up from the bed and began pacing the carpet.

"We are a very powerful organization, Mr. Drake. With many resources. Trust me, we will find a way to make you listen. We always have in the past."

"You mean . . . Christ, you mean you've done this before? I'm not the first person you've—"

She laughed; an angry, ugly sound. "Oh, yes. There have been others. None as popular as you, of course, but there have been others." She waited, then said, "Alex Forrester wouldn't listen either. Do you remember him?"

Jesus, he remembered. It had been in the newspapers. Alex Forrester. Rock and roll musician. Heavy metal. Accused of headlining a satanic movement; using his music to recruit devil worshippers. Paralyzed last year in a highly publicized automobile accident. Brakes failed. *Oh my God.*

"You . . . you were responsible for that accident—"

"Do you know why we chose Mother Earth as our title?"

she asked, ignoring the question. "Because we live by nature's laws. There was a time when this earth was free of darkness and evil; it was pure. It is our mission to make this country pure again; to cleanse it of all filth."

"You're crazy," Drake whispered. "Absolutely crazy." He'd known from the start that this woman and her Mother Earth were a bunch of lunatics. But until now, the real danger of the situation had failed to sink in.

"The choice is yours to make," she said, her voice rising. She was enjoying it now, taking pleasure from the control she held over him. "You still have time to seek redemption for your sins."

"What sins? Have you even read my book? I haven't done anything. I'm not responsible for what ended up on the screen."

"Of course you are, you miserable man. The film is simply an extension of your vision. It is *your* message that must be stopped. Do you think the people see anyone else's name on the movie credits? No, of course not. Only yours. And yours is the only name on the book cover. It is you who is responsible."

"No, that's not true. Why are you doing this to me? You have no good reason to bother me."

"NO GOOD REASON!" She was shouting into the phone now, her voice trembling with rage. "I have a fourteen-year-old daughter, lying comatose in a hospital room because of . . . of filth like you."

My God, he thought, *she is crying.*

"My baby was once an innocent child, a pure person, Mr. Drake. But she was too trusting, too easily swayed. I didn't see the warnings. I failed her. Her group of peers was evil; they read the filthy books, watched the filthy movies, and they acted as characters in those evil worlds. They lied to their parents. They drank and partied and dressed like sluts. They did things with boys. My baby was high on drugs when the car she was a passenger in went over an embankment. Now, she just lays there in that horrible hospital.''

"What is it that you want from—"

"The predators in this world," she continued, "the spreaders of evil like you, think they are powerful and strong, but under nature's laws, we know that evil breeds only weakness and purity offers eternal strength. Remember that, Mr. Drake. Remember that."

Drake sighed. "Just tell me what is it that you want me to do? We cut the signing tour in half. The paperback release is a week away. I couldn't stop that even if I wanted to."

"You must repent for your sins. Speak with your public, to your readers. Warn them. Tell them you have repented. Tell them that the book is wrong, full of filth and lies and evil messages—"

"I'm hanging up, lady. I can't listen to this anymore. And don't try to call back, because I'll have the police put a tap on the phone and—"

"Come now, Mr. Drake. We both know that the police will be of no help to you. They went through the motions for seven days and now you are all alone."

Drake shivered again and walked to the window, parting the white curtains with a finger. The side yard and street were empty.

"Besides, if you keep calling, the police will just think the whole thing is a publicity stunt for the book. They didn't believe Alex Forrester when he called, you know?"

She was under control again, teasing him now, taunting. "Trust me, the police will be of no help. We are much stronger than you think."

"Fuck you."

"Such harsh words." She laughed. "The oldest rule of nature is that the strong shall survive and the weak shall perish. Don't be weak anymore, Mr. Drake. For your own sake, don't be weak."

He hung up, silencing the awful voice, and called his agent and told him of the latest incident. He didn't call the police. Afterward, he left the phone off the hook.

The next morning, Drake drove into town and bought an answering machine. He installed it the same morning and screened his calls the rest of the week. He counted over a hundred hang-ups before deciding to disconnect the line completely.

Things went downhill fast after that night.

Six days ago, on the exact day of *The Prey*'s paperback release, Mother Earth went over the edge and took Drake with them. He found the dog on his way to fetch the morning paper. The black labrador was sprawled on its back, legs stiff, mouth open, and definitely dead. A smear of blood on the walk revealed that it had been killed in the grass—single bullet to the head—then dragged onto the concrete front porch. Stuffed between the dog's teeth was a ball of glossy, colored paper—a wrinkled book cover.

He buried his companion in the backyard, then showered and packed a single bag. He didn't consider, even for a moment, calling the police.

After a trip to the grocery store for supplies and food, he drove downtown to a pawn shop and picked up a brand-new—at least, that's what the owner claimed—.38 caliber pistol and a dozen boxes of ammunition. Then he loaded the car and headed for the cabin.

An hour later, he stopped at a crossroads convenience store and phoned Colin at the office. But instead of hearing Colin's ever cheerful voice, Drake found himself speaking with Colin's literary partner. *I'm afraid I have some tragic news to pass on to you, my dear Thomas.*

Drake immediately knew what had happened.

The police were here this morning. It seems that poor Colin was . . . was shot to death in his apartment late last night. A foiled robbery attempt, the police suggested. There were signs of a struggle and the lock was damaged.

"There was something strange, though. It seems that the killer tried to burn down Colin's apartment by setting a pile of books afire atop his magnificent Persian rug. Now that makes perfect sense: the police saw that the murderer was simply trying to cover his tracks. But what is so puzzling is that every single book on the pile was one of yours. I wonder where they all came from? Don't you find that queer? It's just terrible—"

Drake hung up, cutting him off in midsentence. He felt nauseous and sat inside the parked car for almost an hour before his head felt clear enough to continue.

He arrived at the cabin late in the afternoon, an emotional mess. Anger. Fear. Disbelief.

He was sure they would search for him; they'd gone too far now to turn back. *The disciples of Mother Earth.* He didn't know who or what in the hell they were, but he was sure of one thing: they'd look for him and eventually find him.

And he prayed he'd be ready.

VII

Drake cleared the stairway in two strides and ran for the den window. He could hear the wooden boards groaning, surrendering under pressure. He crossed the kitchen and walked right up on the man who was climbing, legs first, into the cabin. The man's blue-jeans were pushed up above his shins, exposing thick, hairy ankles. He wore no socks, but a leather holster holding a small pistol was strapped to his right ankle. The man was obviously stuck—probably caught on a jagged piece of board or a nail—and was grunting with effort.

Drake stopped short of the den carpet, hoping the man hadn't heard his approach. *Close range. In the back.* He raised the .38, his arms shaking wildly, and took aim. *Steele would never do it,* he thought in a flash of sanity.

He lowered the gun. *Steele would just knock the bastard unconscious and tie him up.*

Drake looked up at the man again, at the gun hanging from his leg, and wondered if the same gun had been used to end his agent and longtime friend's life. He imagined the man breaking into Colin's apartment and pressing the gun barrel to Colin's bald head and firing. He imagined the man stuffing the tattered remains of a book cover into his dog's lifeless mouth, and . . .

. . . he raised the .38 and pulled the trigger twice in a quick, jerky motion. The man spasmed, his legs kicking at empty air, and a pair of red mouths opened near the center of his back. He went limp.

The adrenaline rush was overpowering and, for a moment, Drake felt as though he might faint. He steadied himself against the back of the sofa and brought the gun to eye level, as if he were unsure if he'd actually pulled the trigger.

A loud crash and a flash of light in the next room snapped him back. He moved cautiously through the kitchen, searching the shadows for movement, turned the corner and froze at the base of the stairs. A pile of broken boards lay at his feet, and the bay window stood wide open, the van's headlights shining bright white into the cabin.

The lights were blinding, but Drake leveled the gun and forced himself closer to the window. Holding his breath, he leaned over the windowsill and peered around the right side. Nothing. Then, to the left. Again nothing.

He backed away from the window, shading his eyes with his gun hand. He was about to return upstairs when a long, silver canister flew through the window and exploded with a loud *pop* as it hit the floor. A second can followed, landing with an identical *pop*. A cloud of white smoke erupted with a hiss.

Tear gas, Drake guessed, his eyes already beginning to sting and water. *Trying to smoke me out.* He shaded his eyes and ran for the stairs . . . and tripped face-first on the pile of broken boards. The gun flew from his hand and slid across the floor, settling somewhere near the bottom of the staircase.

Drake crawled on all fours, fingers groping for the lost weapon. The gas was overpowering now; he could barely open his eyes. His throat felt on fire; he couldn't stop the coughs that racked his body. *No,* his mind screamed. *It can't end so easily. Don't panic now.* Suddenly, his fingers touched something metal and cold and he knew it was the gun. *Okay, get yourself together now,* he thought. *Just get back upstairs.* His fingers closed around the rubber grip . . .

. . . and were crushed beneath an unseen boot.

He screamed with pain.

The boot released.

Drake sensed the movement above him, then felt strong hands pick him up and fling him backward out the window, onto the waiting lawn several feet below.

VIII

"It is nature's way, Mr. Drake." The voice was soft and calm. Unbearably confident. "And it is our way."

Drake was stretched out on his back on the dining room table, his arms and legs bound with thick rope. A piece of tape covered his mouth. Jessie sat on a chair at the end of the table. Two men stood behind her.

They'd surprised him at the bay window, and he'd surprised them right back by fighting like a wildcat. It'd taken both men to take him down. One of the men sported a two-inch gash across his forehead and the other man's lips were cracked and swollen. The third man was still inside, stuck in the window; he was dead.

The men rarely spoke, but the woman had spent the past fifteen minutes repeating the same crazy sermon she'd told him earlier over the telephone. "We live by nature's laws, Mr. Drake. It is our duty to make this earth pure again." She motioned to one of the men and he removed the tape from Drake's mouth.

Drake sucked in air, coating his dry lips with a sweep of the tongue. The back of his head ached from where he'd been struck, and he longed to massage it. His eyes were the worst, though: red and raw.

"Kill me now," he hissed. "Just get it over with."

"Oh, but we have no intentions of killing you. We only kill when necessary to achieve our final destination, and you, Mr. Drake, are exactly that. By allowing you to live, by allowing the world to witness our power, we will set the highest possible example and hopefully deter future sinners from walking your path. Mother Earth's message will be heard across the country very soon, thanks to you."

"You're . . . you're all crazy. My God, you killed Colin for no reason. You followed me all over the country because of a damn book."

"Ah, but a very popular book. A book that will, unfortunately, be read by millions. We told you, the film is only an extension of your vision. It is *your* message that must be stopped."

He spoke without thinking: "I'll never stop writing."

"But you will, Mr. Drake. We will make sure of that. I know we have met once before, but allow me to formally introduce myself. I am Jessie Moore. Doctor Jessica Moore. And these two men with me are . . ."

IX

Excerpted from the Monday evening edition of the *Baltimore Sun:*

BALTIMORE—Best-selling crime novelist Thomas Drake was discovered early this morning suffering from shock and severe dehydration at his country home in the Western Maryland wilderness. The local author was flown to the University of Maryland's

Shock Trauma Unit, where he is listed in serious but stable condition.

Though officials declined to discuss details of Drake's condition, the father-and-son team of hunters who stumbled upon the gruesome scene, Jim and Jeffery Cavanaugh of Cumberland, claimed that the local author was suffering from a bizarre wound and was close to death when they found him.

"The first thing I noticed was that both his hands were missing, gone right at the wrist," said the elder Cavanaugh.

"There were bloody bandages wrapped over the stumps, but they were full of dirt and green pus and he didn't even seem to notice. He was crazy as a goat, eyes staring big and wide, slobbering all over himself, mumbling the whole time about his Mother and the earth and something about nature's way. It was spooky as hell."

Ironically, Drake's latest novel *The Prey,* sparked by controversy over the recent film release, debuted at the number one spot on the *New York Times* paperback best-sellers list yesterday and . . .

X

"Stupid." Although whispered, the single word echoed about the small hospital room. It was a small white-walled room; a private room with a washing sink, sitting couch, a single bed, and the usual tangle of hospital machinery. A skeleton of a girl lay stretched atop the white sheets, a clear mask covering her nose and mouth. Her long dark hair, its luster faded, snaked across the pillow. Her eyes were closed.

"How could I be so stupid? I failed you again, my dear Chelsea." Jessie, dressed in a conservative business suit, held a page from the *New York Times* vertically for her daughter to see. Thomas Drake's *The Prey* was still perched atop the paperback list; eight weeks and counting. After a moment, she lowered the paper to her lap.

"How could I be so stupid?" she repeated, as if insisting on an answer. "We knocked him out of commission, sent an important message, but our actions were merely counterproductive. The damn book is selling; even now his filth is spreading to the people." She stood and unlocked the safety rail on the left side of the bed. "What shall we do, sweetheart?" she asked. "Help me see the light." The bar lowered and Jessie leaned down and cuddled against the cool side of her daughter's body. She slipped the mask down and kissed the girl's lips softly, then replaced the mask.

She sat down again on the stiff hospital chair and, as was her custom, began reading to Chelsea. Sometimes she read books or magazine articles, but always the newspaper first ... to keep her daughter abreast of current events. Now, she read from the *Times* entertainment section. The lead article was about New York's revitalized publishing world. Industry numbers were skyrocketing. Hardcover sales were up forty percent; softcover sales past fifty. Companies were expanding.

She finished the article, dropped the newspaper to her lap, and watched her daughter's lifeless face for a reaction, for an answer to her plea for help. Chelsea had targeted both Forrester and Drake, but Jessie knew it was she who had failed in the latter plan's execution. Now, as Chelsea told her what to do next, Jessie's pulse quickened.

"Yes, yes," she said, her enthusiasm mounting, a plan forming in her mind. "We won't fail you, baby girl. We'll go right to the top this time."

She ran a polished fingernail over the black-and-white photograph of Putnam's CEO and vice president, standing together, smiling, then slashed the photo to shreds with a sweep of her nail and said: "We'll go right to the top."

Deceptions

Marcia Muller

San Francisco's Golden Gate Bridge is deceptively fragile-looking, especially when fog swirls across its high span. But from where I was standing, almost underneath it at the south end, even the mist couldn't disguise the massiveness of its concrete piers and the taut strength of its cables. I tipped my head back and looked up the tower to where it disappeared into the drifting grayness, thinking about the other ways the bridge is deceptive.

For one thing, its color isn't gold, but rust red, reminiscent of dried blood. And though the bridge is a marvel of engineering, it is also plagued by maintenance problems that keep the Bridge District in constant danger of financial collapse. For a reputedly romantic structure, it has seen more than its fair share of tragedy: some eight hundred-odd lost souls have jumped to their deaths from its deck.

Today I was there to try to find out if that figure should be raised by one. So far I'd met with little success. I was standing next to my car in the parking lot of Fort Point, a historic fortification at the mouth of San Francisco Bay. Where the pavement stopped, the land fell away to jagged black rocks; waves smashed against them, sending up geysers of salty spray. Beyond the rocks the water was choppy, and Angel Island and Alcatraz were mere humpbacked shapes in the mist. I shivered, wishing I'd worn something heavier than my poplin jacket, and started toward the fort.

This was the last stop on a journey that had taken me from the toll booths and Bridge District offices to Vista Point at the Marin County end of the span, and back to the National Parks Services headquarters down the road from the fort. None of the Parks Service or bridge personnel—including a group of maintenance workers near the north tower—had seen the slender dark-haired woman in the picture I'd shown them, walking south on the pedestrian sidewalk at about four yesterday afternoon. None of them had seen her jump.

It was for that reason—plus the facts that her parents had revealed about twenty-two-year-old Vanessa DiCesare—that made me tend to doubt she actually had committed suicide, in spite of the note she'd left taped to the dashboard of the Honda she'd abandoned at Vista Point. Surely at four o'clock on a Monday afternoon *someone* would have noticed her. Still, I had to follow up every possibility, and the people at the Parks Service station had suggested I check with the rangers at Fort Point.

I entered the dark-brick structure through a long, low tunnel—called a sally port, the sign said—which was flanked at either end by massive wooden doors with iron studding. Years before I'd visited the fort, and now I recalled that it was more or less typical of harbor fortifications built in the Civil War era: a ground floor topped by two tiers of working and living quarters, encircling a central courtyard.

I emerged into the court and looked up at the west side;

he tiers were a series of brick archways, their openings as
lack as empty eye sockets, each roped off by a narrow
trip of yellow plastic strung across it at waist level. There
vas construction gear in the courtyard; the entire west side
vas under renovation and probably off-limits to the public.

As I stood there trying to remember the layout of the
lace and wondering which way to go, I became aware
f a hollow metallic clanking that echoed in the circular
nclosure. The noise drew my eyes upward to the wooden
vatchtower atop the west tiers, and then to the red arch
f the bridge's girders directly above it. The clanking
eemed to have something to do with cars passing over
he roadbed, and it was underlaid by a constant grumbling
ush of tires on pavement. The sounds, coupled with the
oaring height of the fog-laced girders, made me feel very
mall and insignificant. I shivered again and turned to my
eft, looking for one of the rangers.

The man who came out of a nearby doorway startled
ne, more because of his costume than the suddenness of
is appearance. Instead of the Parks Service uniform I
emembered the rangers wearing on my previous visit, he
vas clad in what looked like an old Union Army uniform:
. dark blue frock coat, lighter blue trousers, and a wide-
rimmed hat with a red plume. The long saber in a scab-
ard that was strapped to his waist made him look thor-
ughly authentic.

He smiled at my obvious surprise and came over to
ne, bushy eyebrows lifted inquiringly. "Can I help you,
na'am?"

I reached into my bag and took out my private investiga-
or's license and showed it to him. "I'm Sharon McCone,

from All Souls Legal Cooperative. Do you have a minute
to answer some questions?"

He frowned, the way people often do when confronted
by a private detective, probably trying to remember
whether he'd done anything lately that would warrant
investigation. Then he said, "Sure," and motioned for me
to step into the shelter of the sally port.

"I'm investigating a disappearance, a possible suicide
from the bridge," I said. "It would have happened about
four yesterday afternoon. Were you on duty then?"

He shook his head. "Monday's my day off."

"Is there anyone else here who might have been working
then?"

"You could check with Lee—Lee Gottschalk, the other
ranger on this shift."

"Where can I find him?"

He moved back into the courtyard and looked around.
"I saw him start taking a couple of tourists around just a
few minutes ago. People are crazy; they'll come out in any
kind of weather."

"Can you tell me which way he went?"

The ranger gestured to our right. "Along this side. When
he's done down here, he'll take them up that iron stairway
to the first tier, but I can't say how far he's gotten yet."

I thanked him and started off in the direction he'd
indicated.

There were open doors in the cement wall between the
sally port and the iron staircase. I glanced through the
first and saw no one. The second led into a narrow dark
hallway; when I was halfway down it, I saw that this was the
fort's jail. One cell was set up as a display, complete with
a mannequin prisoner; the other, beyond an archway that

was not much taller than my own five-foot-six, was
unrestored. Its water-stained walls were covered with graf-
iti, and a metal railing protected a two-foot-square iron
grid on the floor in one corner. A sign said that it was a
cistern with a forty-thousand-gallon capacity.

Well, I thought, that's interesting, but playing tourist
isn't helping me catch up with Lee Gottschalk. Quickly I
left the jail and hurried up the iron staircase the first ranger
had indicated. At its top, I turned to my left and bumped
into a chain link fence that blocked access to the area
under renovation. Warning myself to watch where I was
going, I went the other way, toward the east tier. The
archways there were fenced off with similar chain link so
no one could fall, and doors opened off the gallery into
what I supposed had been the soldiers' living quarters. I
pushed through the first one and stepped into a small
museum.

The room was high-ceilinged, with tall, narrow windows
in the outside wall. No ranger or tourists were in sight. I
looked toward an interior door that led to the next room
and saw a series of mirror images: one door within another
leading off into the distance, each diminishing in size until
the last seemed very tiny. I had the unpleasant sensation
that if I walked along there, I would become progressively
smaller and eventually disappear.

From somewhere down there came the sound of voices.
I followed it, passing through more museum displays until
I came to a room containing an old-fashioned bedstead
and footlocker. A ranger, dressed the same as the man
downstairs except that he was bearded and wore granny
glasses, stood beyond the bedstead lecturing to a man and
a woman who were bundled to their chins in bulky sweaters.

"You'll notice that the fireplaces are very small," he was saying, motioning to the one on the wall next to the bed, "and you can imagine how cold it could get for the soldiers garrisoned here. They didn't have a heated employees' lounge like we do." Smiling at his own little joke, he glanced at me. "Do you want to join the tour?"

I shook my head and stepped over by the footlocker. "Are you Lee Gottschalk?"

"Yes." He spoke the word a shade warily.

"I have a few questions I'd like to ask you. How long will the rest of the tour take?"

"At least half an hour. These folks want to see the unrestored rooms on the third floor."

I didn't want to wait around that long, so I said, "Could you take a couple of minutes and talk with me now?"

He moved his head so the light from the windows caught his granny glasses and I couldn't see the expression in his eyes, but his mouth tightened in a way that might have been annoyance. After a moment he said, "Well, the rest of the tour on this floor is pretty much self-guided." To the tourists, he added, "Why don't you go on ahead and I'll catch up after I talk with this lady."

They nodded agreeably and moved on into the next room. Lee Gottschalk folded his arms across his chest and leaned against the small fireplace. "Now what can I do for you?"

I introduced myself and showed him my license. His mouth twitched briefly in surprise, but he didn't comment. I said, "At about four yesterday afternoon, a young woman left her car at Vista Point with a suicide note in it. I'm trying to locate a witness who saw her jump." I took out the photograph I'd been showing to people and handed

to him. By now I had Vanessa DiCesare's features memo-
ized: high forehead, straight nose, full lips, glossy wings
f dark-brown hair curling inward at the jawbone. It was
strong face, not beautiful but striking—and a face I'd
ecognize anywhere.

Gottschalk studied the photo, then handed it back to
ie. "I read about her in the morning paper. Why are you
rying to find a witness?"

"Her parents have hired me to look into it."

"The paper said her father is some big politician here
i the city."

I didn't see any harm in discussing what had already
ppeared in print. "Yes, Ernest DiCesare—he's on the
oard of Supes and likely to be our next mayor."

"And she was a law student, engaged to some hotshot
iwyer who ran her father's last political campaign."

"Right again."

He shook his head, lips pushing out in bewilderment.
Sounds like she had a lot going for her. Why would she
ill herself? Did that note taped inside her car explain it?"

I'd seen the note, but its contents were confidential.
No. Did you happen to see anything unusual yesterday
fternoon?"

"No. But if I'd seen anyone jump, I'd have reported it
the Coast Guard station so they could try to recover the
ody before the current carried it out to sea."

"What about someone standing by the bridge railing,
cting strangely, perhaps?"

"If I'd noticed anyone like that, I'd have reported it to
he bridge offices so they could send out a suicide preven-
ion team." He stared almost combatively at me, as if I'd
ccused him of some kind of wrongdoing, then seemed

to relent a little. "Come outside," he said, "and I'll show you something."

We went through the door to the gallery, and he guided me to the chain link barrier in the archway and pointed up. "Look at the angle of the bridge, and the distance we are from it. You couldn't spot anyone standing at the rail from here, at least not well enough to tell if they were acting upset. And a jumper would have to hurl herself way out before she'd be noticeable."

"And there's nowhere else in the fort from where a jumper would be clearly visible?"

"Maybe from one of the watchtowers or the extreme west side. But they're off-limits to the public, and we only give them one routine check at closing."

Satisfied now, I said, "Well, that about does it. I appreciate your taking the time."

He nodded and we started along the gallery. When we reached the other end, where an enclosed staircase spiraled up and down, I thanked him again and we parted company.

The way the facts looked to me now, Vanessa DiCesare had faked this suicide and just walked away—away from her wealthy old-line Italian family, from her up-and-coming liberal lawyer, from a life that either had become too much or just hadn't been enough. Vanessa was over twenty-one; she had a legal right to disappear if she wanted to. But her parents and her fiancé loved her, and they also had a right to know she was alive and well. If I could locate her and reassure them without ruining whatever new life she planned to create for herself, I would feel I'd performed the job I'd been hired to do. But right now I was weary, chilled to the bone, and out of leads. I decided to go back to All Souls and consider my next moves in warmth and comfort.

All Souls Legal Cooperative is housed in a ramshackle Victorian on one of the steeply sloping side streets of Bernal Heights, a working-class district in the southern part of the city. The co-op caters mainly to clients who live in the area: people with low to middle incomes who don't have much extra money for expensive lawyers. The sliding fee scale allows them to obtain quality legal assistance at reasonable prices—a concept that is probably outdated in the self-centered 1980s, but is kept alive by the people who staff All Souls. It's a place where the lawyers care about their clients, and a good place to work.

I left my MG at the curb and hurried up the front steps through the blowing fog. The warmth inside was almost a shock after the chilliness at Fort Point; I unbuttoned my jacket and went down the long deserted hallway to the big country kitchen at the rear. There I found my boss, Hank Zahn, stirring up a mug of the Navy grog he often concocts on cold November nights like this one.

He looked at me, pointed to the rum bottle, and said, "Shall I make you one?" When I nodded, he reached for another mug.

I went to the round oak table under the windows, moved a pile of newspapers from one of the chairs, and sat down. Hank added lemon juice, hot water, and sugar syrup to the rum; dusted it artistically with nutmeg; and set it in front of me with a flourish. I sampled it as he sat down across from me, then nodded my approval.

He said, "How's it going with the DiCesare investigation?"

Hank had a personal interest in the case; Vanessa's fiancé, Gary Stornetta, was a longtime friend of his, which was why I, rather than one of the large investigative firms her father normally favored, had been asked to look into it. I said, "Everything I've come up with points to it being a disappearance, not a suicide."

"Just as Gary and her parents suspected."

"Yes. I've covered the entire area around the bridge. There are absolutely no witnesses, except for the tour bus driver who saw her park her car at four and got suspicious when it was still there at seven and reported it. But even he didn't see her walk off toward the bridge." I drank some more grog, felt its warmth, and began to relax.

Behind his thick horn-rimmed glasses, Hank's eyes became concerned. "Did the DiCesares or Gary give you any idea why she would have done such a thing?"

"When I talked with Ernest and Sylvia this morning, they said Vanessa had changed her mind about marrying Gary. He's not admitting to that, but he doesn't speak of Vanessa the way a happy husband-to-be would. And it seems an unlikely match to me—he's close to twenty years older than she."

"More like fifteen," Hank said. "Gary's father was Ernest's best friend, and after Ron Stornetta died, Ernest more or less took him on as a protégé. Ernest was delighted that their families were finally going to be joined."

"Oh, he was delighted all right. He admitted to me that he'd practically arranged the marriage. 'Girl didn't know what was good for her,' he said. 'Needed a strong older man to guide her.'" I snorted.

Hank smiled faintly. He's a feminist, but over the years

his sense of outrage has mellowed; mine still has a hair
trigger.

"Anyway," I said, "when Vanessa first announced she
was backing out of the engagement, Ernest told her he
would cut off her funds for law school if she didn't go
through with the wedding."

"Jesus, I had no idea he was capable of such . . . Neander-
thal tactics."

"Well, he is. After that Vanessa went ahead and set the
wedding date. But Sylvia said she suspected she wouldn't
go through with it. Vanessa talked of quitting law school
and moving out of their home. And she'd been seeing
other men; she and her father had a bad quarrel about it
just last week. Anyway, all of that, plus the fact that one of
her suitcases and some clothing are missing, made them
highly suspicious of the suicide."

Hank reached for my mug and went to get us more
grog. I began thumbing through the copy of the morning
paper that I'd moved off the chair, looking for the story
on Vanessa. I found it on page three.

The daughter of Supervisor Ernest DiCesare apparently committed suicide by jumping from the Golden
Gate Bridge late yesterday afternoon.

Vanessa DiCesare, 22, abandoned her 1985 Honda
Civic at Vista Point at approximately four P.M., police
said. There were no witnesses to her jump, and the
body has not been recovered. The contents of a suicide
note found in her car have not been disclosed.

Ms. DiCesare, a first-year student at Hastings College of Law, is the only child of the supervisor and
his wife, Sylvia. She planned to be married next month

to San Francisco attorney Gary R. Stornetta, a political associate of her father. . . .

Strange how routine it all sounded when reduced to journalistic language. And yet how mysterious—the "undisclosed contents" of the suicide note, for instance.

"You know," I said as Hank came back to the table and set down the fresh mugs of grog, "that note is another factor that makes me believe she staged this whole thing. It was so formal and controlled. If they had samples of suicide notes in etiquette books, I'd say she looked one up and copied it."

He ran his fingers through his wiry brown hair. "What I don't understand is why she didn't just break off the engagement and move out of the house. So what if her father cut off her money? There are lots worse things than working your way through law school."

"Oh, but this way she gets back at everyone, and has the advantage of actually being alive to gloat over it. Imagine her parents and Gary's grief and guilt—it's the ultimate way of getting even."

"She must be a very angry young woman."

"Yes. After I talked with Ernest and Sylvia and Gary, I spoke briefly with Vanessa's best friend, a law student named Kathy Graves. Kathy told me that Vanessa was furious with her father for making her go through with the marriage. And she'd come to hate Gary because she'd decided he was only marrying her for her family's money and political power."

"Oh, come on. Gary's ambitious, sure. But you can't tell me he doesn't genuinely care for Vanessa."

"I'm only giving you her side of the story."

"So now what do you plan to do?"

"Talk with Gary and the DiCesares again. See if I can't come up with some bit of information that will help me find her."

"And then?"

"Then it's up to them to work it out."

The DiCesare home was mock-Tudor, brick and half-timber, set on a corner knoll in the exclusive area of St. Francis Wood. When I'd first come there that morning, I'd been slightly awed; now the house had lost its power to impress me. After delving into the lives of the family who lived there, I knew that it was merely a pile of brick and mortar and wood that contained more than the usual amount of misery.

The DiCesares and Gary Stornetta were waiting for me in the living room, a strangely formal place with several groupings of furniture and expensive-looking knickknacks laid out in precise patterns on the tables. Vanessa's parents and fiancé—like the house—seemed diminished since my previous visit: Sylvia huddled in an armchair by the fireplace, her gray-blond hair straggling from its elegant coiffure; Ernest stood behind her, haggard-faced, one hand protectively on her shoulder. Gary paced, smoking and clawing at his hair with his other hand. Occasionally he dropped ashes on the thick wall-to-wall carpeting, but no one called it to his attention.

They listened to what I had to report without interruption. When I finished, there was a long silence. Then Sylvia put a hand over her eyes and said, "How she must hate us to do a thing like this!"

Ernest tightened his grip on his wife's shoulder. His face was a conflict of anger, bewilderment, and sorrow.

There was no question of which emotion had hold of Gary; he smashed out his cigarette in an ashtray, lit another, and resumed pacing. But while his movements before had merely been nervous, now his tall, lean body was rigid with thinly controlled fury. "Damn her!" he said. "Damn her anyway!"

"Gary." There was a warning note in Ernest's voice.

Gary glanced at him, then at Sylvia. "Sorry."

I said, "The question now is, do you want me to continue looking for her?"

In shocked tones, Sylvia said, "Of course we do!" Then she tipped her head back and looked at her husband.

Ernest was silent, his fingers pressing hard against the black wool of her dress.

"Ernest?" Now Sylvia's voice held a note of panic.

"Of course we do," he said. But the words somehow lacked conviction.

I took out my notebook and pencil, glancing at Gary. He had stopped pacing and was watching the DiCesares. His craggy face was still mottled with anger, and I sensed he shared Ernest's uncertainty.

Opening the notebook, I said, "I need more details about Vanessa, what her life was like the past month or so. Perhaps something will occur to one of you that didn't this morning."

"Ms. McCone," Ernest said, "I don't think Sylvia's up to this right now. Why don't you and Gary talk, and then if there's anything else, I'll be glad to help you."

"Fine." Gary was the one I was primarily interested in

questioning, anyway. I waited until Ernest and Sylvia had left the room, then turned to him.

When the door shut behind them, he hurled his cigarette into the empty fireplace. "Goddamn little bitch!" he said.

I said, "Why don't you sit down."

He looked at me for a few seconds, obviously wanting to keep on pacing, but then he flopped into the chair Sylvia had vacated. When I'd first met with Gary this morning, he'd been controlled and immaculately groomed, and he had seemed more solicitous of the DiCesares than concerned with his own feelings. Now his clothing was disheveled, his graying hair tousled, and he looked to be on the brink of a rage that would flatten anyone in its path.

Unfortunately, what I had to ask him would probably fan that rage. I braced myself and said, "Now tell me about Vanessa. And not all the stuff about her being a lovely young woman and a brilliant student. I heard all that this morning—but now we both know it isn't the whole truth, don't we?"

Surprisingly he reached for a cigarette and lit it slowly, using the time to calm himself. When he spoke, his voice was as level as my own. "All right, it's not the whole truth. Vanessa is lovely and brilliant. She'll make a top-notch lawyer. There's a hardness in her; she gets it from Ernest. It took guts to fake this suicide . . ."

"What do you think she hopes to gain from it?"

"Freedom. From me. From Ernest's domination. She's probably taken off somewhere for a good time. When she's ready she'll come back and make her demands."

"And what will they be?"

"Enough money to move into a place of her own and

finish law school. And she'll get it, too. She's all her parents have."

"You don't think she's set out to make a new life for herself?"

"Hell, no. That would mean giving up all this." The sweep of his arm encompassed the house and all of the DiCesares's privileged world.

But there was one factor that made me doubt his assessment. I said, "What about the other men in her life?"

He tried to look surprised, but an angry muscle twitched in his jaw.

"Come on, Gary," I said, "you know there were other men. Even Ernest and Sylvia were aware of that."

"Ah, Christ!" He popped out of the chair and began pacing again. "All right, there were other men. It started a few months ago. I didn't understand it; things had been good with us; they still *were* good physically. But I thought, okay, she's young; this is only natural. So I decided to give her some rope, let her get it out of her system. She didn't throw it in my face, didn't embarrass me in front of my friends. Why shouldn't she have a last fling?"

"And then?"

"She began making noises about breaking off the engagement. And Ernest started that shit about not footing the bill for law school. Like a fool I went along with it, and she seemed to cave in from the pressure. But a few weeks later, it all started up again—only this time it was purposeful, cruel."

"In what way?"

"She'd know I was meeting political associates for lunch or dinner, and she'd show up at the restaurant with a date. Later she'd claim he was just a friend, but you couldn't prove it from the way they acted. We'd go to a party and she'd flirt with every man there. She got sly and secretive about where she'd been, what she'd been doing."

I had pictured Vanessa as a very angry young woman; now I realized she was not a particularly nice one, either.

Gary was saying, ". . . the last straw was on Halloween. We went to a costume party given by one of her friends from Hastings. I didn't want to go—costumes, a young crowd, not my kind of thing—and so she was angry with me to begin with. Anyway, she walked out with another man, some jerk in a soldier outfit. They were dancing . . ."

I sat up straighter. "Describe the costume."

"An old-fashioned soldier outfit. Wide-brimmed hat with a plume, frock coat, sword."

"What did the man look like?"

"Youngish. He had a full beard and wore granny glasses."

Lee Gottschalk.

The address I got from the phone directory for Lee Gottschalk was on California Street not far from Twenty-fifth Avenue and only a couple of miles from where I'd first met the ranger at Fort Point. When I arrived there and parked at the opposite curb, I didn't need to check the mailboxes to see which apartment was his; the corner windows on the second floor were ablaze with light, and inside I could see Gottschalk, sitting in an armchair in what appeared to be his living room. He seemed to be alone but expecting company, because frequently he looked up from the book he was reading and checked his watch.

In case the company was Vanessa DiCesare, I didn't want to go barging in there. Gottschalk might find a way to warn her off, or simply not answer the door when she arrived. Besides, I didn't yet have a definite connection between the two of them; the "jerk in a soldier outfit" *could* have been someone else, someone in a rented costume that just happened to resemble the working uniform at the fort. But my suspicions were strong enough to keep me watching Gottschalk for well over an hour. The ranger *had* lied to me that afternoon.

The lies had been casual and convincing, except for two mistakes—such small mistakes that I hadn't caught them even when I'd read the newspaper account of Vanessa's purported suicide later. But now I recognized them for what they were: The paper had called Gary Stornetta a "political associate" of Vanessa's father, rather than his former campaign manager, as Lee had termed him. And while the paper mentioned the suicide note, it had not said it was *taped* inside the car. While Gottschalk conceivably could know about Gary managing Ernest's campaign for the Board of Supes from other newspaper accounts, there was no way he could have known how the note was secured—except from Vanessa herself.

Because of those mistakes, I continued watching Gottschalk, straining my eyes as the mist grew heavier, hoping Vanessa would show up or that he'd eventually lead me to her. The ranger appeared to be nervous: He got up a couple of times and turned on a TV, flipped through the channels, and turned it off again. For about ten minutes, he paced back and forth. Finally, around twelve-thirty, he checked his watch again, then got up and drew the draperies shut. The lights went out behind them.

I tensed, staring through the blowing mist at the door of the apartment building. Somehow Gottschalk hadn't looked like a man who was going to bed. And my impression was correct: In a few minutes he came through the door onto the sidewalk carrying a suitcase—pale leather like the one of Vanessa's Sylvia had described to me—and got into a dark-colored Mustang parked on his side of the street. The car started up and he made a U-turn, then went right on Twenty-fifth Avenue. I followed. After a few minutes, it became apparent that he was heading for Fort Point.

When Gottschalk turned into the road to the fort, I kept going until I could pull over on the shoulder. The brake lights of the Mustang flared, and then Gottschalk got out and unlocked the low iron bar that blocked the road from sunset to sunrise; after he'd driven through he closed it again, and the car's lights disappeared down the road.

Had Vanessa been hiding at drafty, cold Fort Point? It seemed a strange choice of place, since she could have used a motel or Gottschalk's apartment. But perhaps she'd been afraid someone would recognize her in a public place, or connect her with Gottschalk and come looking, as I had. And while the fort would be a miserable place to hide during the hours it was open to the public—she'd have had to keep to one of the off-limits areas, such as the west side—at night she could probably avail herself of the heated employees' lounge.

Now I could reconstruct most of the scenario of what had gone on: Vanessa meets Lee; they talk about his work; she decides he is the person to help her fake her suicide. Maybe there's a romantic entanglement, maybe not; but for whatever reason, he agrees to go along with the plan. She leaves her car at Vista Point, walks across the bridge, and later he drives over there and picks up the suitcase. . . .

But then why hadn't he delivered it to her at the fort? And to go after the suitcase after she'd abandoned the car was too much of a risk; he might have been seen, or the people at the fort might have noticed him leaving for too long a break. Also, if she'd walked across the bridge, surely at least one of the people I'd talked with would have seen her—the maintenance crew near the north tower, for instance.

There was no point in speculating on it now, I decided. The thing to do was to follow Gottschalk down there and confront Vanessa before she disappeared again. For a moment I debated taking my gun out of the glovebox, but then decided against it. I don't like to carry it unless I'm going into a dangerous situation, and neither Gottschalk nor Vanessa posed any particular threat to me. I was merely here to deliver a message from Vanessa's parents asking her to come home. If she didn't care to respond to it, that was not my business—or my problem.

I got out of my car and locked it, then hurried across the road and down the narrow lane to the gate, ducking under it and continuing along toward the ranger station. On either side of me were tall, thick groves of eucalyptus; I could smell their acrid fragrance and hear the fog-laden wind rustle their brittle leaves. Their shadows turned the lane into a black winding alley, and the only sound besides distant traffic noises was my tennis shoes slapping on the broken pavement. The ranger station was dark, but ahead I could see Gottschalk's car parked next to the fort. The area was illuminated only by small security lights set at intervals on the walls of the structure. Above it the bridge arched, washed in fog-muted yellowish light; as I drew closer I became aware of the grumble and clank of traffic up there.

I ran across the parking area and checked Gottschalk's car. It was empty, but the suitcase rested on the passenger seat. I turned and started toward the sally port, noticing that its heavily studded door stood open a few inches. The low tunnel was completely dark. I felt my way along it toward the courtyard, one hand on its icy stone wall.

The doors to the courtyard also stood open. I peered through them into the gloom beyond. What light there was came from the bridge and more security beacons high up on the wooden watchtowers; I could barely make out the shapes of the construction equipment that stood near the west side. The clanking from the bridge was oppressive and eerie in the still night.

As I was about to step into the courtyard, there was a movement to my right. I drew back into the sally port as Lee Gottschalk came out of one of the ground-floor doorways. My first impulse was to confront him, but then I decided against it. He might shout, warn Vanessa, and she might escape before I could deliver her parents' message.

After a few seconds I looked out again, meaning to follow Gottschalk, but he was nowhere in sight. A faint shaft of light fell through the door from which he had emerged and rippled over the cobblestone floor. I went that way, through the door and along a narrow corridor to where an archway was illuminated. Then, realizing the archway led to the unrestored cell of the jail I'd seen earlier, I paused. Surely Vanessa wasn't hiding in there. . . .

I crept forward and looked through the arch. The light came from a heavy-duty flashlight that sat on the floor. It threw macabre shadows on the water-stained walls, showing their streaked paint and graffiti. My gaze followed its beams upward and then down, to where the grating of the cistern lay out of place on the floor beside the hole. Then I moved over to the railing, leaned across it, and trained the flashlight down into the well.

I saw, with a rush of shock and horror, the dark hair and once-handsome features of Vanessa DiCesare.

She had been hacked to death. Stabbed and slashed, as if in a frenzy. Her clothing was ripped; there were gashes on her face and hands; she was covered with dark smears of blood. Her eyes were open, staring with that horrible flatness of death.

I came back on my heels, clutching the railing for support. A wave of dizziness swept over me, followed by an icy coldness. I thought: He killed her. And then I pictured Gottschalk in his Union Army uniform, the saber hanging from his belt, and I knew what the weapon had been.

"God!" I said aloud.

Why had he murdered her? I had no way of knowing yet. But the answer to why he'd thrown her into the cistern, instead of just putting her into the bay, was clear: She was supposed to have committed suicide; and while bodies that fall from the Golden Gate Bridge sustain a great many injuries, slash and stab wounds aren't among them. Gottschalk could not count on the body being swept out to sea on the current; if she washed up somewhere along the coast, it would be obvious she had been murdered— and eventually an investigation might have led back to him. To him and his soldier's saber.

It also seemed clear that he'd come to the fort tonight to move the body. But why not last night, why leave her in the cistern all day? Probably he'd needed to plan, to secure keys to the gate and fort, to check the schedule of the night patrols for the best time to remove her. Whatever his reason, I realized now that I'd walked into a very dangerous situation. Walked right in without bringing my gun. I turned quickly to get out of there. . . .

And came face-to-face with Lee Gottschalk.

His eyes were wide, his mouth drawn back in a snarl of surprise. In one hand he held a bundle of heavy canvas. "You!" he said. "What the hell are you doing here?"

I jerked back from him, bumped into the railing, and dropped the flashlight. It clattered on the floor and began rolling toward the mouth of the cistern. Gottschalk lunged toward me, and as I dodged, the light fell into the hole and the cell went dark. I managed to push past him and ran down the hallway to the courtyard.

Stumbling on the cobblestones, I ran blindly for the sally port. Its doors were shut now—he'd probably taken that precaution when he'd returned from getting the tarp to wrap her body in. I grabbed the iron hasp and tugged, but couldn't get it open. Gottschalk's footsteps were coming through the courtyard after me now. I let go of the hasp and ran again.

When I came to the enclosed staircase at the other end of the court, I started up. The steps were wide at the outside wall, narrow at the inside. My toes banged into the risers of the steps; a couple of times I teetered and almost fell backward. At the first tier I paused, then kept going. Gottschalk had said something about unrestored rooms on the second tier; they'd be a better place to hide than in the museum.

Down below I could hear him climbing after me. The sound of his feet—clattering and stumbling—echoed in

the close space. I could hear him grunt and mumble: low,
ugly sounds that I knew were curses.

I had absolutely no doubt that if he caught me, he would
kill me. Maybe do to me what he had done to Vanessa. . . .

I rounded the spiral once again and came out on the top
floor gallery, my heart beating wildly, my breath coming in
pants. To my left were archways, black outlines filled with
dark-gray sky. To my right was blackness. I went that way,
hands out, feeling my way.

My hands touched the rough wood of a door. I pushed,
and it opened. As I passed through it, my shoulder bag
caught on something; I yanked it loose and kept going.
Beyond the door I heard Gottschalk curse loudly, the
sound filled with surprise and pain; he must have fallen
on the stairway. And that gave me a little more time.

The tug at my shoulder bag had reminded me of the
small flashlight I keep there. Flattening myself against the
wall next to the door, I rummaged through the bag and
brought out the flashlight. Its beam showed high walls and
arching ceilings, plaster and lath pulled away to expose
dark brick. I saw cubicles and cubbyholes opening into
dead ends, but to my right was an arch. I made a small
involuntary sound of relief, then thought *Quiet.*
Gottschalk's footsteps started up the stairway again as I
moved through the archway.

The crumbling plaster walls beyond the archway were
set at odd angles—an interlocking fun-house maze connected by small doors. I slipped through one and found
an irregularly shaped room heaped with debris. There
didn't seem to be an exit, so I ducked back into the first
room and moved toward the outside wall, where gray outlines indicated small high-placed windows. I couldn't hear

Gottschalk anymore—couldn't hear anything but the roar and clank from the bridge directly overhead.

The front wall was brick and stone, and the windows had wide waist-high sills. I leaned across one, looked through the salt-caked glass, and saw the open sea. I was at the front of the fort, the part that faced beyond the Golden Gate; to my immediate right would be the unrestored portion. If I could slip over into that area, I might be able to hide until the other rangers came to work in the morning.

But Gottschalk could be anywhere. I couldn't hear his footsteps above the infernal noise from the bridge. He could be right here in the room with me, pinpointing me by the beam of my flashlight. . . .

Fighting down panic, I switched the light off and continued along the wall, my hands recoiling from its clammy stone surface. It was icy cold in the vast, echoing space, but my own flesh felt colder still. The air had a salt tang, underlaid by odors of rot and mildew. For a couple of minutes the darkness was unalleviated, but then I saw a lighter rectangular shape ahead of me.

When I reached it I found it was some sort of embrasure, about four feet tall, but only a little over a foot wide. Beyond it I could see the edge of the gallery where it curved and stopped at the chain-link fence that barred entrance to the other side of the fort. The fence wasn't very high—only five feet or so. If I could get through this narrow opening, I could climb it and find refuge . . .

The sudden noise behind me was like a firecracker popping. I whirled, and saw a tall figure silhouetted against one of the seaward windows. He lurched forward, tripping over whatever he'd stepped on. Forcing back a cry, I hoisted myself up and began squeezing through the embrasure.

Its sides were rough brick. They scraped my flesh clear through my clothing. Behind me I heard the slap of Gottschalk's shoes on the wooden floor.

My hips wouldn't fit through the opening. I gasped, grunted, pulling with my arms on the outside wall. Then I turned on my side, sucking in my stomach. My bag caught again, and I let go of the wall long enough to rip its strap off my elbow. As my hips squeezed through the embrasure, I felt Gottschalk grab at my feet. I kicked out frantically, breaking his hold, and fell off the sill to the floor of the gallery.

Fighting for breath, I pushed off the floor, threw myself at the fence, and began climbing. The metal bit into my fingers, rattled and clashed with my weight. At the top, the leg of my jeans got hung up on the spiky wires. I tore it loose and jumped down the other side.

The door to the gallery burst open and Gottschalk came through it. I got up from a crouch and ran into the darkness ahead of me. The fence began to rattle as he started up it. I raced, half-stumbling, along the gallery, the open archways to my right. To my left was probably a warren of rooms similar to those on the east side. I could lose him in there . . .

Only I couldn't. The door I tried was locked. I ran to the next one and hurled my body against its wooden panels. It didn't give. I heard myself sob in fear and frustration.

Gottschalk was over the fence now, coming toward me, limping. His breath came in erratic gasps, loud enough to hear over the noise from the bridge. I twisted around, looking for shelter, and saw a pile of lumber lying across one of the open archways.

I dashed toward it and slipped behind, wedged between it and the pillar of the arch. The courtyard lay two dizzying stories below me. I grasped the end of the top two-by-four. It moved easily, as if on a fulcrum.

Gottschalk had seen me. He came on steadily, his right leg dragging behind him. When he reached the pile of lumber and started over it toward me, I yanked on the two-by-four. The other end moved and struck him on the knee.

He screamed and stumbled back. Then he came forward again, hands outstretched toward me. I pulled back further against the pillar. His clutching hands missed me, and when they did he lost his balance and toppled onto the pile of lumber. And then the boards began to slide toward the open archway.

He grabbed at the boards, yelling and flailing his arms. I tried to reach for him, but the lumber was moving like an avalanche now, pitching over the side and crashing down into the courtyard two stories below. It carried Gottschalk's thrashing body with it, and his screams echoed in its wake. For an awful few seconds the boards continued to crash down on him, and then everything was terribly still. Even the thrumming of the bridge traffic seemed muted.

I straightened slowly and looked down into the courtyard. Gottschalk lay unmoving among the scattered pieces of lumber. For a moment I breathed deeply to control my vertigo; then I ran back to the chain-link fence, climbed it, and rushed down the spiral staircase to the courtyard.

When I got to the ranger's body, I could hear him moaning. I said, "Lie still. I'll call an ambulance."

He moaned louder as I ran across the courtyard and found a phone in the gift shop, but by the time I returned, he was silent. His breathing was so shallow that I thought he'd passed out, but then I heard mumbled words coming from his lips. I bent closer to listen.

"Vanessa," he said. "Wouldn't take me with her. . . ."

I said, "Take you where?"

"Going away together. Left my car . . . over there so she could drive across the bridge. But when she . . . brought it here she said she was going alone. . . ."

So you argued, I thought. And you lost your head and slashed her to death.

"Vanessa," he said again. "Never planned to take me . . . tricked me. . . ."

I started to put a hand on his arm, but found I couldn't touch him. "Don't talk any more. The ambulance'll be here soon."

"Vanessa," he said. "Oh God, what did you do to me?"

I looked up at the bridge, rust red through the darkness and the mist. In the distance, I could hear the wail of a siren.

Deceptions, I thought.

Deceptions. . . .

A World of Eerie Suspense
Awaits in Novels by Noel Hynd

Your Favorite Mystery Authors
Are Now Just A Phone Call Away

HORROR FROM PINNACLE . . .

__HAUNTED by Tamara Thorne
0-7860-1090-9 $5.99US/$7.99CAN
Its violent, sordid past is what draws bestselling author David Masters to the infamous Victorian mansion called Baudey House. Its shrouded history of madness and murder is just the inspiration he needs to write his ultimate masterpiece of horror. But what waits for David and his teenaged daughter at Baudey House is more terrifying than any legend; it is the dead, seducing the living, in an age-old ritual of perverted desire and unholy blood lust.

__THIRST by Michael Cecilione
0-7860-1091-6 $5.99US/$7.99CAN
Cassandra Hall meets her new lover at a Greenwich Village poetry reading— and sex with him is like nothing she's ever experienced. But Cassandra's new man has a secret he wants her to share: he's a vampire. And soon, Cassandra descends into a deeper realm of exotic thirst and unspeakable passion, where she must confront the dark side of her own sensuality . . . and where a beautiful rival threatens her earthly soul.

__THE HAUNTING by Ruby Jean Jensen
0-7860-1095-9 $5.99US/7.99CAN
Soon after Katie Rogers moves into an abandoned house in the woods with her sister and her young niece and nephew, she begins having bizarre nightmares in which she is a small child again, running in terror. Then come horrifying visions of a woman wielding a gleaming butcher knife. Of course, Katie doesn't believe that any of it is *real* . . . until her niece and nephew disappear. Now only Katie can put an end to a savage evil that is slowly awakening . . . to unleash a fresh cycle of slaughter and death in which the innocent will die again and again!

Call toll free **1-888-345-BOOK** to order by phone or use this coupon to order by mail.
Name_____
Address_____
City_____ State _____ Zip _____
Please send me the books I have checked above.
I am enclosing $_____
Plus postage and handling* $_____
Sales tax (in NY and TN) $_____
Total amount enclosed $_____
*Add $2.50 for the first book and $.50 for each additional book.
Send check or money order (no cash or CODs) to: **Kensington Publishing Corp., Dept. C.O., 850 Third Avenue, New York, NY 10022**
Prices and numbers subject to change without notice. Valid only in the U.S. All orders subject to availability.
Visit out our website at **www.kensingtonbooks.com**